THE THOUGHT

Tibor Fischer was born in Stockport, in 1959. Brought up in London, where he now lives, he was educated at Cambridge and worked as a journalist. He is the author of *Under the Frog* (which won the Betty Trask Award, earned him a place on *Granta's* 1993 'Best of Young British Novelists' and made the 1993 Booker shortlist), *The Collector Collector* and most recently *Don't Read This Book If You're Stupid*.

Tibor Fischer

THE THOUGHT GANG

V

VINTAGE

Published by Vintage 1999

10 9

Copyright © Tibor Fischer 1994

The right of Tibor Fischer to be identified as the author of this work has been asserted by him in accordance with the Copyright, Designs and Patents Act, 1988

First published in Great Britain by
Polygon 1994

Vintage
Random House, 20 Vauxhall Bridge Road,
London SW1V 2SA

Random House Australia (Pty) Limited
20 Alfred Street, Milsons Point, Sydney
New South Wales 2061, Australia

Random House New Zealand Limited
18 Poland Road, Glenfield,
Auckland 10, New Zealand

Random House (Pty) Limited
Endulini, 5a Jubilee Road, Parktown 2193, South Africa

The Random House Group Limited Reg. No. 954009

www.randomhouse.co.uk

A CIP catalogue record for this book
is available from the British Library

ISBN 0 7493 9550 8

Printed and bound in Great Britain by
Cox & Wyman Ltd, Reading, Berkshire

For my mother

ἰδιῶται – one's own countrymen

Liddell and Scott's Greek-English Lexicon

The Past 1.1

The only advice I can offer, should you wake up vertiginously in a strange flat, with a thoroughly installed hangover, without any of your clothing, without any recollection of how you got there, with the police sledgehammering down the door to the accompaniment of excited dogs, while you are surrounded by bales of lavishly-produced magazines featuring children in adult acts, the only advice I can offer is to try be good-humoured and polite.

Presumably having blacked out, I whited on to this tableau and assayed amiability as I tried to figure out what all the fuss had to do with me. My endeavour at goodwill was the result of my belief that it is what should be to-ed to all men and, as I subsequently discovered, even if you don't (a) feel goodwill or (b) feel like showing it, because of powerful sensations of ill will, it's all the more imperative to display friendliness and zing since it makes the police fret about having got something wrong.

Do remember, they're only doing what they see as their job, as I attempted to when they lifted me up just enough to make it worthwhile for them to slam me down onto the floor. They then pointed a large number of handguns at my unmitigated flesh (distastefully pale and goose-pimply) as I thought about offering them a cup of tea or something. Soon, it occurred to me I had no idea if there was a kitchen. Where it might be. Let alone whether there might be the required items for the preparation of tea. Having enough vigour for running minimal vital functions, I admired the patch of floor next to my face (and the compliment slip from the Zenshinren Bank), holding on firmly all the time.

Unsatisfactory floors of the East End 1.1

It was very cold.

But still a floor, and, being prone to being prone, I have often drawn comfort from them; they've backed me up in vicissitude. Very stable, floors. Replete with admirable qualities: reliable, supportive, uncomplicated, patient. And no matter how awkward your posture, how pained your joints or points of contact, you know you've eluded serious injury, you've cheated the perils of gravity when you've made it to the floor.

As my hands were cuffed behind my back, and I had a zet at the footwear of my arresting officers, I couldn't help hailing Nietzsche's dictum, *what does not kill me makes me stronger*. One could add that what doesn't kill you can be extremely uncomfortable and can give you a very nasty cold. I sneezed with no hands and discharged some nose marrow across the short distance between my nostrils and the gleaming footwear of the detective in charge of the operation, where it spread-eagled and made itself at home.

The trouble with Nietzsche – who in any case never prescribed instructions regarding conduct while being hand-cuffed on chilly floors in undignified circumstances – is that you can never be sure when he's doing some levity or not.

The Metropolitan Police had the same problem with me. They were hugely unconvinced by my responses to their questioning.

We stalled on the very first question. My name. Coffin. I can't blame them. I can see that it's a name that could be easily categorised as extempore and provocatively preposterous. It is, bearing in mind, the definition that accompanies it in the dictionary, a stupid name.

Not as stupid as say, Pine-Coffin, of whom there are a number running around. Not as stupid as Cock, Dick, Death, Loony, Longbottom, Stutter, Semen, Thick or Vermin (look in the telephone directory, it's stupendous what people will endure for their geniture – not to mention their genitals) but good for a laugh. All through my school years I was a bringer of much amusement and there did come a period when I thought about changing it, either for something bland or for something more pleasingly exotic; but then when I reflected on all the punishment I'd taken, I resolved however difficult it was to spell out, however often I was going to receive letters addressed to Dr Coughing, Dr Muffin, Dr Kaffeine or Dr Co-Fin, I was going to stick with it. You don't want to let the cosmos catch you backing off in any way.

Besides, my father would have lathered mightily at the suggestion that after the Coffins taking guffaws for centuries I was going to chicken out. Also there are eerie significances in the supposed origins of the name: from coffer, as in money-coffers. Certainly, for as long as I can recollect, I've always had an affinity with money. I've never gone through a phase, where, for whatever reason, I wanted to show money the door, belittled it, or pretended that there were more important things (though some entities get parity). Though it might well be that I would have wanted to swan about on ziggurats of tenners even if my name had been Jesus Mohammed McBuddha.

The uncanny significance in the other supposed origin of my name is that it comes from the French for bald (don't ask me how they work these things out) and this is uncanny because not only am I as bald as you get, but I have been since the age of twenty-five. No heroic follicles of resistance anywhere, no die-hard islets round the back spurning surrender.

And while being as smooth as a billiard ball at say forty

or fifty might invite ribaldry, it doesn't look suspicious. When you've been delivered to a police station in a blanket with a shinehead at the age of thirty, it compounds your improbity.

Then came the date of birth. We were all happy about that. No opening for controversy there.

However ... occupation?

"Philosopher."

"Philosopher?"

"Philosopher."

Why ask questions if you don't like answers? This response put a polish on their conviction that I was making things up for my amusement. What relevance did it, does it have? Were they contracted to arrest a certain quota from each profession? "We'll have to let you go. We've already got two existentialists in the tank." Why not ask for your favourite novel, if there's a need to differentiate between two Eddie Coffins born 9-5-45?

I wasn't much help to the police – to their demonstrated irritation. Having been supplied so quickly with a blanket, I did feel a bit guilty. Our dialogues were rather trite and one-sided, with a variety of questions from the forces of law and order, and mainly the same answer from me, with a variety of apologetic inflections.

I told them over and over that I couldn't tell them anything about the set-up at the flat in Zetland Street, because I didn't know anything about it. Or its occupants. The police, I indicated, were informationally advantaged, because they at least knew the address. All I could offer was a minute description of the lino.

The police greeted all this with considerable and much-practised derision, because as anyone involved in the criminal trade will affirm (although I didn't know this at the time) the phrase *I don't know anything about it* is employed almost exclusively by those, paradoxically, who do know all about it; that this concatenation of words is a code, a slang, a camouflaged way of saying: prove it. It is the criminalese for: don't expect me to do your job for you.

Going to a pub, the *Zodiac* in Tower Hamlets, that was where my remembrance was amputated, after I had launched into my ten-minute package on the nature of knowledge, the product of the inevitable inquiry about philosophy. I was, admittedly, already collating collapse before I entered the premises.

After a day of detention, however, I was voided from the police station, because, despite the greatest of efforts, the police couldn't fit this Cambridge philosophy lecturer into the scenario of malfeasance: I didn't know any of the people who were shepherding those wicked goods and also, as it turned out, when some of the culpable were subsequently tracked down and arrested, they knew nothing about me. Ubiquitous puzzlement. Especially as my clothes were never recovered.

The scandal, if there was one, I didn't cognize. A few fellow academics looked at me thoughtfully, but said nothing. Strangely, the Master didn't seem surprised or put out by a detectivy phone call in regard to one of the fellows. "Ah, Coffin," he said when he saw me before zooming off in the direction I clearly wasn't going. Apart from that observation he seemed to have nothing more to say.

Indeed, though it was inconvenient, cold, and many other things drawn from the collection of qualities frowned upon by hazelnut-headed philosophers, I'm quite sure that I only got tenure because I became known in wider academic circles as "isn't he the one who was found in an East End flat with a few hundred grand's worth of kiddy pics?". It gets you noticed. People want to meet you.

Get on with it

One could easily argue against beginnings, bash determination and rub causality's face in the dirt, but that's a good point to point at and say that's where I became trapped in philosophy, encased in the biz.

The present 1.1

So sitting here at the airport about to flee the country, that scene presents its credentials. Perhaps because this is a good point to point at and say, this is the end of my stint in philosophy, or at least the end of my career as a nine-to-five thinker.

When you flee your country, when you are about to embark on fugitivedom, you expect a heightening, dramatic music, a stirred soul.

The plane's late. Outside it's dark. Atrous. The sort of black, miserable, gloomy dank evening that you could expect any evening in England, but it's barely April so you can't really have a substantial rant about how disgusting the weather is. I don't understand why people insist on carrying on the pretence that there are four seasons in this land. What we get is four types of winter, all so rainy they're hard to distinguish from one another.

Most commuting is exciting and glamorous compared to this. Tragically, having run out of reading matter I laboriously write this on the margins of my newspaper. I am surrounded by French businessmen, all so zinjanthropine, that any one of them could single-handedly torpedo the notion that Frenchmen are suave and stylish.

Everything is so forgettable and dull I am surprised my consciousness bothers doing its job. This would be a good moment for a break.

Now that I'm expecting the police to appear, they don't. Surely they'd want to wave goodbye to me and my career? Even more tragically, this gate is too far from a bar to really tank up. I uncap my duty-free bottle and conceal some milligrams of vodka about my person; but there's only one bottle and that's not enough to buy out my awareness.

I catch my reflection in the glass, balancing the bottle like a vast exclamation mark in front of my face. I look like cobbles with too many centuries. A Frenchman glares at me reproachfully but his disapproval is couched in zero since he carries a briefcase so laughable no six year-old would want to burn it. Besides, I'm English: a race known for its feats with lawns, for saying sorry when people walk into us, for queuing in the rain and a miscellany of other traits, but one thing not in the compact is looking sharp in departure lounges, especially as one bids farewell to the remains of one's career.

Not enough future to go round

Shortage of future. Some past that passed me by. Take your pick. I've had significant bursts of black many times before.

When my career as a banker came to an end. A career so brief it was transparent. It didn't even endure twenty-four hours, though it hurdled one working-day. A doomed attempt to flee the university life, to evade the world of nine-to-five wisdom. I had succumbed to a bout of wanting to find the realworld, a vagary most of us are ensnared by at some time or other, that certain parts of our world have more packed in them. Much as dust self-appoints itself into clumps in one corner rather than another, so the idea that the reality is realer over the horizon reels us in. (More about the realworld later.)

The mnemonic gap took place (a) again in the evening (b) far beyond the ten pint zone. I still have a very clear image of myself standing on a snooker table. This snooker table was in the hall of residence where we were being given our introductory course to high finance. My memory is unusually zealous at this spot, almost as if it were concentrating so much on that instant, that it dillydallied too long and gorged itself on that representation and then had to take a short cut to the next morning.

A voice was shrieking at those gathered there about the unexamined life and promising to knock the stuffing out of anyone who disagreed. From (a) the effort being made by my lungs (b) a familiar ring to the voice and (c) the snooker cue I was brandishing in an inexcusably aggressive fashion, I deduced that it was mine.

Then the present wasn't present. My senses were censored. The future stopped supplying me.

Gradually, I was presented with the present of the present, and I resumed recording the thing deemed reality. It was the next morning, and I was first aware that only my feet had gone the full road and made it to my bed. Like a stretched zed, the rest of me was lying on the floor with a numbed discomfort (steadily losing its numbness), and my face was looking up at two of the course organisers looking down at me and releasing raw displeasure.

"That's the one," one said to the other, who nodded.

What exactly transpired I never managed to piece together. However, judging from the regards of horror and amazement that I garnered from my peers as I was escorted, floppy, from the building and chucked into a taxi (given instructions, but not a fare to remove me), it was forgetfulnessdefying.

Years afterwards, I met one of those who had been in the process of getting banked up with me. It was in full commuterdom on a train. "I know you," he said. Despite my fleeting employment I was still anecdoteable in the company he informed me. My reminiscer had to get off but he left me his number (which of course I lost) with a promise to give me the complete story of my antics which he had himself witnessed.

Get on with it.

Summary: what was the upshot of my birthday-suited arrest? What does my memory wish to serve up? It's hard to forget the wicket-gate opening as the entire police station came to see me one by one, the remarks "that's him", the raspings as they revved up their contempt, the comets as they flobbed on me.

I met some interesting people. To wit, a plasterer who had the whole line up of the 1966 English World Cup team tattooed on his penis. He volunteered this information quite readily, after only a few minutes of acquaintance, as well as a lament that he was being stitched up for drunk and disorderly. "Drunk? Ask anyone – I only had eight pints and a couple of shorts."

Having an ornament like that doesn't count unless people know about it, I suppose. I asked why. "You're either a fan or you're not."

I also met Zak, probably one of the greatest, most success- ful smugglers alive. His name isn't passed in public, which is the most cogent testimonial to his ability. He shifted all sorts of things, from the pretty to the unbelievably illegal, and sums that many small nations would quite fancy as their GDP. Appropriately enough he was helping the police with their inquiries into a matter of speeding on the Mile End Road.

You haven't even started yet

So there we have it. When I was innocently unconscious, the police pour in, can't get enough of me, but now I am consciously guilty, they can't be bothered to turn up to stop me leaving the country.
Let's go.

?????????????????????????

I gaze out over Bordeaux, Montaigne's beat.
My view from the café is good. Any town or city is largely flavoured by the people you know, and although he hasn't

been out on the streets for four hundred years (due to death) I can't think of this place as anything else but the town that was mayored by Montaigne. The first great compiler that we know of (though perhaps Athenaeus is in there with a claim). The first encyclopedist of human endeavour.

He was the first to sift through the totality of human knowledge (as it stood then) to see what answers might be sprinkled over the centuries. To crack the code and fillet out the structure.

Sitting down in his vast library around 1560 he asked the question: what do I know? His zetetic method: to choose questions and then to skewer together chunks of thought like a kebab, morsels taken from top commentators and cogitators, spiced with a few opinions and experiences of his own. Mr. Database. The interrogator of history and letters. And not giving an answer, but giving them all.

I add but I don't correct. Anything you say may be taken down and used in evidence. A clever method, a man with a great chateau and a great vineyard that I shall shortly visit.

Montaigne's task was herculean, but possible. Now you could spend your life trying to decide where to start. I heard one of the university librarians wistfully talking of the need for a good book-burning dictatorship. There is hardly an epoch or region whose intellectual door I can't kick down if I want to search for their customs, findings, ruminations. Whether it's a zaotar or the parasites in a pottoo's intestine, I can biblio my way in and demand: "Give me your information, hand over your profundities." My vision is wider, deeper, longer than Montaigne's. Your whole three score and ten could vanish without a trace in one wing of the university library. There comes a stage with knowledge, like a city, where it becomes unmanageable, where it boils over. And even our data-dogs shepherding facts for us won't be able to cope. Word overflow. Shelves of neglected books pleading for readers. Shelves, shelves and shelves. The forests are hiding in the buildings.

What do we know?

I gaze out over Bordeaux fugitively. A very fast peripatetic. Sloping out of town is a distinguished philosophical tradition. On the run, but comfortably seated.

We all need, or at the very least, find useful a model, someone from the past running ahead, whether we follow them closely or faithfully. Montaigne is my pace-setter. Every thinker has teamed up with names from the past even if it's chiefly to rubbish them, every thinker has chosen some page-mates. Even the venerable M was hitching a lift on Sextus Empiricus. The joy of this arrangement is that deceased philosophers can't refuse to dance.

Montaigne can't curl his lip as I make myself comfortable. He can't ask: who is this tubby bald git? (Especially since he gave up using his own hair). He can't enquire or protest about my position in the world ranking of philosophy as I sit at his table. That's the drawback to being dead and published: you're open all hours. Admission free. Anyone can wander in, make disparaging or moronic remarks and stay as long as they want. A textual squat. I put my arm around Mickey, give a crass grin and a thumbs up for the camera. Flash! Phut! A souvenir picture.

The question.

As a pro, people are always asking me questions. Not so much about the biz, but when they learn that I philosophise professionally they seem to believe I have a big bag of answers and that they can cadge a free panacea off me, like a kid fleecing Santa Claus.

People have turned to me as an agony uncle and laid out their anguishes, unpaid bills, dilemmas, emotional zigzags. Outside the biz you find this preconception that there is a mental gadget that can fix unhappiness. More and more, I wonder what good is philosophy? After all these years, what does philosophy, indeed human knowledge, have to say for itself? We're a few years from the Big Two. 2000 makes a neat date for an audit.

Thus I fattify here in the sunshine with a glass of Zédé, surrounded by crumbs, the tracks of two sandwich merguez tucked away in my guts. My physical situation is probably about the same as those who started the biz. Sunshine, a glass of wine, a bit of time.

What advantage do they, who were first to spread their reason over the horizon, who got a faction of facts to back them up, have over me? They were cleverer than me. They got in first, staked out the territory. Indeed, things haven't budged much since the idea tour hit Athens in the fifth century. We're merely Plato addicts, you could say.

My advantage: that I have two and a half thousand years on them. That I have the whole span of recorded history at my fingertips (or I could in a good library). I have the spadework of thousands of brilliants at my disposal, the servitude of gangs of geniuses.

I have a lot of time. No – that I can't be sure of, but what I do have is a good lot of time; time unmarked, uncluttered, ready to do my bidding. An open road ahead of me, albeit a short one.

One of the best books I never wrote was one to cash in on the millennium. I did get as far as a title: *The Two meets the Three Zeroes (Uptown)*.

So delighted with that, I took a year off before purchasing and designating an exercise book to imprison my thoughts on the subject. Ten years on, I flicked through to light upon three terse entries, a squashed ant and an address I had wanted so badly at one point I had completely emptied my study in a frenzy to locate it. Two of the entries were illegible and the third was an attempt at a biography to go on a dust jacket of another book I didn't write.

Granted, the year 2000 is simply another 52 Monday mornings, another 366 days, another batch of 31, 622, 400 seconds, but it's like a birthday, it may be an unexalted day for others, but it tenders a base for reference, a time for stock-taking. Part of my procrastination was down to leaving things to the last moment in case of a civilisation-spinning idea popping up after I'd started work. Of course, this envisaged procrastination might be hard to spot in my monumental laziness, like a fish's tears in an ocean.

There have been times when I've had a lot to say. I had a great deal to say to the police before I left. Was my effusion on that occasion due to feeling guilty about having wasted police time previously? Was it the revenge of my long-lost probity? Or was it my energetic laziness? The thing about lying, even badly or carelessly, is that it takes effort. The truth has this to recommend it: you don't have to think too much about it.

The Proposition

I am working on the assumption that my lifelong sloth hasn't been that, but a well-disguised storage of creative vim for the killer opus to leave known civilisation gaping. One book and out. I'm taking it all down. The trivialities. The ramblings. The drearies. The trites. I'm taking no chances. Rounding up all the usual suspects, and all the unusual ones, picking them off as they emerge one by one.

This is in case I can't spot a vein-bearing line straight away. Not so much for posterity as for satisfaction, though it would be nice for someone to read this in a few hundred years' time. And not come to the conclusion I reach with many musty, speckled works I chance upon in antiquarian bookshops: what a zero, what a waste of ink, what a regurgitator, what a ripple from someone else's imaginative stone. Pages of blank masquerading as writing. Why did anyone bother writing or printing or selling or buying or keeping it? If anyone should be reading this ...

Message to the future

Sorry this isn't more interesting. Sorry if you find this feeble or predictably fin de millennium. Really 2000ish. But I'm glad you've made it, that you're out there. Hope human suffering is at tolerable levels and that situations are an agreeable level of stimulation, with happiness not out of the question.

Ludicrously long postcard home?

This is certainly longer than anything I've produced in thirty years in the thought trade.

Never too late to be late

Naturally, there's no question of suicide as it's conventionally defined. My consciousness may not be much, but it's all I've got.

However, your life has been dull if you haven't at least conceived of it. At one unbalanced, black juncture, I got as far as buying pills but by the time I got home, I'd lost them. I went out again in the rain, bought some more, mumbling on and on "you're born, you fail as much as you can, then you die" in a way that makes me laugh now.

I was on the verge of pulling the R.I.P. cord, when I had a chilling worry that checked me: what if you have to work in the hereafter? Toil after this mortal coil? Floating around nebulously or having my bubble burst, that was fine. I had achieved, at that age, if nothing else, the ability to philosophise with such little effort that I didn't sense it. A decade's worth of philosophical perusal puts you in a position to pulverise students whose reading consists of ten minutes of the nearest paperback. No matter how sharp they are, you can zugzwang them. Yes, I panicked at the idea of labour after death. Elbowgrease. Graft. Polishing the pearly gates, or stoking the eternal flames. Transported either to a place where my studies would be eyewash, or where I would be stripped of my memory, and thence my ability to con a living. That halted the attempt.

On the other hand, apart from eating abundantly, I'm not doing very much to prolong my life. Which will claim me first, the peelers or cirrhosis? Or will it be an outsider, a long shot, a hurtling grand piano, an improperly rooted elm zelkova, a pavementing car, a vicious microbe lurking in a cheese or lounging on a chop?

The police did take my passport. But what they didn't do was ascertain whether I had others. Mislaying passports: one of my weaknesses. I'd apply for a new one (graduate students are excellent for the purpose of waiting at the Passport Office on your behalf) and then would discover the old one under a breakfast tray or book. One even penetrated the vegetable compartment of the fridge.

And of course they weren't expecting me and the two other passports to do a runner. I was a touch surprised myself. My solicitor was holding the promise of a non-custodial sentence. Because I'd put my hands up and because putting people in jail is apparently considered extremely unfashionable these days. But even as an unlikely option, it was still a risk, and even a nychthemeron in the clink is out. The food's not up to it.

Distressing cheese sandwiches 1.1

I still have strong impressions of the cheese sandwich I encountered my first time in custody. Now, the great strength of a cheese sandwich is that it's an item that doesn't require a highly-trained begetter and that you would judge impossible to render inedible. It might be a slovenly cheese, a cheese that doesn't inspire fanatical loyalty, it might be grudging, arid bread, it might not be a cheese sandwich to go down in history, but it should still be a cheese sandwich, however humble.

Thus, while banged up, I approached the provided cheese sandwich with confidence only to discover that there is such an entity as the cheese sandwich which can't be eaten.

I took one bite and, unwilling to admit how bad it was, I took another. I meditated on the great prisoners who would have zestfully wolfed much less savoury objects, I meditated on the great thinkers at ease in hardship who would have embraced that sandwich with open molars. I dwelled on how weak my refusal was, recognised it as such, and content with that self-knowledge, I frisbeed the sandwich back onto its transport. The flavour wasn't so noxious, but it wasn't a cheese sandwich flavour, it had a wet larded carpet tang. That was my main objection: I don't see the use of a cheese sandwich that doesn't taste like a cheese sandwich. But prisons are full of people who, evidently, aren't afraid of bogus cheese sandwiches.

I may well end up there. But they have to catch me first. All in all, I'd rather be sunning myself in a high temperature like a Lord Derby's zonure and tanking up in a superior French café.

What have I left behind? A home in need of so much repair that you'd have to be a fairly senior Third World dictator to take it on. Not much else. You look at the missed appointments, the poorly-peeled potatoes, the failed friendships, the unwashed plates, evenings alone in restaurants, the traffic jams, the cancelled trains, the unanswered phones, the tooth-brushings and you realise they're not just missed appointments, poorly-peeled potatoes, failed friendships, unwashed plates, lonings in restaurants, traffic jams, cancelled trains, unanswered phones and tooth-brushings, they're your life. Many of us, I suppose, see our existences not as lives, but as life-holders, zarfs, waiting for the job, the person, the event to fill it.

I observe my fellow baskers complain, snap, cachinnate, straighten out government policy. That's the wonder of abroad. Even if you're well-versed in the language, well-planted in the culture, conversations too oafish to be worth expending ear-time on at home get a topping of interest from operating in a different language.

Things are more interesting abroad, even dying.

????????????????????????????

Pauillac
Just outside the Château Latour estate

The only frank and remotely pleasant exchange I ever had with the Master of my college was very short, after one of my slips. "I'm flabbergasted," he perorated, "that you have managed to make a career as a philosopher."

"Not, I assure you," I replied, "as gobsmacked as I am."

People have said to me: "Eddie, you're a loafer." People who don't like me very much (Featherstone in particular) and who have assessed my progress uncharitably have said: lush, compulsive gambler, zero, drug-dealer, fraud, disaster, slob. People who like me have said much the same.

Mea Culpa 1.1

For the record, I am well aware that I didn't execute any of the chores, that as a pro, as an official thought trafficant I should have done. I didn't write any papers or books. I didn't do much teaching, though this made me rather popular. People were eager to be supervised by me – when they didn't turn up I didn't remonstrate because I wasn't there either.

I did go to conferences, though, if someone else paid. And I was very hot on subscribing to journals. I did the same lecture, year after year, without yielding to the temptation to make changes.

I blame the authorities. In a half-reasonable world I would have been fired a long time ago. In a sixth-reasonable world I would have been booted out sooner. Even in a hundredth-reasonable world I wouldn't have got far.

I did everything wrong. I got a first. I didn't mean to (perhaps the secret). By the time my finals arrived I had chosen to go into banking and I knew that without any effort

I could pick up enough degree for that. For the last paper, I almost didn't go. It was only because it would have offended Wilbur, my director of studies, who had taken much stick in my defence, that I trudged along. Perhaps the first was a subtle, rigged, way of encouraging me to stay on, as Wilbur had been trying to persuade me to do.

No, I left (though I didn't get far). Nick, who had been on the substitute's bench took the slot for zetting young philosopher, but then topped himself. I was expelled from the towers of high finance and parachuted back into Cambridge, months after vowing never to return.

I made the Ionians my speciality. Very few people realise that you can read the entire extant oeuvre of the Ionians, slowly and carefully, in an hour. Most of them come in handy packets of adages. Extremely important, the first caught having a go with their reason, the inventors of paid thought and science – anything you'll find in a university – and blissfully curt.

Is this the best you can do?

It's not a bad life being a fugitive. I've been avolating for forty-eight hours and I've no complaints. While I have money. That's the thing about embezzlement, if you do it, do it big, enough for a luxurious new life. Unfortunately, in addition to the options of being arrested or liquidating myself with liquids, there is also the more perplexing possibility of running out of dunops. On the run with no more run.

Exile

Well, not really. France doesn't count as exile. Over the years with my consumption of French wine, language and letters, I'm at least half-French. Gallicized inside. I'm certainly more imbued with the culture than any zig here but an *agrégé*. Indeed, since this is the only country in the world where being a philosopher, even with my world ranking, can get you your leg over, I fit in here better than anywhere else. And the boys were always itinerants. Philosophers, like all flim-flammers, have a taste for the open road and new ears.

Château Latour. Peak wine. A wine three times more expensive than my usual plonk. Not three times better, but better. All reputations are over or under; you'd have to be cobra-fast to catch a reputation at the correct level.

I've got the money. I've got the taste buds. I'm going in.

???????????????????????????»»

More Bordeaux

I got out too.

A grey morning, uncharacteristic of the region and the season. A sort of grey that reminds me of Cambridge: sullen and persistent. Why anyone set up a university there in the first place is beyond me, unless it was an act of malice. Someone who relished the sound of clerics coughing in foggy fens. The sensible place for a seat of learning would have been Dover – as far south as possible and closest to a country with a proper climate and cuisine.

En route for my newspaper, I walk past a funeral parlour. I fight off a powerful urge to go in and give myself up.

You never know when your number will be up, but I reflect that those who pass me in the street look better than I do, have more breathing in them. The doctors have been telling me for so long that I should be dead that I got bored going to see them (for a while it was amusing rattling them with my continued existence, but the fun wore off).

My GP, a humourless Zanzibari, was especially censorious. He was hooked on being taken seriously. "Goodbye," he said to me. "This is the last time we shall meet, I think." A last ditch attempt at scaring me into abstinence. He was right though. He was murdered by his wife the week after.

I often wish I could reason with my liver. Doesn't it understand it's cutting its own throat by shutting up shop? I might have some chance, some forwarding address. I can't rule out my soul being recycled, my me escape-podding somewhere new. But my liver and its confederates? They're heading for a redistribution of atoms, doubtfully to their advantage. What shakes me most is my heart is a lot for rot.

Montpellier

You don't know how hard a mug is until you throw it.

That's always been one of my favourites: redolent of domestic violence. I heard it in a pint-point outside Zennor. Adversity's revelations.

The trouble is these days by the time I finish a sentence, I can't remember why I started it.

Trace the movements. I left Bordeaux, making for Vélines, Montaigne's gaff. I don't know how the idea of visiting came up. After all, I knew before I'd started that I'd missed him by four hundred years. The pull of the paraphernalia.

By the time I reached Vélines, I'd changed my mind, and put in a mind that was fully aware that this tour wasn't going to endow me with any acuities. Micky wouldn't be there at the door with an outheld tray: "Here, try some of these profundities." It wasn't going to push a life into my life-holder.

From the car park, I could see Montaigne's study tower. Somehow I had been hoping for a hand-out. A group of visitors meandered out through the gates. Visiting Montaigne's tower wasn't going to do me any more good than scaling the Eiffel tower. Exposure to intelligent folks' furniture doesn't help.

On to Cahors. I picked this circuitous route to Montpellier because I'd never been there. I didn't think it would be of great note, but I always consider every place worth exploring once – just in case there's a thirty-foot flaming sign, divulging the secret of life, that no one has told me about.

I was driving my favourite type of car: a hired car. Fast. I never get comfortable in a car unless the accelerator is right down. This unsettles some people. I often find cars I drive suddenly empty of passengers at the first stop.

Even Zak, a man who collected risks, would decline a lift from me and would always deny me my second favourite type of car: a friend's car. "I know other people who are prepared to drive at over a hundred miles an hour in a built-up zone. On the wrong side of the road. In the rain. After a few drinks. Through a red light. Into a bend. Not many, but I can think of a couple. But you're the only one who thinks it perfectly natural." I would have lost my licence by now I'm sure, if I'd ever bothered to get one.

To avoid tarnishing my repute as a driver, I want to state: it wasn't my fault. All the conditions were there for a successful drive: sobriety, good weather, a straight and vacant road. Unless it was a skilled assassination bid by cosmic interventionists, the car simply had enough of me and wanted to buck me. The left wheel blew. There are times when life spells out how little control you have.

No control

The car rolled as if having a dust-bath, and during this, too rapidly for me to appraise, I was ejaculated through the windscreen, reborn from the automotive womb.

I lay by the roadside, shocked that I still owned myself (or that my self had a body). Apart from a dull pain on my head, my body was in as good a working order as when I had commenced my trajectory. No limbs had deserted. No assets stripped. A bit misdirected getting such good fortune so late in life, when I didn't hugely need it, and I wasn't doing anything to maximize my life expectancy.

The windscreen had defected at the right moment. It lay not far from me, intact, having fared much better than the rest of the car, which had been patted down to dimensions that prevented anyone but an exceptionally short dwarf getting in it again, and was some thirty feet down a slope.

The car waited for me to struggle down to it, my clothes and skin lacerating on the undergrowth. It waited patiently and then as I was about to delve for my belongings, with a soft but forceful whoomph, like a gas ring, it flamed on, causing an excessive application of heat to my front.

As I watched it burn (I noted that the bottles of Château de Michel Montaigne had no retardative effect on the combustion) my passport, my money in various guises, my clothes, my possession entourage paraded through my mind in their unsmokey forms. There was nothing I could have done even if I'd been in an action mood, but it was before lunch so I dispensed with even the pretence of engagement. Too early for that magnitude of calamity.

I fought my way back to the road where I found the suitcase of civilisation which had also been spewed out by the car. I'd had it thirty years ago when I was undergraduating; it had been tatty and at the end of suitcasing then. For at least twenty-nine years I'd been plotting to buy a new one, shopping for non-fluids being another of my weak areas. The new suitcase was ashed along with my currency and credit, but the methuselah of receptacles, like all cheap objects one doesn't want, possessed an indestructible indestructibility, housing my books, which weren't much help in achieving a drinking-yourself-to-death-in-an-unconscionable-zenith-of-luxury situation.

Hee-hee

Luckily, no one had samaritaned along, so I had the chance of skipping the site of the crash, not wanting to be associated with anything that might attract the attentions of the police who couldn't do my liberty any good.

Having created a disassociating distance between myself and my ex-car, I then became most enthusiastic about making contact with fellow motorists.

There I was, a singed, bald, ageing philosopher with a ripped shirt and a frayed suitcase. Four francs twenty in my left hand pocket. In deepest nowhere. I concede I was not the ideal candidate for a hitchhiking post. Certainly the traffic that belted by displayed no hesitation in speeding away.

It started to rain. Like the cars, it didn't stop. I took the time to be sorry for myself while the sky juice marinated me with my suitcase which had grown a heaviness that outdid its volume. Not how I'd envisioned my flight to the South of France.

I walked on, purely because walking in the rain wasn't as asinine as standing in it. I couldn't condemn the cars for not stopping now. Who'd want to give a lift to someone insane enough to be trying out pedestrianism in a storm?

Arizona

I hadn't got so wet since my trip to Arizona years ago. I had automotive distress there too. On the trail of a Zonian student (I've never been worried about being one of those despicable teachers who discharge in their charges; my anxiety was always being one of those despicable teachers who didn't discharge in their charges) my car expired in the middle of what could be described, without fear of legal action, as a desert. A deserted desert, with no other voyagers in sight, only me and the zacaton.

I perscrutated the engine, awaiting a celestial voice to chip in and guide me through the problems. It was off duty. The thought that I was soon to die parched perched, vulturine, in my noggin. Too much imagination isn't much use in a desert. However, I hadn't got a mile from the car when I was getting all the water I needed. It rained without interruption until I had reached the nearest habitation eleven miles away (I got a lift for the last half mile) by which time I had contracted pneumonia. Everyone said it never rained in July. That was all I heard in hospital.

Ha-Ha

My ineptitude at hitching confirmed, I strode on cursing, as the total of cars making their journey precisely so they could not stop for me rose. The discrimination against rotund thinkers was infuriatingly unjust; I had no doubt if my chromosomes had been femaler and younger my sense-data would have been on their sedentary way.

But we all get a fan club.

A lorry pulled up blowily. I couldn't believe it had been ensnared by my wet, cursory thumb but I ran, ready to board, with or without invitation. However, a door ajarred and as I climbed up I was assailed by a reek of long-distanced lorry driver so potent it almost knocked my teeth out. Only the momentum of desperation drove me on. The driver's physiognomy was as enticing as his odour, but I couldn't be deflected.

Wherever he was going, I didn't care. My plan was to jump out when we got somewhere incontrovertibly urban. Problems of a financial nature seem more solveable in a concreted environment. "Montpellier," he told me was his destination. I was relieved to be vehicled and out of the rain, and I didn't add much to the introductory chit-chat because I was zombied by his face.

What had happened to it I couldn't divine, but a world congress of plastic surgeons couldn't have dedisastered what would have looked alarming stuck on a baboon's backside. His nose was awol, and the features that were present didn't cohabit too well. An astounding number of purple hues had made themselves at home on his countenance, not leaving any room for the more traditional fleshy tones. His age was undiscernible from his face (ravages of old age, tough shit) but judging from the looseness of the overample arms that were on show from the mangy vest he wore, this body was a big billionaire of crapulent seconds. His breath gave free passage to many foul things; his teeth were a remarkable refutation of the achievements of fin de millennium dentistry.

"I'm a philosopher," I replied to the ineluctable question, too lazy to lie or invent. He nodded approvingly, complimented me on my French and told me about the bricks he was taking to Montpellier. I'm not very good on bricks, but

I didn't listen to his exegesis, I was enjoying the consumed road.

I was still measuring out our progress when I heard him say what sounded like "you're cute". I thought I had misheard or that he was quoting from a popular song, but then I noticed that he had a hand fiddling in his crotch in what was too protracted a manner to qualify as scratching and which was shaping up to be offhand masturbation. "You're cute, my little philosopher," he added with added amplification, banishing auditory or elocutional doubts. Licking his lips, his hand zedded on my thigh and he commented, penetratingly, that it wasn't pussy, but that driving the unmade road wasn't at all bad. "Why don't we spend the night together in Montpellier?" he offered.

I became incredulity. In my youth, when I still had the factory finish, I had received inquiries, but I honestly felt I was a decade or two past my sell-by date, and long past the era of inciting uncontrollable lust in lorry drivers. Secondly, if I had been anxious to find someone willing to let my todger be a lodger (and women must be familiar with those suitors who go to enormous trouble to make themselves unpalatable and then expected to be snapped up) Gustave wouldn't have got an application form for last place. Even the roughest-tradingest of my acquaintances (and Cambridge has a proud heritage of wild sodomy dating back to the thirteenth century) would have made excuses and left.

"It's kind of you, but no."

"Why not?"

He said this so readily that I had the certainty he had had this conversation before. Because I would sooner die seemed a little harsh as a reply to an appeal for intimacy. Every creature has the right to solicit some events in the genital arena, but if you want to play hostthepost you've got to be in greater proximity to the norms of hygiene and the cosmetic triumphs of the fin de millennium. One might reckon that an offer is always flattering, but you had the feeling that Gustave would fall for anything with a pulse, and while that species of pantophagous appetite has its admirable side (it makes life easier) you don't want to be marooned in a cab with it. Nevertheless, I didn't want to recommence my career as a rain-gatherer, the headlong onset of lubricity not having allowed much travelling time to have elapsed.

"I don't do that."

"This doesn't happen in England?"

"Continually, but not to me."

"We could make the windows rattle," he elaborated. I declined with a smile exteriorizing that while such an offer was a delight and the acme of the day, it was one that I, for a variety of very regrettable reasons, couldn't take up.

"Is it because I didn't go to university?" he demanded, furious. Again, I assume this is a circumstance that ladies become accustomed to early on: when your no isn't working. When you fire no after no and your target still wants to zephaniah you and your no gun is empty.

"Is it because I drive a lorry?" I took refuge in silent contemplation of less road between me and Montpellier. "It's because I didn't go to university, isn't it? This not good enough for you?" he said, unleashing something resembling one of those bruised bananas still in the gutter two days after the market has gone and which he started to manhandle.

"I think I should get out," I announced.

"Oh no. The least I'm entitled to, my haughty philosopher, is an auto-rub." I logicked it up, and considering that it was (a) his lorry (b) not my desire to carry on absorbing rain in the wilderness, I decided that , bearing in mind (c) the famine (d) the slaughter and (e) the less photogenic suffering sloshing around our globe, I couldn't work up a fulmination about one off the wrist. I concurred and placed my gaze outside.

"Hey, you've got to watch," he protested, appalled at my disetiquette.

"I have to listen," I parried, "but I'm not watching."

"But take off your top. Please. As a favour." It was hard to refuse.

Civilisation is, after all, based on compromise. We had our social contract: he wanted a class wank, I wanted to get to Montpellier (though I felt unable to comply with his suggestion that I finger my nipples). "You were superb," he eulogised after evincing the symptoms of a zam-zum-mim of a goodness.

We drove on with new camaraderie and detente, and without incident (apart from Gustave shearing off the wing-mirror of a smaller, softer car as he expounded on the ultimate glory of, at high speed on the N6, galloping the maggot in the centre of Lyon – certainly the only worthwhile activity if you happen to be there).

"We work hard," he emphasised as we parted company on the outskirts of town.

His address was supplied to me on the inside of a choco-late bar wrapper along with the tip that he mostly plied the N6. The writing was in the very careful style of those who really have to think about it. Initially, I had a very intense compulsion to burn it, but then I reasoned it best to keep the information to make sure that I never accidentally (a) visited his town (b) his street (c) his block of flats in the mini future I had.

Money

I didn't know what to do. A bit futile coming all the way down South merely to watch your stash incinerate in the brazier of a wrecked car that I had gallingly just topped up with petrol.

Hunger made a scheduled appearance, but I was unable to push my consciousness through the French restaurant experience. With the spending power I had I might as well have been up the Zambezi.

I've always disliked those who've played down the charms

of money, they're usually the ones a couple of heartbeats from inheriting a castle. Tourists in indigence. The boys have been divided on this question – Bias, Aristippus, and others turning out to praise the good of goods, but a lot of them (usually the well-niched) sniffy; then the Dogs, the no pain no gain school, the be cheerful at your execution troop, Diogenes (himself on the run from Sinope for using moody money) and Crates, the only reason-merchant in world history known to have blown his yennom by giving ... it away to his fellow citizens. But true misfortune always features poverty, because true misfortune involves power-lessness.

I pondered whether any of my chums up North would be in loanable form. I pondered giving some lectures. I had played Paris at the Boulevard Saint-Germain once in my youth. I was drunk as a drunk, but I did get a bulging pocket of francs from a large crowd, annoying some zig on stilts and a fire-eater who had come to milk the tourists and the pavement flotsam. I had wanted to see what it was like to be an itinerant packing only rhetoric. Never let people tell you people aren't interested in ideas, as my careers officer at university once said of philosophy, "one of our problem areas".

But I sensed it wasn't a night for twirling ideas on a street-corner in Montpellier and passing the hat round. What to do? I had been counting on my liver failing before my wad.

Ho-Ho

I found a seedy hotel not far from the station, where you would expect to find one. France has some of the finest seedy hotels in the world. Elegance tends to be uniform: seediness surprises. I like three or four different types of wallpaper in the same room, and not knowing which fixture isn't working or is going to come off in your hand.

I explained at reception that I just had my money pinched

on the train and that I'd like a cheap room. They understood. It was obvious that they dealt with much more outlandish customers than grimy philosophers in grave difficulty with their world ranking, and that weird and dangerous as I thought I was, they handled odder oddities.

A passport excavated from the suitcase of civilisation seemed to satisfy the receptionist. "The English are always welcome here," he said as if there was a reason. It didn't seem any way to run a business. I'm not sure I would have let myself in, but the place didn't seem burdened with customers. A lanky youth in a cheap black leather jacket and half a haircut was slumped in an armchair, waiting openly, as if he were paid to sit there to heighten the disreputability of the establishment.

I went up to my room, opened my suitcase (in the mechanical way one does, although I had nothing that needed unpacking) and lay on the bed. I find I can think better this way, and a horizontal position makes you more streamlined for life. Nearly all the trouble in life comes from standing up.

There was a tapping at the door.

"Who's there?" I asked, perplexed at my sudden social attractiveness.

"You forgot to sign something."

What greeted me when I opened the door was not an unsigned document, but a zam-zum-mim of a gun, pointed at me by the quintessential dangerboy from downstairs.

"Your money!" he demanded with admirable succinctness, a quality much lacking, I feel, in modern philosophy. Untutored as I am in firearms, I could see with the merest of visual licks that this was enough gun to kill me and three or four major philosophers. It has to be declared that moments like this are an excellent justification for decades of gross intemperance. Imagine how great my distress would have been if I had spent my mornings gasping around jogging, abstaining from wine and beer, shunning pâtisseries, dodging rotundity by one square meal a day, only to be plugged like a fairground bull's-eye in a cheap hotel.

I unpocketed my four francs and held them out. The corridorman pushed me back into the room and closed the door to give a little privacy to the robbery.

"Don't mess around. Give me your money."

"That's it," I replied.

"But you're a tourist."

"Yes, but a tourist without any money."

"There's no such thing as a tourist without any money."

"Well, you've met one now. You're welcome to have a look," I said indicating my worldly possessions of the moment.

"But you're a tourist," he insisted, though I was relieved to hear with a tone of ripped credulity rather than menace.

But

His tone reminded me very much of Tanizaki's "but you're a philosopher". Tanizaki's Japanese brain had been splitting at the seams trying to fit in the concept of a philosopher who could defraud. He was a decent soul, and I sympathised with him at that moment. Tacked onto the general Japanese inability to understand anything more than five miles off-shore of Japan was a quite common misconception of philosophy as moral callisthenics. He had confronted me in the hope that I might have some inconceivable but all-embracing explanation to turn a prolonged and messy embezzlement into zany bookkeeping. I didn't lie because (a) it was before lunch and therefore too much effort and (b) because it would have shoved the nastiness away for only a few days or weeks.

The really noteworthy aspect of his presenting me with the evidence of the missing money was that he was the one who was ashamed, ashamed on my behalf. I toyed with making him an offer, cutting him in, since that would have given me a breathing space and you can never be sure when the earth might be clobbered by a shower of planetocidal asteroids rendering my academic pilfering academic. But I realised that the proposal itself would tizzy him to his knees. Even my offer to buy him a drink hunched him with horror since he clearly feared that it would simply be a question of a few more dunops of foundation money slipping from his grip.

"Why?", he asked, which is odd really because it strikes me that the theft of money can only really be motivated by the desire for money. There were two accessories I'd like to denounce by way of mitigation: firstly, I blame the medical profession who repeatedly assured me that my bucket-kicking muscles were in excellent condition. That puts consequences in a different light.

Also, I've never understood why the dangerously crass and stupid trades such as estate agents, television presenters, financial advisers, fashion designers, double-glazing salesmen, nightclub owners and plasterers should have an exclusive relationship with high denomination bills. My needs have always been modest, but my desires, to make up for that, have become increasingly expensive. An old entity needs harder and harder hits.

Rather like my health, I got away with defrauding the foundation much longer than I thought I would. For years Tanizaki's predecessors had come over, nodded approvingly at my administration and directed their energies to acquiring the correct brands of golfclubs and whisky. Ironically Tanizaki would get his arse zaibatsu'd for being more efficient than they were.

I might have acted more honourably in my earlier years. Idealism shackled to faith in my trade went overboard as soon as I went pro; dedication and decency overtaken even before the last lap by a desire to look out on the world from a balcony of cash. Perhaps if I had retained any confidence that there was a great deal left in the way of pathfinding in the biz, I would have reined in my ignobility. But for years the distant rumbling – that as a thinker all I was doing was acting as a museum flunkey, dusting off a few thoughts, shifting around some of the exhibits – had grown to a deafening roar.

I would be delighted to be proved wrong. It would be splendid if some genius were to come along and tidy up the history of thought, to wow us by showing how all the pieces click together. But I fear all that's left is some bitter skirmishing in the footnotes, shoving around some punctuation, shoot-outs in the letter-pages.

Years ago I noticed some domains in which no one had done any work, but the thing about these areas in which no one has done any work is (a) there's nothing to be done or (b) it's extremely difficult to do something or (c) the work's been done but you didn't know about it because you were too sloppy when you checked first time. In addition, as a specialist in the history of philosophy, I can assure you that there isn't a thought that the Greeks didn't copyright; they corralled all the concepts long before Christ. That's a position you could defend comfortably. And any cranial creations that you might maintain weren't spotted by them have certainly been mopped up by the French, German and British crews.

Still, if you think abusing a position of trust is easy you should try it. Dishonesty can be hard work.

Take my favourite researcher, the brilliant John Smith (try checking up on that name) whose hermit-like existence rapidly achieved legendary status. A legendary hermit-like existence that was necessarily legendary and hermit-like because John Smith didn't exist.

When I say he didn't exist, I am using the verb in the crude, layman sense. For example, he didn't exist in the sense that he could turn up on my doorstep one morning to exclaim: "Zeitgeist your mother, I want the money the foundation has been so generously sending me but which has been ending up in a bank account emptied exclusively by you."

As a pro, I would like to stress that simply because John Smith was a bit short on metabolic functions can one say he is any less real than, say, Montaigne?

People have read and, allegedly, enjoyed John Smith's work. They've seen his documentation. He had a room in college (arranged by me and praised by the cleaners for its tidiness). People had distinct memories of him. They discussed the meetings he didn't attend, lunches he mysteriously cancelled at the last minute via bizarre forms of indirect communication. And even if he was, in essence, a figment pigmented by my wit, where did it say on the application form you had to be able to make a bed creak?

And there were naturally bona fide zettists too (electromagnetically discernible to others) who got the peel of the financial fruits. There will be those who will say I was blocking those with talent from furthering the cause of the biz. Good, I'm glad, as the politicians say, that you mentioned that. That's exactly what I was doing. Three years at university doing philosophy is enough for any healthy individual.

Hmmmm

So, a warning against any assumptions.

Charitably viewed: we don't have much else. We have to assume water will boil at 100 degrees next time we try, that the old lady approaching you who looks like your mother, who is wearing your mother's clothes is your mother and not the President of Zambia in disguise, that we will be human beings in ten seconds' time and not contrary to our experience metamorphose into zalambodonts in a poorly run zoo.

Uncharitably viewed: The comfy cushions our liege, Laziness, chooses for its rear.

Anyway, a warning against assumptions about philosophers' morality and tourists' funds.

"You're a tourist," my armed assailant summed up for

the third time, as if this datum were a bulky parcel he was trying to push through a narrow letter-box, "and you haven't got any money."

I apologised, I would have liked to have had some money for him to purloin, but there it was. Thankfully there was no hint of violence, just the murmuring irritation and sulky resignation people demonstrate when they've got on the wrong train.

The gunman didn't threaten me, but neither did he leg it. He sat down and leaned forward to rest his forehead on his palms, making his head look like a mutant golf ball on its tee. "No, no, no," he said. Slowly. With equal zoning. I didn't know what to do. Another lamentable gap in our educational system. The gun was perched at an unsupervised angle in his lap.

"Shouldn't you be careful with the gun?" I offered.

"There aren't any bullets," he said, very quietly, in the tone of a man whose entire family has just perished in a car crash (a family he loved I should say).

"I couldn't even afford the bullets," he elucidated, chewing the black.

I was going to say he had outstayed his welcome but since, technically, he hadn't had one, I suppose more accurately, he was outstaying his barging-in. How does the well-brought up philosopher deal with a failed armed robber? These days I tend to keep quiet about my profession because there's something about the way it's perceived that calls for appeals for free advice (as doctors off duty, I suppose, are plagued by reports of twinges and importunings of pain) and prompts disclosure: the unloading of confidences, most of which you'd rather not hear (in a pub in Leeds, for instance, a gentleman sought my blessing for his predilection for zephaniahing Dalmatians. "Dalmatians! Dalmatians! I love them all"). However, even without the incentive of a known philosophical audience, the gunman proceeded to tell all.

"He didn't want to sell me the gun. I only had half the

money. 'But, ' he said 'Hubert, since you've just got out and since half a gun is as much use as no gun, I'll stem you the credit, as a favour.'"

Without any expression of interest on my part, I proceeded to get a generous helping of his life story. He had been released from prison that morning and had used his start-up money to obtain what he described as a disappointingly small gun. He had then looked around for a suitable victim, nothing personal.

"I'm pleased to think I look so affluent," I interjected to show there were no hard feelings.

"I've got a lot of catching up to do," he said, but there were none of the signs traditionally associated with the process of leaving, and zonitid-like he didn't budge. I wanted to offer him a drink, now that the attempted robbery was over and we were getting down to the tale-baring. I wanted to offer myself one, but alas the room was drinkless.

He gave me an appraising eye and I noticed that what I had thought was a squint was a glass left eye.

Then his right hand fell off and hit the floor with a hand-sized clunk.

"It's always doing that," he said, not making any attempt to retrieve it, or committing any other action that amounted to preparing to leave. His getaway was as flawed as his intended brigandage.

"And you," he said, "you speak good French. What do you do?"

I steeled myself like a pro. "I'm a philosopher," I said, pondering on the present tense. It was going to be very late before he left.

"Ah. Is there any money in that?"

"Depends."

"Depends on what?"

"On what sort of philosopher you are."

"You're not the rich sort? Or did someone rob you before I got to you?"

I led out the less embarrassing parts of my day.

"You had parents too, I suppose?" he asked, jumping theme.

"People tend to."

"Not me."

We indulged in a silence, which I didn't want to break by professing curiosity as to his family tree.

"And how do you like France?," he resumed, finally the zealous host.

I aimed for a nutshell account, but his attention boomeranged back to himself. I got the one-hour performance of the Meet Hubert show. Clearly, there was nowhere where Hubert was expected.

Hubert: a short criminal, but long penal career. Strong on misfortune, weak on working anatomy.

"I came into this world short-changed," he said. "A hand short. Or so they tell me." His childhood: he had been found abandoned inexplicably in a dustbin and taken into care. "They always liked to remind me about the dustbin." An infection removed the left eye. He was sparing about the details of care, assuming I would take it as read that it was infernal.

As I mentally noted that it was a pity I couldn't find a way of making money out of listening – I seem to give good ear – he skipped a bit to eighteen and his criminal debut in the big time. He and an accomplice more senior in the felonious hierarchy had stalked and ambushed a well-known local miser and entrepreneur, whose first reaction had been one of utter terror as they waylaid him in his flat and trussed him up, believing Hubert and his partner to be an active service unit of the tax authorities. When he realized they were common breakers of the law, he just chortled as they kicked him around and threatened him with their knives in an effort to get him to reveal the combination of the safe.

"I won't talk," he had said gleefully. The can of petrol that Hubert had been instructed to bring along was then poured over the bound curmudgeon. Hubert's confrère then ostentatiously lit a cigarette and mimed confusion as to what to do with the match still bearing a head of flame.

The miser talked. He talked so zippily Hubert and his mentor couldn't take down the details as he furiously repeated them before keeling over, cardiac'd out. "This is an interesting legal point," Hubert's chum had remarked, "I wonder what they'll charge us with?" They left empty-handed apart from some postage stamps Hubert had noticed on the kitchen table.

Hubert then reflected it might be a good time to go solo. He went up to the arrière-pays to do some grape-picking and live in a barn, and to brood about his fingerprints being all over the petrol can they had left at the scene of the crime. "And," he observed, "I'd had to pay for the petrol with my own money."

After resting up, Hubert studied a nice, small but fat, bank, where the staff had been powerfully snooty to him when he had tried to get a loan to buy a prestigious firearm (one that would get him noticed).

He expertly stole a car for getaway purposes. Carrying a gun that represented most of his grape-picking wages, he entered the bank and found robbing easy, as easy as breathing (easy if you don't have a medical condition that makes breathing difficult, or some blockage in the windpipe, in which circumstances, I concede, breathing can't be easy – as it can't be, on reflection, if you should find yourself submerged in a great body of water with a block of concrete round your feet; and if you can forget the ordeal of respiration at high altitude, not to mention the struggle to inhale at low altitude if it transpires you're in the middle of being strangled.)

Hubert, thinking that he had found his calling, got the money, cleared his throat and announced to the small gathering of bank employees and two Algerian plumbers: "Ladies and gentlemen, your attention please. You have been privi-

leged to witness my début performance. Your grandchildren
will think all the more of you for having been here; this alone
will make them cherish and respect you."

And then he zoomed out of the bank with his haul to find
that his stolen getaway car had been stolen.

He had left the door open and the ignition key in. A
zam-zum-mim of a nuisance, but with some calm, he could
have found an alternative means of absenting his sense-data
from the vicinity – hijacking another car or whatever. "I
flipped." He started running. The police followed a series of
pointing fingers which led them to the frozen food section of
a supermarket where Hubert was huddled amid frosty peas
in a futile attempt to reduce the visibility of his surface area.
He surrendered on demand, dropping his gun, causing it to
fire a bullet into a policeman's leg.

Here, Hubert insisted his luck changed drastically, because they didn't shoot him. He got ten years instead. Prison
was better than the children's home. "No one pretended you
were free." And: "I knew I was going to get another chance."

Night. I offered to go out and find something to eat for
four francs. The brotherhood of hunger. Hubert accepted.
He gave me his franc and suggested I borrow the pistol if I
wanted. "I'm not risking another flop tonight." There was a
late-night grocery which was willing to trade some baguettes
for five francs. We ate them, and having distracted his
hunger, Hubert (after politely asking for permission)
grabbed some bedcovers and a cushion and gave up verticality for the day.

??????????????????????????

More consciousness

I awoke aware as I always am now, that my wakings-up are an endangered species. Aware that if I wanted to bring civilization to heel, it was time to get up and with it. But the truth was I wasn't feeling zetetic or ready to get tectonic, to shift those continents of thought.

What I felt like doing was going for a fry-up at a greasy spoon in Leytonstone, where the grease is just so. Not any greasy spoon, but the one in Leytonstone. This is one of the most terrible agonies, one of the cruellest blows contingency's got, the desire to devour something that can only be found many hundreds of miles from where you have succumbed to the yearning.

Without warning, in the middle of crossing a courtyard in Cambridge I would become contorted with the craving for *moules bonne femme*. Not *moules bonne femme* in general, not a well-prepared *moules bonne femme* that might be found in any number of quality restaurants a fast taxi ride away, but the *moules bonne femme* from a small restaurant near Le Levandou.

Or if you're in Le Levandou besieged by the finest cooking in the world, what happens? You're assaulted, twisted by the need, a desperate need for the chocolate terrine that only exists in an out of the way foodie haunt in South London. Some might say: go and buy a bar of chocolate, you faffing fat failure, chocolate's chocolate. I say you eat this terrine, you know there's a God because you can see his face. The proof in the pudding. Something that good couldn't possibly exist in a universe that was just there to be a universe.

Hubert was lying sedately on the floor, almost making it look comfortable. I could tell from his breathing he was awake too, but not eager to confront the day either. Why endure verticality when you can be horizontal?

The day had slipped a sample of its wares through the

curtains on to the ceiling. I wasn't impressed by the sunshine. I wasn't falling for that old trick.

Bits of Hubert adorned the room. His hearing-aid was enthroned on his leather jacket. The artificial leg, in a manner that didn't speak well of its legness, leaned against the alleged chair. The hand was on the basin, with a head start as it were, awaiting the order to turn on the tap for morning ablutions. With an assemblage like that, I could see why Hubert wasn't bounding off the floor: he was no doubt pondering how to scrape his world ranking off the ground.

I was deeply bogged too. My plan to dissolve myself out of life was scuppered without reasonable, if not inordinate, amounts of cash. There comes a time when you consider yourself entitled not to have to worry about yennom any more. (A little struggle in one's youth, okay, that looks good.) I had reached that point.

Some universals

I may be wrong on this, but it seems to me that there are certain impulses of a non-fleshy nature that occur to everyone, or nearly everyone in a minimally developed civilization.

In no fixed order: the book. I go along with the view that most people have one book in them. Many are kind enough to keep it under skull arrest. It might be memoirs, fiction, love effusions or a guidebook to Zululand, but most people toy with leaving their brainprint behind. Mercifully for publishers and those of us constrained to read for a living, only a fraction actually go the full road authorially. (Some people succeed in making a career out of the one book by changing the title on a regular basis.)

Another common brainwave: the restaurant. Who wouldn't like a tenner for every occasion an associate chimed in at a meal with the idea of opening a restaurant, café or some species of catering service? (x) it looks not too difficult

(y) we all like food (z) you tend to see the better side of people when they're at the table.

The third unfulfilled recurrer: bank robbery. The charms are obvious. Almost all of us, most of the time, find ourselves short, or painfully short, of dosh. The solution: the dosh-houses rarely more than a few minutes walk away. You saunter in and run out with handfuls of remedy in its most naked form. A U-turn of fortune. The financial peep-show, just glass between you and those thin, coloured slices of freedom. A couple of pounds of pounds, a few kilos of the local figureheads, those pocket portraits, and you're on your way to wherever you want to go.

Then as lawbreaking activities with long jail sentences go, bank robbery seems fairly blameless. Banks seem to have more money than they need – it's just lying about all over the place. And everyone hates (a) banks and (b) bankers. It looks rather victimless. Of course, the people who aren't doing the bank robbery pay, but they do in a hard-to-notice fashion. Furthermore, because of (b), the idea of sending a wave of terror down the lower reaches of bankers' digestive tracts is appealing.

What stops us in the main is not a belief in order or a palliness with ethics. No, we are shackled by the likelihood of punishment – fear's bilboes. On top of which, pragmatically speaking, it's unlikely that one bank job would set you up for life; whatever its benefits, they're short term. You can't get rich robbing banks. The big money and the shorter sentences naturally lie in fraud, where with a bit of luck no one will even notice that a crime has been committed. But fraud lacks the directness, the plain beauty of bank robbery.

At various thin-walled junctures of my life, the temptation had swung through, but now, abetted by Hubert's presence, I invited it in for a drink, to sit down and tell me all about it. Bank robbery's other merit is that it scores highly in the I-can-do-that stakes. Great bank robbery might demand some flair and dedication but not bank robbery.

Apart from the need for wonga, there was also curiosity ... and there was no alternative I could think of to make or acquire money. There wasn't much call for a blubberous English philosopher with a six-figure world ranking on a Friday morning in Montpellier. My chums were out of convenient reach, and anyway I didn't want to gash my friendships with unwarranted demands. I wanted to keep as much of my address book as possible in good shape.

The Ultimate Truth: On the Blag

Like water swirling round the plug hole, my speculations wound into the idea. There's nothing like death on the horizon for shrinking inhibition. And the zetetics were prodding me to check the still unexplored corners of existence.

My main objection to poverty is that it's boring and just sands you away; I've done my share of that. Being poor is the same everywhere. I'm not sure being rich is: my embezzling only trampolined me fleetingly into those heights. But I was willing to investigate further. I had little to lose, so little I couldn't see it. I was looking at a stretch inside anyway, and if I was out, I wanted to spend.

Gear

I was lucky in that misfortune had provided me with the hardest-to-get ingredient of a bank robbery kit: a gun. "Pass the gun, Hubert. I think I'll go out and rob a bank."

"It isn't that easy, Prof."

Demarcation. Closed shop. Initiates don't like outsiders to think you can just decide yourself in.

"I didn't say it was easy, but there comes a point in life when you've got to go out and rob a bank."

"You can't get money somewhere else?"

"No, I haven't got a penny. And I'm on the run."

"On the run? From the bobbies? Scotland Yard? Prof, I

knew when I set eyes on you there was something agreeable about you. And it's much more agreeable to rob agreeable people, you know." Hubert fixed on his leg, stirred by my proposal. "I haven't had much success, that's true, but I recommend starting with some tourists. Not succeeding with a tourist is better than not succeeding with a bank. Or can't you philosophize or something? How have you made your living so far?"

"I could philosophize, but I don't think we'd get any lunch."

Hubert tried dissuading me all the way to the bank. (The receptionist said "Double room rate" as we left.) He insisted on accompanying me although I indicated association with me in my bank-robbing capacity wouldn't do his liberty any good.

"What would you say to me, Prof, if I decided to be a philosopher just like that, eh?" Hubert repeated, stressing my lack of background. I certainly was unsure what the signs of an eminently robbable bank were; I was tempted to sound out Hubert for his advice, but I didn't want to expose anything that looked like irresolution. I circled around, scrutinizing banks, Hubert quietening and showing approval that I was taking the trouble to appraise the merchandise.

But I realized that I would always find grounds to hesitate: the ideal bank certainly didn't exist in Montpellier. Or, as Plato would maintain, anywhere in this world. I could have chosen a bank further away from the hotel, I could have waited till the afternoon when there was less custom, I could have pandered to a dozen other considerations, but thinking about bank robbery doesn't make it any easier, and I couldn't face lunch-time without lunch.

I plumped for a branch of the bank where they had been the most offensive and most unhelpful over the years. What do you do if a bank is rude to you? Go to another bank. Which will have the same rates, same services, same A to Z of rudeness. Bankers have a cartel of disdain, an agreement to treat like dirt all customers who are not markedly rich; their revenge, no doubt, for having to go through life as bankers.

With bank robbery, the first decision you have to make is where to hide your gun. In an act of tremendous symbolism, I had emptied my suitcase of its books and placed the gun inside. The second decision you face is whether to make an entrance or to join the queue. Inside the bank were three harried, badly-dressed figures (with hairstyles a decade or two out of fashion) who looked like teachers taking time out from their crises to carry out some financial transactions.

One woman with a number of small za-zaing infants was letting them crawl and invade all the space around them – her air suggested that she wouldn't be unduly bothered if she lost one. Hubert did some tricks for a couple of them with his detachable hand. One looked up at me with curiosity; perhaps he was expecting me to be interested in him (as young children tend to assume everyone must be, not long having lost the twenty-four hour attentions of the womb), or perhaps he had never seen a philosopher revving up for a bank robbery.

I decided to let the customers go about their business; I didn't see why I should ruin their day. There were two tellers. One, a grizzled veteran who was going badly into baldness, over-indulging the few scattered strands left, letting them grow long into absurd squiggles which merely underlined the shortage of pileous action. He moved briskly, with contrived jollity, as if he were trying to convince us and himself that he really enjoyed being a banker, that he was doing what he wanted to do.

The other teller was a woman. She had that look.

I know. It's wretched. Still a slave. There I was: skint, fallen off the edge of middle age, a career careered off the road, undertakers eyeing me up, about to wallow in villainy. And yet I took the time to think about the possibility of getting work for my jubilation specialist. Instead of concentrating on my blag, I found my sentient space becoming crowded with amorous plans.

I stood in the queue and prayed that I would get the strand master and not the belle. I've often thought that locating the seat of thought in the head is wrong: in men it's closer to the seat, down there in the soft head that dangles, with its loose hemispheres, zone of the secret capital. What sits on our shoulders is a front.

For the male, you only lose interest when you're (a) dead, or (b) very nearly dead. Boxed in the gonad's monad. It's always been a good rule of thumb for judging how ill I am – if the concept of a young blonde wearing nothing much doesn't make the blood chuckle, I know it's time to call the doctor.

It was odd; I wanted to board her acquaintance, but at the same time I couldn't help surmising that robbing her bank wouldn't be the best way of presenting myself.

Also, as a reason handler, I was nudged by the notion that I should be able to convince people that this was a bank robbery without the banal aid of a gun. As a nod to my world ranking. There was, I noted, a video camera. Hubert zapped it with a big smile. The teller a few hairs' breadth from baldness copped the extended family.

I walked up to her.

"Good morning, Madame," I said. "This is a bank robbery." I wouldn't have been surprised to have been told I was at the wrong counter.

"A robbery?" She wasn't bothered. Not lackadaisical, not shrill: a stoic. I could have been asking the time. That look was still there, like jam smeared around the mouth. Past the years deemed to be the best for female beauty, but there are women who can make a mug of time, especially when they have that look, a constituent of which might be prosified as hard to shock.

"You're sure about this?"

"I'm sure," I said, opening my over-large holster to reveal

the cash-hungry maw and the gun. She started plunking wads of yennom into the suitcase, not slowly, not fast. I rested the gun on the counter.

"Do you want the change as well?"

"No thanks."

"Yeah, leave something," said a tetchy voice behind me. "I drove in this morning especially to make a withdrawal. Some people have to earn a living, you know."

Quasi-baldy next door hadn't grasped it was a robbery. He was arguing about some technicality of money orders with the much-zygoted woman.

My dispenseress packed all the visible cash, then added a small slip of paper she had scribbled on. "That's it. My colleague has some more."

"No, don't bother him," I said. That would have been greedy. "Thanks very much. Sorry to have troubled you. See you."

"See you," she said, waiting for the next customer. Hubert and I walked out, Hubert billowing admiration; I could sense he wanted to unload some comments but refrained from doing anything so out of place or unprofessional.

Outside he looked at me expectantly, waiting for me to give the lead, clearly thinking, now what do we do? I remembered there was a very good fish restaurant around the corner. I chose to head there. Hubert whispered edgily: "Aren't we going to run a bit?"

"No," I said. Hubert obviously hadn't twigged that I was (a) too old (b) too fat and (c) too lazy to run, and that if I was going to be caught by the police I wanted to be collared in a dignified posture and state.

The police were slow. We were already scanning the entreés and sipping an aperitif when the first police car sped by, easy to observe from our table by the window.

The waiter didn't get on well with Hubert. Hubert seemed to me to be a stranger to first-class fish restaurants and the waiter had formed the same opinion. He had no doubt that

Hubert should be conducted to an open field and napalmed.

"Let me tell you about the specialities of the day," the waiter urged.

"No, I don't want to hear about the specialities," said Hubert, "I want the zarzuela. We aren't tourists, you see." He concluded by curling up his lip in the manner one associates with very aggressive dogs about to bite someone.

We were asked to move tables when another party arrived. Hubert was brought the wrong dish and had to ask five times for his beer. For us, criminals in a criminally expensive restaurant, the service was rubbish, despite the place being half-empty, my caving in and taking one of the specialities of the day as a peace-offering and our drinking a small fortune. This is another heart-squashing element of life: no matter how good or expensive a restaurant, sooner or later you're going to be the recipient of offhandedness. The waiter rounded it off by pouring some buff-coloured sauce all over Hubert. I thought Hubert was going to hit him, but instead he insisted on leaving a tip as large as the bill.

"That'll teach him," he said.

"I don't follow."

"He thinks I'm a prick, and there's nothing as grating as a prick with money, not even a smack in the mouth."

In among the cash, I found the piece of scrap that she had put in. In large writing so exciting that each character was worth a thousand pictures was the name Jocelyne and a telephone number. I showed it to Hubert. He had noticed that look too.

"Phew!" he said, shaking his undetachable hand as if it were on fire. "Now there's a woman … a woman who's hard to shock."

On the way out, Hubert lifted someone's cap from the coat-rack and passed it to me. "We mustn't push our luck," he said, as I muffled my baldness.

The police were making up for their earlier absence by a lot of presence, standing around, looking serious, talking into radios and acting as if they had important things to consider and do. We waltzed through them, only stopping when Hubert asked one motorized copper leaning on his bike what had happened.

"Bank robbery."

"Did you catch them? Or have you got a good description?" asked Hubert in his public-spirited voice.

"They won't get far," was the response.

"Why did you do that?" I asked once we were out of earshot.

"Just checking."

Back in our room, Hubert kicked the cushion into the wall.

"All I want to know is, are you a genius?" he exclaimed. "Or is this what philosophy can do for you? In one morning you knock over a bank, invent the getaway lunch and you're in danger of being siphoned away by a woman who could drain the Zuider Zee with a straw. I've never seen anything like it."

Après-blag

Who can say no to praise, however unearned? Nevertheless, the robbery hadn't done anything for my hollowness. It had been like withdrawing money without the encumbrance of a cheque-book and I was surprised to have come out the other end without having deployed the zetetics.

The problem now that I had money was that I couldn't worry about not having money. There was no pecuniary emergency to keep me from the pandect, the last say, the round-up, the $E=mc^2$ of ideas. A universal history on the lines of the composition of Johannes Zonaras (he had it easy being a twelfth century Byzantine bureaucrat) is something I fancy; but a universal history in one sentence. Maybe two (to give people the feeling they're getting value for their money).

Shame I've jeroboamed my life away. Ah my youth, when the zet was good. It's not something you tell anyone, but I went up to university confident I could take human knowledge, that I could be the zeb, the beachmaster, the big swinging dick of the biz and all that jazz. Forget being number one. I'd just like to get on the scoreboard.

The haul had only been the monthly take-home pay of a bank manager, but it was enough to keep me in contact with sommeliers for a while (getting the wine right was something to chafe about, I suppose).

What looked like about half of the money, I gave to Hubert (I'm past the age for counting money). After all, it had been his gun that had taken me over the hurdle from sigher to yennom-collector (and he had been giving me immoral support).

"I'm off to do some shopping, if that's all right with you, Prof," he said keeping me promoted, "we'll have to talk about philosophy later."

I didn't share Hubert's optimism about the outcome of dialling Jocelyne's number. Getting arrested wasn't so bad, but getting arrested bumpkinly: no one likes to make policemen laugh. Visions trooped in of the guffawing in court, as it was related how I had phoned Madame X in the expectation of colliding loins and how the police had been waiting for me; then came the hovering into view of those zones that I wanted to lip onto. I reached for the phone.

There was no reply. Perhaps still at work, or still being debriefed by the police.

Do we care about this?

Well, I'm taking it all down.

When you're out of control, you're out of control. Later, the phone was answered. I hadn't had such awkwardness making a call for decades.

"Hallo." One word. A sonic sample from a voice, poised,

confident, unhurried; a single utterance that carried its begetter's qualities in its plumage.

"I hope you remember me," I said, but it was a voice with such emotional trunk, that received so many calls, that was so weighty, that I felt obliged to make it clear beyond doubt who I was, "I robbed your bank today."

There was no rush to reply. "Ah, yes. Of course I remember. We only had one today."

"I would like to apologise for any inconvenience."

"I was hoping you'd ring. I presume you're not working this evening."

We agreed to meet at what I had been assured was the best (and most expensive) restaurant in town.

"Are you sure? It's very pricey, and, let's face it, you didn't get that much."

I had time to go out and buy some clothes. Presentation isn't something I fuss much over lately. One of the few benefits of slapheadom, of a chrome dome is there's (x) no need to wash (y) no need to comb (z) no need to worry about the vogueability of your locks. A bullet head can save you hours in a week, weeks in a year, years in a life (if you manage to hang on long enough). The savings on shampooing and snipping aren't to be snubbed either.

Perhaps providence has shorn me deep, beyond the roots, so that I wouldn't have to fritter away my time fretting about extracranial arrangements, giving me more chrono for idea spinning. Bad luck, providence.

Reflecting on my reflection 1.1

Making sure my reflection still worked, I logicked that one of the few benefits of extreme middle age (or apprentice old age) is that you know there's nothing much you can do to improve the package in a few hours (you'd need to get a deity in for a week for the retouching alone); satisfaction can only be obtained by encountering worn-philosopher fans.

The repast 1.1

I rolled in late, reasoning that if the police were there to bag me, I could have the pleasure of having made them wait (though on route incarceration had begun to look tempting – it might give me the inclination to do some writing to right my written-off career).

She was already at the table – once I got over my apprehension of apprehension, I started to enjoy the prospects of the evening.

"My name's Eddie."

Re past repasts

In her sitting opposite me, I saw, as when a mirror mirrors a mirror, a string of identical couples, dining couples tailing off into imperceptibility. Suddenly I was aware (x) how much money I had expended on women in restaurants and (y) how little joy had been afforded and (z) that I was too old and tired to be on the pull. But there was none of that firing of verbal vacuums (words with nothing inside) when social reconnaissance is taking place, when no one wants to say anything lest it frighten the other person off.

"It's a tedious place," she said giving me the stare of a sex-army sergeant. "I hardly ever work at the counter. I'm the assistant manager. But I'm glad I was today, it's hard to meet interesting people."

Company

The truth is, even for the most outgoing of people, finding people to whom you can adhere to is tricky. Even when you're young, one of the most important considerations is the pph (people per hour); but as you age, not only do you get receipt of wizened, deflated years, the clocks tock too much (or so it seems to us reality-junkies who need greater and greater volumes of chronal space to get the same effect we partook of in youth) and many of the platforms of experience are blocked off, the huge tubes of adhesive: going to school together, going to university, first jobs, first loves, first abodes, first treks. Friendships need to be seasoned with seasons of ascent and fall to girth up.

But you do get your slots. At a busstop in Taipei I was next to a fellow European, and his mean mien messaged that we would laugh at the same things, be outraged by the same things, that we would be kicking off with five years on the clock. However, without sounding either doolally or stern-hungry I couldn't just say "we're going to friend brilliantly". A bus bussed him away.

The repast 1.2

"So is bank robbery your main occupation?", she asked, not terribly worried about what the answer would be.

"Very rarely. I'm a philosopher."

"Is that a tough way to make a living? Did you need to buy some new ideas? Or is it simply greed that brought you to us?"

"Greed is a need. The police were slow."

"That's because, in my alarm, I forgot to push the alarm button."

Your face or mine?

Amid my animadversions on philosophy, and the forecasts of full-time decay swooping in my mental hangar, and the quivering engines of conversation, there was also speculation about what my dining-companion had underneath her dress (although at my age you do have a shrewd idea, but you can never dispel the curiosity). Despite having an iffy vitality, a world ranking not dissimilar to any spotty student who's read half a paperback on Zenonism, I couldn't help postulating lapping her lap. The idea of my trying it on I immediately dismissed as bollocks from my bollocks: who would want to take me home? (Unless they had a fascination with the Ionians). Jocelyne liked unusual table talk, that was it.

Zzzzzzzzs need not apply

But there is always that moment when desire breaks cover from amiability.

"Where are you staying?" she asked as I walked her to her car. "My place is quite far out of town. I think we've waited long enough, don't you?" This is the turn of phrase you ache for at twenty, pine for at thirty, but you don't expect to hear when you're half-centuried, overbellied and frazzled in a Montpellier car park, with two police forces seeking to jug you.

Anticipating a handshake, I found a dickshake (one that it occurred to me might kill me).

Moral: go deeply middle-aged, scupper your career, embezzle vast sums, head for a foreign country to jeroboam yourself to death, knock over a bank, and your love-life will pick up no end.

To be honest, I've always been surprised when women have intimated that intimacy is on. Even when I was more marketable, even with the less pursued ones, the why? was big between my ears; but then women have this great allocation of kindness.

Get your romances out 1.1

I hadn't been forsaking much, when I quit England. The last pressions of warmth were from a French secretary in the City, who railed her way to Cambridge for weekends from time to time. She would talk by the hour, reviling the weather, the food, the people and her lodgings (to which I didn't have the grounds or the opportunity to demur) before we would seek to improve the world. By and large I had the impression that it was the audiencetial aspect of the visit that was most needful. How does that look? Discuss with reference to your life.

Fact sheet on Jocelyne

1. 35
2. Twice divorced.
3. Possibly fatal to philosophers with over-lived livers.

As we went into the hotel, I saw two toughs outside and I had an urge to ask them in to give me a hand, since I was afraid improving the world with Jocelyne might cost me my life. Dying right is important for your career. Let's be frank, Socrates' name for one would have covered a lot less paper if he'd expired on account of a bad oyster or a vicious cold. Bruno's only remembered at all because of his pre-death cremation, and Seneca salvaged himself sharpish by slashing his wrists in the bath.

Jocelyne unclothed: not too quickly, not too slowly. No matter how much of a veteran lecher you are, there's always something about that last item of garb, clearing the working surfaces. She removed her panties, stretched back the elastic on her thumb and fired them across the room, catching me, sniper-like, on the forehead (a forehead, as someone once remarked, that has conquered its way to my nape.)

What did my decades of rhetoric, eristic and idea-prodding provide me with? All I could do was gape like a zonked zonkey and croak like a juggernauted frog: "All night."

I filled up with sensuous sense-data.

Get your romances out 1.2

I haven't really had much success with women. What a single status testifies to, you can argue either way, but the truth is they want you, they get you. However, you do become more hawk-eyed about which berthings have hope and which don't, though this acuity is often evicted by the desperation to have your consciousness crossed by pleasure, however ephemeral or marred.

I haven't really had much success in Montpellier before, even decades back, when, in the right light , I didn't look too bad. The reason I remember my lack of success in Montpellier is that it was a nose dive that pissed in the mouth of forgetfulness.

It had been that stage at a party. I: twenty-two, prepared to do anything to bring the jubilation specialist to a zephaniah, virtually the only non-couple, certainly the only buck standing and unbonded.

This is a seduction stratagem I have often utilised: keep drinking, certainly, but keep standing because even women who are inclined to lower their standards truly low find it easy to overlook someone slumped at their feet.

What I said at that party I can't summon up, but it wasn't anything pithier than "Could you pass me that half-empty glass of vodka that no one is drinking?", but without warning I found hoops of attention being placed around me by a young lady, who must have had a powerful imagination to fashion wit out of my banal conversation. She was extremely attractive, and I emphasise this, not because I attract the attractive, but because I don't. Every fat philosopher gets an attractivette once a lifetime (if he keeps upright at enough parties).

The room was fuggy, heated with indulgences of all sorts; many of my fellow wassailers had keeled over and had retreated to view the inside of their skulls.

"It's cooler outside," she said, climbing out of her jeans and out onto a window ledge. Eulogiseable thighs: were I to be executed, I could happily spend the eve rotating them in my electricity.

I craned out of the window and watched her flounce along

the ledge and swing onto a flagpole that belonged to an adjacent municipal building. From our brief conversing, I had gleaned that she was a keen mountaineer – her waifish body in a white top (that advocated her brownness) swung effortlessly, like a trapeze artist or a human flag.

"Come here, Edouard. Let's make love."

From that time on I've been very wary of women who call me Edouard. The years throw some small change of enlightenment into your outstretched hand, and you know what will work and what won't.

Now, I would have stressed the unsuitability of flagpoles for improving the world and I'd have tried to coax her back from the air.

But she was far more beautiful than a callow philosopher with my world ranking had a right to. I had had no distressing experiences with flagpoles, I was exceedingly drunk and like most males of my age I was amenable to going to any lengths for my length.

That it was three in the morning, fifteen feet or so above a public square, that I had been repeatedly characterised as an orangutan but wasn't one, I paid no mind. I zestily unleashed the hyperhypo and essayed the pole.

I dangled in a way which would have been a credit to any primate. For around six seconds.

The flagpole didn't snap, but my grip did. She had wrapped her legs around me, and for those brief breaths when I was a qualified suspendee, I received the warmth and fragrances lounging on her skin. I was however unable to relish my erotic harvest because I was completely occupied with the sensations of strain and discomfort that had taken up residence in my arms. I had no chance to warm up her warmth.

What I had was a brief moment to admire her musculature from underneath, an even briefer moment to ponder that that might be the picture I'd be taking with me to eternity, and a couple of chronons to play the thought what a monkey my desires had made out of me (not a very good one) (but one shouldn't be monkeyist).

If I'd jumped of my own volition or timed my letting go, the drop would have severely injured me or broken my neck, but since I had not participated in the creation of the fall I rejoined groundlevel fairly amicably. Plummeting from pussy, I landed with cat-like grace (assuming a cat overweight, drunk, clumsy and into landing on its head).

Thoughtfully, she lobbed down my trousers and I worked my way back up to the party, but the moment, the momentum was gone; just would-be rutters who passed in the night on the sky's sole.

???????????????????????????

Hubert entered as we were busy colliding loins. Jocelyne looked at him with curiosity as if he were an unheralded part of my technique.

"Sorry," he said, "I need the gun." I surmised that would be the last of Hubert, but he only vanished until the morning when he rereturned to catch me making use of the bed for zeds, and Jocelyne getting dressed to go to work. The concept of the knock had eluded him. It was that sort of hotel, that sort of end of the millennium.

"It was a pleasure robbing your bank," said Hubert, unpacking weapons from a hold-all as Jocelyne carried on packing hers up.

"Glad you liked it," she replied with as much courtesy as a mortuary slab (directed at Hubert or merely part of working up to office hours?). "You have business, I see. You know where to find me."

Woman: God's last job. The zeb.

Hubert was very excited. I was not. He held up a circular clip of bullets. "It's a full moon," he said. "I went to see my armourer to buy some ammo, but then I thought why buy it? I helped myself to all this stuff. He didn't scratch my back when it needed scratching."

"I would have thought your armourer, as someone who arms armed robbers, would have been well-prepared for his customers."

"He's a cunning bastard, all right, Frédéric, I had to wait until he wasn't looking."

"What distracted him long enough for you to whip all that?"

"Two bottles of pastis, on the head."

Hubert twirled his weapons. "Oh, and I've hired a flat." Which was his way of telling me, as I shortly discovered, that he had also made available to himself what remained of my money in the suitcase. When I rose to grapple with the universe, I found I had four francs in my pocket again (though different ones). My crime had tickled two good meals out of life, and I had a roof over my head for the foreseeable future.

The flies buzz round my world ranking.

"It's a full moon," said Hubert, slipping the clip of disquietingly large bullets into a disquietingly large revolver. "When it's a full moon, bank robbers rob."

Still Montpellier

I've never understood why Plato pushed the examined life so much. That the unexamined life isn't worth living, let's leave that alone, but the same could be said of the examined life. You zet your life and you see it's a steaming pile of dung: it's one thing to see the worthlessness of your existence, to dunk your finger into the slime of your soul, and another to work some amelioration. It's easier to transmogrify a banquet into excrement than it is to make excrement toothsome.

Or the Delphic oracle: know yourself. What if you're not the sort of person you want to know? Going to the mirror and firing your face into yourself, it's not unquestionably congenial. We are forced to stew in the juices of our own self, whether we break down the flavours precisely or not. It is, I suspect, more often than it is admitted, like having to stay in the same bathwater for your span.

Image without a home:

We wade through questions and answers that come up to our waist; they have inundated the world, there are so many that to pair off even a few is good going. And sadly hard work.

Still Montpellier

It was an inauspicious morning. The goat cheese that Hubert had been raving about, and that I had fancied for breakfast had mostly gone, apparently rodented away. Hube's lair was in the old part of town – the wallpaper had a dull patina that messaged living and dying unpleasantly and unmemorably, ironed-in encrustations of misery that were far more dispiriting than bare walls would have been.

Hubert kept trying to talk about philosophy, much as my students had, and much as then I wasn't in the mood.

He also urged me to do another job. "We have a reputation to maintain. We are undefeated." I thought about (x) protesting (y) lunch and (z) not wasting Hubert's time by making him persuade me.

Robbing banks seems to be habit-forming.

We could have gone a bit further, but since it was eleven o' clock, I was loath to infringe on lunchtime by exploring for a pukka bank, when we knew there was a branch around the corner.

"What philosophical method are we going to use?" insisted Hubert.

"You're serious about this?" I commented as he produced a notebook. I speculated on what I could impart in the thirty feet to the bank. "All right. We'll draw on the common sense school. A much underrated nodule of zetetics. It was hushed up by the boys as it could have put the biz out of business. John Locke, 1632-1704, was big on it. The work of Thomas Reid 1710-1796. Read Reid's *Inquiry into the Human Mind on the Principles of Common Sense*. Backed up by Mendelssohn's *Gemeinsinn* in his *Morgenstunden*. Believe me, I could go on. Common sense tells us to go in there with a big gun and take the money."

Doing wrongdoing right

There was none of the sense of occasion for number two.

A small queue had awaited us and just as we were about to be served, someone scurried in front of us. "Sorry, I'm in a rush." This wasn't an apology or a stab at an apology; the import was heading rapidly in the other direction, so much so that most people could have made a fundamental rudeness sound ingratiating in comparison.

"Where are you going?" said Hubert, grabbing the zig by the arm.

He was bulky, he could have made two Huberts with some left over to construct an eight year-old Hubert. He looked down on Hubert, not only physically but morally. He had a flash suit that spoke of high finance while Hubert's apparel shouted workhouse.

"I'm in a rush," he snarled, staring at Hubert with repugnance as if he had scorpions coming out of his nostrils, and addressing the harridan behind the counter: "I've come for the dollars, Madame Robert."

"Let me show you something," proposed Hubert as the queue-jumper tried to shake him off his arm like droplets of rain. Hubert stayed calmed while his gripee got shirty. It was as if they were performing some modern choreography (by one of those companies that succeed in diverting public funds without any risk of a jail sentence). Funnily enough the man was threatening to call the police when Hube folded him up like a deckchair by the fast knee to groinsville.

"Let me show you something." Hubert bared the gun. "You see this? Do you have one of these? If not, you're going to have a bad day."

We took his dollars, and his suit.

"When did you push the alarm?" Hubert quizzed the note-shepherdess, who acted as if she had swallowed an alarm-clock. "Don't worry, I just want to time them."

We perambulated out, peripatetic blaggers, environmental friendly culprits; we cut through a block of flats and waited for the sirens.

"Ten minutes," exclaimed Hubert. "Can you believe that? It's outrageous. I'm so wise not to pay taxes."

Hubert went off to do some more shopping, I to call Jocelyne.

Have you learned anything?

Amongst the sparse, useful data I have collated during my internment in this Eddie Coffin: no matter if they have the thousand dick stare, there are few women who don't prize (w) flowers (x) invitations to posh restaurants (y) playing I-lick-you-scream (z) solicitous phone calls.

Still Montpellier

Having been home-cookinged, I returned to the flat the next day, pondering how for many twenty-first century couples, the personal culinary experience is the final stage of bonding.

Hube vigorously recommended that I try some of the goat cheese he had repurchased. Opening the fridge door, I found a rat eating the cheese. My dealings with rodents, particularly those tagged verminous, have been few, but generally the pattern has been one of man, the boss, the caretaker of creation, the namer, appearing and the lower orders hitting the road.

The rat, glossy and as comfortable as if it were in a zendo, was mantled in the wrapping paper and didn't desist in munching when I loomed. I glared at the rat, waiting for it to slink off but it wasn't intimidated by never-been philosophers.

I called for armed assistance: "Hube!" The rat deigned to react now but acted in a way which reminded me of Hubert asking about the alarm the day before: the rat brushed its whiskers and then, in a sedate fashion sloped off to the back of the fridge and a small gap through which it had disappeared by the time Hubert turned up, infuriated to see the loss of another cheese.

He spent most of the day, shifting furniture, auscultating the walls with a glass and ripping up floorboards, and even, having applied a silencer, firing off some rounds into one section of shoddy masonry.

Then it was getting to be the time when I had to choose between auscultating civilisation or going for a drink.

Not a long choice. Hubert suggested his local, where he assured me I could find Blanche de Garonne.

Booze

They say alkys can give it up; I say if they can give it up, they're not alkys. You can space out the spaces between drinks, but once you're a prisoner of the bottle, you're not getting out. True marriage.

I have despaired, not because of being a sot (because in the gradations of degradation it's not so bad, it is possible to drown yourself quietly with small lakes) but because I couldn't do anything about it.

Feeling it couldn't make things worse, I did attend a meeting once, where I was encouraged to talk about what I found so alluring about booze. I must have had a glib tongue in, because we all went down the pub.

Still Montpellier

Hubert's local was the sort of place you'd imagine it to be: easy-to-hose-down walls, gnarled, zany codgers clutching the one drink that was the pay-off of their day.

"People know me here," said Hubert proudly.

Since I wasn't at home pandecting, I was forced to drink several beers. Feeling bad about drinking, I drank some more. They had a store of Trappist beer which, short of banging your head against a wall, is the most efficacious way of getting that detachment necessary for meditation.

Hube was certainly right about his celebrity in the hostelry. As he emerged from the toilets, he was stonewalled by four pugilists and hoisted up the wall by his jacket lapels and frisked. "Guess what, Hubert?" said the leaderly one, "Frédéric would like his stuff back. Here's the deal: you give us back everything and your money – we only break your leg. No stuff, we break everything." He pulled Hubert's hand off and tossed it over his shoulder. "You're really fragile, Hubert. Has anyone ever told you that?"

Bar-room brawls

I've never had much to do with them. I think the word brawl implies giving (or at least attempting to give) as well as taking; I've only ever been on the receiving end.

Of course, there are certain parts of London where having a drink is asking for it. By some bureaucratic oversight these zones aren't marked and you are only aware that you've stumbled on one when you're on the floor with the dog-ends and you're trying to be considerate and bleed internally as you take the boot.

I remember lying on the pavement in Catford (where the police had left me after dragging me out of a pub) watching the Christmas Eve snowflakes whirl down, thinking how beautiful they were and how, if I had been sober, I would have been too concerned with my pain and dignity to enjoy the sight.

The only time I tried to take part (in an advisory role) was when Zak was being strangled on a pinball machine. Zak was one of those Americans who was incapable of making it back to his country. He had served in Vietnam (while his entire family had died in a car crash), doing three tours of duty, his final posting being as instructor in unarmed combat.

Clearly his antagonist had no idea that Zak was trained to kill with his bare hands since he seemed to be having no difficulty in throttling him. I was sitting back enjoying it, because this sort of commotion was not what you expected in Cambridge, and because I was looking forward to Zak sorting him out.

After a while, as Zak was going blue, it occurred to me that his self-defence skills might be having a night off and that I should do something. I tapped the strangler on his shoulder. "I think it only fair to tell you that my friend here is an expert in hand-to-hand combat."

Doubtless, the strangler didn't realise my participation was purely cautionary. Suddenly, I smelt broken nose. However, in belting me, he unperfected his choking giving Zak the chance to hospitalise him by unQueensberry numbers.

Still Montpellier

"I'm warning you," said Hubert, speaking through his jacket lapels, "you don't want to do this." The quartet laughed. Not false laughter. This was evidently an old favourite in their line of work.

My philanthropy swollen by the beers, I had a conviction that I could persuade everyone to sit down and enjoy brotherly love. Looking at the leader, he didn't seem a bad sort. He probably had a family. This probably wasn't his idea of a good time either. He probably didn't relish spending his evenings looking for people, threatening them, pulling off their artificial limbs, and then beating them up. He would have preferred to have been at home watching television or helping his kids with their homework.

I walked over to intervene, but my legs had gone a funny shape so it took me longer than foreseen to get me there and I didn't have the best posture.

"There's really no need for this," I counselled in my jolliest voice as I gained their presence thresholds.

"We're in trouble now, lads," said the leader. "It's the bouncer." I tried to maintain cheerfully that there was no need, while the leader opined it was necessary and stubbed out his cigarette on my head.

"Having three friends isn't going to save your teeth," said Hubert, still jammed half way to the ceiling. The leader found this very funny and parted his henchmen to prod Hubert with a heavy finger. "What are you going to do, cripple, bleed on me?" There was the shortness of breath in this question, known to those of us conversant with tavern conversations as presaging lashing out.

Hubert caught the eye of the barman. "Sorry, Jean," was what he said.

They had made a mistake. They had left him with one hand.

Hube was incredibly fast. He grabbed a bottle off the zinky table and hit himself on the head with it. He had been so fast, it wouldn't have seemed a problem to have, say, hit the leader with the bottle instead. I, and everyone else assumed he had got it wrong. The bottle shards fell as an octopus of blood advanced down his brow.

"Bravo," cackled the leader, in danger of wetting himself, "are you going to break your own leg for an encore?"

"I have something, very fatal, very fashionable, transmitted by blood," said Hubert. Expertly, he paused for a second or two for this to sink in. Then, leaping up, he headbutted the leader. It was the headbutt of a worldfamous headbuttist, with the distinctive sound of crumpled face and a closed consciousness. A fine tribute to the power of the mind when applied properly, behind a thick forehead.

The others didn't run off. Reflex, I suppose.

They were strapping figures, so if they'd hit Hubert they would have mashed him. But they didn't. One of them did hit me, persistently, but I was glad to be kicked around while Hubert dealt with the other two. One sagged down yelping as Hube probed his thigh with penknife and struck artery (they hadn't frisked him thoroughly). The second got two fingers further in his eyeballs and zonules of Zinn than is normally considered acceptable plus Hube's teeth in his neck. My assailant had his nose bitten off, and then along with his companions, preoccupied with pain, they got boot treatment from Hube, shooing their sense-data temporarily away from Montpellier.

"Don't forget," he said, "I was with the perpetuals." This reminder was squandered.

Even at his best, Hube didn't look his best. Now he looked quite ghastly, doused in blood and panting out rage; a good example of how in unlicensed fighting, he who goes nuclear, wins.

He helped me to my feet, while the barman presented him with his hand. I noticed in the mirror that I had the makings not just of a black eye, but a black face. I stood half up: I couldn't straighten up. The floor was looking good.

"I warned them," said Hubert. "He conned me. That's why I did it. The gun he sold me? Didn't work. He told me when I went back to get bullets." He chucked the barman a wad.

Beating up and being beaten up is tiring work. We withdrew leaving others to work out whose blood was whose.

?????????????????????????

"Just give me the short cuts," Hubert kept saying to me.

Because we profess that it takes years to study philosophy at university so we can have a job, is it really so? Surely if you know something, you should be able to disseminate it in a cut-price sampler.

Charitably viewed: Eddie's edited highlights, Eddie's ed-ifications, the best of the West, semi-skimmed.

Uncharitably viewed: Christmas cracker, spoonfeeding, garden gnomes of the intellect.

It occurs to me that with the demands that are made on our leisure time, a wallet-sized, handbag fitting Top Ten philosophical hits might be a profitable venture. I scrawled down some of the most salient prosifications:

1. "Hoc Zenon dixit.": tu quid? (Seneca)

2. On ne saurait rien imaginer de si étrange et si peu croyable, qu'il n'ait été dit par quelqu'un des philosophes (Descartes)

3. ... και παντ ειναι αληθη (Protagoras)

4. Stupid bin ich immer geweßen (Hamann)

5. Σκεπτομαι (Sextus Empiricus)

6. Themistocles driving a quadriga pulled by four harlots through the agora in Athens at the height of business.

7. Wenn ich nicht das Alchemisten-Kunststück erfinde, auch aus diesem – Kothe Gold zu machen, so bin ich verloren (Nietzsche)

8. I dine, I play a game of backgammon, I converse and am merry with my friends; and when after three or four hours' amusement, I would return to these speculations, they appear so cold and strained and ridiculous, that I cannot find it in my heart to enter into them any further (Hume)

9. Infirmi animi est pati non posse divitas (Seneca)

10. For how few of our past actions are there any of which we have memory? (Hume)

11. God knows all (Ibn Khaldûn)

12. Secundum naturam vivere (Seneca)

13. Si fallor, sum (St Augustine)

14. La lecture de tous les bons livres est comme une conversation avec les plus honnêtes gens des siècles passés . (Descartes)

15. Impera et dic, quod memoriae tradatur (Seneca)

So there's the squad I have to whittle down. It's interesting that Seneca charts so often. Zero as a thinker, a failure on the new grey juice front, one has to own up that as a commentator and idea salesman, he's unbeatable.

1. This is arguably the top sentence in the biz. The maximum maxim. "This is what Zeno said, but what about you?" You might have some trouble deciding which Zeno Seneca was referring to, but this question unquestionably captures the gist. It's not the enlightenment that counts, but the taking part. The great heavyweights of antiquity are not there to be admired but to be lifted, to be tested against your brain's brawn. The prosifications of the greats are no more use than dumbbells under the bed if you don't pump them.

4. Stupidity, that's me: Hamann doing his Socrates number (as well as issuing a reminder that no amount of intelligence can save you from stupidity), and unless you're lucky enough to be portering a massive arrogance, a quotidian sensation, one neatly glorified by St Augustine in 13. (If I'm in bed with the hippopotamus, I am) then covered more successfully by René, producing one of the greatest one-liners. You've got to get the monostich right. Posterity won't bear anything that can't be fitted on a beer mat. You need the catchphrase. For the T-shirts.

12. Live according to nature. This is an evergreen one. You get this everywhere: the problem is making up your mind what nature is. Get someone to tell you and give them your money. Great all-purpose line massive with con-men and fakes of all nations. Also this Senecaism encapsulates the old style phil which promises to make a real man of you, to deagonise your life, to give you a tonic, as opposed to Ludwig's light for hire and what you see is what you get clarification.

11. God knows all. Always a popular cop-out, and a good one to stick in to avoid lapidation, burning at the stake, being machine-gunned and so on, unless you're living in a society where the clerics have gone in for social work. This should be squired by: "audacter deum roga" – Seneca. Call boldly on God, a move hardly limited to practitioners of the biz, the only recourse most of us have. The striking thing about the biz is that despite the wielding of rationality, the brouhaha over proof, the bravado of the nous, you can't turn in the history of philosophy without tripping over mysticism, spectre-spectaculars and bleatings for celestial authorities to sort out our riddle-riddled universe.

6. Themistocles zooming around the agora in a tart-powered chariot. Nothing to do with philosophy of course. But what an idea!

????????????????????????????

Still Montpellier

The only advice I can offer, should you purchase a newspaper before you're really awake to discover a well-composed photograph of yourself on the front page, identifying you as a hardcore malefactor and calling on all law-abiding citizens to shop you, is not to walk into a lamppost (which is what I did). One shouldn't overreact to regional newspapers.

I was curious where they had got the photograph. It was old, and I looked quite dashing (for me). You could still see around the eyes the faint hope of doing the business in the biz. The promise hadn't completely evaporated. A head not pronounceable as one that's not going to make it.

Soon, I realised that it was the publicity photograph from my book. My publishers must have gleefully furnished the snap.

Pass the past 1.1

The literary game. The drawback to a career in philosophy is that you're expected to paper: you are your black and white. Quality doesn't do you any harm, but shelf-space counts. Your stature is raised by the slipping of papers under your feet.

I rerererererereturned[10] to Cambridge from London one Monday to find a letter enclosing a contract for me to write a history of thought. Perplexed, I surmised I had impressed someone at a party. It was a period when I spent a lot of time blathering at parties. Money, a zam-zum-mim of an advance for a signature? That seemed a good deal, a bonus for being rat-arsed.

However, it soon transpired that more was required from my pen than my mark but a quick tour of philosophical bloodshed through the ages? A doddle.

The advance for the book was unnaturally large and caused pleasing amounts of resentment amongst my colleagues, with Featherstone in the lead. I bought a case of Château Lafite '61 and put it down for two days (the irony is that I don't even like Château Lafite; I'm not sure anyone does). I consumed it in one sitting and lying on the floor. I pissed the money away – mostly through my best suit. I was a middle-aged home for the world's griefs, homing in on me.

Boozology

Why do you drink? I have been asked. Because (a) I like to and (b) it's hard to stop. When you've got the hole, you can't go to the corner shop and ask for a couple of pounds of meaning, a packet of panacea, a can of resolution. A solution for one's plight is hard to find, but solutions aren't. You can't go a hundred yards without a pick-up point for zymurgic solutions: off-licences, pubs, supermarkets, restaurants. Civilisation is a careful construction for the production and distribution of alcohol.

The profundity cupboard is bare

Two thousand five hundred and seventy-nine years and counting. A long time to go without a drink or to be waiting for a bus, but not even a blink for the planet, our host. Not even a Babylonian saros. I take the date of 585 BC as the starting point when Thales foretold to the Ionians an eclipse.

Thales, card holder number one, citizen of Miletus on the Ionian coast, the first man caught thinking systematically by posterity, the premier philosopher. Naturally, he lifted his ideas from someone; you don't hit the ground running like that, but we don't have the evidence. Whatever the Kmt, the Mesopotamian, the Indus and Chink crews got up to, they don't feed us directly. Everyone in the biz, whether they look up to him or not, has taken the baton he proffered. For those forgotten labourers in the good grey juice works: get better PR or hardier writing materials.

Though of course 776 BC is also a good candidate: the establishment of the Olympic Games. Many cities, one language, competition. Cheers for the victors, jeers for the also-ran. Elbows and abuse fuel civilisation. Vying, from the meadows of Olympus to the arid fields of the moon. The Greeks and the Persians. Athens and Sparta. Rome and Carthage.

If there was supposed to be a crunch to all this, I've forgotten it.

Letters' fetters

The publishers eventually tracked me down and asked me about the book, how it was, where it could be found. I countered by asking for more money, simply so I had something to say apart from, I can't find the typewriter and even if I could find it, it doesn't have a ribbon, and the a and the z don't work.

I don't know whether I have unwittingly the knack to sound charming, or whether I had latched onto a singularly profligate publisher, but more money was sent.

I bought ten crates of tequila, true brainwash, which would have cleansed the life out of me if a cohort of crack barflies hadn't volunteered to spend the weekend with me at a cottage near South Zeal.

It's not a fact that's been widely marketed, but that weekend we created, over three hundred square feet, for several hours, intergalactic euphoric eternal fraternal just benevolence.

The thing about signing a contract is that it can mislead people into thinking something has been agreed.

In reply to their missives, I snarled for more money, more rudely. I trusted they would get tired of me, but no, the cheques came unabated.

To an extent, I did bring it on myself. I did weaken and send in an outline (knocked out for me by a most junior research fellow). They responded by sending me their catalogue, announcing my forthcoming title. The arrival of the catalogue became an annual event. There is a part of me that likes to make people happy so when they asked if the book would be ready I said "yes" granting them an epoch of contentment.

Alternating with the catalogues were telephone calls from distraught females, some bursting into tears, some threatening me with that hushed, knotted hatred that precedes fevered stabbing with a good quality kitchen knife. My guilt was such that after four years I went to the university library and copied out a few pages of a nineteenth-century work on medieval thought by a Reverend, updating a number of the verbs.

Then one day I got a call from a Scottish voice introducing herself as my new caseworker. "Why don't we have a drink?" A woman who knows how to handle crabby philosophers, I thought.

Hence, I arrived at the offices to be the target of those regards that only someone who is seven years late with delivery of a book and who has been the beneficiary of small, but accumulatively obscene and ruinous, advances, gets.

My arrival at the publishers and holding a glass of zinfandel was my last usable memory for some time. I misplaced quite a bit of time mnemonically. I have a hazy thought on why planes have to be too hot or too cold, and more distant sensations of discomfort and disorientation.

Of cold and discomfort, more reports were submitted by my body and as my consciousness gave them serious consideration, my senses gave me an image of myself handcuffed to a radiator in a bare, white-walled cottagey building. The handcuffs seemed an official philosopher-restraining device, so I assumed I was in some backward, hard-up clink. I wondered how the nearest British Consulate would react to me.

Then the young lady who was my current editor walked in.

Benders – uncharitably viewed: among the many penalties to be endured for bendering is the inconvenience that of being easy to kidnap.

Benders – charitably viewed: one can't refute that the consummate consumption of the juice gets you around, very often to places to which you'd never dream of booking a ticket.

I once had breakfast on the concourse of Zürich railway station (and I do mean on) with a Glaswegian poulterer, who, before we were moved on by the police, extolled the globe-trotting effects of special brew (I translate): "You're only in trouble if you sober up; then you don't get the free travel. And it's true if you want to get home, it can take a while. But keep on drinking, you'll get there." He had been cruising down the longest river in the world, the Booze, that flows through every city in the world, disembarking at Oslo, Tangiers, Suva, Alice Springs, Venice.

Benders – promoting universal understanding: In Seoul, at a party, where either the people who had invited me weren't present or simply didn't live there, I was seized by a gentleman who took me into the neighbouring flat and began pointing out his electrical goods (he had ranks of radios, alarm clocks, cassette-players) and then opening his fridge, motioned at the copious amounts of meat he had there. His wife watched television. I can't be sure whether he understood that I didn't understand a word he said, because he was tanked-up too. Whether his discourse was economic or philosophical, I couldn't tell, but I was drunk enough to find it gripping.

We then drove at high speed for two hours to another city, where he left me, in the middle of the night, with no money, nothing to drink, not a clue where I was, not a word of Korean. The smile he gave me as he drove off leads me to think he thought he was doing me a favour.

Benders – make friends: I met a Nobel Prize winner once on a park bench in Kilburn. It was the Nobel Prize for chemistry or physics for 192something in the name of Zsigmondy I believe; my fellow benchee had won it in a card game. "If anyone goes to France after my divorce, they'll be killed," he said among other things, giving his lips the repeated opportunity to clasp the neck of a meths container.

It was a real mire: I felt as if I had been dropped from two thousand feet, and I accepted a swig of meths, spitting it out before it got halfway down my tongue. I was disgusted with myself both for trying it and not being able to ingest it. The academic life, reading Zegabenus on Z, I realised, had made me too effete to hack it as a real alky. The winner offered me a Vitamin-C tablet: "You've got to look after yourself, eh?"

Handcuffs versus philosophy

Certainly, in an attaching-a-philosopher-to-a-radiator situation, the handcuffs win; they are the supreme rhetorical device for attaining juxtaposition.

Being kidnapped

If you must do this, I do endorse an attractive young woman as a kidnapperess, though preferably one that doesn't want you to write a book.

Letters' fetters

So, I was bereft of booze, captured in a cottage, devoid of the hyperspace liquid that could gain me access to tickletless travel.

"Dr Coffin, you are lazy ... thoughtless ... crapulent ... contemptible." I was biding my time until something came up to which I could object, but nothing surfaced in her disdain that I could really contest.

"You're on Barra. You're miles from the nearest off-licence, even if you could decuff yourself. You have a problem: me. And I have a problem: you. We can unproblem ourselves. I enjoy working in publishing, but you're impeding, indeed threatening my career. No one has ever been so reluctant to blacken paper as you, no one has been so absorbent of funds. Now I have the task of getting a book out of you. I didn't ask for it, but my job depends on it. I've tried being friendly, I've tried being stern, I've tried leaving you alone, I've tried pestering you -"

"I can remember the being left alone, but I can't place the pestering or -"

"Your memory is extremely selective."

"All memory is extremely selective," I said, attempting a wriggle, "otherwise we'd be in a mess, that's what memory's there for, to not remember otherwise we'd be weighed down with telephone numbers, tooth brushings, zouk, nose blowings, ceilings, furniture, shopping, waiting for public transport, our work ... " I petered out, being poorly and unable to mount a rhetorical blitz from the floor.

"At the risk of wearying your memory, let me reiterate the salient facts. You've had seven years and the largest advance we've ever given. We've had thirty, badly typed, treble-spaced pages, which don't make much sense."

"Let's hire someone to hunt down some nice illustrations ... to fatten it up a bit."

"Dr Coffin, we, but particularly I, need a book. Books start at four times the length you've submitted."

"We could be different."

"No, we can sit down and write. Ten pages a meal. When you've done two hundred you can say goodbye to the radiator."

I have my faults (there aren't many I don't have) but in many ways, I'm reasonable and unflappable. With good humour, I had been conducting a colloquy from a cold floor, abducted and manacled to a radiator. Perhaps my personality hadn't been switched on; but suddenly my ego bounded out of its kennel and barked. I went berserk and had a good zob.

Do you know who I am?

This is a risky ploy. Akin to parachuting, you've got to be sure it's going to work, otherwise all you're doing is outrageously multiplying your discomfort. It was the only time I made a claim to importance; my play for dignity only resulted in pure indignity.

Still, if you're going to lose all dignity, look utterly ridiculous and be stripped of all cultivated attributes and blub pathetically, there are few places better than a cottage in Barra with an audience of one to get it out of the way.

We all have moments we'd like to have concrete-shoed and sunk in deepest oblivion. If in any afterlife, my existence were to be replayed in duplication time for any panel, this is the only patch that would really burn my skin (along with an adolescent episode involving a watermelon, after I had been assured that romantic liaisons were possible).

Letters' fetters.

I frothed for four minutes. Then I was too knackered to rant, so I did enough sulking for a small town in five minutes. However, being a pro, I couldn't delude myself about the rapidly approaching craving for a drink. I had a go at negotiation. It didn't work.

"I haven't kidnapped you, Dr Coffin. No one could believe that a slip of a lass like me could force a beachmaster of erudition such as yourself, a man with a history of violence, to do anything. There are plenty of witnesses to your travelling up here zealously, bottle of malt in hand.

"I can't make you write, but I warn you, I'm on holiday for two weeks and that's a long time for a man in your position."

I weighed things up: which fork had "indolents this way" posted on it, fuming and refusing and enduring, or capitulating and scribbling? Perhaps this was the induced birth of a mighty opus.

"Forget the food," I said in heroic stoic, "get me a drink."

We had a new contract. I remained on the inclement floor and with a volume of the Shorter Oxford English Dictionary (Marl-Z) as a desk, tried to write the bottle of whisky opposite me across the room, onerous when you feel as if you're under thirty feet of water.

Using big words and big letters and a deal of repetition, I had reached the furthest reach of page ten when she reentered.

"That's the Renaissance," I said, sullenly indicating the papers, "bottle please."

While I badgered, she scrutinised the sheets. "I can't read this," she pronounced, "I can't read a word of this, apart from one that looks like geranium and that can't be right." I reminded her, whilst thrashing about on the floor and worming down to new depths of abasement, that she hadn't asked for ten legible pages. She fetched a typewriter and a low table.

I threw another zam-zum-mim of a tantrum because typing out the pages wasn't appealing, and I had an even more harrowing moment when I realised I couldn't read my own writing either. I sprinted across the pages, because whatever you do, the desire for a drink remains patiently.

My smell was beginning to torment me but she stood there painstakingly reading the stuff.

"Do you do this for a living? Am I mistaken in thinking you are a specialist in the history of philosophy?" By then the residue of dignity had gone, and I simply slumped on myself in the way you see people do in disaster areas when they know they'll never enjoy themselves again.

Darkness came and I was given a bowl of porridge and a banana. I smouldered through the night like a harshly-treated primate, having come to terms with perishing on Barra. But the next morning when she turned up with some toast, she handed me a chapter.

"What do you think?"

"It's very lucid," I commented.

"Fine," she said unlocking me. "I take it you have no objection to me writing your book for you?"

"I cannot agree to such a subterfuge, unless you give me a cast-iron guarantee that I will get all the royalties."

?????????????????????????

Come on in, Montpellier

Also, when you are greeted by your mug on the front page of a newspaper, make sure you're wearing (as I was) your disguise of rich facial bruising. Whether it was the effectiveness of my black eyes, or the failure of civic zest in our neighbourhood, I made it back to the flat to find Hubert, a box of hollow-nosed rounds next to him, on rat-vigil with a cocked revolver fitted with a silencer and tumuli of goat-cheese strewn around the rooms.

I was coming to the conclusion that it wasn't such a good idea leaving Hube on his own. I tossed him the paper.

The thing about approaching your sixth decade is that, apart from a few small mammals and a bunch of invertebrates (zyzzogetons, zoraptera and suchlike) you feel you've seen it all and that whatever problems you're going to encounter, you're not going to be pelted with surprise. How right Solon was in saying that the match isn't over until you're back in the changing room. I could have spent the next ten years trying to guess what had happened without getting it right.

"It's a good piece," was Hubert's verdict. "The whole page."

"How did they get my name? And what's this Thought Gang business?"

"I told them."

There are times when despite the general reliability of your ears, you have troubling feeding things to your credulity.

"You told them?"

"Yes."

"You told them."

"Yes. Yes." This was contrary to the principles of good blagging as I understood them. Hubert was operating under some strange categorical imperative:

"I phoned them after you went. It's very important that

we start right. If I hadn't let them know it was us who did those two jobs, they might not have put them together. And if you don't supply a name, the journalists or the police'll do it anyway. It should be our privilege."

"The Thought Gang?"

"That's right. I told them that we're advised by a distinguished philosopher on how to rob banks without any risk of getting caught."

"And you gave them my name?"

"You should take the credit that's due, Prof. And you did say you were on the run anyway."

I was on the wrong end of a Socratic dialogue. Hubert could certainly make a case, but I couldn't help suspecting that the French authorities might make more effort to ensnare an armed robber than an absconding philo with a wonky zet.

"Don't fret," Hubert exhorted. "We're not tourists."

Immobilised by the acceleration of events, I could imagine them back in the big C reading the papers. "I see Coffin has been knocking over some Frog banks." "Ah, yes, he was always as crooked as a zed, but he still hasn't published anything of note, has he?" Sniggers all round. The trouble with taking writing seriously, is that the more seriously you take it the harder it is to write. Possibly I take writing more seriously than any other human being that has ever lived. That could explain a lot. O for something short. That would be nice. In and out.

What will people say about me? Mostly nothing. Or wasn't he the one who robbed banks? Or he was the one who ate amazing amounts in amazingly expensive restaurants and drank an amazing amount of amazingly expensive wine – and got laid more than the average logical positivist?

Maybe I shouldn't ferment. After all, there have been bad boys before in the biz. Take Dionysius the Renegade. His one-liner: pleasure is the end of action. And as a lapsed stoic, it wasn't namby-pamby stuff like lolling around contemplating or merely dodging pain that was his cup of tea. He frequented houses of ill repute and indulged in all other excesses, without disguise, and lived to be eighty. Now there's someone you'd want to invite round on a Saturday night – but he still managed to tome.

Although carrying some indifference to prison, I made a note to allow my beard to beard, a brush being the hallmark of committed thinkers in the ancient world and the first recourse of the determined fugitive.

And let's not forget the example of the immortal Agrippinus, the only Roman in my opinion who's put something in the kitty. When he heard the Senate was discussing his case, he had a bath. When he heard that he was to be exiled his only question was "Have they confiscated my property?" They hadn't ... so he went off to lunch.

I made myself his disciple.

??????????????????????????????

I did try to seek help.

I set all the tripos questions one year. In the faculty office stealing some stationery for a book on the Zodiac I never wrote, I was cornered by the Prof. His ideal conversation with me: "So sorry to hear you've lost your job, Eddie." His ideal form of contact with me: him in a large, extremely hard car with no brakes motoring at double the speed limit, me in front of it.

However, he was off on a millionaire hunt, and needed someone pronto to set the papers. My saying yes surprised me as much as him asking me. It wasn't hard at all though. Far from it. For the philosophy papers you just stick question marks on. On anything. Morals. Morals? Plato. Plato? And with the philosophy papers a certain incomprehensibility, a dash of opacity is quite chic. Zaire? Jeroboam? Zedoary? After all it's the answers, not the questions that are important.

I also marked the papers. Apocryphally, examiners toss papers down those charming staircases in Cambridge and grade them according to their altitude. I wouldn't have minded adopting that method, but gathering up all the scattered papers sounded onerous. I went through (without reading them, since that would have been judgemental and unfair on those who were lazy and underbrained) mechanically going up and down the grades from third to first to third. It was a time when I was praying to be fired, but no one contested my marking.

The Ethics paper I had taken some trouble over:

"Can a skint, clapped-out, fat philosopher have any right to self-respect?"

No one attempted that. Even some jejeunery would have been welcome.

"If you slipped the examiner, Dr E. Coffin (1 Tennison Road) fifty nicker to boost your marks, would it make your life any unhappier?"

No envelopes

"If it weren't for suicide, we'd have all killed ourselves long ago?"

No goes.

???????????????????????????

Here's Montpellier

Lunch's shortcoming is that one can only have so many in one day. A chink for thought prevails. I make a few notes on a napkin, reach for the jeroboam and behold my bloatedness.

But I yield to Hube's promptings in the hope that some fresh air will alleviate my self-disgust, and that I might find something zettable in a bank.

We hired a car, using one of Hube's aliases (he was collecting false documentation as fast as he was acquiring firearms).

On the way to Frontignan, in the glorious sunshine, Hubert explained how philosophy had changed his life, when he had paid a visit to Frédéric.

"I was going to shoot him. I was going to shoot off his chopper. But then I thought more philosophically. I thought would that really teach him anything?

"So when he woke up to find me there with the bags of cement, he shat himself. It's true, man is most afraid of the unknown. He knew my gun could kill him; he didn't like that, but he knew all about that. What he couldn't understand was the cement.

"He didn't understand why I made him shave off all his hair, his chest, his eyebrows, everything. It took some time, I tell you. You could have filled a sofa or two with all that hair. He didn't understand why I made him mix up the cement in the bathtub. But we had a couple of hours to talk while the cement set around him, so I spelt it out for him that this was a lesson and his losing all his hair was a symbol of his rebirth and that I hoped the new Frédéric would be a better man.

"I had brought a rubber duck for the right touch. Then when Frédéric was entombed I went down to the bar and invited everyone up to his bathroom for a drink. He was foaming. I said: 'Frederic, can't you see where you're going wrong? Are any of your friends helping you? Can't you see that you lived your life so badly there's no one here willing to chisel you out? They're drinking your cognac, but they're not lifting a finger.' I hope it did him some good."

I wondered about that.

Our selection technique for finding a bank we could zip open consisted of motoring until we saw a bank. Hube insisted on another phil pill before the job, so having primed him, we did a Socratic.

"So, Hubert, what are you proposing?"

"I am proposing that we find some honest jobs."

"What, Hubert, would be the motive for this?"

"To earn money."

"Do you think it likely that you, an unskilled, unschooled wreck, and me an unskilled, overschooled wreck could obtain posts that pay reasonably, or indeed, unreasonably?"

"I doubt it very much."

"And would it not be more efficacious to walk over to this nearby bank and strip them of their lucre? For is not money an indispensable aid in achieving the highest good, namely a life of contemplation?"

"Should I protest a bit more?"

"That's plenty. Let's get zet."

Heigh-hc

It was already getting to be a bit of a grind. We didn't bother waiting, we traipsed in and Hubert announced what was what. One of the customers hailed Hubert.

"Hubert! It's been years. What are you doing these days? Sorry, I'm not embarrassing you, am I?"

They shook hands and Hube chatted while taking the yennom from a most charming young teller.

We evaluated our performance in the car. "One minute twenty-seven seconds to do the job, and twenty seconds to relate ten years of my life," reflected Hube.

"I'd have thought ten years inside would have been quite memorable."

"It was, especially with Emile."

"Emile?"

"He was someone in my last prison, Les Baumettes. They called him the king of the perpetuals. But all these things, you can't explain what they mean. And even if you could, you wouldn't want to."

His tongue desisted. I needled him about the charmer, asking him why he didn't get her telephone number.

"Come on, she was good-looking."

"She was good-looking. But I want a girl with nothing. Not even looks."

The police had pulled their socks up. We spotted a zarp car coming towards us on one of the narrow coastal roads. I assume they were after us since the lights were bluing. It wasn't much of a contest – they wanted to live. As I drove straight at them, they signified this desire by veering off the road.

I hadn't planned it, but I realised if they hadn't chickened out, I wouldn't have moved the wheel. The police didn't make it back into the world of my rear-view mirror. We burned to the outskirts of town and then took a bus back home.

¿¿¿¿¿¿¿¿¿¿¿¿¿¿¿¿¿¿¿¿¿¿¿¿¿¿

The phone rang a lot at Jocelyne's.

"You're becoming quite a celebrity," she said, after she had received her second proposal of marriage for the day.

A hot cop, she explained, an anti-gang expert, a Corsican, had been called in to take charge and make sure that the Thought Gang was brought to some Zaleucusian justice. He had been visiting the scenes of our crimes, and had taken a great deal of time interviewing Jocelyne. You couldn't blame him.

"I like you," she said. "You don't tell me that you love me."

I kept quiet around Jocelyne, because that (a) reduced the odds of my saying something that might irritate her and richter our union and (b) my silence could induce her into believing I was thinking the right things. Being the thinking woman's bank robber didn't alter the fact I had enough love handles for an amorous suitcase factory.

Update on Jocelyne

1. Made money modelling, modelling her body rather

than clothes. Then went into banking "because I thought finance would be interesting."2. Authorities refuse her real power because of earlier career. "They're trying to bore me out of the business."3. First husband. "He was boring. I thought he was kind. But he was too dull to be cruel. He would always ask before. You shouldn't always ask."4. Second husband. "He never asked. He never said please. He never said thank you. He never came home. I had wanted the complete opposite, and I got it. He was intriguing at first, but even total bastards get boring."

5. Wedlock ruptured after she went to bed with husband's best friend, at husband's suggestion. "He enjoyed that. But what upset him was that I enjoyed it too."

The long dick of the law

There was a tringing from the doorbell.

Jocelyne didn't use clothes much. She went to answer wearing a long vest, not really doing the duties that apparel is supposed to carry out.

What would it have been like if we had met before we were both so charred, semi-cremated? In any case, she was too ordered, too much a success at womanning to bother much with me. A little mothering agrees with most women but who would want to adopt the sextuplets of trouble I represent?

Jocelyne was talking quietly, matterly of factly, not as curtly as one would with, say, a Jehovah's Witness or a pusher of products, but not as warmly as one would with a friend or acquaintance.

I approached the window and looked down.

There was a zig trying not to spill his gaze over Jocelyne's torso. Instinctively, I knew it was the Corsican. You could hear him sizzling like a piece of bacon, despite Jocelyne having the mortuary slab out.

He was shooting: "I have this problem you see, Jocelyne,

I have to track down a number of extremely dangerous criminals but all I can do is think of you. My work is being severely hampered. As a good citizen you should help me."

Jocelyne was granite-irised: "I've told you. I'm spoken for."

"No one's perfect," he retorted. I had to salute his stamina and front. "You should have pity on me. Before I do something to disgrace myself."

I could see that the time of door-slamming was at hand. He wasn't unattractive so it was rather funny that he was being kept out of the running by an older ziphiid of a philosopher with a world ranking which in car park terms would be level-20 with oily slicks.

"You will force me to go home and to make love to you on my own."

"My boyfriend's waiting for me upstairs," she said as incisively as a coroner's saw.

"Another time," he said, unbashed by his failure to gain a foothold.

"No is what I'm thinking," said Jocelyne, letting the door say goodbye.

"I'm not sure I'm going to do you any good," I, an old lag of catastrophe, observed as she came back upstairs.

"Now there's discussion," she said smiling.

???????????????????????????

This is a brilliant philosophical work disguised as a sentence.

???????????????????????????

Back home, Hubert was lying on the ground inside a huge trunk, covered by a blanket, like a big-game hunter in a hide.

The rodent commando had come out of retirement during the night, taking my truffle paté, shunning the rat poison that Hube had dished out, and leaving some metabolic souvenirs.

Hube, through his grapevines, had already been appraised of the Corsican getting on our trail. He was incensed to learn that the Corsican had been hanging around Jocelyne's since (a) it was unprofessional and (b) he had, wearing one of the outfits supplied to him by his costumier mate, been looking for the Corsican at the police headquarters.

"Why?"

"Because I was curious to meet him. I wanted to size up our opposition."

"Wasn't that risky?" I wasn't worried, we were past that stage where worry had any use – like a bottle of water at the bottom of the ocean – I was just zetting out Hubert's behaviour.

"We're the untouchables. We're invincible."

"But only until we aren't. Anyway the idea is that the police chase us, not that we chase the police."

"More books," said Hube breaking cover. "I'm not feeling cultured enough. I can feel my stupidity growing."

I wasn't keen on going out but it occurred to me that a couple of heavy tomes would incarcerate Hubert nicely and sloth him up in his trouble-making and bank-robbing. Hubert read very slowly (but very carefully – you could see him becoming one of those dangerous students who tried to make you work).

"You choose some things for me," he said as we entered the bookshop. I advocated some Diogenes Laertius – that would shut him up. But it was a small bookshop, with lots of books on dieting and memoirs by politicians and actors, and some novels with nakedish women on the cover.

Hube scanned the shelves and then drifted over to the assistant who looked and dressed like a junior sociology lecturer.

"I can't see the philosophy section," said Hube, with the

faint resonance of what I was coming to recognise as his scene-making voice.

"There isn't one," replied the assistant, extremely unassisting and minimalist in reply since he was directing his consciousness into a magazine.

"So where will I find Diogenes Laertius?" asked Hubert, with what I could now confirm as a slight hope that DL wouldn't be making an unexpected appearance. The assistant was behind a low counter and it occurred to me that I might be about to ocularly take in the much-celebrated counter kick.

"You won't."

"You mean you haven't got any Diogenes Laertius?" said Hube, outraged and pleased at the same time. A zeb zob in the offing.

"Who has?" said the assistant not prying his pupils from the magazine, or varnishing his words with any veneer of regret, or doing anything like offering to order up the DL, or recommending a place round the corner that might stock it but employing a tone that aspired to roadblock further enquiry or conversation. One of the traits of advanced capitalism is that it's generally staffed by people who aren't very concerned about selling anything – one of the consequences of a society where, sadly, people don't starve to death if they lose their job.

There was a zam-zum-mim of a pile of books on dieting.

"How do I lose weight, Prof?"

"Eat less, exercise more." I'm fine on the principles.

"Did you hear that? This man knows about knowledge. Why don't you clear away this rubbish and get in some books. If people need advice about losing weight, you can give it to them in that easy-to-remember formula. That way you can serve both your customers and letters more efficiently."

"They sell."

"So you call this a bookshop?"

The assistant perked up here. His eyes swept round inquisitively. "Looks like one to me."

I was surprised that he couldn't see the danger signs: Hubert had that unfed and fed-up stray dog look.

The counter kick, I guessed, had to be coming. Hubert had been elaborating to me how he had spent years of his detention perfecting it. The splendour of the kick resides in those behind counters not really expecting a boot in the chops. I was rather looking forward to it, despite having two decades of much greater professional misconduct and idleness under my belt than the assistant but years of shopping can make you very cruel.

"You've got eyes in your head, you have," Hube responded, reaching into his tatty but commodious leather jacket. "I have a question for you. Would I be right in calling this a gun?" He had a sub-machine gun, the 9mm Mac-10 out, and training it on the diet books, slimmed them down along with the adjacent scoria, by firing thirty-two rounds from its Zytel magazine at 1100 rounds per minute (I was getting something in exchange for the phil pills) his hand zedding from the recoil. The books jumped around like jumping beans that are unquestionably in the mood for jumping.

There's nothing like the threat of serious injury or plentiful death to get people's attention, particularly on a slow Tuesday in a small bookshop in Montpellier.

"You're completely right," said the assistant, with what I have to credit as swift and exceptional sycophancy, which had come rushing out of nowhere, propelled at Mach-10 by the Mac-10. "Righter than right." Sequelling with "I've never met anyone as right as you."

"It says bookshop outside," homilized Hubert. "If it said crapshop, I wouldn't be bothered. But when people come in here, they're expecting something. Beauty. Truth. Escape. You're selling glued paper, not books. I recommend you change your stock or broaden it considerably. You need a philosophy section. Something to quiver the heart and to heat the scalp."

"We'll check. And it won't be next week, it won't be when the police are around, it won't be when you presume it will be. And if things haven't changed, it won't be the books that'll get the holes. That comes to a thousand francs for the bullets and the consultancy."

There was five hundred in the till, but the assistant only had three hundred on him, so Hubert took his bag of groceries and a dictionary.

We evacuated ourselves with a little less zip than after banking, but smartly.

"We should have charged more," Hube hindsighted, "stars like us shouldn't work for small change. That cretin will wear his tongue out telling that story. We just gave him the most exciting moment of his life." I imagined that Hube was minded to go back and fix up a weekly payment.

"Unless people pay for things, they don't value them. Only threats can be free. They cost nothing, but they can work."

I had an odd sense of achievement, that for once my shenanigans had abetted good. Hube was dissastisfied with the proceedings. "It was too easy. An ape could have pulled the trigger." He unclipped the magazine, cleared the chamber, and then flung the weapon into a litter bin. "We'll have to think some thoughts about this ... how to achieve that effect without bullets."

We walked on. "I don't feel at all well," he said.

?????????????????????????????

Still Montpellier

I am worryingly healthy. I must be really ill if I don't feel ill.
I even got the rat.

Hube came in and announced that we had to move on. Frédéric, who was still apparently picking cement out from between his toes, had put an unheard of bounty on Hube's head, indeed every part of his body. Since people in the neighbourhood were asking Hube for his autograph, he finally acknowledged that the time-honoured technique of putting a distance between yourself and your problems was appropriate.

"But I'm not going until I get the rat," he insisted.

"Don't be a hindmind, Hubert. Why hand over what's left of your life to Frédéric? We should have made ourselves scarce a long time ago."

"The rat reminds me of Emile," he said.

I ordered him to go out and hire a car. While he was gone, for my own amusement, I set up the cage that had been left by the previous occupant, who had kept a parrot. The previous occupant had obviously allowed the zygodactyl the flap of the flat, since its feathers and droppings were all over the place, mostly in places where you didn't want to find parrot feathers or pellets.

I set up the cage in the ancient trap form, baited, with a long length of string. I went into the other room, and I had barely commenced thinking about pandecting when I heard the sound of scuttling in the cage. I tugged on the string and heard the whup of cage on carpet.

The rat was unrepentant and looked very upset at having fallen for something so obvious. Little did the rat realise that I was more upset by the thought that this incidental foray into rat-catching was one of the most achievementous moments of my life. I served a last meal of fresh rye bread.

When Hubert returned, I presented him with the caged rat to be blasted, so we could move on.

"No, that's no good. I'm not going to shoot him like that," Hube protested. I protested that there wasn't the time for him to chase round after the rat. If he wanted to give the rat a sporting chance, I suggested he either pass the rat a shooter or take it with us to arrange, at a later date, an equitable environment in which to deal with it.

"Did you know that in India there are people who venerate rats, who see them as guardian spirits, porters of good fortune." India's a bit like New York, you're going to find anything you look for.

This de-voiced Hubert. We packed our chattels, we packed the rat (ever vigilant of zoonosis) and we drove off without Hube sprinkling his thoughts about. He chewed his lip, and dragged his vision along the passing streets.

"I thought it was you who had changed my destiny, Prof. But you know, my luck changed the moment I took that flat. I met you after I got the flat."

"I thought you got the flat after our first outing."

"I paid for the flat after our première, but I had already signed for it. That's why I was out, I was looking for the deposit. In Les Baumettes there was someone who had a good-luck gerbil. A wall fell on him after Emile boiled the gerbil in coffee."

Thus the idea that the rat might be ratifying our success came to stay with Hubert. The rat was christened Thales.

Triptych

Naturally, it doesn't make sense to go on a long drive without doing some banks on the way.

As we sped towards Marseille, I had been cherishing the sabbatical from villainy.

"I'm glad we can take it easy for a bit," I remarked. Hube looked out of the window in a way that conveyed he wasn't looking out of the window entirely out of a desire to look out of the window,

"I had to take care of Frédéric," said Hubert, which was his way of saying that he had (x) located the cash I had cached in my suitcase lining and (y) purchased and planted two decas of heroin in Fred's toilet cistern and then (z)

drawn its existence to the attention of the police.

"If it makes you feel any better, Prof, it took me a minute or two to find your stash."

"So how much have we got left?"

"We're okay for lunch. I'm not very hungry."

Ergo we zapped three banks on our way to Marseille.

Methods used

I was getting, I own up, slapdash.

1. Marxist: "You decide you're the vanguard of the proletariat and then you can do whatever you want because history will back you up."

2. Stoic: "Stay very calm."

3. Positivist: "Yes, I'm positive I want to rob this bank."

The redistributions were dull, apart from number three in Arles which strictly speaking wasn't a bank robbery, whatever it was; I don't think the word has been invented yet.

We got off on the wrong foot. Hube got very shirty over a purple shirt that one of the tellers was wearing: "How can you wear something like that to work? It's unreal."

The teller was a school-leaver who had no idea of how to treat a blagger. "Sorry, are you a bank robber or a fashion journalist? The jacket fooled me, it's real PVC isn't it?"

The takings were too much for Hubert, they were too little: four thousand francs.

"Where's the manager?" Hubert demanded furiously. He duly materialised from the back.

"Listen, your staff are rude and they can't dress."

The teller cut in: "Hey, my grandfather is blind, he's never left his village but he still wouldn't wear rubbish like that. There are people starving in Africa who've got a better wardrobe than that."

"I'm a bank robber, right? These are my working clothes. How can you people pretend this is a bank when you've only got four thousand francs. I'm carrying more than that."

"You didn't let us know you'd be coming. It's market day." The manager was swooning on his feet, doing the zonked zonkey, but the teller refused to give ground to Hubert, who blew up.

"You know what? You can keep your money. We wouldn't steal your money if you paid us. It's a privilege to be robbed by the Thought Gang. A privilege, do you hear? We won't touch any of your shitty branches with fire tongs. But let me help you out this time," Hube said tossing them a couple of thousand.

We reached Marseille. Separating, we worked on a schedule of odd rendezvous at the platforms of the railway station: number one at one on Monday, number three at three on Wednesday and so on in the event of one of us not showing. Hube loved it all.

??????????????????????????

I miss my Lexicon.

Best purchase ever:

My buying Liddell and Scott's Intermediate Greek-English Lexicon. A zeb zet.

The greatest danger of being gifted, is that you may never learn how to make an effort. Not that I consider myself gifted, but I've never understood the hardship some people have learning languages, digesting the grammar, memorising the words. I always breezed though my exams, that was my problem.

I recall how hard I had to work delivering newspapers to get the money. Of course I was fired from the job, but not before I had saved up.

You couldn't buy the Lexicon in Macclesfield, you had to order it. That was half the fun.

Worst purchase ever

I was thirteen. When I received the Lexicon, I had only acquired the rudiments of Greek. But I ran home with the book and stayed up late taking it in. I would cram my clothes by the foot of my door so my parents couldn't detect the light from my reading into the morning. I felt I was getting something you couldn't get anywhere else and which hardly anyone else knew about. One word would lead to another. A semantic circle. I couldn't stop. I used to sit in school thinking – great, I can go home soon and hit the Lexicon.

This frenzy was the foundation of my career; my doctoral thesis on Ionian vocabulary was half ready before I even got to university. I picked up such Greek speed that even though I had taken my foot off the accelerator, I crashed into the end wall of tertiary education.

Slaves

Their control, like the best control, is invisible to the majority.

But their colonies are everywhere. They colonised the Romans, the Arabs, the Persians, the Indians. Using other languages as a front, they now operate globally. They were the first, and they are the greatest multinational. Their dust has settled evenly over the orb.

Every university is one of their foundations. In every corner of the world eyes clamber over alphas and betas, zetas and etas; everywhere scientists reach for psi's and omegas.

No imbecile, no mugger, no doctor, no politician anywhere in the world can open their mouth without uttering some pidgin Greek.

The Lexicon, in all my years where there has only been a smattering of mattering, has never been devenustated. Never been devenustated.

???????????????????????????

Jocelyne picked up my copy of La Mettrie's *Art of Enjoyment* from the bed. I've always thought that *les philosophes* were somewhat spoilt by having their careers pulled for them by that monster, that zam-zum-mim of sex 'n' violence, the Revolution; but La Mettrie has always excited my admiration for making a vocation out of his self-indulgence and toming his sensuality; a demon eudemonist who ate himself to death and died with his cutlery in hand.

"That's it. The theories are theories. The universe's real secret is being able to enjoy it. To enjoy what you have. That'll make the heavens heave."

We did our best.

Already out the door, she stopped, studying me as if there was a floor show on my brow. Then she slapped me.

"What's that?"

"It's an advance. You'll do something to disappoint me, and then you might not be around for me to do that."

???????????????????????????

You lie in bed thinking, I should really be out drinking myself to death.

I contemplate the possibility that I have an indestructible liver, one that will be a medical prodigy for centuries, and that long after the rest of me has melted away, my liver will be transplanted from patient to patient, like a family heirloom.

So I revved myself up and went to rendezvous with Hubert.

We went for a drink in a place recommended by him. I couldn't see why anyone would recommend it, it seemed to have been blasted out of rock and had the sparse disposable fittings of the previous bar where I had been pasted. The clientele had the incurable thinness and malice of zoa who have only experienced poverty and especially restrictive penal institutions.

Hube was up and up, elated by the IDs he had procured. He passed me a passport. "Still warm from the tourist. That's one that will really suit you."

But it wasn't a bar that welcomed globular philosophers with wheezy world rankings. Two beers in, I heard a hiss near to my head and a wet, formicating sensation on my nape. I saw Hubert staring behind me like a stretch of bad road.

I turned round to see a aerosol can of blue paint held by a diminutive North African; the paint had been applied on the virgin canvas of my skull. The sprayist was ably supported by six, much larger, chortling friends. As always, it's the runt that likes to throw his weight around, standing on others' shoulders to play the jester.

"I'm painting," he elucidated. "Do you have a problem with that?"

Deathless beat-up lines 1.1

It is, of course, a classic of the genre. From the moment in whatever valley the first hominid gripped a clobbering tool and made the first pate paté, to the swishest watering hole in any city now, it's a line that's always been in attendance.

Bearing in mind the wars, the starvation, the mountains of misery that clutter our heavenly body, bearing out mind some paint daubed by a half-pint wanting to ponce with your bonce isn't so terrible.

"It depends on what you're painting," resorting to philosophical evasion.

"Blue hair. It's pretty."

"We aren't tourists," Hubert intervened with what I perceived, but the others didn't, to be the last ministration of restraint.

"And you," exclaimed the dauber squirting Hubert zedily in the face, "you need a new complexion."

Hubert picked up a bottle from the table as the seven got on their marks for a good kicking.

"I've got a disease, very fatal, very fashionable," he said, slamming the bottle onto his head and slumping onto the ground. It swiftly became clear that his furthering his acquaintance with the floor was not an elaborate ruse but an over-application of the bottle.

In a flash, I was down with Hube, sadly not estranged from reality. If you're going to be forced to impersonate a football, a skinful first.

On taking boot

Pain, as the billing vouchsafes, is painful.

Our career as a dance-floor came to an end and our assailants went off to get a drink; it was an establishment where no one fussed over well-kicked patrons littering the floor.

They left me booby-trapped with supplementary pain every time I tried to move. I wondered if the stiff-upper lippers of antiquity would be quite so sanguine about taking boot.

The etiquette seemed to be to let the vanquished bleed quietly in their pools. The mob showed no inclination to move on; it was quite a while before I managed to crawl over to Hube and grope in his jacket for what I was looking for. Then it took several minutes for me to accumulate some verticality and to have Hube's gun visually chronicled by the revellers.

I had never really experienced the delightful anticipation of inflicting great harm. I ruminated on what great teachers such as Zoroaster, Confucius, Socrates or Jesus Christ would have done in this situation, but then, of course, none of them had the benefit of a Desert Eagle .50 Magnum (Standard

Black Oxide, polygonal rifling to enhance obturation between bullet and bore – hey, when I have the film, I have a photographic memory) and seven rounds of 325-gr jacketed hollow-point ammunition that Hubert had explained to me made such huge embrasures in flesh their way out of the body, that it had the doctors reaching for their cameras.

Call in a classical precept

Democritus: a wrong unrighted is a double wrong.

Violence gets a bad press. It's not so terrible if you're on the right end of it, it's rather fun, which probably goes a long way to explaining its enduring popularity.

"Mmmmppff shhyyy zzeezz kkkoontts yi ghhhad," I said, and I wasn't surprised they couldn't understand me. My teeth had been widely distributed; my mouth had become half the bar, if the oral boundary was marked dentally. Catching sight of myself in a mirror with my slit vision, I was wearing spectacles made from violet bagels, my lips had become a life raft. This perspective in tandem with the increasing pain didn't dispose me to understanding and forgiveness, which in any case, can deprive you of a lot of enjoyment.

I mimed for the barman to do something to bring Hubert round.

Trying to reassemble his shattered hearing-aid, and having unholstered another, smaller pistol (but nevertheless an adequate deporter of souls) Hubert took over the ceremonies.

Our captive audience had the I-knew-I-should-have-brought-the-gun-out-tonight look.

Hubert fiddled with his shattered hearing-aid, although it was obvious to those of us with no hearing-aid design knowledge whatsoever, that whatever the future held in store for the fragments, hearing-aid work wasn't on. It was a dumb-show of the irreparable state of our relations.

"You," said Hubert finally, indicating the performance

artist with his gun-barrel. "Did you have a bad childhood? Deprived? Abused? Without opportunities?"

"Yes," came the uncertain reply.

"Good," said Hubert, "that's a start. We're going to conduct a little experiment tonight; let's get zet. My first question; who evicted my friend's teeth?"

Silence. Resolution? Ignorance? Collective guilt?

"Ah, is this loyalty? Is this friendship? Outstanding virtues. Let's put them to the test."

At Hubert's request, the barman managed to get hold of a hammer and some nails. "Okay, this is how it works – I ask you to nail the lip of one of your friends to the bar counter. If you refuse as a stalwart friend, I am impressed by your loyalty, and I blow your head off. Any hesitation, it's one through the leg."

Our grisly appearance (I looked like a runny Union Jack on acid and Hubert was worse) gave this prolegomenon some clout. However when Hubert instructed the painter to go to work, one of the septet baulked and Hube had to shoot him in the leg.

"You should get that looked at, you could bleed to death," he remarked.

The nails went in. Finally, there was only the painter left, looking as worried as a man should be when he has recently nailed the lips of six, much larger, demonstratedly aggressive individuals to a bar counter, sprayed their faces blue and hammered out the teeth responsible for public relations, and who still has to worry about a trigger-lover such as Hube.

"Okay," concluded Hube, "now, can you give me a good reason for not shooting your chopper off?"

"It would make a lot of women unhappy," offered the painter which I thought quite glib for the circumstances he found himself in.

"Sorry. Can't hear you," said Hubert loosing off a crotch shot. "I'm sure your friends will look after you."

"You're a very dangerous man, Prof," Hubert complimented me as we left.

"Nnnahh bhuull agg gwaan."

"Yes, but an unloaded gun isn't very dangerous. They could see you're all edge."

"Nngggaakk sluup poorrr zaapoor."

"That's why that gun was unloaded. I wouldn't dream of using a loaded gun for bank robbery – they can go off. We are philosophers not criminals. I only carry the other one for self-defence."

I hailed a taxi. "Wah wsshii idokk beema. Sdunee ddeenntrist."

"Time alone, to think up new methods? Illustriousness."

"Ddjja reelii grodggd eed?"

"That's what the doctors say. It could be a nationwide medical hoax, I suppose."

???????????????????????????

Jocelyne was fascinated by my face. "If that's a disguise it's brilliant. I wouldn't have recognised you."

After improving the world, she went into the kitchen and produced a bottle of Zédé.

"Wish me happy birthday."

"If I'd known, I'd have brought you something."

"Some wisdom would be nice."

"Believe me, if I had any I'd be hanging on to it with both hands."

"We all get some. I should have started reversing my ageing at twenty-six. Now I could do a good job of being sixteen. Now I know how to identify a good man and reel him in."

She started to varnish her nails. They had used some of my memory when I was robbing her bank. Each nail had a different colour. The black was the most striking, but I had noticed that its position changed every week. "I started it for my first boyfriend," she said. "He was clever – he died before I could find a reason for disliking him, before he did anything to hurt me. He became a somewhat harmful ideal. I resolved a part of me should always be mindful of him, in constant mourning. Eventually I added the other colours, the range of the spectrum: red, orange, yellow, green, blue, indigo, violet and white. As a reminder that there are other things, and because it annoys the hell out of the boss."

"And the unpainted nail?"

"You can say that's because no theory can cover everything. Or you can say that that nail has the colours you can't see."

Eavesdroppers' Arms

"After the second divorce, I decided I should study the traffic between men and women. You know the significance of the number three; you know what having three marriages go down makes you. That's why I'll never marry again, even if it means passing up something viable.

"But I wanted to go beyond my own experience, to study it as if it were a proper discipline. I wanted the private lives of others so I could make comparisons. That's why I opened a small hotel."

"What did you do, bug all the rooms?"

"Exactly."

"Did you find out anything interesting?"

"Mostly no. The biggest lesson was how hard it is to keep tabs on people. I'm not surprised that police states tend to be poor. It takes so much *effort*. The results were so boring. What came out of the two years was how zealous couples are for disputes, they can argue about anything. You could fit a hundred arguing couples on the head of a pin. That and the bathrooms; you can never be unamazed by the state people leave them in."

She went over to a chest of drawers and took out a sheaf of bound papers and handed it to me.

"But I sold up after this. They were a couple in their twenties. French I would have said. But when they went into their room, they switched to another language."

"So what is it?" I asked, reviewing the pages which were a phonetic transcription.

"I don't know, and what's interesting, no one seems to. I've sent the tape and the transcript to universities all over the world. Name a language department, I've tried it. From Albania to Zaragoza. No one has a clue."

"What was the couple like?"

"Like a young French couple. They stayed one night. Average activities. I tried to follow up the address they gave afterwards, but there was no more trace of them than their language."

"Leg-pull?"

"Angels."

"Well-gallicized extra-terrestials."

"An all-inclusive pair. A nation of two."

More revelations

"I have to say, when I saw you in the bank, I did think you were out of place."

"No, when I saw you in the bank, I thought you were out of place."

She went over to the chest of drawers again. "I keep my whole life here." I can believe it; she was very tidy. She fished out a picture. A clumsy square, a black 'n' white photo taken in a booth: an out of centre visage, a young guy's face, with a roundness, unshaven, out of position collar, eyes going to four o' clock, pursed lips halfway to a smirk – interesting trouble.

"That's him. The one who took a motorbike ride into eternity, leaving me unsatisfied with other men. When I saw you, queuing, despite the fact you were older, fatter, foreigner, I knew you had come back to me.."

?????????????????????????

My friends lose their telephones 1.1

I rest my consciousness on the phone. I pick up the receiver and hear its electronic purring.

I'm aware, more and more, that the only thing I'm going to miss are my friends. Apart from the deluge of terror that attends the prospect of turning carcass, what bothers me is the idea of losing the handful of people I can have a decent conversation with. It takes you a lifetime to acquire them. Losing life isn't so bad, but losing them is.

The tone of the phone changes, impatient with my lack of use.

Bring on the Popes 1.1

There isn't (to my knowledge) a patron saint of bank robbery. Saint Callistus (bubble burst 222 AD) would be a good nomination. Put in charge of a bank, its funds evaporated, and he fled Rome. But despite this mishap, Pope Zephryinus put him in charge of a cemetery, especially popular with ex-bishops of Rome, and in due course Callistus pulled the short crozier and became Pontifex Maximus himself. Moral: sticky fingers don't necessarily impede you going all the way in this world and the next.

Bring on the Popes 1.2

There isn't a patron saint of lost causes (to my knowledge). A good nomination would be Saint Zosimus. During his expiration he was so still, they had him in the box several times before he was boxable. Moral: just because it looks as if it's over doesn't mean it is.

The Popes ain't working. I either have nothing or too much to say; nothing is in store that would slot in to phone call duration. In addition to a feeling I or they have been transferred to another planet.

I return the receiver to its receiver. A Z of sorrow is stuck in my throat.

???????????????????????????

Blagging has this in its favour – you can work the hours you want and you can check, whenever you want, that your bed is working properly. (If it weren't for the question of lengthy jail sentences in the company of people whom likening to excrement is grossly unfair to excrement.)

Disadvantages of staying in bed 1.1

Fifty years in, haven't found one yet. Let me know if you can think of any. Laziness rarely gets its due. I suppose it's because its votaries are just too lazy to compose panegyrics in its honour. It's the free lunch, the easiest of the vices. Limitless, free, inexhaustible, the cold fusion of debasement. The zeb. You can do it anywhere, and if done right, no one need ever know you're doing it. Everything else requires some time, some outlay, some money. Laziness, like some ideas of God, is everywhere. And you can't overdose.

Disadvantages of staying in bed 1.2

Truth be told, you can't drink in bed; unless you're on a drip. The bonus of staying in bed all day (hoping that brilliant ideas will make their way into the world through your mind) is that when you get up you feel virtuous for not having had anything to drink, so you can go out to celebrate by having a drink.

I suspect that most addicts don't really want to give up (because you're unlikely to be addicted to something you don't like or which doesn't chuck some value at you) but want a working relationship, the compromise necessary in all long-term partnerships. I don't want to be liquidated by liquids. Sometimes.

I sortie barwards, the Zouave. When you want a drink, a drink, and nothing but a drink will do.

Closing in on the bar, I pass an ambulance, flashing, stopped in the middle of the road. A good crowd has formed. Someone on the asphalt is treated with a blanket; death just shoots out. You know from fifty yards and without a medical degree that the victim isn't going to make it.

I traverse the arc of watchers, glance at a car's pedestrianed windscreen, a couple of policemen note-taking. There's a light drizzle but the congregation doesn't budge.

I don't know why those who coagulate at such incidents are so often castigated as ghoulish. It's not that at all. We've all seen broken bodies – they have little fascination. It's not the lure of the splattered: no, no one likes to see the Big Bumper Offer pull one off. Not gawping, but supporting. One of those duties, like directions or fire, that one cannot refuse a stranger.

Inside the bar, no messing about, double Zamoyski. The interior is dark, but at the tables there are candles to give romantic illumination.

Without any preamble, my soul takes the express lift to the minus fortieth floor. My jollity is left a long way behind.

One thought

One thought jumping up and down in my skull: please, please, please tell me what's going on here, I beg you.

You would have thought that after a few thousand years

of high-class thinking from the hottest domes, the biz would have a foothold. We're still confronted by the front, the extent of the extant, the same flame burns for me as for Thales, and we've got the ologies, teleology, alethiology, eschatology, but we don't have a gnat's hair of evidence about what's going on here. Old wives' tales, old philosophers' discourses, old divines' sermons, a few hand-me-down outlooks.

Zut alors

I gaze into the candle. It seems so real. I seem so real. It's a small flame but boisterous, confident. One day a flame like that, with a few hundred companions, might abridge me to my real worth. Dust that's lost the knack of not being dust. Zud. Perhaps I should leave instructions for my disposal, but what happens to my remains is of no more concern to me than the fate of a Zairian pot-hound. That I may not have a body to wake up in, that does worry.

What are the real units of measurement? How do you do a spiritual push-up? How do you do anything good and how do you know you're doing it? The two is meeting the three zeroes, and we still have the choice between self-abnegation in others' woes (prison visiting, planting trees, leper colonies, old donkeys' homes, raising kids) or self-abnegation in an off-the-peg world-wrapper from the men who had heaven whispering in their ear, or you can go for an ism.

From their refoundation in 1883, the Zutistes of Paris would meet at 139, rue de Rennes (usually on a Thursday evening). They were poets who would say zut to everything. All isms are zutisms; a cerebral gizmo, that gives you a response to any situation, a filler.

The Universe and Me

Still, nine times out of time Heaven's reps can take Reason's boys when it comes to insulating the mind, fear-proofing, proof-proofing. And let's concede that God electing to incarnate in AD 0 in a carpenter's family in Judea, or tipping off some camel-trader is no whackier than the sub-atomic japes of z bosons.

Since the unveiling of civilisation when folks lost the chilblains of the ice age, the holocene scene has been, once you decorticate the refined language, what the zet is going on and what can we do about it?

Are we just trick dust? Apex apes? I mean the universe seems an awful lot of trouble for a practical joke.

What do we idea-jockeys have to show for all our concept squeezing? It's the spin-offs from philosophy, mathematics, astronomy, biology that have covered some ground, made some comfort. Wisdom has never been able to extend beyond the span of a life. Facts snowball. Take 10^{83}. According to the bath-pourers that's the number of electrons in the universe. Assume they've got it wrong, let's top it up to 10^{100}. A googol. Can the biz produce a figure, a scrawl as powerful, as encompassing as that? So true. So shapely. But we've got more how than we know what to do with; our why colons persist empty. And if Zubiri is right in asserting that those who work over the physics, the fish-slitters and mote-bulliers leave us metaphysically famished, I can't go along with him when he says that the biz has the refreshments.

I've been paid to examine all this, unlike those who delve into the lining of the world after bereavement, loss, failure. I'm glad no one is in a position to ask for the money back. I haven't got much to show: a pile of books, and the oldest cliché: what are we doing here? But then clichés tend to be the truths we're bored with.

You can struggle with it till your mind pops; it's like trying to lift a bucket you're standing in.

We find out.

I sit in this bar full of unhappy people, conducting themselves as if happy. I would vouch for this moment being so strong it could tire eternity. People tell me it won't. Perhaps it's all a stunt. Perhaps, suddenly, everyone will turn around and say: surprise, Eddie! We're just jesting about you being mortal. We just blindfolded your immortality.

Present. 3.1 (or something like that) Return of the lawful sledgehammers 2.2

The only advice I can offer, should you wake up vertiginously in a strange flat again, again with a thoroughly installed hangover, again without much in the way of clothing, again without any recollection of how you got there or why, as the police are again sledgehammering through the door and you are encompassed by bent gear and bales that are never going to make it to legality, while you are at the height of enjoying a reputation as the scholar's bank robber, is: (x) you'll find you're less worried about the tea-bags (y) you mustn't attempt to work out what the odds are on this happening again since you'll only give yourself a headache and (z) you have the consolation of knowing that in a finite universe there's no way this can happen again.

Naturally, I assumed it was a jumble of bank robberies that had led them to me.

They were a well-mannered bunch. The way they threw me about was rather half-hearted, but then I don't suppose I posed much of a threat: bleary, aged, tubby, grubby, not enough works published to have a real rep, wearing a baseball cap (with a hand coming out the side and bringing down a fabric sledgehammer on the summit of the cap) and a pair of underpants featuring cartoon zebras. The cartoon zebras bothered me slightly.

I know it's rather late in the day to express concern over dignity, but the cartoon zebras niggled. When you get to the end of the road, you don't want to look silly, or rather although you might look silly, you don't want to look too silly. The underpants had been mysteriously allotted to me in a launderette spin dryer, and, you know, I have nothing against cartoon zebras as such, because it's perfectly possible to have cartoon zebras that are stylish but these were naff zebras from a naff mind in a naff reproduction. When you're terminally nicked, you don't want your arresting officers sniggering at your undergarments. I've been called many things: boozologist, the rogue elephant of the archaeology of knowledge, the hard man of philosophy, but never a wearer of risible, failed cartoon zebra underwear.

Then the police started speaking to me in German.

Hard man of philosophy 1.1

Most of the things you get credit for, you don't deserve. For others, this is balanced out by things that they deserve credit for, but don't receive; in my case I am unaware of any unrecognised, unapplauded feats, but I'm open to anyone suggesting anything. My rep as the bootboy of the Ionians was acquired quite fortuitously.

Oxford was the setting, a long weekend conference on Ancient Philosophy, the last morning finishing with a seminar on change and the Ionians (Thales, the Anaxs, Heraclitus). A clash was eagerly awaited (by everyone except me) since my views (shruggy as they were) were fervently opposed by Zwanziger. Believe it or not, it's the sort of thing that can get people geed up at a philosophy conference. Heraclitus' flux: I for process, Zwanziger against. It's one of the most popular philosophical pantomimes, the refinement of "Oh yes, he is," "Oh no, he isn't". An academic keeper-off-the-streetser.

The night before, I had been retiring to my room agonising whether I should go for the square of coke there first and then polish off the Polish vodka, or warm up with a joint first, and whether a bottle of wine should be harmonized into this ensemble. Deep in this reverie I ascended the staircase and went through a fire door (these fire doors are envisaged to elevate public safety I'm told). Because of my calculations on which stimulants were becoming on the eve of a seminar on change, I didn't verify what was happening to the fire door after my using it.

What happened to the fire door after I used it was it reverted to its usual position and in doing so kapowed Zwanziger who was just behind me, carrying a tray with twelve minutes of Dundee cake and a pot of steaming tea as a goodnight snack. My attention was drawn to Zwanziger by his shrieking as he tumbled down the staircase, with the clattering pot. A fractured skull, a broken arm, a broken leg and a scalded scrotum was the sum of his somersaulting journey down the stairs.

Rather gracelessly, as he was wheeled away to an ambulance, Zwanziger took the time between groaning in agony to denounce me bitterly as the cause of his injuries. What was interesting about this was the looks I got from the others as Zwanziger was carted away. Far from being condemnatory or reproachful, the looks I clocked were sly glances of admiration and wonder: someone gets in the way of your exposition, you take him out, you break him into pieces. No messing. Did I get invitations to conferences.

Lawful sledgehammers of the present 2.21

When the chief zarp spoke to me in German, I was a bit alarmed. Had I really bendered myself as far as Germany? I responded with a few Teutonic grunts from the floor. I wondered if they had any Schiller or Hölderlin at the nick because I'd never ever got round to reading any.

But as I was dragged out into the sunshine of Marseille, still not really the master of my mental processes and the sense-data gushing in, I realised that I had been nicked by the French who were for some reason eager to practise their German.

That my arrest was for any other reason apart from my

unapproved withdrawals from French banks, never occurred to me. I was rather relieved. Marseille was getting to be a bit much for me. I was almost looking forward to a bit of bird since I was by now forced to the conclusion that the only way I would do any serious writing was via incarceration.

For me, it was too early in the morning for conversation: all I was bothering about was whether I could grab some zeds once I arrived at the station. My captors weren't very garrulous either, apart from asking me where a certain Angoulême was. I didn't do much apart from grunt, and then spew and retch in a careless manner (doubly odious when handcuffed), a rather tardy and misguided gesture by my body to evacuate hop venom and save my liver a shift. The drinks' comeback put a dampener on our colloquy, and brought communication to a halt.

Granted that I patently looked like the old wreck I am, they were almost cordial. I gained enough awakeness to feel sorry for myself, my liver, my world ranking and (in a beauty-queen style) refugees of all nationalities.

Wisdom of plasterers with tattooed penises:

I forgot the sermon I received from my co-incarceree in the Mile End nick. "Never confess. Never shop yourself. They get paid for what they do; don't do their job for them. And never underestimate their stupidity. If they had any brains they wouldn't be working here now, would they?"

I would have cheerily holographed anything taking responsibility not only for the bank robberies, but for the state of English cuisine, denosing the Sphinx, the South Sea Bubble, the Schleswig-Holstein crisis, putting the spots on the natterjack toad, torching the library at Alexandria, spifflicating Rasputin.

Which just goes to show, be careful when you start thinking you know what's going on. E.g.:

More lawful sledgehammers of the past (no extra cost)

The only advice I can offer you when the police are sledge-hammering down the door (and you're not in a strange flat, you're sober and dressed, and you're recollecting like a genius your recent criminal activities) is to make sure they don't have a good reason, or indeed any reason, for storming in.

The police thought they had a good reason. They had trailed me from the airport. I had flown in from Columbia, carrying four kilos of cocaine in a specially gutted edition of Diogenes Laertius' *Lives of the Philosophers*.

Zak, for whom I had been acting as mule, whose one brush with the rozzers had been because of an over-enthusiastic application of the accelerator pedal, but whose infractions carefully totted up could have earned him a million years of chokey, looked as if he had swallowed a whole cormorant, unplucked and uncooked.

Why did I do it? One always likes to share one's interests and Zak was keen to educate me in the contraband trade (although he viewed narcotics as the riffraff segment of the market and he characterised the chief virtue of a mule as unwithering stupidity). It was the summer vac and I didn't have a foundation to swindle.

I was as surprised as Zak to see the law but, as they threw me to the floor, I was rather pleased to see them because I had been feeling monumental awkwardness about having to explain to Zak that I had lost the four ks on the tube making my way to his place.

When I say lost, I can't authenticate its lostness. The carrier bag could have been stolen. It could have spontane-ously annihilated itself. When I was on the escalator coming up at Belsize Park struggling with my luggage, I looked down to check for the bag as I had done a hundred times previously, but there was nothing to check. The bag was beyond my ontological detection.

My credulity left in disgust. I sprouted Corinthian columns of disbelief. Even after having lived with myself all my life, I couldn't believe it.

Neither could the police. No floorboard was left unturned, no body cavity unilluminated. Neither could Zak. He later owned up to being floored by my legerdemain in ditching the snow without the peelers clocking it: "You're a natural." His gratitude was unending. I just mention this because if no amount of intelligence can save you from stupidity, stupidity can occasionally save you from intelligence (one of Zak's contacts grassed us up).

Let's not forget the lawful sledgehammers of the present. 1.1 or

Digging yourself out of the grave 1.1

So there I was, woozy 'n' boozy in one of Marseille's finest police stations, facing my interrogating officer who had just walked in and slapped down a passport on the table.

A German passport. "Your full name?" Then I twigged and shifted gear. I had just been about to be polite and to felicitate them on catching me, give them as much confession as they could take, and then have a kip and some grub, or some grub and a kip, I wasn't fussy.

But the passport. I looked at the passport, and realised it could be my passport out of jail. It was a close thing. I had an unbridled desire to give in (because I was half-asleep, half-dead, half-witted and half-hearted about my current position in the universe) to give the zig a career, to fortunate him. I had a hangover, and it seemed preposterous to try and bluff my way out.

It was a moment of heroism unseen this millennium but luckily there was a part of my committee which didn't fancy being banged up, and I had already been in custody long enough for the novelty to be flaking off. Thus I rallied and turned my back on the impulse to surrender and lied if not effortlessly, satisfactorily.

"My name is Robert Oskar Kruger," I responded.

The sight of the passport was all I needed to guide me out, my guide book. The lack of laughter from my interlocutor, the absence of a sarcastic smirk, or any rebuttalish mien, encouraged me. I declined the offer of a translator (I didn't want anyone turning up who spoke good enough German to spot my bogus krautness) and tried to open rather jammed drawers of my mind to see whether I had had any incriminating evidence on me when I had gone out for my crate of Belgian beer. I was sure I had carried one of my own passports (which would have been a bit of a giveaway) but perhaps I had lost it.

Robert Kruger: a very convenient German with a loose passport:

Hubert had given me his passport, in great excitement. "Still warm from the tourist." He was really hooked on false documentation. And, of course, the best false documentation isn't false. That was why Hubert had been so pleased with his latest acquisition, fresh from the pocket. Because Herr Kruger's specifics were right on mine and he had correctly considered him a good match for me.

Admittedly most old, bloated, calvous Germans could double for me, and even if he hadn't been doppelganger material, with the beard I had started growing and the two black eyes, you'd need x-rays to spot the difference.

With constant praise for my French, I recited Kruger's details from my memory. He was a Gemini like me. I gave his office address and telephone in Zirndorf, his home telephone number, his hotel in Marseille. Irregular verbs, addresses, telephone numbers have always been my forte.

I may have mislaid what others would term frightening amounts of my life (1987, for example, is a bit of a puzzler), but I still remember the telephone number of the first girl I asked out. I remember the number and that she said no, although I can't remember her name. I particularly remember that number because I dialled six-sevenths of it two hundred times over a week before I had the guts to add the last digit. This is a party piece of mine, rather forced on me by the continual losses of address books, papers, diaries where most folk have the possibility of storing such information. Also, I would like to say in defence of the seat of learning where I worked that it might be possible to get a job at Cambridge if you're workshy, dishonest, repulsive, unimaginative, tedious, inadequate, alky, insane, badly dressed, smelly, or a combination of any or all of the former but not if you're thick or you haven't got a memory to draw on (however intermittent).

Then, still receiving tributes on my French, I explained how I had been beaten up a couple of nights before (no, I hadn't reported it – I didn't want to bother the police which was true) and had gone wassailing and taken the wrong turning from reality (largely true) and had no idea how I had finished up in that flat displaying inferior cartoon zebras; obviously I had, inadvertently, fallen in with bad company and I deeply regretted not being able to provide more assistance to them.

They asked me a lot of questions about Angoulême and the goods. Then they asked me again just to see if I had changed my mind. I was quite good on this since my version was a massive no, topped with no, and a free souvenir no. I would have been wobblier on my adopted self, but the numerals seemed to have satisfied them. "Oh, I'm freelance now, I dabble in banking and finance," I had said in response to profession since the information in Kruger's wallet hadn't delineated what he did.

The Suit took it all down. He was young, dapper and he must have saved up half a year for the suit. It was the sort of suit that excited the admiration of those with little or no time for fashion (such as myself); not to be merely worn, but to cane forgetfulness. All in all, he was too good-looking (he had a profile you could have broken rocks with) too broad-shouldered to be a policeman. The suit was a dead giveaway; the police, like the Army, entices in those who don't want any sartorial tribulation or effort. The Suit had the traits of man who comes to work from a different direction every morning, but despite all these boons, he was very proper with the lumpy philosopher coming the German opposite.

The Suit took his disappointment well, but that's the blessing of a healthy climate; you can't get too worked up. If I'd been bagged in Boulogne or some other grim Northern city that's a hyetologist's delight, I would have been stuffed and mounted on the wall. They weren't stupid, but they were the vice squad, they had their preoccupations, other goals stained on their windows.

But I gave good answer. It was one of those two-tone occasions when before your eyes you see incredible good luck and bad luck switching around. On the face of it, being collared robed only in cartoon zebras you wouldn't wish on your worst enemy (even allowing for my being prone to being prone, and prone to being prone in unsuitable venues) is weighty misfortune and would be enough to drive most people to renouncing the bottle. On the other hand bearing in mind the zeal with which two police forces were seeking my physicality, I had to count myself at the front of the fortunate, that I ended up walking out of the police station.

If anyone had spoken really good German my hopes would have been julienned and sautéd in shit.

Breakdown of detention:

A number of things baffled me: they took my fingerprints. Well, they couldn't have checked those properly. How come they didn't know Kruger's passport was swiped? Taken from his room, had Kruger not noticed? Not got round to reporting it? Or were they all working their own beats? The passport squad worrying about passports, the Suit worrying about Angoulême, the Corsican worrying about bank robbers, and no one talking to each other? The question marks were really having a day out.

Despite my signal failure to do my job properly (or indeed to do it even improperly for a lot of the time) for over twenty years, I found it outrageous that others were coffining it. The desire to shout "Isn't it obvious who I am?" strained at the leash.

I suppose they could have phoned the numbers I gave to verify the existence of a Robert Kruger; they might have checked the hotel Herr Kruger was at, Kruger conveniently being out.

Perhaps efficiency, like a unicorn or the ziphius, only exists in the imagination; or it is a mirage, only apparent far away. I must confess to this if nothing else: I was a trifle disappointed.

I had a tasty omelette for lunch. This was accompanied by two helpings of salad because the luncher in the next cell didn't want his. Hearing his refusal I immediately offered my belly as a destination. I wanted another go at analysing the elements of the dressing and was contemplating asking the chef for the tricks because there was something that teased and eluded my gustative disquisitions. That salad was a doughty champion of good cooking not being much to do with cost or complication, but simply caring. I ate it while tracking a zebra spider (salticus scenicus) roaming my cell in search of a bite.

The Suit and his minions, once they had decided I wasn't court material, were very solicitous. They offered me a lift back and a phone call to my wife. I declined saying I needed a constitutional. We parted, they lauding me on my French, and expressing the hope that my setbacks wouldn't prevent me enjoying the rest of my holiday in France. I thanked them courteously and left the baseball cap with sledgehammer to be claimed by its rightful owner.

Out

I had mixed feelings as I hit daylight and fresh air. I did have a temptation to yell "Pushovers!" but the salad dressing hadn't been that intriguing. My manumission was so outrageous, that if ever I were caught I could use it to blackmail my way to freedom or to one of the more luxurious jails.

But another idea strolled into my mind as I ambulated out. That the peelers weren't out to lunch, but were ultra-astute, and had released me to bag the other half of the Thought Gang: Hubert. They would follow me and fold us up together. This idea that I was tailed suddenly swelled in my idea pot.

The central police station had a marvellous set of stairs outside and, as I was lowering myself thinking I must avoid Hubert in case police eyes were sedanning on my shoulders, I spotted a figure coming up the stairs that looked remark-ably like Hubert, because it was Hubert, wearing a trench coat, which looked rather eccentric in the heat. I also spotted Thales peering out of the trenchcoat pocket.

"I should have known," he said exultantly, "that you had too much edge for any police station to hold."

I walked past firmly, pretending that Hube hadn't had any auditory or ocular impact.

But he zeroed in on me. "How did you give them the slip, Prof? I was coming to spring you," he said with a volume and a clarity astonishing in a very wanted bank robber on the steps of a major police station. He pulled back the lapels of his trenchcoat to reveal a small arsenal of weapons. "But I should have known you would be too much for them. You make the perpetuals look like old women."

"Go away!" I side-shouted, making a mini-mouth. But

my attempt at disassociating myself from Hubert didn't work.

"What's the matter?" he asked.

"Get the hell away," through unopened lips.

"That's nice," he said, umbraging up. "There's gratitude. I come to risk my neck to save you and all I get is being tossed aside like a used match. What's wrong with you?"

"Nothing's wrong, you idiot! I'm trying to be professional!" I said blowing up. We zobbed at each other, as a rotund man, who reminded me of Kruger walked up the stairs, giving us the wide berth you do to people whose hobby is shouting furiously in public.

Hubert's version

When I had failed to make our rendezvous that morning, he had called Jocelyne assuming I was entangled there, hurling my acreage. Jocelyne had explained that she had been worried since receiving a call from the Corsican who, apart from his customary bids to inveigle his loins closer to Jocelyne's, gloatingly announced that they had found the fat Brit who had been recognised by a bank employee of a Thought-Ganged bank, staying at a pension and that arrest would take place as soon as he returned. Jocelyne had driven around all night trying to find me, but since I didn't know where I was, it wasn't surprising that she couldn't find me.

Discreetly ringing round, after trying the hospitals to see if I was in the jug, Hubert discovered that there was a Kruger in custody. He decided to come on in. "What was your plan?" "To see what happened."

Hubert had also been circumspectly to visit my pension and had seen the undercovers strewn around.

Eddie's edifications:

The best way to avoid being arrested by someone who has a

hankering to give you a lonnng jail sentence, is to get arrested by someone else.

"How long do you think they'll wait?"

"A long time. The overtime's good."

Bank Robbery

We were late because we couldn't find the out-of-town bank that had been recommended to us by a friend of Hubert's as eminently picturesque and run by his brother-in-law whom he hated. "I don't see why we shouldn't do requests," said Hubert. We drove around banklessly: either we were lost or the bank was.

Hubert was driving; he insisted that we stop and ask for directions at a police station. He went in with Thales in his customised cage while I slouched in the car (still sorely sore from my body versus boot contest) knowing protest was futile. Despite his new-found fascination with reason he was as reasonable as a Gutian from the Zagros range. But Hube did come back.

"Just checking. So I had to wait ten minutes, before they stopped doing important things like shuffling papers and checking the coffee. I ask them the way. They don't know. They ask each other. They telephone. They radio. They make little circles in the hope that will provide them with the answer. They ask about the rat. 'It's an experiment,' I say. They've been thinking about it long enough so they make the joke: 'We thought you were going to report a lost rat.' Finally, because they want to get rid of me, they invent some directions.

"I go and stand by my poster. 'That's me, ' I say. 'How much do I get if I hand myself in?' I say. 'We're busy,' they say, going to pour an important coffee. And people say that the prisons are full of the stupid.

"We're invisible. Invincible. We're rolling."

He pulled away and lobbed Thales a chocolate raisin. That's life – you sire Western science and philosophy and some two and half thousand years later two jokers christen a rat after you.

We found a man carrying two infants, in tow behind two women who had a wife and mother-in-law air, who gave us the right route to the bank and added in a conspiratorial whisper: "If I'm not too late, whatever you do, lads, don't get married."

We had been discussing La Mettrie's use of the word voluptuousness, and Hubert wanted to do the next boj en philosophe, but I couldn't really fashion an angle.

For a firm which made such a name for itself, they actually did very little in adding to the hill of ideas. Les Philosophes. I know it's rich coming from a man who has trouble writing out a shopping list, but still eurt.

Zozo Voltaire: a man exempt from original thought. Agreed, he did a lot of actresses, gave good salon and will be read a long time after Eddie Coffin and his world ranking are blowing powderously across the streets. Rousseau: a man who made a career out of spite and who could bore a balloon to Mars. Then the others: a bunch of inept chemistry set-handlers, who, unfortunately, unlike Bacon, didn't manage to kill themselves. The only two I have time for are Diderot (not because of his thinking, but his writing) and La Mettrie, because anyone who foods himself to death has to be taken seriously.

And, unquestionably, the reason the boys are well-known is not because of their deposits in our idea-vaults, but because they were the putative producers of one of the greatest shows on Earth: the French Revolution. As any author knows, sex 'n' violence are a zeb combination.

Historians and letterists like a bit of carnage and carnal carnivaling because their lives are so dreary and pond-like. And unquestionably what makes the slaying 'n' laying even more tasty is that it's fellow alphabet-fiends, the biblioparous class, idea-junkies at the wheel. Despite the Terror getting householded, getting a capital letter, we're talking about a few thousand aristos and advocates getting topped; why don't we hear about the tens of millions of Chinese peasants starving to death?

Well, because (x) they're peasants, (y) it wasn't archived, (z) there were no novelists in the vicinity, and (zz) it's more fun doing research in a city with sharp restaurants.

Why the modern (a word with nothing in it) era is so often pegged at 1789 (although I like to frequent French restaurants as much as the next academic) is beyond me. If you want a better date, try 1776. Now that's an idea that worked: The United States of America, the only country in the world's history to import the poor, to court the zany, the dissenting, the only country in world history that had the power to impose its will on the world but didn't.

Nredom World

It's not the most successful of facts, but the opening of the modern era, for me, was in 1759 in the East Prussian town of Königsberg, (now degenerated and degermaned) at an inn called the Windmill.

Oh Yeah?

Yeah. The Windmill was the meeting place for three Krauts: Hamann, Berens and Kant.

This was some nineteen years after Hume had released the *Treatise on Human Nature* and some sixty years after Locke had unloaded *Civil Government* and *An Essay Concerning Human Understanding*. The British firm's henchmen were making ready to launch civil wars in America and France, both to be called revolutions because that sound makes killing easier.

And Germany, tired of being dispraised by the French (Leibniz, their top idea-tamer, had even written in French) was about to make its move, detonated long-range by Hume and Locke. In that one boozer was Hamann, a twenty-nine year-old layabout, recently returned from London where he had spent, on non-stop whoring and banqueting, an unfeasibly large sum of money (and was thus ready for religion) provided by Berens a businessman, who, like all straights with too much money, wanted to buy some cool 'n' cred and who had brought in Kant, the forty-five year-old philo and dipso whose rank was rocketing, to reform Hamann over a few glasses of zwetschenwasser.

This is not just a meeting of three frankfurter-handlers; this is the contents page of our times. Hamann toting faith, Kant the great spider, tooled up with reason, and Berens the man of affairs, bankrolling the whole exercise. The meeting was designed to snatch Hamann from the ranks of the pietists. They loggerheaded: Hamann arguing then and later for faith in faith, Kant arguing for deliverance thru reason, that the mind can lick the universe. Both flows producing, downriver, banks with a lot of pistols at the back of a lot of heads.

The tradesmen do the work of creating affluence, ease and variety; the real heroes are the ones who don't do very well in the posterity stakes, their names at best on portentous doors for a few lifetimes. Do we give a fig for the olive merchants, the vintners, the slavers of Rome or Hellas?

Reason was mostly novelty in the Ancient world, a branch of entertainment; only in the eighteenth century did reason start to earn its keep, to get you from London to Edinburgh faster. That gave the boys extra oomph, riding on Newton's back. It was the first time that the thinkers said, stand back we're going to sort everything out. The zeb theory is at hand. We've really cracked it this time.

The closure of the labs and the final packing away of the bunsen burners have been announced every few years since then.

Reason has had its finest moments in getting us from London to Edinburgh (and in deadening any pain that might result from such a journey). It's not so good on whether it's worth going. We are on the same road as Hamann and Kant, – just further down. Arguably we've always been on it but haven't noticed it. Reason has whelped the Cray computer, but the choice you have is one or the other. To Cray or to pray.

And significantly, despite the thrust of their gust, both Hamann and Kant, idea-surfers extraordinaire, were devotees of throat lubrication. We're frail, baby. The bottle to leave the bottle is given to few. When you drink, you drink in illustrious company.

Bank getting ready to be robbed

When we arrived at the lost bank, Hubert dished out two periwigs. I baulked at this: somehow it seemed too absurd, to rob a bank in a peruke and to try and foist off such an action as having some philosophical muscle.

I snapped at Hubert. "Don't be so ridiculous."

Hubert adjusted his wing, slid on his sunglasses and then admired himself in the rear view mirror. "It's the fucking Enlightenment."

I stayed to sulk in the car. But it didn't take long for me to parse my predicament, and to demonstrate that whether I wore the horsehair or not when I robbed a bank or not, my work as a philosopher was over. Getting grumpy is to no avail when you've become the galactic capital of preposterousness. The oceans might as well object to the tears of zeiformes and other fish.

Hubert sloped over to the bank. "Don't close the door on the Enlightenment," he yelled to a man who was closing the door as Hubert closed in, perhaps closing the door with a tad more urgency to prevent the whacko with the wig from having any chance of getting in. He might well have been justified in barring Hube solely on the strength of his aberrant appearance, but (not that it did him any good) he motioned to the sign indicating that the bank closed at 5.00, while Hubert expostulated that the universe hadn't reached that point; my babylonian certainly said 4.56.

The closer didn't accept Hubert's assertion or didn't care, but acted as if it were 5.00 and put his back into closing the door, which he was having difficulty doing since the mechanism hadn't been designed to take account of Hubert's foot. Tussling broke out, as times and shoulders vied. Hubert announced: "I'll bet you fifty francs, I can persuade you to open the door."

The closer shook his head firmly, but drastically relented on the door-pushing when Hubert produced the infallible door-opening utensil, the bandit's PhD.

"I'm getting tired of dealing with these people," Hubert remarked getting in the car, slinging the hold-all onto the back seat, a fifty franc note peeking out of his jacket pocket. "They're so unprofessional."

More unarrested time

We watched the Corsican bound out and rev up his car. Such zest for work was heartening to witness, all the more at the start of the day. Hubert would have made a good detective – he had tracked down the Corsican's den by means of looking him up in the telephone directory.

The original tip-off had emanated from Jo.

With military precision, I could call in feminine ministrations whenever I had a base (a bed with a space margin). Some suitable pad found (by the grace of tourist information) I would get on the estimable dog and bone and, within hours, a blanket of assistant bank manageress would be dooring.

Jo was incredibly resilient. If I had been forced to do a day's work, I would have been incapable of doing anymore, but she would cheerily travel over to help a philosophical bank robber unwind. All in all, when you ponder how men get women, and women get men, it seems rather unfair. The nullipara stalking the nullity's stalk.

The Corsican's persistence I sympathised with. Jocelyne would walk out of the bank to find the Corsican lurking with another lunch invitation, to escort her home, to propose sundry services. Her initial impulse had been to stamp him out like a loathsome crunchy hexapod but she had refrained. She thought it worthwhile logging his verbal spillages, as they might yield information beneficial to the liberty of blagging philosophers. "He's very keen for someone supposedly so busy." But she couldn't determine whether he wanted to expound zygite-like a grunty commentary on her because of in-built lust or whether her denial was fuelling his devotion. "No can do funny things to some men."

Amongst the wisps of data that Jo had minuted was the area he lived in (with the recommendation that it would be an unparalleled site for the sight of entwined bodies).

The address having been serendipitied on, Hube was all for going along and turning him over. I wasn't keen on the we, and when I discovered what time he was proposing to form our journey, I was (a) perplexed and (b) outraged. But the evening before I had found a crate of Trappist beer (along with St. Aug in the first rank of Catholic achievement) and feeling that the clientele on the premises wasn't fit to drink this murky marvel, in the manner of Cambridge dons who selflessly drained the college cellars during the War to prevent the claret and vintage port falling into enemy hands, I worked yeomanly to transmute the liquid into tonguewilding memories or a smooth obliviscence.

The bar went on all night. The night went all bar. They closed inasmuch as they locked the door at one o clock. It was the yeast or whatever but I found it harder to sleep. I have no problem staying in bed, the charm of being mattressed is undiminished, but I find it harder and harder to take an invigorating burst of blackness, put the dark in the park.

Perhaps this is just a natural attribute of ageing or (possibly the same thing) the feel of soil in the skull, the advent of darkness slotted in permanently.

Not feeling very prehumous though (despite being un-somnolent), I hobbled home to find Hube making ready to sally out. Not really having much else to do apart from flattening a bed, I thought it might be amusing to get the zet out.

The Corsican's flat was in a neoteric block, light, not cheap, but not palatial either. Hube dealt with the locks, if not swiftly (being out of practice) without much ado.

"It's a disgrace that a senior police officer should have such shoddy security," Hubert commented, "he might as well have a neon invitation over the door."

The flat had the tidiness of the long-distance bachelor and investigator, ordered if not well-thought out. There were two book shelves, with a predictable number of classics (studied at school) presumably to certify the fact he had read books once. A dead giveaway. As I skimmed his tomes (by his spines shall ye know him) I noticed Hubert heading for the kitchen and starting to meddle with a percolator.

"Do you want a coffee, Prof?"

"Didn't you say you wanted to pinch some stuff?"

"Yes, but one doesn't want to act like a criminal. Relax, ease up, take the weight off your feet."

"What if he comes back?"

"I suspect he's gone for the day. But you have to show life who's the boss. Anyway, if he turns up, that's all right. I'd like a word."

Taking up a newspaper (yesterday's), Hubert gave the sofa his weight. If he was going to twiddle his thumbs, I was going to bed to twiddle my thoughts there. The Corsican must have been feeling optimistic because he had just put on fresh sheets, black and dandy; so I hit the horizontal. I hardly ever decline a recline.

In the end was the word

But despite my night with light, I couldn't jettison my self.

It's an effort to sleep in an alien bed anyway, but a hundred-fold, when it belongs to the man who is in charge of hunting you down, even if you try counting zebras.

Voices: the uncharitable view

Perhaps it's been a little harsh of me, a little dismissive, but whenever folk talk of seeing things or hearing voices which aren't there (i.e. which others can't perceive) and unless there is solid evidence of powerful hallucinogens at play, fly agarics, ergot, I scrawl down: lunacy or deception, with lunacy in the lead. Over the cultures, and over the centuries, pointing out things others can't discern has generally not been an earner – going for sainthood, spiritual signposting, is a perilous gambit as one thing that has never been in short supply is kindling for burning people who are acting strangely.

Also, although I don't make claims for my knowledge, frankly, I've catalogued unutttered utterances as utter bollocks. Load of joad.

That's why it was a bit of a shock to hear a voice, a voice that wasn't mine, speaking chez moi, in-skull, in the medias of my res, a voice that had taken up residence in my head, a voice speaking without the help of sound.

The Brain: Left 'n' Right, Hemi 'n' Semi:

Our mind double acts which may be why double acts have triumphed through the ages. Think of the great double acts of history: Adam and Eve, Cain and Abel, Romulus and Remus, Romeo and Juliet, Zoser and Imhotep, Laurel and Hardy. We have domiciled in our domes two speakers, mantled as good and bad, sighted as him and her, and perhaps because contraries are the foundation of our evolutionary escapades. We know these voices (and their understudies), we know these counsellors, even if one is stronger than the other.

But this wasn't a home-grown message, this wasn't the tone of the usual thought emissaries. This was crisp, clear voice, much bolder than the usual inter-ear banter, like a radio sunk in my head, as if I had tuned in to someone else's thoughts.

I was scared. Petrified. Because (x) hearing voices isn't like catching a cold, you can't get rid of it with lemon tea (y) it's inside, it's not some naevus, an epidermal blemish you can cover up or cauterise (z) I had no control over it. It was there of its own volition, just stepped in and (zz) I was going bananas.

This worried me a lot. Terrified me terribly. Horrified me horribly. I hadn't been that scared when I had been buzzed by a Soviet gunship in Afghanistan. Somehow falling apart wasn't too bad as long as I was aware of it and had some say in it; I could still go nephalist and eat lettuce, that would have some effect, even if it were akin to spitting against a wall in an effort to demolish it; but that I might not know what was going on ... that roused the glands' bands' hands.

This is what the voice said:

"Hello."

Act naturally

I rose and, responding to the dictates of lunchtime, let my taste zigzag in the fridge until it discovered some devilled chicken livers, prepared and provided with a covering note in handwriting that was the product of an age when calligraphy still mattered, from an aged female relative step-by-stepping how they should be warmed up to the greatest effect.

Which we did and ate them with some fresh baguette; they intercoursed each other so exquisitely I would have blissed myself, were it not for the fact that my appetite had been unwhetted by the fear of my marbles rolling around the kitchen floor.

Two bottles of quite good bottle were consumed, not quite as dear as the plonk I had got accustomed to since turning to open crime, but the discrepancy didn't matter since I only ended up drinking a bottle and a half out of worry about the harm that bibation might cause.

The voice had rather marred my pleasure, but Hube was overflowing with the joys of humiliating his adversary. The old 'nous avons νους', had catapulted him into higher space.

Afterwards, we watched videos of the Corsican on the job, that Hubert had unearthed as he had ransacked the nooks of the flat during my mental interpolation. They evinced the cackhandedness of the amateur, but doubtless the Corsican considered that his loin work deserved electromagnetic prolongation. The camerawork was rather static as the camera had been left on its own, and cameras aren't known for moving around much by themselves. The lighting wasn't much either, and, in any case, it was an almost instantly dull wide-shot of the Corsican's rear rearing and veering on partial women zedded under him. The soundtrack was similarly dreary 'n' weary, with impatient breathing and male and female snorting, plus the odd, often increasingly desperate, "are you coming?" from the Corsican as he wiggled his pelvis in his quest to activate ecstasy in his companion.

"Gold. Solid Gold," Hubert verdicted.

If you're to film yourself torpedoing the swimming pool, you really need to invite a close friend around to do the camerawork, or spend a mint on a bank of cameras. Sequences such as the Corsican unravelling a condom onto his nose (obviously a humorous attempt to impersonate an elephant) and wearing black stockings and suspenders (the panel's out on that one) might have rendered him too bashful to invite a neighbour around. "Twenty-four carat gold," verdicted Hubert.

Hubert was extremely meticulous about spinning through the cassettes to make sure he didn't miss anything. For myself, I had gotten to know the Corsican better than I wanted. Hubert had all his financial details, a squeaky pink hippopotamus, and a photograph of a young attractive girl on the beach, topless and toothy, who, Hube had established in a forensic fashion, was the Corsican's sister on a honeymoon beach.

The phone had been connected to the talking clock in Japan for four hours at this point (peak rates). Hubert had offered me the use of the phone to make any extremely long-distance phone calls. Getting in touch with the foundation had appealed to me. What would they say if I rang up to give them my best wishes? "Ah, Coffin-san, you are in France now, robbing banks?" Japanese etiquette and language are wide in scope (although I didn't get far – only five hundred kanjis' worth) with different forms of address for water-carriers and royalty; I was piqued whether the range would stretch to dealing with someone who had absconded with large sums of your money and who phones up between blags in the South of France.

Foundations: how to take them to the cleaners

It's easy. You just find a foundation which wants to give you lots of money, then you walk off with it and indulge yourself remorselessly. The world is full of rich people who are in a dither about what to do with their yennom; the thing is that they're usually monotoners who've made their money with decimal points, and who, with zilch in the fascinating bank, want to stand arm in arm with epithets such as deep and bewitching (as, once we've filled our bellies, we all do to an extent I suppose). The difference is they can buy it. The only difficulty is obstructing their thought path, tying yourself to the tracks of their cheque book. It took some practice.

One of the main problems about having a drink problem is that people tend to treat you as if you have a drink problem. This was brought home to me, when Featherstone ...

Featherstone 1.1

... who had come a long way with me. We adjacented as undergraduates; I used to complain that he would rise too noisily and disturb my sleep as he went off to lectures early in the morning. If you're a physicist, you have to do stuff like that, as well as pushing around particles, zirconium. I suspect that the getting up early and working hard and not going to the hot parties seemed a trifle punitive to Featherstone as after all that he earned himself a position in the college which also employed a certain E. Coffin, a man guaranteed never to have got up early or worked hard or missed a party, or your money back. In his dealings with me, I sensed, barely beneath his demeanour, a resentment. It was he ...

Foundations at the cleaners 1.2

... who was the designated millionaire-stroker (every college has one). That time, he addressed me in the following terms, "No drinkee, Eddie, no bottle for one evening. And big, big, money." He was also making oodles of big, big yennom gestures to reinforce the message; this made me realise that I was getting far gone, that a fellow don thought it necessary to parley with me in such terms.

Hanging around yacht clubs, wine tastings, operas, as was his wont, Featherstone had trawled a billionaire who was (to his annoyance) digging philosophy. I was required to turn up, philosophize mildly, get out some blandishments and collect the cheque, as so many disc jockeys of thought, impecunious, empty-handed, have turned up at the tables of the well-heeled to do so in the past. "He's dying to be philanthropic; he's going to do a couple of million at least ... and he likes your book."

It was Featherstone's application of pidgin English without a drop of irony that frightened me into teetotalling, as much as the promise of cash without end.

Be Yourself

Perhaps that was my mistake. I should have been my usual
self. If I'd turned up cradling a bottle, I'd have done some
seven figure charming without a slip. I was off the bottle for
a week before the meeting. The world looked strange, ubiq-
uitously fresh, newly painted. I was intoxicated (after feeling
like dud mud for two days) by the lack of intoxication.

I arrived in Hampstead at Long's, (taking care to station
myself away from the walls, the Ming bowls and Zoffanys
so that if I slumped or swivelled nothing priceless would get
it) where Featherstone was awaiting me anxiously in the
hallway, trying to ascertain ocularly whether I was pickled
or not. I wasn't, but that didn't stop me tripping over
headlong and decking Mrs Long who, as she dominoed over,
broke her arm.

"It could happen to anyone," Long assured me magnan-
imously.

Mr Long was suspiciously gracious about my hospitalising
his wife. She was whisked away by the chauffeur for medical
treatment and we mealed on, although I was a bit edgy about
sitting next to Featherstone who had that sort of glare people
have prior to inserting a fish knife into your neck.

Mr Long was also most gracious about my vomiting
violently over his zeb porcelain. He hosted superbly, since
the needlessly rich usually have the manners (as well as the
looks) of wart-hogs but he had good manners to spare as I
yawned lumpily to the east, to the west, to the north and to
the south. I hadn't eaten much in expectation of a free satiety
but there had been enough to do 360°.

Mr Long conducted me to a room where I ailed for a bit,
keeping very still, in case I demolished a wall or combusted
the house. By the time I came down, I was in control, eager
to try and shine a bit. Instead I ended up scuttling to the loo
since I felt promptings from the invisible enemy at the other
end.

Eddie vs. the unflushable turd

I stared at it. Somehow, despite all that had preceded, deranged by my ordeal, I felt it all rested on this: getting rid of this object. Whatever else they reviled me for, I didn't want them saying I wasn't a house-trained philosopher. I don't give myself airs, but even *I* have some vestigial self-esteem and I felt it could be torpedo'd by this. Despite the luxury of the house it was a very slow-filling toilet. Every flush cost me ten minutes. I had a lot of time to reflect on the slothful plumbing. I was in there for half an hour before the search party came. It was Featherstone, hoping I suspect, that I was dead, or at least dying, so he could enjoy it, and then go for the tragedy card.

"Are you all right?" he asked.

I affirmed this. Somehow I couldn't bring myself to impart the news I had created a monster that I and fin-de-millennium sanitation couldn't control. The trouble was there was no brush to insinuate the log round the bend, and desperate though I was, I wasn't going to give it a helping hand.

Naturally, if it had been in the guest wing or some remote part of the mansion, I would have left it for the servants to deal with, but this installation was on the main drag, and I could imagine Long coming in and beholding my bottomwork, and somehow, it just seemed terribly wrong, even in a world where children starve to death. I was in there for another hour giving it the handle. They must have started to fear that I was moving in because the chauffeur announced himself eventually.

We didn't get the loot.

But when the Japanese turned up, we all went down to Soho to a tatty dive with the head zori, played drinking games and behaved so disgracefully I forgot I was in the UK. At about three o' clock when they wanted to throw us out, Hiroshi (who is so rich other millionaires faint when he comes into the room) bought the place (and presumably gave it to his driver as a tip). "Japan and England are both islands," he said to me. And that was it. I had the big money tap open.

Featherstone, incandescent with rage, stroked on. He had gone to America to woo another millionaire. On a standby flight, he spent a day at Heathrow waiting for the flight. He was picked up and taken to the moneybag's home. The home was a twenty-room mansion, in which seventeen of the rooms were completely unfurnished and bare. There was no heating in his room and it was January (although his host, Nash had a bar-heater in his). "Make yourself at home," he said.

Featherstone investigated the kitchen and found an open pint of long-life milk and three ancient Hershey bars. The evening meals were delivered pizzas: "I love simple food, don't you?" Featherstone also uncovered a stash of special offer pizza vouchers in a drawer while Nash went out for lunch leaving Featherstone "to work".

Then there were the conversations.

"I've listened to students' drivel, but this, this was ... unbearable, untreated blether; it was only the possibility of largesse or food that kept me in his company, in addition to the fact I had nowhere else to go."

The mansion was ten miles walk from the nearest food outlet and Nash maintained that the car was out of order, offering to call Featherstone a taxi. One day Featherstone walked into the kitchen and found a dead rat. "I understood at once; the rat had died of despair."

Leaving without a cent, Featherstone discovered that Nash was a serial bore. That he lured academics to his place to air his theories on history, economics and American foreign policy which they would be forced to endure because they were stranded, or because they were hoping in vain for a handout. Nash's reputation was such that he had had to commence flying people in from London, Berlin, Zomba. Featherstone had to pay for his taxi to the airport as the car was still out. He had actually walked ten miles to the shops the previous day. "I had to get out and see some people." With wadologists, you've either got it or you ain't. It's a knack.

Gashing the Corsican's gaff 1.2

Hubert had gone down to collect some of the bags packed into the car. He was helped with a hefty bag of cement by one of the Corsican's neighbours. "We're just making a few modifications," Hubert explained.

It was a two-bedroom flat, and Hubert was meticulous in his modifications. The lounge was covered in an inch to two inches of tapir dung (one of Hube's orphanage crew ran a tapir farm in Britanny). "It's important to be original." He drilled very large holes in all the walls with a power drill he had found. He burned out the wiring. An orange tree, the result of careful years of nurture, greenly growing in a pot, was doused in cognac and immolated. The toilet, sinks, basins were fully cemented. He glued several items of furniture to the ceiling. It was not hostility; Hubert was very good-natured about vandalising the flat, it was merely the way things were.

I scanned a volume of early erotic photos by Zipette, a touch of fin-de-siècle frippery for a fin-de-millennium. Still bewildered by my contact with the unexpected voice, I couldn't read much more than a few bare bottoms (though the Corsican actually had a rather fine edition of Montaigne).

Lighting on those photographs from the age when Paris was the world headquarters for tits 'n' bums, gave me strong draughts of mortality. These women, the finest platforms for gratification of their time, for whom men paid for, for whom they did or would have done anything, are gone. Posteritied posteriors, neither living nor dying. Testimony that no matter how powerful your passions, you pass like a quiet breath.

I met their gazes and ruminated (x) that in painting it is the artist that filters what he wants, but in photography the model always has a say. I reflected how sparse our vocabulary is for the nomenclature of the regard, the configuration of mouth and eyes, the nets of muscles that catch emotion, how good it would be to write a book on this, as well as (y) how rare are the words reserved for climax, how abundant the names for the tools of delight, how plentiful the vocabulary for their exploitation and how few for those finest seconds of release and how good it would be to write a book about it and (z) how if you leave something long enough, people take it seriously.

However, vivisecting myself, I know this is all over. Done pandecting. Pandect no more. No one said it would be easy. Ysae eb dluow ti etc. Why me? Em yhw. Get zet. Tez teg.

I'm a too-late developer. Life, things, one's position suddenly switches from having plenty of time, too much time, to having none. I can't perceive a patch where time was gleaming right.

Where my life went wrong 1.1

It was one of those moments where I was unable to zero in on the origin of my zeroness, because it seemed that my whole existence had never gone right; I couldn't single out a fragment of sense.

You can't keep a perpetual down

The collapse of my self didn't impede Hube in his campaign. Taking a pad to the telephone, he started making notes: "I don't want to forget anything." Then he picked up the receiver and dialled, asking twice for the Corsican.

"Salut! It's me," Hube announced, having presumably been passed over to our host. "I'll keep it brief because a long conversation could be very damaging to my freedom. Okay, here's the situation: we've got the pink hippopotamus, as well as the three thousand francs you hid under the cutlery. We've viewed and reviewed the tapes.

"No ... no ... you can't say that. How can you know who I am? I've lived with myself for thirty years and I don't know who I am ... well ... well, you might think that, but whatever I am, I'm not someone who takes two hours to make a woman come. Anyway, we must get on. We've drunk your wine; I thought it was okay, but the Prof said it was a little sorry for a senior police officer ... and we've got that picture of your sister ... pity she's married... but I'm certainly going to study it closely and I'll make sure that all the perpetuals in Les Baumettes get a copy for those long winter evenings ... and we'll be sending a list of items to the insurance company so don't try and invent any claims to fatten up your cheque. To end ... we continue to micturate all over you ... m-i-c-t-u-r-a-t-e all over you."

We were out the door faster than zebras after Hube's farewell. It was only in the car, as Hube shredded up irredeemably the picture of the Corsican's sister, that I questioned him about micturate.

"Yes, he'll have to look it up. There's nothing, nothing more annoying for a policeman than someone who spent ten years inside having a choicer vocabulary than him."

Farewell to Marseille

News of the Corsican was slow; Jocelyne found his lascitivities had vanished. But she was summoned to the police station because they had a very confessy individual who claimed to be Eddie Coffin; they were fairly confident he was a chimera-breather but they asked Jo to come and give him a lookover and an authoritative no. She said the Corsican had hoared overnight; no manifestos of lust manifested themselves.

Hubert had returned all his property (along with an inflatable doll – a deniable but still besmirching item) to the local newspaper and our tame journalist, the sports club membership card and bank statements giving indubitable authenticity to the package.

The impostor threw Hube into paroxysms; he immediately wanted to go out and put on a platter the unquestionable nature of a Thought Gang job. I agreed, but only on condition that we upped sticks. I had an inkling, in spite of our unblemished luck, that it was wise to shift.

Also, I wanted to see Toulon again, which was singular since it was a cesspit (and not much of one at that). The likelihood was that if I experienced anything it would turn me into a melancholy flavoured person but one aspect of my ageing is that, more than anything else I want to feel, even if I feel bad.

We zoomed down to Bandol (surely one of the best entries in the Good Bank robbing guide) where the air is so fresh, the sunshine so sunny you'd think there were three suns on duty. I really am perplexed by civilisation's strides in the Mediterranean since I never want to do anything but collect the photons hot from the sun and nibble an olive or a grape. The heliasts were so right to worship the sun; there's something worthy of idolation, you need so little else. The stoics were amongst the earliest beach bums.

Beach scene

But a sadness lurked for me in Bandol. One of my favourite restaurants had gone. There are few things more sorrowful than the closure of a good restaurant, or (more pernicious, but equally devastating) a change in management, the replacement of a chef. It's inevitable, but you can't steel yourself completely. More and more as you deyouth, after forty or so, a switch occurs in your social arrangements and you find yourself spending your consciousness at funerals (and if you have distinguished acquaintances the double burden of memorial services) and tramping to restaurants that no longer exist, and you have to effort again to find an establishment worthy of your custom.

The most galling thing about the human, is not the sadness at the passing (the disappearance of your favourite actuals) but the exertion of relacing new information in your mind, relearning, re-reifying again.

Back in the centre of Bandol, I was outraged to see it verging on the unrecognisable. There's nothing like towns being swapped like that, to heap age on your shoulders, to feed you the zaqqûm of deyouthing. I wished they would have the decency to wait until I was dead before they redeveloped my memories. Man may be the measure of all things, but we need a measure too, we need a mnemonic yardstick. However much we enjoy change, we need that yardstick, a high-street where the library, the restaurant, the shops, the police station are fixed; a home to come back to, where people say hello even if they hate you and you hate them, where you can borrow money, where your absence will be present. A prompt, an aide-memoire for your youth.

Unquestionably, you don't get rich robbing banks. It's a slog and these days you can't expect more than a few thousand a go, because there usually isn't much more in the till and because it takes time to stuff mostly small denomination bills into bags. It's a comfortable income and can keep you in Chablis, but you can't put your feet up for good and retire in a style that would satisfy your imagination.

Back in blag

Ironically, I wasn't in the mood; I was miffed about the restaurant. Essentially the world is divided into two categories, those people who are looking at a much longer than life jail sentence, and those who aren't. If you aren't it's very easy to dragoon reasons for not knocking over the nearest bank; if you're already mired in iniquity, turpidutinous to the zth degree, it's not so easy to glib your way out. 'I'm too lazy' just sounds soft and reprehensible. But Hubert's youthful verve dragged me (limping) along.

The bank was one of those with a buzzer system on the door. "I don't know why they bother with these," derided Hubert. "They don't pay any attention. I'll show you." He gave me a beret, and he reached in his bag and pulled out two small pistols which he fixed onto the rings he wore in his ears, so they dangled like the most extravagant earrings ever devised. He cradled the Desert Eagle in his other arm.

"People simply don't expect anything as exciting as us to hit town. Especially in a place like Bandol, where someone breaking wind is a major event," He pressed the bell. "They could never be ready for the hottest philosophic duo this side of Zama. Only Plato and Socrates could give us a run."

As he prophesied, despite an unquestionably bank robberish air, we gained ingress as I ruminated on Hube's gluttony for erudition.

"This," promulgated Hube, "is a neo-Platonic bank robbery. You'll have to pay close attention if you want to tell the difference between this and a Platonic job. Ask the Prof if you have any questions."

I doubt if anyone noticed any neo platonic elements (though if really pushed I could always concoct a few) or could tell the difference, or cared. There were no questions. A good-looking girl marshalled the notes for us while Hube joked: "Forgive me for being so forward, but you're so beautiful we'll have to come back here again." He was developing into a very entertaining criminal. Had there been a vote for bank robber of the year he would have walked it.

The manager was old, even by my standards, although he will doubtless be doing more decades than me.

"I suppose you've come for the money out back," he said extremely voluntarily.

"No, thanks. We won't bother," I said. Our expectations were modest, and to be honest, the bank looked like a joke bank, barely much evolved past the level of having a sign saying bank and a door, but Hube was ravenous for more robbery. He laughed:

"You can read our minds. A telepathic bank manager. You should advertise."

"It's in a safe but when you threaten me, reluctantly, I'll have to open it for you."

We were conducted to an alcove where there was a laughably ancient safe. The manager, cowed by our aggressive exhaling, opened the safe. I have to say it took invisible amounts of threatening from where I was standing. "Please don't point that gun at me," he said in a very loud voice and very unnecessarily since we wouldn't have had the ill grace to do so.

Inside the safe was a hard to credit amount of money in five hundred franc bills, beginning with serial number Z.341 50701; it brought back that pristine elation of bank robbing. "It's four million francs," he said putting a figure to our speculations.

"Do you often have this much money?" Hubert inquired.

"No. We've never had a pay-in like that, but then we've never had a bank robbery before. I've been working here for thirty years. More's happened today than in the whole of before. Never had anything like it. It's been an staggering last day. I retire tomorrow. Not that I want to. But when are the wishes of people who've worked loyally for thirty years taken into consideration?"

He was a pleasant man. I felt like asking him for a drink, but we didn't have time so I said: "I'd like to invite you for a drink, but we don't have the time."

Hubert dipped into his bag and produced some T-shirts ("Perhaps your children or grandchildren might like them?") bearing the legend "My Sense Data have met the Thought Gang" and "I rob, therefore I am", as well as a handful of badges, "I want to know.." or "The zet's good".

We shook hands and then drove onto Toulon.

Civilisation's greatest boo-boos

Perhaps I've been going about this the wrong way. We're all used to the congratulatory reviews of civilisation, perhaps mankind's greatest massacres, the top butcherings, all-time greatest pillagings? Or humanity's finest idiocies, our world's most serene daftnesses; philosophy's out-takes, knowledge's backfirings. Posterity's posteriors.

Know-all:

This is a standard one. The 'it's all sorted' sensation. Diderot (*Pensées sur l'interpretation de la nature* – 1754) pontificating that mathematical science would soon come to a standstill. Then there was Kant reckoning the ink had dried on the subject of astronomy. Not to mention Rutherford at the beginning of the century jeering at the universe, logicking the savants had done the business with Newtonian physics. The physicists and abacists are still at it. It rains guts and toes. The horizon is always in sight.

Every generation has this image of itself as the edge, the edge that will cut all the way. It starts with everyone, it starts with the Greeks, and although they admit there are things that are hazy, there is the cheque in the post atmosphere. The chiliasts 'n' seers 'n' millennarians, along with the bath-pourers 'n' physicists 'n' abacists, they all always agree that IT is at hand, the WHY is nigh. With civilisations, with us, it's the same thing, we itch for the pay off, for the real thing; what we get is a burst of blackness. Civilisations' bones are bigger than ours, the disappointments the same. I admit I feel as cheerful as a Zwickau prophet.

The bottom ten

1. Johannes Van Helmont's recipe for making a mouse. (I admire the modesty of scale.)

2. Fourier's notion that the seas would turn into orangeade in the new era of justice.

3. Voltaire's condemnation of Buffon (thereby making a buffoon of himself) arguing that seashells discovered on mountains had been left there by picnickers and not antediluvian seas.

4. Aristotle's view that the chest is the seat of the intellect.

5. Duret's anatiferous trees.

6. The alchemist Paracelsus' recipe for growing a man. (Fuck a pumpkin – leave it to rot and you get your homunculus.)

7. Gorgias the supersophist declares nothing exists then erects a statue of himself in gold.

8. Condorcet – *Esquisse d'un tableau historique des progrès de l'esprit humain* (1794). His idea of the tenth epoch (1789 –) the abolition of stupidity. (We're almost there, it's just round the corner).

9. Saint-Pierre's Projet de paix perpétuelle (1713). No more war in Europe. (The cheque's in the post.)

10. Life: solitary, poor, nasty, brutish and short. No. Sometimes the cheque is in the post. Life wasn't like that for Hobbes; he limed with Galileo, Descartes, Harvey. Had a nice pension. Lived to be ninety-one. In fact, if there's one thing to be said for philosophy is that it seems to promote longevity.

Which of our beliefs or practices will split their sides in the future? Maybe the future won't get a chance. Maybe we won't give the future a chance. We're due for a stupendous catastrophe. For all the stick it gets this century has been quite generous to a lot of people. A bellicose first half, but while there are galores of wars, disasters, diseases, zadrugas butchering zadrugas (the cruellest disputes always being between those who are indistinguishable to outsiders), evil's weevils in their innumerable forms, they're most popular in countries lacking crack French restaurants, and therefore of not much weight; things have eased up on the apocalypse front, which is always a bad sign. Teiuq oot s'ti, ti ekil t'nod I.

Première porte de guerre

As we suburbed into Toulon, I gave Hubert strict instructions: "I want to stay in Toulon. For at least a few days. I want to look around. No robberies. No bother. No regrettable incidents. No brawls. Nothing to write home about. No head-butts. No experiments. You're allowed to do some shopping and watch some television."

"Okay, Prof. I'll go along with that." There was a pause while Hube gave his assent its moment of glory. To show the give and take of our partnership. That was the give; then came the take. He continued.

"But I've been thinking. We have to do something to make things spicier.We should publicize our next robberies. We'll double back to Montpellier for it. What we do is to announce that we're going to do five jobs on one day. To add another thick crust to the police's stupidity. And we also warn them: when we come into a bank and announce we're the Thought Gang, if they respond with a citation from one of the greats, we leave the bank in peace. Our slogan: only learning can save you from The Thought Gang. Don't call the police, read the classics. Don't buy an alarm, buy a Zeno.The perpetuals will be hospitalised when they hear about this."

I presume all human history is paved with the thought: this can't be happening. Gnineppah eb t'nac siht. The Huns. The Black Death. The Mongols. Syphilis. The Turks. The Bomb. The Conquistadores. Germans invading France again. Millions of men and women stand up: this can't be happening again. Did the dinosaurs have a saurian equivalent when the terminal boulder from outer space hit?

In any event, I've left my common sense in another galaxy.

"We could even have a philosopher of the month," Hubert honed.

??????????????????????????

Toulon 1.1

We rented a flat near the beach in an area that was aching to be bourgeois but, since this was Toulon, wasn't going to make it. We had a flat downstairs, while our landpeople lived above.

I'm surprised the banks haven't stumped up a reward for us yet. Hube, I can tell, is slighted by it and is harbouring architects of revenge and penalty, but he reasoned it away: "They haven't got any money left for rewards, have they? We've stolen it all."

An old guy swept in front of the flats. He was so elderfied that he could barely handle the broom. There wasn't much to sweep anyway, and he had swept it yesterday, but it gave him something to do. I guessed he was a venerable relative of the family put out for an bit of exercise, but he was on holiday, and renting the flat next to us, sitting inside silently, occasionally popping out for a stimulating sweep of the empty yard.

M. Thomas explained this to me as he showed me around. He was the only Frenchman I've ever come across who looked ridiculous in a beret. Jut as some people assume elegance in any attire, he had the talent of eradicating any style hidden in a fabric. He should have been hired by fashion houses to destroy their rivals' lines. Anti-model.

Madame Thomas gave me an enthusiastic sale spiel too, inconscient that I was taking the flat because it had more than three walls and because it had been at the top of the list given to me by the Tourist information office. I felt like saying, "I'm a bank robber, I don't give a toss about the new showerhead." She explained they had had to get rid of the previous tenant, a young Zelenogradian, because she kept on inviting marines back and having quartets in the bed. I wondered how she knew that and, if she could observe, why she was so put out.

They were pleased they had a German professor (from

Tübingen) in the offing; that put a zocle under their respectability. The ink had barely dehydrated on the receipt when anxiety exploded as Hubert appeared. He gave them the predatory and felonious look that was his face, making them fear for their silverware and standing. His very posture signalled that this was someone capable of burning down their home merely to warm his hands.

With the appearance of Thales they were torn horribly between a desire to call in an air strike, and the hunger for wads (I had paid in cash that was not going to be fed into the tax system). They spoke disparagingly of rodents while Thales gazed on them contemptuously. An elephant turd in a blue bow-tie would have surprised them less and would have been more welcome. Unlike most wild animals, alleged to be implacable against captivity, Thales, in the great freeloading style, was getting plump and had a proprietorial affection for his cage never roaming more than a few paws from it. As if anxious he might be barred from his barred suite and he'd have to go back to being a rat.

I introduced Hube as a professor of neurology from Montpellier university. "I do apologise for my colleague but neurologists, as you probably know, are strange folk."

Jocelyne turned up after Hubert had gone out, parting with my injunction. "If anything happens, however accidentally, however fortuitously, don't come back. Explanations are the wrong shape." I handed him a note to the same effect, so it was in writing, so he couldn't claim he'd misheard or forgotten. Much difference wasn't going to be made, but it might brush a sheen of discretion on him.

We changed into the livery of lust.

I ran the bath. Indicated we should embark. "We can't fit into that," she said, but of course we did. Her splendours were undiluted; the water gave a gleam farm to her chest, her coasts. "I've never done this before," she said (emitting splashy ziraleets), a sentence I never expected to catch emerging from her lips.

"What?"

"Have a bath with someone else."

That surprised me. But it pleased me. I was pleased we had firsted, that Eddie had set foot in an experience others had not. Years from now she would say, if nothing else, "Oh yes, Eddie, he was the bank robber in the bath."

I was getting very fond of J. One of the few boons of deyouthing is that I really expect so little, that I can value things as they arrive. An evening with Jocelyne. Even if I were never to see her again, I'd still be 14, 400 seconds ahead. That's what you get to appreciate: good company. She never fussed, never conversed about navigating the fourth, never waved a contract, unpacked the verb *to regulate*.

"You never married?"

"One mistake I never made. Life is too short to make them all. Unless you stay up at night or get up very early"

She had legs that seemed timeless; skied into shape to get me into shape.

I shaped.

"Life is short; but your dick's long."

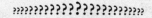

Gérard's cafe

Would Gérard be there I asked myself? Would there be a Gérard time of day to catch him? I chose to just go, to launch myself on the impulse to see him. Either fate's a mate or it's not. It was no use trying to be clever after such a long time.

Towns are people; if Bordeaux is Montaigne, then Toulon is Gérard.

I hadn't heard from him for over twenty years. Hadn't seen him in thirty, despite the pleasure I had always received from his company.

He was likeable for a number of reasons; despite his flourishing in areas where I failed, he was one of the few people I've come across, more untidy, more impractical, more absent-minded, more of a fervent zymometer than me.

First Gérarding

It was the year out I had in France. After serving two years in Cambridge my faith in the biz was wilting, so Wilbur, as my director of studies, suggested that I go abroad to refresh my love of wisdom:

"Have a year out, distribute some bodily fluids. Do whatever you want, just don't talk about finding the truth or anything like that. I couldn't bear that. If you want the truth you have to attach electrodes to people's genitals. You get the truth pretty damn quick then.

"You lucky bugger," he valedicted, "I wish I could get away from this dump for a year." I was a bit taken aback by that since I had always regarded Wilbur as the personification of urbanity and poise, both bizwise and in person; but I didn't appreciate that in all long-term matings, no matter how much you love, you have the rucksack of vexation.

So I got a job as an assistant at the lycée Zola in Toulon, a job which suited me since it involved little more than opening my mouth and talking to teenagers who were weary of life.

"I had to spend the weekend in Normandy," Gérard told me fifteen seconds after I first encountered him in the canteen. "I was trying to be faithful to my wife, but it was no use." Gérard had problems with that. Not as bad as Nick (who was?) but he did keep on discovering these naked women on the end of his jubilation specialist. A surveillant at the school (paid to shout at the teenagers when they stopped being weary), he was working on his agrégation in philosophy.

The things that impressed me were his genius in talking the clothes off females and his unremitting reading. He had read everything that wasn't self-confessed crap, and he always carried books of remarkable worth that I had never heard of in French, German and English, and he always carried at least one spare, just in case he ran out of book, or if he judged that the book he was perusing didn't deserve his consciousness. Three years older than me, he was limbering up to be one of the great French philos. I like to think I can look after myself dialectically, but he broke my noetic legs, bushwhacking me with German mystics, wringing hidden grey juice out of the Ideologues, and zapping me with portions of the American pragmatists that I didn't even knew existed, and that no other human being had read since 1913, all during the lunch breaks.

The sophists ride again

Gérard had the Frog sophistical tendency of taking unlikely material and making it walk. Unlike the boss, Gorgias, who was kind enough in his encomium of Helen, to end, after having praised one of the most reviled women in ancient history, by saying "this is just for laughs". Many of his disciples leave that in ellipsis. But Gérard would terminate with a little smile.

Gérard was also the only other person I've ever seen to have that look that I occasionally catch on my face, when my eyes seem divorced from each other, the left and the right in their own zones, being not seeing. Introspecting. It looks extremely stupid, and I always tore up photographs where that look appeared. But I saw it a couple of times on Gérard's face. People used to think we were relatives (admittedly, people who were dim).

Last try at a Gérarding

Quite a long time ago. I tried the last telephone number I had for him twenty years ago, knowing that it was liable to be unviable. The upshot was a conversation with an aggrieved landlord, who emphasised at enormous duration that he would like nothing more than to find Gérard, since the flat he had been renting had gone walkies leaving behind only a few smouldering embers. "I've had people take cutlery, or run off with some furniture, but I've never lost the whole flat."

Losing other people's houses

It can be embarrassing ...

I suppose we've all found ourselves running brothels in Amsterdam without the proper training at some time or other.

I did it quite inadvertently one summer when I was entrusted with a splendid five-bedroomed home in the centre of town. A Dutch surgeon gave it to me to facilitate me in writing a book on Spinoza; I do seem to have this gift of charming people when I don't want to, or need to.

But I snapped up the offer of a palatial residence. Then, jeroboaming, I got chatting to a young lady in a cafe, who it turned out needed a place to stay; chivalrously, I offered her a temporary roost (but next to the chivalry in my skull was an idea not averse to some uterine guest-starring).

Although absorbed in not writing my book on Spinoza (there was no point starting until I got the title spot on) I couldn't help noticing the number of young American males that started milling about the house after she moved in, asking where the bar was and if there were any zapotes. Philosophy does sharpen up the faculties. Similarly, I had noticed that the young lady, Olenka, had a number of other friendesses who also seemed to be in a need-a-bedroom predicament.

Fine; I'm irresponsible, but I'm not totally irresponsible. It did occur to me that running a house of ill-repute wouldn't do my world-ranking much good, and that the wear and tear of priapic males wouldn't do the house, which had been in a shockingly immaculate condition when I moved in, any favours. And I was unsettled by one of the girls recounting that one of her most popular routines was singeing off her clients' bodily hairs with a blow-torch.

I had spent a week, or maybe ten days, perhaps a fortnight, deciding that the next day I would have to think some hard thoughts about what to do (and how, if I were a white slaver, how come I hadn't been provisioned with visions of not very dressed women hollaing "do it! Eddie, do it!") when the house burned down.

If you have to have your house burn down, I recommend a balmy summer evening so you don't feel too uncomfortable as you stand there wearing only a pair of Union Jack underpants (another story). It's like a log fire, but much bigger.

A fireman handed me a joint and I lit up from the combusting stew, and mused on what I was going to do. From Amsterdam I could always hijack a rowing boat to return to England, change my name and run an off-licence in Dundee, Zakro, Zante, or some other place people and agents of retribution never go.

But the moral of this episode is this: just because you're responsible for setting up a knocking shop, spreading moral pollution, destroying one of the finest buildings in Amsterdam, lost all your property, been caught in public with a pair of absurd underpants, spent more than two months without writing a line or even a very, very short sentence about Spinoza (indeed you haven't even joined the library yet, let alone taken out a book on Baruch), don't be so sure that you're in trouble.

The owner turned up unexpectedly to witness the final glimmers of his property. What do you think happened? Assault? Attempted murder?

I got three new suits, as well as a variety of other clothing, first-class travel home, a generous cheque for further research, a zoetrope, an indefinite open-ended invitation of hospitality and pampering in any part of Holland, and an apology for any inconvenience caused to me.

If you can't work it out, here's the conversation:

Vandermoor: My God, are you all right? I tried to phone you to let you know I was coming back but the phone was engaged all the time ...

Eddie: um

Vandermoor: This is terrible. You must have lost all your belongings.

Eddie: ... well.

Vandermoor: And your work! Your work, where's that?

Eddie: ... well.

Vandermoor: What, three months work gone up in smoke? God, I feel so guilty ...

Eddie: ... sorry ...

Vandermoor: I feel so guilty. I should have warned you before I left, but I was so busy. We've had slight blazes because of the bad wiring before... but nothing like this... don't worry I'll take care of everything ...

Motives for seeing Gérard

I had always felt heated up, had the cogs spinning at full blast, when I was with Gérard; I danced cerebral zapateados, I had the laurels burgeoning at my ears. Perhaps he could work a last minute transformation, give me the missing ingredient, give me something for the millennium.

So I can do something for the big 2. Very few people hit a millennium. Especially the two. That's a marketing opportunity, a cash-in. Eddie presents the culmination of history. You've got to have your own turf. Intellectually the field seems played out, but (as far as I am aware) there's never been a second millennium.

Also, I was worried about Gérard. Ever since he had had his problem.

Admittedly my concern hadn't extended much beyond probing French philosophical journals for signs of Gérard. I was counting on him to bag a post, to come out and trounce the Nanterre brigade, mullah the deconstructionists, slap around the Collège crew. But he never black and whited, which surprised me since he was good, a two-figure world ranking, no sweat. When Nick had delifed himself, I had persuaded Wilbur to try and sign G, but Wilbur had been obsessed with reeling me in, and Gérard was making himself uncontactable.

At the old port, in what was largely the same café where we had loafed about (give or take a few coats of paint), I saw him. The café was virtually deserted, and he sat, alone at a table in his usual posture. I recognised him almost straight away, although his features had let him down, slouchy skin like rouged porridge. An old man. A zostered old man.

What was more remarkable than my locating him was that he recognised me, despite my shades and a forage cap. Our eyes butted at twelve feet.

"My brother," he said, "you always were late, though twenty years' tardiness is phenomenal. But I knew if I were patient you'd turn up and pay the bill."

Sitting down, what was most striking was the bookless-ness of his table and no volumes were visible or perceptible about his person or down by his side. He would carry three volumes at a time, over a thousand pages on his person; the book in his hand had been so customary it had seemed like an evolutionary innovation. I remembered him saying that one of his greatest fears was a free consciousness and no text to plunge it into. He could talk, walk, do everything with text; even his paramours probably shared the pillow with a book.

Our eyes traded.

"Yes, no book. I have plenty to occupy my mind. I find it rather hard to concentrate on literature; dying has that effect."

Gérarding: what's in it for me

Lessons on how to end. Termination classes. Is there anything to be done apart from calling in the zucchettos? Gérard wasn't much older than me, but he was older, and brilliant. I was curious about what he would say. Whether I could copy some profundity, whip some of his tips. What galls me is that after all this bio, I'm no wiser. I don't expect much, but something.

Death beds 1.1

Wilbur regained his sanity just before he passed away. I went to see him. He didn't say a lot. "You're supposed to say something memorable, pithy, illuminating at a moment like this." Pause. "I must say I don't feel memorable, pithy, or illuminating."

That was about all he said for the half an hour I was there. Then: "There's no question that people who are really good are trouble; those who are good can be orderly and considerate; Gorgias didn't really upset anyone. But Protagoras did. Anaxagoras did. Parmenides did. And so on. Above the truly talented hangs the plume of strife. What I can't adjudicate is whether you're talented and troublesome, or just troublesome."

This too, skulking in my skull, behind other thoughts, was there: to see if Gérard didn't have a slice of revelation to pass to me, to check that he hadn't got up on the scoreboard, to verify that here was another promising, or indeed promisinger philosopher who hadn't made it.

Gérard at the old port 1.2

I was looking at Gérard in the way I suppose people have gaped at me for the last few years: is there anyone alive in there? The amazement that anyone could be in such appalling physical condition, done humaning. G sized me up sizing him up.

"Repeat after me: Gérard, you look awful, most people look better at their funerals. Stop drinking. Gérard, pull yourself together. Have some dignity. I suspect, Eddie, that you've heard it all before too. Good, now we've got that out of the way, let's have a drink."

The solution of solutions

That's the problem: for most problems, you can't find a solution by popping out round the corner, but in most civilised circumstances, you can't go a hundred yards without crossing some bottled oasis, you can find a solution to dissolve yourself in.

Gerard at the old port 1.2

"So, Eddie, how are you? I spotted your books; they were quite enjoyable. Who wrote them for you?"

I couldn't fault Gérard.

My editor had been forced to write the first one owing to my taking uselessness to the z. My second book had been equally untaxing of my creative juices: clearing out Wilbur's room as his executor I unearthed a manuscript, which he must have forgotten, because he had adamantly denied having anything over a paragraph left.

It had been on the dreaded medieval logicians of Paris (in 1136 – that's one year before Emperor John II pushed back Zangi – John of Salisbury studied logic there, and returned twelve years later to find them discussing the same question as when he had left. Indeed, I wouldn't be all that surprised to learn they're still in some garret, bickering, so obsessed by their endless subtleties they forgot to die. You have to go to Padua and Aristotelians such as Marcus Antonius Zimara or Jacobus Zabarella and their overdicing of the immortality of the intellect to get that sort of tail-chasing.

220 pp. Ta very much.

Getting a book published isn't that easy. The manuscript, although perfectly respectable, was not a great work, but its outstanding merit was it was typed. My first impulse on discovering it was to send it off immediately and collect some kudos 'n' kash, but I relented and didn't yield to this base impulse straightaway.

First, I mislaid it. A year later I rediscovered it in the middle of my armchair. A fortnight retyping the cover page with my name and address before I could send it off to the publishers. A weekend, stricken with guilt about my buccaneering, zamboning the prose and making a contribution by penning in some trendy verbs. A month to buy an envelope, which I misplaced. A month or so excavating for it and then another month or so trying to buy another one and then another month to entrust it to the postal services. Well, I never actually got round to mailing it. I left it on a train (I suspect) but someone was kind enough to forward it on as I then received a contract. I can be very persistent when I want to be.

Featherstone's credulity was locked out. All the philosophy graduates and undergraduates were invited round to his rooms; they supped on champagne and abundant smoked salmon and venison as he vainly interrogated them to find out who had been bribed, blackmailed or cajoled into writing it for me. But he was sifting the wrong people; the man who knew had (a) forgotten and (b) died.

What I won't write about 1.2:

Gerard at the old port 1.3

Gérard was walking all over me. I filled him in, shifting uneasily in my chair; he shifted into English.

"No sudden movements, Eddie. A bottomless pit can take our bottoms at any time. You can go to hell, direct, non-stop, anytime, anywhere. Without warning. In the arctic. In the deep blue sea. Hell – for one person, from top to toe, like a single bed, without a drop of sulphur falling onto the next person. A hell as infernal as the desert of Zungaria, without the person next to you getting a grain of sand. Shut up, Gérard, shut up."

What I won't write about 1.3:

Gerard at the old port:

Then he switched to German. "Come on. Order something expensive. Remember, you're a philosopher of the first echelon and the bank robber of the moment." I was a little surprised about this. Even when he had been a voracious reader, he had never had much time for news or newspapers. "If it's of consequence it'll get into a book."

Gérard had been living in a cottage up-country, the last time I had got intelligence on him, without electricity or running water, even more indifferent to the progress of history and civilisation, with only industrial transfusions of grape blood for company. During our time together in Toulon, he, like me, had been working on a little corpulence. Now we were polar: I was at the height of girth, and he looked (zootomically) as if he had been filleted, the meat binned – or to use a vegetarian figure, he looked like a closely nibbled apple core. In take-away terms, Gerard's reappearance (or my reappearance if you prefer) was your favourite sandwich, with a thick slice of friendship, but also a dash of a unfamiliar (unwanted) condiment.

"So Eddie, are you going out in a blaze of judicial gunfire? I am going to enjoy being you." He extricated an overfolded newspaper from a pocket (he had always referred to newspapers as the small ads) which he unsquared into a front page, flaunting the news of our upcoming tour of the banks of Montpellier. "Hell, Eddie, hell can uniform you, tailor-made, anytime."

I wanted to ask about his problem, but what I said was: "I see you have your old table."

"Yes, there is something to be said for a world where you can hang on to your table, but you're lucky to find me. I've only just resumed residence after a ban of many years. Longevity has this for it; it can outstrip bans. There's a whole new generation of victuallers and beveragists in Toulon whose first reaction is not to call the police when I walk in, or to slip someone a few francs to flatten my nose."

He looked at me: "So. Aren't you going to ask?"

Gérard's problem

His problem: he had made a mistake. His biggest mistake. He hadn't slept with a girl. He hadn't committed adultery. He had made the classic error: decency, loyalty.

He had married young, but as an intellect about town in a country where ideamen are celebrities, he laboured under more female admiration than he knew what to do with.

His wife was unusually tolerant, but she had a flair for uncovering his antics, though sometimes G was extremely unlucky.

In a field, he had been about to improve the world with a companion, when his wife had parachuted in on top of them, having been blown seven kilometres off her target area by freak zephyrs. This was especially dejecting because he had been the one to suggest sky-diving to his wife (in order to keep her out of his hair) and because "you don't get any less punishment for being caught in a field with a naked woman you haven't made love to than for being caught in a field with a naked woman you have made love to and I had to be caught in a field with a naked woman I hadn't made love to."

You could tell when Gerard had been in a scrap. He would be pale, quiet, secretly penitent and refraining from romance, until his wife moved back in, when he would perk up and restart being brilliant and irresistible to the opposite sex.

A new surveillante started work at the lycée. He dazzled her with his frayed paperbacks, his one-liners, his overview of Hegel. He took her to a restaurant, fed her oysters and then offered her a lift home to score the gooey goal.

Then, as he related to me later: "I said to myself – no, not this time. I simply saw how pointless it was. I was merely working to make three people unhappy. For what? A pleasure most familiar, and not that dissimilar to the conjugal. Underneath, once I had rubbed off the novelty I would find an inferior wife. Perhaps I had grown up; anyway the serving of pleasure and pain seemed wrong. And the morals: they're worth a mention."

Furthermore: "I could see she was willing. My vanity had collected its payment."

He dropped her off at the corner of her street.

"She was a little surprised I didn't try to come in. But she thought better of me for it. He's not like other married men her eyes said. He can enjoy a supper without anything more. You know what? I liked that. I didn't want her to find out that, like most men, I'm a life support system for a phallus."

He drove home congratulating himself on having found a new kick. The next morning she was found in a garage near to her home. Zedded. Murdered. Raped. The police pathologist estimated her time of death as within half an hour of Gérard dropping her off. Her throat had been cut.

"Have you seen anything like that, Eddie? It's sadder than you think possible, clotted sorrow. It leaves language a long way behind."

Here comes Afghanistan

The only advice I can offer when someone invites you to go to a war, is to bawl no, and if they're smaller than you and unlikely to respond in kind, belt them in the mouth so there's no risk of them asking again and you changing your mind.

If you want to know what it's like, don't eat or sleep for three days, jump in some mud, visit a mortuary and then blindfold yourself and walk across a motorway (give yourself a chance: do it at three in the morning); if you survive, it's cheaper and easier. When Zak asked me if I wanted to go to Afghanistan, I said something like: "why not, oh, and pass the salt." So much for a lifetime of philosophical study; q.e.d. no amount of intelligence can save you from stupidity.

Reasons Zak and I get on

1. We were both in Mile End nick.
2. We both did Vietnam. He, as a grunt, myself as a guided-missile-finner (a summer job in Plymouth).
3. Our common interest in philosophy
4. Our common interest in the fine wines of France.
5. Our common interest in the dusts of paradise.
6. Whence our mail-order scheme for expensive editions of

the Greek classics from Columbia with free concealed gift of nose candy.

7. I've never had a problem about being friendly to people who are wrecked.

So what's a failed philosopher like you doing in Afghanistan?

Zak wanted to go shopping for rubies which Afghanistan even during the war was coughing up. Zak, I should explain, is a doer of things the hardest way.

On holiday in Switzerland, he would rise at dawn and start scaling a peak. I would rise at lunchtime, take the cable car to the summit, and sit in the most expensive restaurant I could find, where I kept a seat ready for Zak, and a volume of Plato on stand-by (since I was there as private tutor) while without the benefit of safety harnesses or anything else that might reduce the risk of death or serious injury he made his way up.

And what's Afghanistan doing in Gérard's problem?

We were a week in. I was living in a fog of terror, exhaustion, and illness, so much so that when the village we were passing through was bombed, I wasn't much bothered, because I really had no room left to be worried; I was terrified out.

On the outskirts of the village we found a girl who had been collecting water, lying by her buckets. She was eleven, twelve. Very pretty. Well turned out for a penniless peasant's daughter in an especially brutal war zone. She looked fine, no blood, no dirt, no sign of injury apart from that fact that the top of her head was gone; she looked like a photograph someone had taken a pair of scissors to; a pretty girl, snipped.

I sank to all fours and wept, sobbed, cried. I cried and wept and sobbed and shed tears and puled and made with the lacrymation and everything in between, my emotions leaked from my eyes; freefall grieving. I wept for the girl, but also, I think, I wept for myself, being in a world where something like this could happen. Gerard would certainly argue that I wept for myself completely. Believe me, even for people who are infinitely tougher than me, dignity is usually found around room temperature. Don't find out for yourselves.

Gérard's problem

So Gerard had met an insurmountable sadness in the form of the slaughtered surveillante.

Naturally his wife left him. Their biosphere had been irreparably zykloned. Gérard had fed her a cover story to cover his time regaling the surveillante in the restaurant. She didn't accept that there wasn't more to it than a pleasant evening out and she couldn't believe that if nothing uniting had taken place, it was because G had abstained from infidelity.

Naturally the police gave him the honour of being chief suspect but he was cleared after the divination of the fluids.

I had seen him in Paris not long after that. G had been in a bad way, but I had logicked that he would sort things out. "If I hadn't had that sudden attack of virtue, she'd be alive. My rectitude sponsored her death in fear and pain. You should have seen her family." The police had produced no results. "It's someone local," said G, "I know it is. Someone close."

The police continued running on the investigative spot. No suspects, as G heard from the family. So G started to look for the killer, although he had no idea how to. "Odd that there is so much in the Greeks about so many things, but no method for locating murderers."

What Gérard Did

He got out the zet, launched his own enquiry. He interviewed all her friends, all her acquaintances. Nothing. He talked to them again and again, searching for scraps. He followed her old boyfriends. Where do you go to find out about crime? You go to criminals. "I spent a lot of time in bars, making the most unsavoury acquaintances; it's much, much harder than it sounds."

Gerard started to do a little informing for the zarps, to get a little income as he'd lost his job because of the enquiries, and didn't have the time to hold down anything else apart from the odd barwork. He investigated other attacks, violations, deaths in the region.

Gérard's nuggets of information without my prompts such as 'what happened then?' or 'why?'

1. Months sneaked past. "A year had gone, with nothing to show for it. I thought, Gérard, don't be weak. A real philosopher should be up to a challenge.'
2. Years flounced past. "Every year, I gave myself a year. Like waiting for a bus: if, at a bus-stop someone would tell there isn't going to be a bus for an hour, you'd walk on. But once you've waited ten minutes, there's no way you're moving. If I'd stopped after three months, that would have been it. But the longer you do it, the harder it is to stop. After one year, if I'd stopped, it would have been a year wasted. If I had stopped after two years, it would have been two years down the drain. I had to keep going; all I had to do was find him and I could trade in my wasted years for dedication and triumph. If I'd known at the start how bad and how long it would be, I wouldn't have bothered."
3. He persevered: opened a bar, carefully fingerprinting the customers' dead glasses. He also got work at a blood bank, keeping an eye out for the killer's type. "I was on good terms with the police. They gave me all the information they had: lots of nothing."
4: He became suspicious of someone, a psychiatrist, who,

well, was suspicious, with the right blood. "There was something not right." He investigated. "I couldn't find a past for him." Gérard followed him, observed him, opened his mail, rifled his flat (finding some zuclopenthixol) and put in a bug. Depatiented, Gérard finally kidnapped him, beat the stuffing out of him. "I'm not the police. I'm not interested in justice. I want to know what happened." After a day and a half, the shrink confessed that he had been born a woman. Gérard got a surprisingly short sentence.

5. Gérard infiltrated bondage, SM clubs and other unsavoury circles and started dropping hints about how he had murdered successfully, citing a few known examples, plus several the police hadn't expressed an interest in. "I thought it might flush him out. Enthusiasts always like to share." But the killer wasn't drawn to him.

However, the police came to lift up his floorboards, dig up his garden and in relation to one unsolved slaying would have been in very serious trouble, had he not had the alibi of being in prison for his abduction.

6. Finally, after fifteen years of trawling Toulon, he moved to the countryside, to a ramshackle cottage, with miles of isolation. "All the time, I felt he was there. But in town there were too many people, too much confusion. I needed to be in solitude, somewhere clear where I could bring him to me. One night I heard sounds outside and I waited for him to enter, but they faded. My will just couldn't reel him in – I rejoiced for a moment and he slipped away."

Gérard's nuggets with Eddie's prompts restituted

"So there was never any sign of the killer?" I asked.

"Oh, yes. He finally proclaimed himself – two months ago. A deathbed confession. He called in the police – there's little value in a successful crime if people don't know about it.

"A carpenter. Ugly as a zho. He only did it once, which

I'm told is unusual with that sort of crime. They asked him why: 'I would never get a chance with a girl like that otherwise.' 'Why not go to a whore?' 'I didn't want a girl like that.' He had one of her rings – it had been enough for him, slowly feeding off the dead like a slow-living insect. The cop asked him if it was remorse that had made him confess. 'No, it was great. You should try it sometime.' The policeman who was dealing with him told me that if the carpenter hadn't been three quarters-transferred to the other side and only had some hours left in considerable pain, he would have emptied his service revolver. He lived two streets away from the girl."

The word problem comes from Greek and it's cognate with a shield.

Gérard and I left the old port, and wandered into the Chicago, the maze of narrow streets, bars and restaurants where the matelots liked to go to have a few drinks, demolish a few buildings and where the police were never ever seen. The zone was curiously quiet; either the fleet was out, or there was a boot-polishing festival of prodigious magnitude in the barracks.

We strolled into a dive that we had haunted in our youth: the management and clientèle had changed, the disreputability hadn't. We reheated the past, traded information on those that had peopled that period, but it didn't take that long.

Life's work, please

His eye fell on a half-caste girl, rough even for a low-class prostitute: no looks, no charm, no intelligence, no radiant attire. She wore sandals: her feet were callused and dirty. She laughed unattractively.

"I shan't enjoying being her," said Gerard. "Or I didn't enjoy it. No, I shan't or I didn't enjoy being her."

"What?"

"It's my one aperçu. In my pursuit of the carpenter, I

sensed I understood him. Perhaps the qualities I attributed to him were obvious; but I felt I understood him. Then I started to think about previous lives, how people say they recall being King Arthur, an Egyptian brewer, a zilladar. It was like that – as if I had chunks of his life. I could see his wife... his job... his holidays, but I couldn't see him. It was like a badly-remembered life, but he was my evil coeval."

Gérard's response to these mental events, a surfeit either of universal truth or booze, was to throw reason aside like a child's toy and to take passage on what was coming in. I nodded, thinking how difficult it is for sanity to hire body-guards, as he insighted: that in the many versions of the soul's roles, no one had suggested that there's only one conscious-ness, not a collective one that's spread out liberally like jam on a giant brioche, but one awareness that races back and forth across the ages, that travels both time and continents; that consciousness is a hapax, a one-off. That it is in a vast tunnel composed of everyone's lives.

"You are in furs in a dark, antediluvian cave in France charcoaling the walls," he said, downing a Zubrowka, "then someone bashes your brains in. You shoot to San Francisco to be a debugger in Silicon valley; then, despite being a vegan, you die and become a hunter in New Guinea in the middle of the thirteenth century. Then a Norwegian flaybottomist in a small coastal village in the nineteenth, followed by a span of rope-making in China, before getting back to the penum-bral cave to grow up and smite the charcoaler. The evil you do, you do to yourself.

"Everything, from every angle. You worry less, because when you see the starving child, the freezing pensioner, the mangled soldier, you know it's happened to you or that it will. A revelation like this does terrible damage to your curiosity, because you're going to get everything in such detail it would bore the fussiest accountant. So, Eddie, my brother, my dentist, my flower arranger, what do you have to put on the table?"

It's never been easy, I suppose, up close, deciding whether you're dealing with staggering originality or someone who's hanging onto their sanity by their eyelids.

"Well," I said, using one of the phrases that must be well into the Top Ten most used phrases by Eddie Coffin. "I'm thinking of writing a book on the millennium." Then, with the frankness one only offers to an intimate intimate. "But I can't think of anything to say."

"Eddie! There's so much to say," Gerard shot upright. You can't be a French idea-jockey all your life and just stop like that. And (a curious phenomenon) book-writing is always much easier in other people's lives. "There's always so much to say. There's always in any civilisation a large box marked: things not to be said. You've spat on society, Eddie, now you can write all the things that people think and know, but won't say. Chapter one: Nuking Greece. The decline and decline of the greatest culture into third-rate waiters and the most repulsive bureaucrats in that metropolis of repulsive bureaucrats, Brussels. In a world where culture and learning earned any respect, we'd nuke Greece and get down to the really import-ant work of serious archaeological examination of what lies underneath, finding Homer's shoes, his lost manuscripts."

He then indicated the tart. "Or take Sandrine. Four, five, six children by different fathers. It's four, five, six children because she's never sure how many of her kids the state is looking after. She's unemployed, officially; a most modern notion, paying people to do nothing, but her work unoffi-cially is enough to keep her in booze and drugs." (I couldn't help feeling that he could be describing me.) "About the only time she sees her kids is at her court appearances; she gets upset when the kids are put in care. She's a good mother in that respect."

Sandrine was having her neck nibbled zigzaggily by David, who, Gérard explained, was her current. The two of them cuddled like spoony teenagers, instead of a worn prostitute and thug. I wasn't going to enjoy being him.

"They have these rare get-togethers when they're both out. It won't last. But it's amazing, this billing and cooing, isn't it?". Gérard was making his unflattering remarks loudly as if he were studying animals at the zoo; a fact that worried me since you could tell David's chief method of communication was the knife. "It's so hard to wring out the last drops of humanity, it's hard to gun down that last illusion. There's a romance that's bound to end very badly, probably fatally. Just a question of how soon and where."

"Perhaps that's why they enjoy it so much," I offered.

"What do you do with the useless now? Now the useless are really useless; now we have not only have useless classes, but useless countries. Look at Africa: we feed – they breed. We have as much stupidity in this century as in any other; it's just been moved around. Believe me, I'm concerned about the suffering in the world, I don't want to be sitting in a dustbowl in Africa. I won't enjoy that."

He got another round, then giving me a double-pupilled blast, said:

"We haven't got long, you know. I don't know why they call life life; it's just a moment with memories. Come on, Eddie, what do you say? Haven't you thought about the Big Curtain?"

Return of the peanut-butter lobbing mujahedeen

We've all been in the sights of a Soviet helicopter gunship in Afghanistan, I suppose: that was my most direct look at the Big Curtain.

We were in a lorry, a old vehicle carefully constructed to cause the maximum cruelty to my already withered, lacerated and contused frame. I had been separated from Zak, I didn't know where I was, I didn't know where we were going. I had lost a quarter of my body weight. No one spoke any of the languages I could. We were going somewhere, that was enough.

The muj were pelting each other with cans of peanut-butter. This presumably had been supplied to them by their backers, but none of them was remotely interested in eating it, though they regularly ate things that would have been incinerated anywhere in Europe. I had exchanged my wristwatch, the only item of any value I had left (apart from my clothes and they had spectacular holes, rips and stains, and could have stood up on their own) for a bottle of Coca-Cola that one of my companions had been carrying for days, waiting for the right price. You carry a bottle of Coca-Cola long enough in Afghanistan, you'll get a good price. Someone had kindly opened it for me with their teeth, when the lorry screeched to a halt. I dropped the bottle (losing half its frothy contents) and everyone piled out, caterwauling and waving their weapons in a way, that despite my near-collapse, perturbed me.

I recovered my bottle and looked out of the lorry to see what was up: what was up was a Soviet helicopter gunship, chopping above us.

A word about the muj. Around the world you get a lot of people who talk about fighting to the death, but few of them turn up for the appointment. Some of the muj I met talked about fighting to Moscow, to Nova Zemlya; this at a time when they were fighting the most powerful army in the world with stuff little better than water pistols. The muj, who normally laughed at gunfire, were running around in small circles yelping, not so much out of fear, as frustration at dying impotently, because at that stage there was nothing you could do about gunships.

A word about gunships: if you haven't seen what they can do, you won't believe it. They can erase villages; if you didn't know the village was there beforehand, you couldn't tell; you walk on metal casings. Big black full stops.

The muj fired at it, but it had as much armour as a tank; they might as well have waved. We were in a desert, no cover.

Essentially, it looked bad. I was already two days late for

the start of term. I was in the middle of a desert and a war with half my Coca-Cola spilt, no money. My odour could have stripped paint. Strange bacteria and protozoa were using my colon as a race track. Amoebae trickling down my leg. My world ranking wheezing.

Woebegotten philosopher vs helicopter gunship

The gunship was close enough for me to see the pilot.

What did I think

"Oh dear," was the sum of my thoughts. I wasn't very frightened because I just hadn't had the time. I raised my bottle in greeting. The gunship wheeled away.

Hindsight on the Hind 24 gunship

1. Amazement at the banality of my intellectual and emotional response.
2. Amazement at not getting zapped. I thought perhaps they had been out of ammunition; I raised this with a spook back in Peshawar. "They have unimaginable amounts of ammunition; it was orders they didn't have. In the Soviet army you go from A to B, and it doesn't matter how glittering C or D is. You weren't on the menu."
3. I didn't appreciate it at the time, but I was witnessing the end of an empire. That was 1983. It was all downhill from then. They really should have blown me away. A tip for end-of-empire watchers: do it from home. Fragments of empire can damage your health.
4. The trip wasn't entirely deleterious to my health. I was so angry with myself for my boozily letting Zak talk me into going, I didn't have a drink for two years. Yes, I did write two years. Though I made up for that.

Back with Gérard now

"The Big Curtain? What do I have to say? Whatever I say, it's all lung work. It's not knowledge. We don't know a sausage, and I'll probably end up yelling for a priest. But you've worked it out."

"I could be wrong. I am my evidence. All the goodies are on the other side, where the answers are stored."

"We've obviously gone downhill from Gorgias and his claim to answer any question."

"Protagoras: everything is true. Or Gorgias: you can make anything true. No, my constitutional amender, my usherette, my dancing instructress, we have to go beyond human knowledge; that's where the paycheque is. And there's only one way to do that: go behind the Big Curtain. It's getting to be that time."

Do-it-yourself 1.1

Florence Justine North (1963-1982) had had the same views as Gérard. Perhaps it reflected badly on the Philosophy Tripos at Cambridge, but she left a note explaining that she found the systems of knowledge intriguing but ultimately rather inadequate and predictable, filled with language rather than wisdom, and not to take it as a personal slight or as any form of disrespect to me, but she had concluded that she wouldn't be attending any more of my supervisions and that her only recourse for intellectual satisfaction was suicide (turning to the end of the book for the answers). You don't get many students with commitment to scholarship like that. She had even made her own funeral arrangements.

I wanted to lob her a posthumous doctorate, as a nod, but this was viewed as (x) drunken rambling (y) tasteless and (z) encouragement.

Vintage do-it-yourself

Then there was Nick. A day or two before I went off to start my banking career I got a call from Wilbur. "I'm very worried about Nick."

"What's the matter?"

"I don't know. I thought you could talk to him. He's been acting very strangely and he's only been a junior don for two days; I think he's going insane."

This, of course, was one of those phrases with delayed irony since Wilbur, within a year, was regularly dining on the most powerful sedatives known to man in a sequestered sanatorium.

Grudgingly I found Cambridge on my sole again, since I had taken a vow never to use my feet there again. I knocked on Nick's door, and got stillness as my reply. No one had seen him for days. I got the key from the porter's lodge and went in: cooped-up philosopher spoor, drawn curtains. I pushed open the bedroom door very gingerly, wondering whether I was up to discovering a body no longer bodying or something equally unpleasant, when the television set that had been perched on the door missed smashing my head by a zorapteran's inch.

"I've got a knife." I heard Nick's voice, slightly muffled, as he was sheltering under a table in his bedroom under a protective mound of mattresses.

People (chiefly women) have often accused me of extreme insensitivity, but even I could tell at first sight that Nick wasn't well.

Coaxing him out of his impromptu bunker took three hours and required my locking the outside door, piling some furniture up against it, and stripping down to my underwear so that Nick could be confident I didn't have any concealed weapons or communications equipment. Not only did he have a survival knife, he had three kitchen knives (long ones), a meat cleaver, a baseball bat (through which he had driven a variety of nails) milk bottles filled with petrol, some tripwires, and a length of cheese wire.

"So, Nick, is there something you need to say? Anything worrying you?"

He was sitting in the armchair as if it were travelling at six hundred miles an hour and at thirty thousand feet.

"Tell me, Eddie, has there ever been a happy man? A man truly happy, who has never, not once encountered unhappiness, misfortune?"

"History's rather quiet on that subject," I conceded.

"You see: no one, but no one, gets away with happiness forever. You know what my life is like."

I did know what Nick's life was like. Everyone in the college did.

Nicholas Dexter Nebuchadnezzar McClanagan-Standish. More commonly known as Nick the Dick. Brilliant, good-looking, rich and despite all that, charming. His effect on women was so extraordinary, you couldn't even be jealous. Wealth, wit, warmth and well-madeness didn't even begin to account for his success. He could have any girl he wanted as well as her mother and friends, even in an ensemble. He would say something like "hello' and strong-willed married women of high moral conviction would leave their families. The world his zenana.

And they were all happy. He went through vistas of women like a combine-harvester, but not one of them was bitter or dejected about getting the hours, days, or week that was granted to them. No torn hearts in his wake. They understood that a phenomenon as extraordinary as Nick was for the whole of womankind. Out of curiosity (not desire to emulate or learn) I quizzed one young lady. "He does ... everything," this twenty year-old said, with the fond air of a grandmother looking back on her lost youth.

"I didn't work to get into Cambridge," he continued. "Others sweated for years. I read two books and got an exhibition. I drive a car that any ten philosophers clubbing together couldn't afford. I don't need to work at all. I never had any illness more serious than a head cold. I row to Olympic standard. I've never been refused by a woman; frankly if there's only one in my bed it feels empty. Wilbur wanted you to have this job, your hired light is better than mine, so what happens? You leave: so Wilbur has to give me the job, the post I've always wanted from the age of eleven. I don't think I've even been rained on, apart from a few summery occasions when I was in the mood to get soaked. It's not natural. Hence my question to you, Eddie: why should I be happier than other men?" Zumbadors of panic hovered around him.

I turned it round and sent it back: "Why not? Why shouldn't you? Why shouldn't one of us make it?"

"I'll tell you why not. Because there's never been a completely happy man and there never will be. I acknowledge those who lead unremarkable lives who have no terrible pain in their lives, who are jilted, who lose a handbag, who have a difficult boss – minor inconveniences – and who lead a contented life because they're wise enough to enjoy what they have. But the really fortunate man, as Solon says indirectly, ain't here, Eddie. I'm not happier than other men: I'm just being fattened up for the kill. This is all to put me off my guard … for something. I don't know what's coming, but I know it's something … unique. Pick a biography, any biography, you get people who have two years' good fortune or ten years' good fortune, but it never, never, never lasts. Enter the badness. Exeunt goodies. We're surrounded by sadness, it's all around, how can I be exempt? Immune? You always have to pay the bill, for knowledge or pleasure, and I don't think I can afford the bill that's coming."

My light for hire didn't do much good on this occasion. I left Nick in his warren and went to Wilbur to tell him he was right to be worried.

What I won't write 1.6

How much good I did for Nick?

Within three months, I was to return to Cambridge to be strapped into the contemplative life, taking over from Nick, who had put his idea pot into a gas oven to dodge his terrible doom. Wilbur, having wangled me the appointment, was having long appointments with six foot cyan toothbrushes from Zubenelgenubi who were trying to sell him life insurance in one of those rooms where there were no sharp objects or other items that make harm easy. All in all, not an outcome that did much to commend philosophy, and certainly many of my colleagues (forefront Featherstone) did time Wilbur's loss of sanity prior to my appointment.

More Gérard to go

"What are you thinking of?" Gérard asked, seeing that my thoughts were aligning elsewhere.

"Paying the bill."

"Good idea. Listen – you pay for these drinks, and I'll make you a deal. When I go behind the Big Curtain, if there are answers no one has suspected, I'll come back (if there's any way of coming back) and dictate them to you. That would put you back on top. That'll teach all those smug philosophers who aren't piss artists or bank robbers."

"And I'll do the same for you. I'll give you a briefing and you can write the book and publish it my name."

"That would upset a lot of hardworking pen-pushers. Okay, we're agreed – whoever goes behind the Big Curtain first, slips the gen underneath to the other. Why hasn't anyone thought of it before?"

Paying the bill: Afghanistan style

Nick, I think, was right, you can't expect things for free. The closest thing to a free lunch is a mother's love (and you have to endure strictures on attire). Everything else comes at some effort or cost – even that noblest of physical pleasures (greater than most of us deserve I warrant) requires a bit of push.

I reached Peshawar, in a lorry full of wounded men with legs missing, stomachs gashed, rotting prehumously. I got out, and had a surge of satisfaction. I had emerged from a war zone in one piece, intact. In truth not; I had hepatitis and amoebic dysentery that was to weld me to the bathroom for months but my exhaustion was such I couldn't tell. I had spent all the waking hours in the last four weeks swearing, continuously, continually, swearing at the world and myself. I had seen things no one should ever see. In a way those four weeks are as large as, say, the thirty years I've spent thinking thoughts professionally, if not larger. Fear on a national scale.

I leaned against the lorry and the driver slammed shut the door, not noticing my hand in the doorframe, breaking three of my fingers. I screamed and rolled around on the ground, my ears opened as wide as my mouth with the pain. The wounded muj looked at me perplexed, imagining I must have heard some terrible news, involving death of the near and dear, to lose all manliness like that and to roll in the dust like a dog.

It was an admonition: the fee, the zakat, for what I had learned.

And most annoying of all, because it occurred in Pakistan, I couldn't even have the kudos of bragging I was wounded in Afghanistan.

Bit more Gérard

We went out into the night. A night. Slightly cool. Like

thousands of others. But more and more this banal night might not just be a dull night in Toulon; it might be my last night. My last moments might well be spent thinking: it's quiet tonight, and what ugly, unremarkable buildings they have here. I had an eructation from the bottom of my mind-bed, I felt it was too much. I wanted to be excused from the world, spared from this test, this trial, whatever it is. I wanted my mother to sort it out ...

Friendship can survive. There are long-distance friendships. The truth is you don't get a huge selection in life. "I'd say I'll see you, but both as a philosopher and a drunk, I think it unlikely, so I shan't. Who was it who said your closest friends are the ones whom it takes you longest to discover that you don't like? Well, obviously it was me, somewhere, sometime."

He kissed me. "Eddie ... Eddie..Eddie." As he said that I had a flash, the asterisk of a footnote, the beating of a Zildjan cymbal. I've had it at odd moments in life. I've sensed when people have said things to me, that I wouldn't truly understand them for a long time. Some things that are said to you take ten, twenty years to unfurl their entire significance. Often very innocent words, pedestrian and pedestrian, but they stick like a burr and it requires years to stumble on the secret passage, to see the message on the obverse, just as you do with the words of the great ones.

Rob five banks in Montpellier and die

And then there's always that morning when you have to get up, harrowingly early, and go and rob five banks in Montpellier. It probably says a great deal about me that what really bothered me about this project was getting up early. I had vaguely counted on Hubert forgetting about this scheme of his, or taking up some other hobby or interest – but he hadn't. It had been announced in the papers we were going to do it, so we were going to do it.

I went along with it, chiefly because I had nothing else to go along with.

To start the day I shot a bar of soap out of Hube's hand, from over twenty feet, and through the bathroom door. Which would have been fancy gunplay had I been attempting to shoot the bar of soap out of his hand rather than rummaging in a bag for a comb to charm the wig Hube had supplied.

"You're dangerous, Professor. You're all edge. I don't understand why the police don't all just resign." An inauspicious or auspicious start. Take your pick.

"I thought you had abjured violence?" I asked.

"I have. But the people who sold me that haven't; they thought they were doing me a favour giving me a ready-to-rob item."

We took the train, lugging huge suitcases full of disguises (enough to stage all of Zeami's plays) and Thales in his carry-cage (the sort designed for cats or small dogs). Thales freaked one or two old ladies who were anticipating a larger feline furry object inside. "You can stroke him, if you want. He's very friendly," Hube ventured.

Hube was, in fact, very exercised. The evening before, the Corsican had appeared on television, replying to questions about our forthcoming hand of robberies. "I vaticinate a shortened career for these gentlemen if they show up tomorrow."

Hube was outraged, not only by the aplomb of the Corsican, (who it did look to me had grown grey hairs), but also by his vocabulary.

"Vaticinate? I *vaticinate* a shortened career? I'll bet he can't even spell the word. That's it. We're not messing around anymore, we're buying a bigger dictionary. In the meantime, you'll have to give me some me some high-powered words."

All police leave had been cancelled in Marseille, we had heard from Hube's narks. As preparation he had paid a couple of acquaintances (one of whom had had to shave his head and learn several phrases in English) to act Thought Gangish and blatantly suspicious around a number of banks in Marseille, as if casing joints to feed disinformation about our presence and intentions.

When he thought I wasn't looking Hubert also looked rather ill. Amid the ziggurats of false documents, firearms, costumes, clothing, there were more and more phials of pills, zidovudine.

We checked into a hotel in the centre of Montpellier. "I don't want you thinking you do all the conceptual work, Prof. Today, I create the getaway siesta."

We did have a bit of fuss over the rat. Hube and I had worked through metempsychosis, Pythagoras to Gérard. "My dear sir," said Hube in an authoritative manner to the receptionist askancing Thales, "first of all, we aren't tourists. Secondly, this isn't a rat, this is the present embodiment of the spiritual leader of millions of people in India, a sect I shan't name since you won't have heard of them; we are transporting him back to his rightful place where he is needed to pronounce on several important doctrinal matters." Hubert's outburst didn't cut much ice, but some thin slices of freedom did.

As we entered our room Hube remarked: "It occurs to me that actually we don't know that Thales isn't the reincarnation of some sage."

"If he were a spiritual leader of any consequence, or at least a spiritual leader of any consequence who felt like saying anything, by now he would have tapped out a message in Morse code on the bars of his cage."

The Banks

Creatures of habit, creatures of nostalgia. We started at the beginning. We went back and rerobbed Jocelyne's bank. To my relief, Jocelyne wasn't there, having a day off or out. I was under Hube's orders for the day (a zabuton for destiny). He was convinced it would have pleased Jocelyne. "They love attention, you know."

We went in wearing Nietzsche masks.

Hube's costumier friend had had them made up, having chosen Nietzsche, I hazard, because he's one of the few recognisable philosophers, an easy mask to make because of the bog-brush moustache. One of the most important things in the biz is being recognisable; having a trait, it's almost as important as a catch phrase. Diogenes: the barrel; Socrates: the hemlock; Aquinas: fat; Kant: indescribably boring. You have so little time to catch people's attentions, that's why people latch onto Nietzsche: he's the one with the bog-brush moustache. The masks had bulging eyes, which was spot on; if you ever take the time to flip through portraits of philosophers, you'll find you get a lot of white, an alarming amount of protuberant white.

We had a quick tutorial. "So what can we say about Nietzsche?" inquired Hubert. "He was very interested in masks," I said, "he's the quick-change artist of the biz. Also if you want something to chew, we can also consider the question of whether all learning isn't stick-on."

"That's not bad," said Hube, "but help me out: I can't go in there without some vocabulary."

Create a jargon, create a livelihood.

"Good morning, ladies and gentlemen, let's get zetetic

and see if you have a few thousand francs you don't need."

Lunch can never be too early

What else could we do, but go back to the fish restaurant afterwards? If it works once, do it again and again. And again, until you're forced to think.

Wilbur was adamantly against any sort of routine or pattern. He used to walk to the college every morning by a different route (his adherence to this enrolled him on half hour detours to cover the five or ten minutes' distance to college). "The mind is ready to go blind at any moment." He refused to teach the same supervision twice, which caused fear and consternation in the idea-jockey trade, lest his policy become an unwelcome precedent or standard. He moved house every year, and was, in addition to putting books in and out of boxes, always studying new languages, new hobbies. "The mind will put its feet up given half a chance. If it's easy there's no point in doing it." Being a being is tiring enough for me.

I had the zander and introspected on the many other groups of dishonesty and deleteriousness who avoid the police's attention: estate-agents, politicians, plasterers, the chairmen of multinational organisations, dentists – the obvious suspects. Indubitably, if, for example, all the used-car salesmen were rounded up in a meadow somewhere and properly machine-gunned, the world would be a better place; such behaviour is rather looked down upon in academic circles, but it's a most effective amelioration if you're machine-gunning the right people.

Bank robbery, if philosophically carried out, harms no one. We thrill. We entertain. We stimulate the economy. We race hearts. We provoke thought. And, unquestionably, bank robbery is an illusion. You take it out, but where does it end up? In a bank. Like water, money is trapped in a cycle, it moves from bank to bank. We take it out for some fresh air.

Numbers two and three

I hate to say it, but after a while bank robbery becomes a bit boring. A zensho is no show. "See how much money you can fit into this bag." The most stimulating aspect was the costume changes inbetween.

No one tried to fend us off with by reciting a snippet of philosophy. Hube, I think, was chagrined by this. He would have quite liked to have walked away from a bank thwarted by a quotation. I was glad we weren't challenged because, what, for instance, would I do if it was something I didn't recognise or couldn't remember? I didn't fancy an 'Oh yes, it isn't, oh no, it is' job.

Numbers four and five

We popped back to the hotel; in the streets the howl of police sirens on the prowl. Hube watched some television, I worked on the mini bar. Then a man turned up carrying a surfboard and leading an Alsatian. He seemed to know Hube and they exchanged a few pleasantries.

I discovered that I was assigned the surfboard.

"I think it's safe to assume that the police aren't sitting in their canteen playing cards at the moment," said Hube, "so we need some extra cover. We play on their assumptions."

The Alsatian gave my hand a friendly lick, as if to say, Eddie, I don't care about your world ranking. I used to have contempt for those (chiefly the zoolatrous English) who overfunded their fondness for animals, but I have discovered as I age, the joys of being liked, and causing joy, even if it's only a dog who bestows his wags to anyone who doesn't beat it.

"Yes?' I said.

"What do you think when you see a man with a surfboard? Do you think, there's a man just back from holiday? Or there's a man going on holiday, or there's a man just taking his surfboard to his car? Or there's a man taking his surfboard to be repaired – I quite fancy a weekend windsurfing – or do you think that's a fat British philosopher on his way to rob a bank and just carrying a surfboard to fool us so we'd better check his papers?"

"And the dog?"

"When you see a man walking a dog, do you think-"

"– epiky, let's go."

Number four was a cynic heist. "Goods aren't good. Money isn't necessary – so put it in this bag." I left the surfboard there, because I was coming to the point of view that prison might be good for me. The discipline of prison might get me writing. There was simply too much Trappist beer and zander in the non-prison world. You slide without difficulty from not having enough money to write a book, to having too much money to write a book.

We sauntered through the botanical gardens on the way to target number five. "This is the life," said Hubert, "no one wants to live forever, but I could take five hundred years of this."

Hube strode in to the last bank with the confidence of an entertainer who is the darling of the day. We didn't bother waiting in queue anymore, we just took over the whole place.

"You don't have to wait any longer," Hubert announced, "we're here. We'll get zet; we'll take all the money, but first a reading from the Ancients." I had just wanted to promulgate a few words from memory, but Hube had been against this, saying you needed a book, as a monstrance (whatever the book was) to create the sense of occasion. I was toting my Loeb edition of Diogenes Laertius and was into the first line on the origin of philosophy when I perceived that one of the gentlemen who had been in file and who had been clutching a large, cellophaned bouquet of flowers, started ripping it open. I wondered whether he was going to offer Hube or myself a stem out of some perverse adulation, but what he was scrabbling for was not a bloom, but a boom.

He uncovered an ugly-looking double-barrelled shotgun, sawn off, while the guy next to him shouted out: "Get out of our way, dickheads. Don't touch a sou. We're doing the robbery here."

This was a bit much for me. Hube leaned against the counter. He appeared rather amused by this unforeseen conflict of interests.

The mouthpiece of the other duo had unsheathed a sizeable knife – that wasn't going to make much difference to the proceedings, but the shotgun worried me. It was worn, nasty, rusty looking and the setaceous individual carrying it looked the type to pull the trigger not only if that action would procure him no benefit, but indeed even if there would be a most unpleasant outcome for him too. His face went in on itself as if he had been given a pound in the kisser with a golf club every birthday from the age of six. If hideosity gave any leverage, we were in deep trouble.

"Do you know who we are?" asked Hube.

"Two cretins who are going to get shot, that's who."

"I'm sorry you feel that way about it," replied Hube. "But we do have priority. We've already booked this robbery – we reserved it last week."

The guy with the knife was mostly clean-shaven; but he did have this rich ginger goatee, not as most people prefer them, on the chin, or under the chin, but for some reason had it sprouting bristly from his Adam's apple. You don't want to be judgmental, Zoilitical, you've got to have respect for other people's tastes and cultures (and I am aware that my showing on a presentability gauge would be low) but he looked bloody stupid.

The line-up

Hubert with a handgun, me with the Loeb and the Alsatian on the one side, the slipped goatee with a knife, and concave face with the blaster on the other. We also had some superiority in that they couldn't work out whether Hube was being flippant or flipped.

" ... anyone can say that," said the goatee, since anyone can say that. He palpably didn't have much practice at this sort of discussion.

"It was in the papers," Hubert countered.

"I didn't see it."

"You don't read the papers?"

"I read the papers."

"Well, if you'd read the papers you'd know."

"I didn't see it. We're taking the money," he shouted, looking shaky.

"I can divide it up for you," volunteered a cashier. But no one moved. It was one of those situations where no one was in a rush to be first to do something since there was a distinct possibility of being decommissioned, losing your grip on the universe.

"You know," said Hubert, still leaning on the counter, "you looked worried. Maybe you should try some sort of outdoor job, nice and healthy."

"I'm not worried," he yelled in a pitch which revealed that he was. 'Get out of our way." I was perturbed as well. I wasn't in the mood to be blasted in half by a shotgun. Perhaps one never is. The guardian of the shotgun and the roaming goatee didn't radiate professionalism. And call me a snob, but I didn't see why I should be dismembered by an individual profoundly zozo and amateurish. As a veteran of blagging, I didn't have much tolerance.

"All right, let's be fair," offered Hubert, snapping open his revolver and taking out the bullets. "If you can prove to me that you deserve the money, that you've suffered more than I have, you can have the lolly. Let's have a trial by ordeal. The most deserving will surely win." Casting the others onto the floor, he took a single cartridge which he held up for inspection and then loaded into the revolver, giving the chambers a good spin.

Then he put the barrel into his mouth. Pulled the trigger.

A click, quiet but unforgettable, without the deafening detonation. He shook his head as if he had downed a stiff whiskey. "Ahhh, that was fun. I think I'll have another go." So he did, and then offered the gun to the goatee. "Have a taste of that, my old mucker."

What they were dealing with was becoming beholdable. "He's a n-n-nutter," declared the shotgun supporter.

"You don't have to leave empty-handed," consoled Hubert, "you can have an autograph."

They didn't know what to do. Like Buridian's ass, they were immobilised and being asked to cope with events that nature had not given their natures the gear to cope with. They couldn't go back, because that would make them look banjo-brained and would render squandered the effort and time that had brought them there; and the risk with going forward was the bloodshed and the feel of zephyrs in the gutshangar. It was getting close, armpit-wettingly close to chamber-clearing time and letting the ballistics sort things out, when we heard sirens, the sonic harbinger of the filth.

We waited for the shotgun-supporter to push it out. "It's the p-p-police."

"Great," said Hubert, still not partaking of the general perturbation, "we can let them decide who's robbing the bank. Let's see who they arrest."

They may not have negotiated well with Hube, but the pair suddenly came to life and made a startlingly rapid and spirited exit; they exhibited no doubt in their total lack of inclination to be arrested. They used their twenty-foot feet to get to the door, which wouldn't open for them, and convinced they had been trapped by some security device, they exacted punishment by giving the door both barrels.

Eventually, they desisted in pushing the door (perhaps having noticed the sign that said pull) and gained egress. This was shortly followed by shouts and the bulletins of bullets out.

"All right," said Hube, getting back to work. "We'll take some of the money and the back door." At the rear we could still hear commotion and sporadic gunfire. We strolled in the direction of away. From behind his ear, Hube pulled out the cartridge (the one that should have been in the revolver).

"I shared a cell with a pickpocket, or street magician, as he preferred to be known. You get a lot of time to practise tricks. It was clear that our competitor loved life too much. He was only robbing the bank for money. The perpetuals would have had him standing on his head in a second."

???????????????????????????

Back at the hotel, Hube decided to go back to Jocelyne's bank and open an account with some of the stolen money. We had so much money that it was quite heavy. "They've been good to us; we owe them some business." He went out dressed as an Arab woman in full chador. I don't think he actually did this because it lessened the risk of apprehension, though it may have done, but because he found it a hoot. I lay on the bed, thought about Zenobia, and her generals, Zabbay and Zabda.

When we arrived at the railway station, our train was nearly an hour late, so Hube wanted to deposit our burdens in the left-luggage. I was worried that the staff might take a peek, and discover some of our bank robbery items. "Nonsense," he snorted, "we're agents of destiny. We're invincible. We're invisible," he said, shouting out at the top of his voice in the crowded railway station: "We're The Thought Gang. Arrest us!"

We weren't arrested (the magnetism that railway stations have for the deranged and the shouty sheltering us perhaps) and we ended up ambling around and visiting a sex shop next to the railway station (another seemingly inevitable concomitant).

To be honest, despite my debt to this trade, I find I don't get the flare of amorosity that coupling couples would have engendered in my younger years. I do feel I've seen it all (apart from some Zantedeschia and Johannesteijsmannia) so that I had little predilection for browsing. But nevertheless, I did have a butcher's at the flesh in case there was something I hadn't seen: you should never think you know it all.

But I didn't learn anything there. Indeed, rolling my eyeballs over the magazines, I couldn't help thinking that the depiction of conjugation hadn't moved on from Corinthian mirror cases of the Fourth Century BC, when rump-rumpus was king of sales.

Troilism ... minor orgies

The drawback to going to bed with two people is, of course, that it doubles the odds of you pressing up against someone you don't like or really don't find attractive. These occurrences are not a testament to my amatory success; they are not really erotic victories, rather the opposite ... and tellings can better things.

Portrait of Young Eddie as one half of an actress sandwich

A winter night, the Cambridge mists swirling, as on the corner of Silver Street stood Trixy, Arthur, the laughably bad poet, and myself. Myself, smooth-skinned, belocked, promising, twenty. Trixy was tossing a sixpence in the street to decide, after a lengthy party, whom to take home. This was one of the earliest instances of my keep-standing-at-the-party-and-someone-will-come-along technique.

Trixy, nominally a student, was in fact an actress, and generations of undergraduates will be very familiar with what that entails, and why the Church had a very sensible policy on not burying them in hallowed ground until recently it gave up all standards.

With all homage to the monkeys and their typewriters, there are laughably bad poets like Arthur of whom you can divine within fifteen seconds, incontrovertibly, that they have not only written nothing of any value to any one, but who will never, ever, under any circumstances, write anything of any value (not even accidentally) and who will spend benighted lives in poverty, remorselessly seeking audiences to torture.

But not Arthur – he went on to make several fortunes (worth a mob of swindled foundations) by writing lyrics for West End musicals. Lyrics so bad, you wanted to call the police. Lyrics so bad but so profitable it made it unquestionably evident that we're riding in a universe where Truth, Justice and Taste get walk-on parts; where they are of no more import than minor planets like Zachia, Zerlina or Zeissia.

Arthur was also a zwitterion, someone who didn't mind where his dick ended up as long as its destination had a blood supply, and he didn't mind being described as such. He also wrote children's books. I'm not going to enjoy being him at all, even with the money.

But on the evening in question, we were both waiting to see who got to play immersion-heater. The sixpence was snatched from the air, and put in a pocket, unexamined. "No, it's no use, I want to go to bed with both of you."

I thought at first this was a joke, but it wasn't. I have never, despite years of restudying the scene, worked out whether it was on the spur of the moment, or whether she had worked up to it. "I want to be fascinating," she had said once to me in the way some people say doctor, merchant banker, zoologist.

"A philosopher and a poet," she licked her lips, "what a combination." Typecast again, but most educated women go through a phase for a few weeks where they think philosophy is important; you've got to get your timing right. Oddly enough, the proposal didn't much appeal to me (perhaps because of Arthur's poetry) but I was at that age where not only could you not be seen backing away from any form of gratification or decadence, you were obliged to zoom towards it at full speed.

I was at the bottom of the pile, and as I lay back, all I could think of was how Arthur's poetry should disbar him from this. Trixy aura'd enjoyment, but then she was an aspiring actress. My lack of ecstasy was misconstrued as over-used dick. "You're so cool, Eddie, I suppose you do this all the time."

Still waiting for the train

I shifted my gaze from the scrums of legs, the fleshy spiders, the angiportal crammings, the juice on the loose, to the bit of babylon on my wrist. We only had a few minutes before our train.

Hubert had browsed around but he kept being drawn back to one magazine (of the tamer class you could find at any newsagent or bookshop: soloing women) at a reduced price, remaindered, in the event of any of the clients wanting an old-fashioned, uncluttered wank. The girl on the cover was brash, unoutstareable. Men seem to get sheepish in a dong-dangling state, while women are head-on into the lens and usually look dressed naked (whatever that miseryguts Schopenhauer says about the female physique). Hube gave his consciousness plenty of time to gain the cover, then reshelfed it languorously.

Halfway back to the station, Hube said "Hang on," and trotted back towards the shop. He returned with the magazine. "It's the eyes."

Ipsation

Cheiromania. Self-service. Making love with the invisible

lover. Nature's consolation prize. The arms are just the right length for it.

The Getaway Train

There were road-blocks all around Montpellier. Hube waved at them from the train. Sirens. The police unquestionably felt they had to be seen and heard doing something. For some reason, I thought of the Zaporogues conquering Azov in 1641. It was three hours to Toulon, so I took out my Loeb and started to read.

"It was a great day,"observed Hubert, "but the thrill is diminishing. It's becoming too much like work."

"And we're running out of philosophical methods. Unless we start inventing them."

"One more. We have to finish neatly. Big. We have to finish bank robbery. One more that will close the subject. We must finish in such a way that no one will ever attempt to outdo us. Perhaps we should close our show in Paris. Then I can do something else." Gradually, he dozed off. I hadn't seen him sleep for a long time.

I returned to the Loeb. Normally, I pack a Teubner or an OCP (why mess about?) but when I had done my bunk, I couldn't trace the OCP edition of Diogenes Laertius, so I'd gone for the Loeb with its toupee of dust. As I read it, one of the thank you notes fluttered out onto the ground.

Any laws untrangressed?

The best way, of course, to prevent a young vulnerable girl who has run away from her provincial home and who has come to London penniless from being corrupted by unscrupulous and dastardly ravishers, is to do the job yourself.

The thing about zephaniahing a young girl is that while you're doing it (a) you know exactly where she is so she can't slip off clandestinely and unbeknown to you fall in with bad company and (b) there's no possibility of her having a carnal carnival with anyone unsuitable, because you'd notice them trying to get in on the act; it's really a foolproof method of safeguarding a girl's morals.

We've all had that moment, though, when having enjoyed erotic communications with a young girl (of more charm and beauty than one has a right to) and she is having a shower, you pick up her passport and inspect it (I read everything including cornflake packets) and you perceive what you hope is some sort of serial number, but is in fact her date of birth and when you have triple checked the figures on paper and on your calculator, you understand that what you've done is not only immoral, which is liveable, but also illegal, which perhaps isn't.

I could visualise the prosecuting counsel tearing into my protestations: "So, Dr Coffin, you bought her a ticket to Cambridge and offered her unlimited board and lodging purely out of concern for her welfare; what a generous fellow you are!"

I also, oddly enough, felt shame; it was only a few months out of season, but what a difference a few months can make to your criminal record.

She stayed for the weekend. We discussed the Ionians, and devoted a great deal of time to the first extant fragment of Ionian philosophy, of Greek philosophy, straight from the phil's mouth. Anaximander, Book one, Chapter one, line one, quotation number one: live and direct from Miletus, circa 550 BC; Anaximander's fragment being one of those overlooked by those who rave about the clarity of Zeus's boys.

Anaximander's fragment embedded in Simplicius is a classic kernel of philosophy: "..as necessary; for they do right and give reparation to each other for their wrongs according to the order of time."

1. Slasherama: turning on Thales, his teacher and kinsman, and rubbishing him. Criticism, the Greekest of

Greekness, as opposed to other knowledge-accruing cultures comfortable with ipse dixitism, thus spake Zarathustra, Confucius says, Pythagoras says. When criticism (idea racing, concept matches, noetic fisticuffs) was overlooked we had the dark ages. A bit of bile on the Ionian Coast and we're on our way to the stars.

2. Succession. There are very few philosophers outside a succession. There are self-taught poets, painters, writers, scientists, but virtually no self-taught philosophers. It's a closed shop going back to the port of Miletus.

3. Be a shade vague (or if you have the balls, unrepentently obscure). It allows others to insert their ideas and preoccupations into your work; this is a biz where people love to pull rabbits out of your hat. If you're too clear it makes it a take it or leave it proposition. Be interpretation-friendly.

All that weekend, I ate nothing, my appetite flung to Zacapoaxtla by my fears. My guest enjoyed her stay, piqued by my expositions. Before she leaving, she cut a sheet of paper into small rectangles, and having inscribed "thank you" in live letters on them, stowed them away in arcane places, in books, in drawers, in the interior of my hoover (five years to find that one), inside my typewriter; I stumbled on them one by one, like the one that had bailed out of the Loeb.

That weekend was the extent of our sense-dataing together. To my relief, neither outraged parents, nor smirking police came through my door (not through my door, and not on account of that). I received three epistles from her: when she started to study philosophy at university, when she graduated and when she received her doctorate in papyrology.

I never replied. Letters, like books, I'm not much good at writing. Now cheques, I'm your man.

?????????????????????????

Hube was buying all the papers. Some days later, idling through one of the local papers I espied a notice announcing Gérard's death from something resembling natural causes – there was no mention of foul play.

Sample of cranial traffic on Gérard's demise

A good example of someone who had no more need to live. Mourning is pointless, but that's exactly its point. Why isn't everyone running down the street screaming, "we're all going to die?" Life fist-fucks us all, and we provide the lubricant (not to make it easier, just possible). Death punches through creeds like soggy tissue paper. Late at night, even in Jesuit dormitories, fear smears. Nothing rational is jacket enough to take the rounds of death. You need to be on some wild delusions to cope with that. Life or death, one or the other gets you. Nice cop, bad cop. Someone please help me. Help. Help.

How do you feel?

Sad. Feeble. Cowardly.

And what's worse, it's not my inconsequentiality, my feebleness, it's everyone's.

Training back from Montpellier, I catch one of the passengers voicing that international platitude "mustn't grumble". A standard gambit of everyday conversation but what's so funny is that the finest cranial exertions, once you file off any refined encrustations, are just that. From Sisyphus 'n' Ziusudra 'n' Ptah-hotep, "mustn't grumble" is the axiom, the bricks and mortar of most philosophical systems and wisdom ladders. Elbmurg t'nsum. Don't whinge. Don't whimper. What you'd get from a busy G.P. Make the best of it. Be nice to people. Enjoy yourself when you can. Drink moderately. Exercise. Don't slouch on the way to the firing squad.

What do you do? There are sadhus in Zira who think it most important to sew coconuts onto their skin – that that's the really important thing in life.

It's easy to jeer at the thought anthills (too easy). In spite of it all, even a nullifidian like me has seen goodness, bravery, even intelligence. The really decent people I've known, no one else would have heard of; decency seems to bar you from high office and prominence. But they're there. Those who spout concern for others, the welfare 'n' solicitude fiends are the ones who bully waiters, neglect their children and who pay their gardeners pittances. Could be goodness is like an aquiline nose, or a bushy eyebrow.

The head head

The best mind I ever encountered was in a pub in Cambridge and belonged to a Colour-Sergeant in the Parachute Regiment. He did the gaps in my crossword for me and sorted out some problems I'd been having with the Wolffians (admittedly I'm not hot on the Wolffians, but I had to explain who the Wolffians were before he stripped 'em bare). He also made me aware of one or two intriguing elements in Indian philosophy I hadn't spotted before (he had read a paperback ten years previously while on service in Aden). It was a black day for my sense of professional competence, and although we chatted about other things (by which sort of machine-gun was it best to be shot at) my heart wasn't in it.

Regret

Of course, what I should have done was ask him the question of questions, the BIG ONE: what's it all about? Perhaps it would have caught him out, perhaps he would have said something interesting. It's not that we don't get opportunities, it's that we don't use them.

Achievement: Eddie's pride

There isn't much I can be proud of. Hindsighting, the only thing that was sensible and a cause of no regret was buying my house. The most important thing about living in Cambridge is being as close as possible to the railway station so that you can depart swiftly and easily, and should you make it back from London (Afghanistan, Zeebrugge or anywhere else) out of it, and without a penny you don't have too far to stagger. I had the sixth closest house to the railway station (and I kept a spare key in the station manager's office). Stuck in Cambridge for thirty years, I never managed to get the bottle to leave, but I was always close to leaving.

This is not a joke.

???????????????????????????

We were lying low in a new flat. Even Hube with his notions of our invulnerability seemed for once to be happy with the doctrine that a stay-at-home-bank robber-is-a-less-likely-to-be-arrested bank robber. I wrote my notes. Hube put his nose into some books, and wrestled with creating the bank robbery to end all bank robberies. The zeb.

I discovered Hube was sneaking out at night. I rose one morning to find him surrounded by a variety of pictures, prints colour and black and white, transparencies, contact sheets. The pictures were of a young lady, in various grades of undress; they seemed to be of the same her although it was difficult to tell from the carpet of likenesses around him.

"Knowledge – it's hard work; especially investigating the past," he said.

"So who's this?"

"This is the mademoiselle who was fronting the magazine I bought."

"Where did you get them?"

"The photographer gave them to me. He also managed to give me an address for her."

"That was kind of him."

"It's difficult to refuse a man who is ramming a pistol into your left nostril."

"I thought you had renounced violence."

"I have. I rammed the pistol into his nostril very gently. And I didn't say anything, but people in these situations imagine all sorts of things. The end of my pistol was so cold and his nostril seemed nice and warm, and I was curious to see whether it would fit in. And you know, he must get all sorts of zombies ringing up and calling around. His caution was well-founded and … admirable.

"And it was quite a search. That magazine was old, the pictures were old, the trail was old. I had to talk to the manager of the shop, the owner, the supplier; they were all very helpful. I only had to nostril my pistol once, which I think in the circumstances shows great restraint on my part. So anyway, the photographer turned out to be full of info."

"So are you going to ask her out?"

"Why not? But I have to find her first. The address is no good. But I'll hire someone to find her. The rich get short cuts." He studied a close-up. "You can see it in the eyes. I'm sure she was in the homes." Looking at the picture, that wasn't my first thought.

"How can you tell?"

"You can tell. You look into those eyes, you can tell. There's a special … lack of expectation."

Hubert's good day

He said he had had one good day when he had arrived at a new home, when he was thirteen. He had been sitting outside the director's office when a beautiful girl had sat next to him. Very beautiful. They hadn't talked but Hubert had noticed they were instantly sitting as friends; the place started to zing.

"But they were doing the paperwork for my arrival, and they were doing the paperwork for her because she was leaving."

Hubert revisited the picture ocularly.

"I think it's her."

????????????????????????????

Jocelyne's very good, but then women tend to be with children, even if they are masquerading as bank-robbing philosophers. It was her idea to try a medium.

Selfishly, I had been hankering for Gérard to reappear and, like the crib that Hube had pleaded for on the ten most important things in the biz, give me a shopping-list length insight on existence: the really important thing in life is to tie weights to your penis and stretch it to eighteen inches. Beat everyone whose name begins with Z with a zope. Whatever. But clear, simple, short. But Gérard, the selfish bastard, didn't get in touch; I kept an eye out for any insect or animal that seemed to be trying to tell me something. On my desk I maintained paper and a very light pen for spectral hands. Nothing.

Jocelyne clicked her barbell on her teeth. I was watching her closely for signs of collapsing romance. Her tongue was pierced, (a process, she had elaborated, that had taken two weeks of painful healing) and it put me in mind of the tongue-piercing ceremony endured on October 28, 709 AD by the principal wife of Shield Jaguar, Blood Lord of Yaxchilan (Lintel 24); i.e. to my eye, pointless, but if it's good enough for the Mayans …

"Why did you do it?"

"To punish my tongue, for saying things it shouldn't have." Click.

"But surely it was only obeying orders?"

"It has to learn to be warier of its mistress. And it's also a symbol." Click.

"What of?"

"That changes from day to day. It's a multi-purpose symbol."

Best of things symbolised by Jocelyne's barbell

"It's a symbol of the need for symbols."

"How life shrapnels us."

"Assistant bank manageress on the outside, primitive on the inside."

"Of whatever I feel like."

"That you can do stupid things at any point in your life."

Jocelyne was a believer in the physical school of reflection. Once she slapped me zealously around the face without any warning. "Don't you feel better?"

The thing is she was right.

"What have I done?"

"Nothing, but you will – I thought we should get it out of the way; I'm sure you'll let me down eventually. I might not be in a position to act then. That was just an advance."

Jocelyne on Gérard

"A friend of mine tried a medium,' she said. My initial reaction was one of withering contempt; whatever its short-comings, philosophy is taught at university. At least we con intelligent people intelligently; if there's a group associated with hoaxery, charlatanism, low-grade bamboozling and simpleton-collecting it's mediums: on the other hand, the evil they do compared with philosophers (especially German philosophers) is rather negligible.

But my social calendar was empty, and is the idea of mediumship any more far-fetched than my having been employed as a philosophy fellow for over twenty years? I think not. You've got to try everything once, except those things you don't like, or that involve a lot of effort and getting up early (I have no intention of trying to be European ice-dance champion). If it's not too much trouble, never call a halt to the zets. Who knows, maybe the medium might give me some hand-outs, chunks of eternity?

Time for a classical precedent?

Yeah, why not. Even Socrates, Mr Analysis, Mr Reason, Mr Point that light over here, used to hang around with old wise women.

Jocelyne fixed it up and we drove over to Hyères. I was dressed as a priest (another one of Hube's innumerable disguises; I made a big mistake letting him measure me up). Not because I felt a need for camouflage, but because I awoke to find I had no other clean clothes. Jocelyne thought the zucchetto suited me. "People would want to hear confession with you; you look as though you'd understand."

The medium welcomed us with a big smile (as well she might considering what she was charging; Jocelyne had suggested we pay double to get some action). The medium was jolly and fat (many of them are – someone should zet up on the link between the occult and obesity) and her consulting room was covered with tiny bottles of liquor; the one-snort size you get on aeroplanes. There were hundreds of them, standing on preposterously thin shelves, no more than two inches in breadth, obviously specially commissioned; her garnering of the cultural diversity of the world.

Is collecting small vessels of alcohol any more absurd than collecting first printed editions of the Greeks? Yes, yes, yes, and more yes.

We put in a bid for Gérard.

"I'm expecting a message."

Madame Lecercle held my hand a bit. And chatted non-consequentially.

"You want to get in touch with a friend. I'm not getting anything. I see a small, furry animal; I see money, but it's not what you want. I see someone, rather strange, he isn't all there."

"Is he saying anything?"

"I'm getting something about tourists, not liking them. Does that make sense?"

If Gérard was hanging around waiting, he blew his chance to pass the dope under the Big Curtain. Madame Lecercle chatted with Jocelyne about her perceptions for several minutes. There weren't any career-resurrecting deliveries being made here. I remember Wilbur's view: "I can predict anyone's future, particularly in regard to the issues that really matter; I can safely predict that they will either live or die."

"Can you request particular individuals?"

"Well, that's not how I normally work, but we can try."

Guest star, flown in from ...

I meditated on the choices. I fancied a bit of Greek. I've always been very happy about my era, if not about my circumstances in this juncture. But given a time-machine I'd go back to the Ionian coast circa 585 BC for some sun, fun 'n' zythum, to mingle with the boys, to find out where they stole their ideas from. As Featherstone remarked: "You'd be ideal to send back; you speak the language and one can't imagine you having any sort of influence, or doing anything that would change the course of history. You could communicate to us via red figure Attic vases."

If I couldn't go back, the next best thing would be to get them to drop in. I had a yearning for Thales. Why not go back to the beginning? I had just been responsible for naming a rat after him and if Thales had the ability to hit town, he had the ability to give me stick about the rat. The next obvious candidate was Plato, but somehow I didn't want to try and summon him up; he must be pestered all the time, his celestial phone must be buzzing all the time. And even if he were available for PAs, I didn't fancy being kicked around the floor by him: I know my limits.

I reflected and determined that I didn't want a philosopher, and I didn't want one of the big names. I lighted on the bad boys of Greek poetry, the iambographers Archilochus, Hipponax and Sotades who rocked the Greek columns with their abuse. Sotades, the leading figure of the kinaidologoi, the specialists in indecency, who insulted all the monarchs in the known world, and was put to death by one of Ptolemy's generals, who put him in a lead jar and dropped him overboard on the high seas (to be safe I suppose), was very tempting. But as I logicked, I thought more and more of Hipponax, older, banneder, exiled from his home, whose targets committed suicide, an Ionian thug whose very tomb it was said was dangerous to walk past. Now, there was someone worth inviting to a party and it struck me that if there was someone who would respond to a failed, bank-robbing philosopher's invitation it was Hipponax.

"How much do you need in the way of details ... ?" Jocelyne had brought a tape recorder which I now saw her switch on. The ceremony was simple.

It was a warm afternoon. Madame Lecercle fell silent and closed her eyes. She was silent and shut-eyed for so long that I suspected she had fallen asleep. I was getting so bored I almost dozed off. I had powerful sensations of time-wasting. I wondered whether Za Dengel, Emperor of Ethiopia (1603) had ever done this sort of thing.

Then she opened her eyes. They seemed clouded and then slowly, like a car's headlights hoving into brightness through fog, a look came into her eyes. You couldn't be sure at first, it flickered in and out. Then suddenly it was there. A hard look, the look of a truculent docker who's had to fight in five too many civil wars. A look you wouldn't have associated with the eupeptic Madame Lecercle.

The hard look looked at me.

"So what are you looking at, son of barbarian shit?" The

voice was that of Madame Lecercle, but hijacked, hoisted out of key, dragged over coals. "You asked for it, you've got it."

Her nostrils flared, and took in spoor.

"I can smell a philosopher," the voice said. Another inhalation. "You all reek like Thales. You couldn't stink a little more to the left, privy-lizard?"

"So, you're Hipponax?" broke in Jocelyne.

The look transferred its force to her. "My name's not Homer." Pause. "You're not going to go hungry with a mouth like that, are you? You must be popular in the alleys."

I didn't quite know what was going on, but it was distasteful. Miasmic. I thought it might be time to leave.

"Long time, no see," resumed the voice, "and then what do I see? A blubberbag and a whirlpooled-mouthed tart. Well, what do you have to say, and what do you have to offer me? Or have you brought me all this way just to sit there open-mouthed as if you're wanking off?"

"How are things?" I ventured.

The voice didn't respond. The look was making its way around the room slowly. It looked down into Madame Lecerle's lap, the folds of her zodiacal skirt. The look concentrated on her body. Then the voice started: "I should have known you were a philosopher. All the really ugly fat ones are philosophers. Trying to tell us that the mind's enough; that a good body isn't. So why are you bothering the dead? No one alive willing to tolerate you?"

I could see why people were advised to give his tomb a wide berth.

"I just wanted a chat."

"You're so boring the living don't have time for you, eh?" The voice hissed like a gas leak about to ignite. Then it completely changed tone, going right up the scale. "Who's the mouth? She looks like a seventh-generation slave." The voice was now so soft and high it was almost impossible to make out. "A sucker of steaky straws. Better than lashing an octopus to your dick, I'll be bound."

Jo didn't know what to make of this either. Madame Lecercle's right hand started pinching the loose flesh of her left arm, languorously, and then started fingering the top of her blouse. "Marvellous. Brought back by a fat-collector and a drudge, a you'll-have-to-burn-your-dick-after-humping woman. What do you want? What do you want? If you want advice on how to be more disgusting I can't see how that can be done: and if you want advice on how to be less disgusting, I don't see how that can be done"

"If you're busy," I rejoined, "don't let us keep you."

The medium's blouse was slowly being undone. The voice, back down to basics, wasn't in any rush to answer. "You people never bring back the philosophers, do you? Got enough ox-shit of your own. No matter how poor or unfortunate a country is, it's always got ten times more philosophers than it needs." A knocker flopped out, and then the other was turned out of its enclosure. Madame Lecercle then held one of her nipples between thumb and forefinger as if it were a small, dead, and unappealing animal (such as a Zapodida).

"Thousands of years dead, and I can tell you that that looks truly revolting," was the voice's pronouncement. The stripping carried on lethargically, revealing the weathered flesh of the unforgivably obese, which has a peculiarly artificial air to it. The look wasn't any more enthusiastic about the sight than me. "So I'm back, and back in this. How can anyone be this unlucky?" Madame Lecercle's pudenda was concealed by overhaunching haunches; a hand drilled in between the fat.

"Nothing. No news. As dead as me. You fat people are so greedy; I suppose one only has to look at the amount of space you take up. You invite me in and nothing to eat or drink. A drink, I think." Madame Lecercle swayed over to the bottled wall. "This is booze, is it?" I nodded assent. The medium then took two of the bottles, uncapped them, pushed one up into each nostril and then threw back her head letting the bottles empty. The head stayed back for quite a while, then the voice resumed. "That was a waste of time." It's tough being a spirit keen on spirits when you can't taste anything. "Why is it I can smell you, but not taste the booze?" Call in Zwaardemaker.

Madame Lecercle then came over and rested one of her globes on my head. "So they still haven't found a hair tonic that works?" the voice adduced. She walked over to the fridge and started liberating items from the food-prison. The voice continued its work over masticated items. "Know what I said to Thales, to Heraclitus, to every sophyphiler?"

Well, I didn't.

"If you're so clever, how come you're going to die? And how are my books doing?"

"Not too well, to be honest. Most of your work has been lost."

"What I wrote will never be lost; at worst it rolls on under other men's names. I could go anywhere and find my stuff. I know what the punters want." Splodges of food which had suffered the initial treatment of digestion flew across the room.

"But your work was suppressed. The Emperor Julian thought it unsuitable."

"Unsuitable? Beetles on their bollocks. My iambs iamb forever."

I contemplated mentioning that, by contrast, the Emperor Julian's writings were excellently preserved (three volumes in the Loeb) but it would have been pissing in the Zamzam.

"These people, can't they see they're transparent, that my work will show through them? Don't they understand that writing was created to carry profanity all over the world; so that a man could vilify the man over the hill; so put in stone his curses might march to the end of time. Nothing tastes of anything," the voice commented, as a selection of foodstuffs, over-frisky in Madame Lecercle's mouth, went along with gravity and made tracks across the double chin and the quintuple stomach.

"What's it like on your side?" I asked.

"Ah. So you do want something. I want to know: what's in it for me?" Madame Lecercle's finger went into her ear. "I can't even feel that. You'd think I could have a good ear-scratch. Look, I'm sure this maggot paradise here has been handsomely rewarded for her services. What about me? I don't sing without silver."

"What were you thinking of?"

"See here, we're discussing things that are deeply deep, things as a philosopher you should be able to work out, but since the best your brains can do is to be something amusing for flies to shit on, I'll trade you. You know, you remind me of someone I knew. I can't remember his name, but I do recall he trained his dog to lick his balls."

I thought about the world ranking, had the memorial service been too long ago? "What do you want?"

"I haven't been accorded much in the way of fun-facilities. I want to see some rutting. And I'm not talking you and the orificist here." Madame Lecercle rechaired herself and started crisscrossing her breasts, in a way that would have had the Kabbalists of Zefat empty of words. "I want some vast fornication. I stipulate young boys. Girls. Boys and girls. Very young. Very numerous. Very blonde. You know, actually, you remind me of another bald humbug. Can't remember his name. But I do remember he was the only person ever to be exiled from Ephesus for farting. There's not a lot to be said for the Ephesians, but they didn't put up with nuisance from baldies."

"Could you give us a sample of the wisdom on offer?' inquired Jo.

"Orgy first, wisdom after. And make sure they're fresh and on their toes. I don't want anything half-hearted. Something choreographed." Madame Lecercle started banging her head on the table in the way that must have been painful for whoever was in charge of those nerves.

"That could take some arranging. Let's have a taster." Jo negotiated.

"You do remind me of someone. No. No. No, can't remember his name. He used to be a tomb-robber. Wrote a treatise on optics, but then who hasn't? I iambed him to death. It wasn't the valuables that attracted him to the tombs, if you know what I mean."

"What's death like?"

"Let me put it like this. This I'll give you for free. It could be a lot worse. I could be a bald, fat, ugly philosopher with no chance of getting a tripod. I've been spared that."

"Let's speak to Madame Lecercle," interposed Jo.

"What do you think this is? No pay, no play. Bring me the bodies."

"Something up front, please," I said, curious. "You haven't given us impressive credentials."

"You time-waster. You outline. Tripodless. The One and the Many. You can lick my arsenious arse."

Madame Lecercle walked over to the window and parted the curtains slightly to admit the hazy afternoon light. No more babbling. The look stared out for a long time. Perhaps because of the brightness, the eyes moistened as her hands rested on the window sill. This posture was maintained while Jo and I looked at each other not sure what to do. Then Madame Lecercle fell on herself like a dropped dress (her Z-bars gone) her head announcing its arrival on the floor with a hair-muted crack.

?????????????????????????

"Well," I said, after we had taken the contused Lecercle to hospital. "We got our money's worth."

Jo clicked her barbell.

Rue the rue

The idea of visiting my old haunts in Toulon had haunted me for a long time. Despite my loafing and using my loaf on almost every inch of French soil since I had left Toulon thirty years earlier, I had never been back.

At first, it was just circumstances, my presence was demanded elsewhere. I was offered accommodation or money to be in other places, or the loin compass directed me north, south, east and west, and the variants in between, but not to Toulon.

Once, I passed through Toulon en route to Nice at three in the morning in a sleeper, but my feet were by the window, the blind was down, the night was too dark, my feet too eyeless. Then I began to be frightened of Toulon.

"You're frightened of Toulon?" Hubert had asked me as we had driven into town.

"It's my youth." The truth of youth.

Verity's Severities

I've lost everything, I imagine, at one time or another, except my way – in a streetplan sense. I've always known a left from a right, if not a right from a wrong. I've lost (in no particular order) pens, wallets, books, documents, suitcases, cars, a zibet, and a fifteen-year sentence, but never my bearings.

Although I hadn't been there for three decades, I worked my way through the sidestreets without hesitation.

I reached the street where I used to live. It was as if I'd popped around the corner and returned from the shops. The street and the building were unremarkable, except for this: this was where I had lived.

I had been dreading this return, because while I had revisited many other loco loci of my youth, the other locations had been so well-visited, it was as if the memories had been trampled into the ground by my returns. Memories scrawled over others, tangled until they blacked each other out.

This was why Toulon was so different. A mint memory. I was unbottling a year of youth. You're supposed to miss your youth. The poets are quite firm on that. Zimbalom playing time.

What was Eddie like?

The younger Eddie (twenty) had health, future and morals.

Beautiful women I refused to sleep with 1.1

This is a very small category, and even if it's extended to women I refused to sleep with, there's only one entry.

This was one of the teachers at my school in Toulon. She invited me home for tea. When I arrived, I had trouble looking at her, since I was terrified that my attention would get stuck in her cleavage, her skin was getting lots of say. I had to aim to the side of her or above, and just catch her in my peripheral vision.

We were alone in the flat. Her husband, a radiographer, was much older. Absent. The conversation went like this: "Edouard, I like to play tennis. My husband doesn't. Do you like tennis, Edouard?" Then "I like to go out dancing, Edouard. My husband doesn't to go out dancing. Do you like to go out dancing?" Then "I like to go to the beach, Edouard. My husband doesn't. Do you like to go to the beach, Edouard?"

The direction of these questions was unequivocal. But no, I drank up and withdrew, because she was married. This was something sacred into which my dick shouldn't slither. It's impossible to believe that that person has anything to do with me. No one had explained to me that marriage is taken seriously by hardly anybody, let alone the married. Now, I suspect that if ten seconds of my pleasure hinged on it, I would be prepared to see the entire population of a medium-sized nation vaporised.

Was it right?

A bone often in my memory's gnashers ...

Most of the time I do think I should have deferred to the deferens (because it has to be said, checking with Zurvan, I don't think I've ever regretted the act, the consequences, frequently, but not the act). I console myself with the thought that my rectitude might not have been one more delivery to that great warehouse of untaken opportunities. Perhaps my refusal saved me from being murdered by a disgraced husband, or avoided events which would have resulted in a biography even more appalling than the one I already have.

Naturally, my decency was predicated on my having sufficient opportunities for gratification without the need for trespassing; decency is sold mostly on the concept that decency is waged. If it had been laid before the twenty year-old Eddie that invitations like that would never again be forthcoming (I discount the flagpole business) and that he would spend years of his life standing at parties waiting for less fetching women to fetch him, well ...

Belief causes problems, it reduces your flexibility, but it's a spiritual skeleton – difficult to move without one.

Time for an aphorism

Evil's weevils: a diversity of pain. But useful though pessimism is, it can't cover it all. Even in Afghanistan they laughed. Amid the slaughtered infants, the triumph of the untalented, mirth sneaks in. Efil always makes you think, keeps you on the zet, which is a bit of bind for the laggards amongst us.

Back in Toulon in a street no one cares about

When I turned into that street, I was expecting to be mugged, to be decked and given a good kicking by regret, and a frantic craving for youth, when, however problemed you are, you have the consolation of decades of rectification to hope for. You're meant to blub uncontrollably.

But I didn't feel like that as I looked at my old home.

I had come to France at twenty because I'd had doubts about the wisdom of doing philosophy. My falling-apart dates from here.

A bit feeble?

Agreed, misgivings about the exactitude of philosophy scarcely counts as the most terrible ordeal, it doesn't rank with the greatest agonies. I've had my share of zaps, but I've never had any of the big breakers: seeing my family burn to death, having to eat my closest friends. Perhaps my real misfortune is that I've never had a real misfortune.

Thus as I faced the rue des Lauriers Roses a faint jet was emitted by my heart, a plea to be young and have another go; but I saw that what I wanted was not youth, but plenitude, accomplishment, not the chance of accomplishment. Youth would be too much like work. No resits. I'd only end up in bed with the hippopotamus again.

An unexpected victory over one of the most redoubtable pangs the heart gets to tackle, the entreaty for another helping of youth. One Eddying is enough.

Doing okay

Yes, apart from the nets of two police forces swirling over my head, and a number of organs closely allied to the maintenance of consciousness about to go kaput, I wasn't doing badly. I was companied. Friendship gets harder and harder, as you get older and older; people your own age with whom you would have most in common with are strapped into their own contraptions. And friendship takes time, but as you age, your years aren't years. Too late to master the zampogna too.

Make your point

About the only thing I'll really miss, what has taken me a lifetime to amass: people I get on with. That's the thing I fear most about death, losing them.

I was to surprise myself once more.

As I walked down towards the old port, I crossed the main road, a major carbon monoxide releasing zone, and I could see Hubert with a suitcase at his feet, apparently in the act of importuning passers-by. I decided to join him on the basis that two can be arrested as speedily as one.

I was halfway across the road, which had been bereft of cars as far as the eye could see, (the lights in my favour) when I was almost mown down by a car which had screeched out of a side-street, shedding rubber and travelling at a speed that could only be characterised as fatally inimical to philosophers.

It missed me by a lot less than the breadth of my collected works. If it had had another coat of paint a glorious career in bank robbery would have been curtailed.

Being almost run over

Being almost run over is an excellent gauge of one's attitude to life. Perhaps there's something in the wassailing lifestyle that promotes almost being run over, that turns you into a motor matador. I seem to get almost run over a lot. Of late, I've discovered a refusal of my intellectual and adrenal forces to get worked up about it. Pulse unchanged. Full up. No more room for time.

This time, it was remarkable how concerned I was for my corporate identity. Long unpresent sensations of self-preservation and of annoyance unboxed. I made an obscene gesture, recognised probably in two-thirds of the world, after the rapidly shrinking car.

To my surprise, there was another expletive from the tyres as the car slammed to a halt, and then started reversing with extravagant acceleration and mechanical fanfare. It bumped into me as it stopped and the driver leapt out, slamming the door with one smooth, practised movement.

He marched up for nose to nose contact, and in spite of our propinquity, shouted: "You've got something to say to me?"

He was in his early thirties, and heavily built; one could guess that he spent a lot of time repetitively lifting heavy metal objects, and that he was quite capable of pulverising me even if I had had two or three brother philosophers backing me up (say Bacon and Von Hartmann with a couple of pick-axe handles and zaxes): as authoritative on smacking folk in the gob, as I am on the Ionians.

Across the road, on the pavement, I could see, worryingly, Hube with that attentive air that habitually presaged an imprudence.

It wasn't a question of whether Mr Bulk was going to hit me, but when. No need for Zener cards. Usually, I would have had to waddle very fast, taking the ignominy or a duffing. But it's not usually when you're carrying a gun.

The street was empty. I did it (a) because I didn't feeling like eating my teeth and (b) I knew that my span was almost spun and it was against the odds (since this was the first occasion in fifty years) that I would have the chance to shoot the shit out of a shit's car.

"No, I don't think so," I responded with a calm that would have earned me full marks from several schools of philosophy. Raw ataraxy. I unhid the Desert Eagle (the .50 semi-auto Magnum with, as Hube had informed me, 60%

more stopping power (whatever that is) than the .44 Magnum, (whatever .44 is)) and loosed a round. Fortunately it fired at my prompting, since I had no idea whether it was cocked, loaded, or safety-catched. It was shockingly loud and almost blew itself out of my hand.

The round removed front and rear windscreens of the car. Mr Bulk seemed to have trouble assimilating the sight of the pistol, the report and the glass confetti. "He's got a gun," explained his friend who had also discarred (no doubt to have a good view of the bloodsport) and whose distress moved at a greater rate than his companion's.

"Why don't you lie on the ground and put your hands on your head. You'll feel better."

They bit the bitumen while I put two more rounds into the bodywork. They plunked in, and while they may have caused some expensive destruction, it didn't look particularly destructive. (Hube later pointed out that if you want to ventilate a car, you need a rapid fire weapon, not a man-splatterer like the Eagle). However, I gave the car two more, and one of these ignited some petrol. Not a dramatic conflagration, but the flames did their bit to reduce the car's roadworthiness and retail value. His insurance claim form would be interesting.

The thing about brute force is: it works. Brute force gets a bad press, because the people who press aren't much good at it. Rhetoric has its merits, and perhaps it would have been more of an achievement to have persuaded him of the folly of belligerence, but it would have taken a long time, and we were blocking the traffic.

Also, it has to be said that the snootiness of the boys towards physical persuasion goes a long way to elucidating their over-familiarity with dungeons and pyres while the thickies ended up with the thick gold jewellery, the zedoary and the good-looking women on the end of their prongs. Violence dissolves all known problems. Ask the Carthaginians. Ask the Greeks who ended up as secretaries. Ask the Philistines. Ask the Sybarites. Ask the Milesians. Ask ashy Alexandrian library. Grill the Gomorrhans.

I bestrode the planet-hugging duo. "Yes, now I think of it, there is something I'd like to say. Did you imagine when you got up this morning that you would die in inimitably humiliating circumstances?"

"No."

"You don't have much imagination." The thing about a gun is, it's like being on the right side of a Socratic dialogue. "A man should ponder his worth, treating every day as his last. Now, can you give me a good reason for not shooting your chopper off?"

"It would be against the law."

Mr Bulk would never work out why I laughed so much. Hube watched quietly. "Fuck[5], I've never seen a car shot up so discreetly."

????????????????????????????

We hastily left the scene on foot, a technique that was proving oddly effective against carred police. We went into the Chicago, a zareeba where the normal laws of France came to a standstill, where a moral blackout operated, and where the inhabitants would sooner see their loved ones marinated overnight in a chilli and ginger sauce, then barbecued and devoured by people they didn't really approve of, rather than do anything to make the lives of the police easier.

I ruminated on Mr Bulk and on the fact that I might have changed his life; that his tasting tarmac by the old port might have made him see the error of his ways. That my whole life's purpose might have been that one action, all my meanderings had been a route to that spot, that I had been carefully trained up to carry out that one task. But probably not.

Not looking well, Hubert. He wasn't complaining. He hardly ever complained (would he know where to start?).

One of the most interesting features of our universe is that the more you have to complain about, the less you do.

"What have you got in the suitcase?"

"Money. I was trying to give it away."

Hube had been by the old port, an area comprising mostly cafés, encouraging the onlookers to help themselves to some of our hard-robbed cash, displayed like huge pearls in the oyster of the suitcase. People had milled around, but no one had made it across the space between themselves and the spondulicks. Maybe the sight of Hube in his caftan, wide-eyed wide-boyness, was not conducive to helping yourself; a self-taught mad professor. "They all woke up that morning, praying for money, but when it was there ...."

We went to what Hubert had been assured was the hardest bar in the Chicago, which I knew very well was the hardest part of Toulon, which has no reason not to hold its head up with the hardest ports in the world. I demurred, pointing out that my holdings of teeth and unfractured bone zones were exceedingly modest, and that if we needed a drink, couldn't we find somewhere where the odds of assault were lower?

"You don't find the perpetuals in reference libraries," Hube snapped (in an odd way as proud of his time in maximum security, as in the right mood, I was of Cambridge. After all, you can't walk into either institution). "I might see some people I know."

"I thought you didn't get on with them that well."

"They're not my brothers. But you know, ten years. You have to talk to someone. You don't always get to choose your company."

The bar was dark, to further detente, prevent recognition or perhaps to save on the electricity bill. Though it was almost empty, someone bumped into me, outing as I was inning. He apologised with extreme courtesy, the sort of manners you could wait ten years for at Harrods or Covent Garden without sighting, but then people in those places are less likely to wheel round and sink their teeth into your neck. Suddenly, I thought of the puritan Zachary Crofton (d.1672) and his sons, Zachary, Zareton, Zephaniah and Zelophehad.

There were postcards on a number of the walls from inimitably unstable countries with governments whose quality and duration might be likened to that of the cheapest elastic bands. Hube said several coup d'états had been facilitated over beer in the premises; gossip that was hard to confute when you studied the fuzzy snapshots of people in combat fatigues standing over other people who didn't look as if they were ever going to get up again. A large glass jar, full of blackish sand, was parked on the bar with a card strung around it "Powdered Republican Guard – you can add water, it won't make any difference."

They served me with a Blanche de Garonne, and I must make room for the peerlessly refreshing and relaxing effect a favourite beer can have. Opening the suitcase, Hube started pawing the money thoughtfully.

"Repetition," he said, "more means less. We have to move on. We're just doing the same thing; what we need is something unique. The bank robbery that's never been done."

"Such as?" I inquired, knowing in advance that I wouldn't like the answer, an answer which would unquestionably be bringing zinging lawful bullets my way.

"I was thinking of something big. A huge job. But they take a lot of planning, a lot of people, which is why they nearly always get caught. The amount you have to steal to get to the top is getting larger and larger. There's no end to it. Sooner or later someone makes a bigger splash than you, even if inflation's taken into account. And the sums are so huge you need a lorry to take it away.

"I thought about different banks, the highest bank, the largest bank, doing a musical bank robbery, but they're all variants on the same theme. I've looked at the history of bank robbery; it's been the same, more or less violence, more or less money.

"What no one's done is the publicised, bring your family bank robbery."

"You announced the robberies in Montpellier."

"We announced that there would be robberies, we didn't say exactly where they would be, or exactly when they would be. Montpellier's big. Lots of banks. This time we say: we'll rob this bank on this day."

"It's a good idea, but it will make it ... more difficult. Even the police might be waiting for us. Despite our dedication to philosophy our liberty kicks sand in the face of miracles; why don't you take some money and enjoy the parts of life you can't from a cell?"

"It's kind of you to pretend that you mean that. No, my life has been these two months. After this. ... there's some tidying up. It would be nice to say something else ... but I can't. I'm not lying to myself so why I should lie to you?"

What befell in hell

I had plummeted into hell. I miserabled until I was wholly miserable. One likes one's misfortune to be misfortune and not part of a universal material. At this point, globally I'm a lot better off than most people: alohaing a'a- chippers, bheesties in Bombay, cattle herders in Kenya, yak-butterists in Yangi, zaptiehs in Zile. What excuse have I got to be low?

The season comes where cleverness and flippancy are wiped away. You tremble with the knowledge that you're going to be fed unhappy ending until it comes out of your ears. What people think of as happy endings aren't, of course, endings; endings are by their nature unhappy.

The well-hard ant

Terminally: all the emotional and noetic artefacts, the resolves, the tranquillities, the creedal graces, all our Zimmer frames of dogma, all the poses of the mind; they are the ant (a soldier Zacryptocerus) declaring "I'm well hard" as the boot comes down on it.

Pulling the sledge

You've got to pull the sledge, every day, all alone, with an ever-growing weight of jumbled disappointments and didn't-work-outs; there is nothing on the horizon.

Powdered philosophers, powdered bank robbers, powdered mercenaries

I look around the bar. By the end of next week, by the end of next year, by the end of this century, indisputably by the end the next century, no one here will be left. Powdered philosopher. Adding water won't do any good, though maybe a drop of vodka ...

Here we are again

Yhw? Yhw? Why do we get out of our celestial beds to come here. If it's pointless, what's the point ? If there's a point to it, what's the point?

Beauty Queens

I had a bad attack of the beauty queens. Happy endings all round is what I'd like to buy. A universal embrace left my heart, for everyone, even the oaf with the recently shot-up car, because the one thing that unites us, that conscripts us into the same army, is mortality: our common enemy.

Last words?

I wish I'd done more good. I'd gladly sacrifice myself to sprinkle some redemption onto others. To give them protection from insurance salesmen, unshaven men with banana-clipped guns.

Pulling the sledge in a Toulon bar

"So how do you plan to rob the anointed bank? A bank which will have more policemen than the largest police station in France when they're serving Christmas lunch?" I needled Hubert. "They'll be standing on each other's shoulders. We won't even get in. And surely posthumous arrest with a head full of lead doesn't count. To qualify as robbing the bank, we surely have to get some money and and survive for a few seconds. We've already monopolised all the luck in the nation. It's impossible."

"The impossible lives next door to the possible; people ring its doorbell by accident all the time."

Hube had obviously been spending too much time with philosophers and the heady-headed. How right to attempt limiting texts like the Zohar to those married and over forty.

"So how are you planning to do it?"

"I don't know. But you'll think of something while I handle the publicity. We'll give them a month to sweat a bit. But I leave the philosophy and the vocabulary to you."

"And which philosophical style should we use?" I asked idly, convinced that Hube had gone so far into the woods of would-be he was never going to make it back.

"For the Big One? For the ultimate bank number? The bank job that will shine both ways through history. A bank job so big that Plato will have felt it in his water. There's only one method fit for this." He looked at me expecting me to supply the line. I shook my head and plateaued my palms in perplexity.

"What's that then?"

"The Coffin method."

???????????????????????????

While Hubert huberts, I restaurant (as a German restaurant critic) testing the hypothesis that stuffing your guts produces unthinkably brilliant innovations in bank robbery. But now I have unlimited restaurant time, I find I no longer have the attack I did even a few weeks ago.

Eat now

I subscribed to the eat now, because the terrible is waiting outlook. As an incurable deipnosophist, I would drop everything and hasten to a nearby restaurant, just in case civilisation was about to go for a Burton before I'd had a chance for a really good troughing. And the thing is, that no matter how often you're wrong, one day you're going to be right.

Classical backing

I always ran to Antiphanes, the playwright of the 4th century BC: "For who among us knows the future or what any of our friends is fated to suffer? Quickly then take the two mushrooms gathered from the ilex, and cook them."

This is antiquity's value; it can be used to sanction anything. If you go into a restaurant and say the man next door thinks a profusion of fusion, a deuterium (Z 1) blow-up is imminent so you would like to have a blow-out – unless you're very rich, people will think you very strange. But bring in a few words from the writings (those denoised soundbites) of a Greek whose bones are well-mineralised and you have put wheels on your stupidity. That's the popularity of proverbs: cut-price, anonymous doctrines, back-up.

I don't see how I can help Hube take the crown. Also, skilled as I am at conceptual prestidigitation, I can't advocate bank robbery as an activity that will usher in an era of unfailing justice, ubiquitous love and copious gratifications.

Money's a sort of counterfeit worthlessness; not real worthlessness, but hard to tell apart. It's a pity it can't buy happiness, because that would be very convenient for everyone. The poor could save up.

????????????????????????????????

"What I like about you is that you don't say you love me," Jocelyne said.

It's good to be doing something right. To be a hit, as big as Zajc in Zagreb. Each time I see her I keep thinking, she's too attractive, intelligent, organised, well-dressed to be here. She homes in on my home, time after time, wherever, whenever. I dread to think how stunted our liaison would be if the seeking had to be done in the other direction: a sloshed philosopher trying to find car keys, trying to remember where he left the car, trying to find the keys again once the car has been found, running out of petrol, taking the wrong junction, tormented in one-way systems, losing the address, not being able to find a parking space.

"Were you frightened when we robbed the bank?"

"No. There's something very gentle about you. You remind me of a bruised apple."

"Any particular sort of bruised apple?"

"Like a bruised apple left in the gutter after a street market. Soft, full of goodness, but battered and unwanted, not looking the way an apple should. You can't hide that. Your untidiness is hair-raising, but not your bank robberies."

Pedigree

Why the degeneration? My father was heroic. He faced a boring job, day in, day out; suffered a job in an insurance company for forty years. Never whinged, even though he was perfectly aware that lazier, dimmer, nastier people overtook him in his company and that lazier, dimmer and nastier people outside his company earned twice what he did with half the effort. He didn't bottle out. Stayed in a job for life, a job it would have taken me a maximum of a week to get fired from. Though once or twice I did catch the but-I've-done-everything-you're-supposed-to look crossing his face.

My mother: I remember her dusting a chair before she took it to the municipal tip, I didn't even have many chairs in Cambridge to start with (it encourages students to hang around). As for the chairs I do have, I certainly can't recall ever dusting them (I got as far as purchasing a duster). Meritorious of being taken to the dump, I never had any intention of taking them there, because (x) I didn't know where it was and (y) if I had known where it was situated, (z) I would have been more tempted to remove furniture than to dump it.

Here I am, two police forces looking for me, my clothes strewn all over the flat, my wet towel bundled up on the kitchen table, an ingrown toe-nail ingrowing, because at the age of fifty I haven't competent toenail cutting, and a row brewing with my partner because of the two treasured pistols he entrusted to me – one on the floor by my bedside lacquered with honey (the result of a late-night toast and honey session) and the other presumed forgotten in a department store toilet.

Am I the progeny of a dying civilisation or just a common slob?

I wonder if I'm going to live long enough for my toenail to cause deep pain.

"Can you guess what Hube's latest idea is?"

Jo scratched her left nipple (bring in Zingg) as an indication I should continue.

"He wants us to do an invitation bank job. We inform the bank when we're coming along to rob it, to give the police a chance."

"So why don't you think of a way of doing it? You're the philosopher after all."

I hadn't expected this. I went to the fridge to get a drink wondering whether Jo would interpret this as getting a drink or as a first step to getting blasted.

Non-sequiturous prosification:

If this fat philosopher goes down the drain, he hopes he'll block it.

And one more:

You can't kid yourself anymore as you get older

That's it.

"I'm touched that you have so much faith in me as a philosopher but I've never claimed to be any good. An also-ran. Or a never-ran. Besides which, my expertise is in the history of philosophy; more precisely, the history until the Emperor Justinian closed down the Academy in Athens in 529 feeling that the philosophers were more trouble they were worth along with assorted charlatans, fakes, geloscopers, the cartomancers, the capnomancers, the ichthyomancers, the oneiromancers, the belomancers, the catoptromancers. And there would have been doubtless the necromancers, the alphitomancers, the axinomancers, the tephromancers, the ornithomancers, the alectryomancers, the cheiromancers, the rhabdomancers, the halomancers, the cleromancers and the haruspices. A stadium's worth of soothsaying and divination. Odd they didn't see it coming really."

Zonaras suggests that Justinian did it to save money by losing teachers' fees. The Neo-Platonics buggered off to Persia to stroke King Chosroes I, but he wasn't buying. We got, depending on how generous you're feeling, five hundred or a thousand years of mumbo-jumbo.

"The solution seems obvious to me," Jo said, "you rob it, but not in the way they're expecting. Surf on their assumptions" I was surprised to hear such naked encouragement from a naked assistant bank manageress.

"Any ideas?" I was curious. The unsurprise party didn't loom that large on my mindscape but we all enjoy being well-thought of. Satisfaction is usually being well-thought of by a small group of people. Hube was one of the remarkably few people who thought well of me, and although I felt like a grapefruit tumbling from the Eiffel Tower, heading for the Grand Kersplat, I wanted to try and retain his regard.

"You need to be there in spirit, but not in the flesh."

She then told me her idea.

I yelped, not a eureka at her ingenuity, but a reflection of the acuity of the carving knife that I had used the previous night, which had made itself comfortable in my bed, and on which I had placed my body weight.

>>>>>>>>>>>>?>?>>>>>>>>>>>>

Big Date

The announcement was made by computer which zapped out our communiqué by fax to several newspapers and finally to the central police station in Toulon. Joseph-Arthur, Hube's costumier, was a computer fiend, so he fixed it. Hube broke into the office of a local lycée, and left the computer there to fire off the missives, along with hundreds of editions of the sophists for the students ("arm the youth"), as our calling-card and verification. Simply sticking it in the post would have been too easy. Hube left a polaroid of us grinning, wine glasses aloft. We wore our shades and togas for the portrait, although as Hube snided:

"This is one picture I don't think they'll distribute."

The statement: "Even the best things come to an end. A bank. A date. A gang. We inform on ourselves, to make things easier for the police. When the eight meets the eight, in a month's time, the Thought Gang will commit the last bank robbery; there will be no more. We will foraminate any police hindrance. Autographs will be available. Toulon. The main square. The bank. Wait all day, stay away, we do it anyway."

We were in a cottage: Hube came in to tell me that the word had gone out, but that he couldn't stay because he had to build a swimming pool.

؟؟؟؟؟؟؟؟؟؟؟؟؟؟؟؟؟؟؟؟؟؟؟؟؟؟

What the week shows about soon-to-be ultimate bank robbers

Monday

Hube watches a film of a woman taking a shower. It was very ... authentic; terrible lighting and the showeree took a long time taking her shower. It turned out it was a home video.

"It's amazing what they can do with fibre optics, whatever they are," said Hube. The video was part of the investigation by the private detectives Hube had hired via Joseph-Arthur; obviously very familiar with unrequited love. The detectives had done, from Hube's point of view, thorough work, ripping away all elements of mystery and indeed clothing. They had intercepted her mail, bugged her phone, talked to her neighbours, pulled her medical records, peered into her bank account, rummaged in her dustbins (moisturiser containers, zucchini etc.) and typed it all up for Hube who was working his way through the stack of documents, while looking at the video.

We were three weeks from the robbery and Hube hadn't asked once about how we were going to do it.

"This lot are expensive but good. It's taken me all morning to read their report – a mixed bag; they've found out things which are pleasant," he gestured towards the picture, "and things which aren't."

"So what's the balance?"

"She lives in Paris. It is her. Or at least she was in care for six months. What's deflating is what she's doing since she left modelling. It'll give you a laugh. It's the last thing you'd expect. Do you want a go?"

"She's not a philosopher, is she?" I had visions of her unrestrainable career, her frontal propelling her up the world-rankings.

"No, ' he grinned, although I wouldn't have found it so amusing in his shoes. "No, she's a policewoman."

He rose: "I'm off to check on my swimming pool."
Tuesday
Time timed.

I thought, an inevitable consequence of being awake, but nothing of a bank robbery genus paced in my idea enclosure. Much privilege has descended on me over the years, a pity I can't seem to put to much use.

I haven't done much in the way of furthering the biz. I've been quite acerbic about the profession, but then, in my defence, the history of philosophy is a series of brainroom brawls, a grotesque daisy chain of jaws fastened onto the legs of predecessors, like linked piranha. This is a profession where the knives come out quick.

I was off-putting to students. Few could take more than a term of me. Few had the zeal for that long dark walk to Tennison Road, where the supervision might be conducted with two unconscious Australian backpackers that I had drunk onto the floor. One young lady arrived for a dose of Brentano, took one look at the stuffed zorilla (nothing to do with me, the only object left by the previous owners of my house) said "excuse me," walked out, went to the end of the road and turned left to the railway station and London, abandoning her university career and philosophy, within forty seconds of coming into contact with me. My greatest smash.

But still they came. The universe seemed to generate philosophy students faster than I could swat them. Though I did begin to suspect that Directors of Studies did target me for their problem cases: got a deadbeat, a failure, a bone-head? Ship 'em over to Coffin. Something amusing always happened when the students struck Tennison Road and I put Z-bends in their lives.

The best way to get rid of them was to get them to learn Greek. Perhaps despair at the intellectual worth of your students is an indelible feature of pedagogues; there's nothing that terrifies present youths more than the sight of an irregular verb (though it has to be said that most of them couldn't identify a regular verb). Most eight year-old Danes have a better grasp of grammar than the undergraduates I encountered. And they know nothing; they can talk endlessly, but they know nothing.

Wilbur would recount how at school his masters had made the pupils memorise huge passages of Greek poetry or prose, and then they would construe it in the penumbra of the bomb shelters, while representatives of the nation that had produced the greatest Greek professors flew overhead trying to drop two thousand pounds of high-explosive on them. "It's out of fashion to learn anything," Wilbur once said to me. "If I sat here chanting some mantra like Hong Kong Dong in order to obtain a new lawn mower or to purify my spirit no one would bat an eyelid. If I recited fifty lines of Aeschylus, I would be thought most eccentric. It is the greatest privilege to be able to think, it's the greatest privilege to study Greek, the words of Gods and God. It's important to put greatness into your mind."

I did take my privilege seriously in some respects. I always felt so bad about selling drugs to my students for instance, that I always did so with a hefty mark-up to discourage them from making further purchases.

Wednesday
No pandect. No solution.

I think of the battle of Zutphen (1586). I think of the boys, reaching out, reaching out. It's always been a very male enclave, which is odd in a way, since the Ionic Tonic has had remarkably few transactions with power. They've flitted around the mighty, they tried to wreak some effects on the big scale by ruler-fawning. Plato, Plotinus, Buridian, Leibniz, Dio, Heidegger, Descartes, Aristotle, they all had a turn at backseat ruling. So much so that a monarch's perineum might as well be marked philosopher's tongue rest.

Women, of course, had better things to do.

Consoled by the failure of my predecessors to achieve anything despite the size of their ideas, I went to bed.

A shaking, rattling sound woke me, like a washing-machine in a spin cycle. Roused, I went into the kitchen where I discovered Hube, stripped to the waist, holding onto the kitchen table and trembling violently. I hung onto him and after a couple of minutes, the jerking ceased.

"It's okay," he said eventually. "You know, I've often had the feeling that someone up there is against me. There isn't much of me left, and I've had to work hard to hang on. I've had to work harder than anyone else. I'm not going to give up now."

Unbelievably, I of all people, asked if he were seeing a doctor.

"I'm seeing a lot of doctors; you know how I love to talk. I can afford to pay for an educated audience these days. Some of them could be wrong. Most of them could be wrong. All but one could be wrong. But I don't believe all of them could be wrong. It's a strange business to pay more and more money to hear worse and worse news."

Thursday

The next morning Hube looked gaunt.

I made him breakfast and tried to get him to eat heartily. He chewed on one croissant, slowly.

"I'm going to check on the swimming-pool, and then I'm going to Paris to see Patricia. If anything should happen to me, don't worry, just carry on with the job."

Swimming-pool: he had learned the whereabouts of M. Gaboriau, his least favourite director of children's homes, and upon ascertaining that he was away on holiday for a fortnight, had gained access to his house and had built a swimming pool in place of his lounge and kitchen because (x) it would cost Gaboriau a small fortune and a lot of trouble to rebuild the house and (y) no insurance company would believe a claim such as "went away on holiday, came home, opened the door and fell into a swimming pool" and (z) Gaboriau was so routine-ridden and boring that he would probably expire from the shock.

"What are you going to do in Paris? Are you going to charm her?"

"No, I can't talk to her. She'll be good at her job, she won't make any exceptions, not her. But I'd like to be near her, to spend a little time in her neighbourhood."

Friday

I introspected and fought with the problem. No ideas. Idea bag looking like a wilderness of Zin.

I tried to fortify myself with examples from my life where I had overcome apparently insurmountable obstacles, but I couldn't think of one. Reviewing my life, there was only one problem I had dealt with, and that had been a problem of my own creation, so I'm not sure whether it counts.

Parish

We were taking bets at high table as we did every year on which of the freshers would fold or commit suicide. Names were raised and then Parish was mentioned. "Yes, he's weird," said Featherstone, "but it's the weird that slimes out, not that turns in on itself. I hear he was in a monastery before he came here; everyone left the order to get away from him."

I hadn't known this, but secretly I was rather pleased. I had had the presentiment he might be trouble when I had chosen Parish for admission to the college. Why they gave me some responsibility for admissions that year is of course a mystery. No, not a mystery; Featherstone did it every year convinced of his touch. However, just before the interviews, he got food poisoning and was in intensive care, unconscious and in no position to object to my taking over, which I was forced to do since no one else was willing to do it.

So I admitted some bathukolpian girls, Parish, everyone over six foot, and everyone whose name began with Z. I had found Parish odious at his interview, but I had had no idea how accurate my assessment was. One morning, heading home after a colossal binge, I walked past the river as they were taking the college boat out for a row, Parish got into the boat and then the rest of the crew fell into the freezing water. I couldn't work out how he did it.

Parish's profile grew. The Dean, who didn't noticeably have much interest in God, and who loathed being in the same room as me since I had mentioned that I'd had a summer job in a munitions factory, started saying things like "Daniel Edward Parish – all six letters, six, six, six." Perhaps we should have listened more closely because he ended up trying to kill Parish with a shotgun, decollating a portrait of a seventeenth-century bishop. No one worried too much, because (a) if there's one thing that our college wasn't short of, it was portraits of seventeenth-century bishops and (b) no one would dare suggest that insanity should be a hindrance in the academic world or for a man of the cloth. Sedated to an extent that made me envious, the Dean was packed off to the Holy Land for a sabbatical.

Lots of books (Zypaeus, Joblot, Leeuwenhoek) had been walking out of the college library and taking the train to London with an alacrity incredible for eighteenth-century publications. Unusually, one London dealer realised their provenance and Featherstone went to investigate. "It must be Parish," he concluded, "the fellow described him as studenty and revolting."

"That covers half the college."

"No, I'm not doing the man justice, he didn't say revolting, he said re-volt-ing-uh." But damning as that testimony was, Parish couldn't be nailed.

Then there was the strike of college staff, allegedly masterminded remotely by Parish, which resulted in most of them being sacked.

"I've never seen anything like him," said Featherstone, one evening in the Senior Combination Room. We realised we were under siege, that no one wanted to leave – because somewhere out there was Parish.

But the Wing-Commander was the crunch.

Parish had started inviting many of the numerous vagrants in Cambridge back to his room. This was not out of compassion you suspected but because he knew it would contort the authorities who preferred the spewing, raving and not washing around the college to be done by people with doctorates. Technically, his running a vagrants' hostel was in breach of college regulations, but no one wanted to be caught chiding a student offering a home to the homeless. Significantly though, none of the tramps stayed more than one night.

Vince, a local character, had been one of Parish's clients and had spent decades slumped around the market square, mollified excessively by booze, and when not would denounce students and foreigners, the two groups he importuned most for cash. "What about me, eh? What about me?". He probably earned more than I did. When he died, the local paper ran a piece on him, complete with photo in mid-obscenity, explaining how despite being a fighter pilot during the war (havoking the Zerstörer formations) he had achieved vagrancy. No one in college paid any attention to his demise, until Parish produced a well-lawyered will in which the stinker left his mortal remains to Parish, who let it be known that he intended to have the ex-Wing Commander stuffed; there is no law specifically against taxiderming gentlemen of the road.

There's a great deal of latitude at university but no college wants to be known as "oh yes, that's the one with the stuffed tramp". Featherstone came to see me. "You mustn't think I'm saying this because I want to see the back of you, because everyone wants to see the back of you, Eddie. Either Parish and his over-sized gnome go, or you do. You brought him in, you take him out."

What Featherstone was hoping was that a huge parcel comprising myself, Parish and a deceased tramp would be posted out of Cambridge

Normally, I would have countered such an ultimatum

with derision and a callous laugh, but this was just when things were shaping up nicely foundationwise, and I didn't want to lose the chance of milking it. There are alkys who can live cheaply and dispense with food, finding the wherewithal for the juice and nothing more, but not me. It dawned on me that however unfit I was for my position, I was a hundred times more unsuited for anything else. Parish and his conversation piece were standing between me and my crates of Chevalier-Montrachet and high class zoophagy. Bad luck.

Nevertheless, as I walked over to Parish's room, I felt a little trepidation. It was unaccountable that someone who had been stared out a Soviet gunship should be unnerved by a pimply pipsqueak.

Ruminating en route

1. His nickname was Prince of Darkness.
2. He would be thirty-three in the millennium, a popular choice for Antichrists.
3. He had inhuman resilience. Informed sources stated that he could go regularly for three days without sleep or food. He would stay up all night and then go out for a run in the morning fresh as a daisy.
4. He was a success as a director. Unlike most people who went into directing, because of interest in the theatre, maltreating literature or a cushy job after graduating, Parish had taken this route because it gave him a license to be massively unpleasant to innumerable people. Stories circulated of his gruelling preparations. During auditions for Sophocles' *Antigone,* Parish brought a cage of rats and said "choose one and bite its head off". General laughter until Parish topped one. A vegan passed out. More hardy troupers objected that the rats might bite them. Parish had responded: "if you're not the predator you're the prey." This occasioned a walkout. But that had been in his first term.

Success is a much-welcomed commodity anywhere. Using ample funds (probably the proceeds on the Proceedings of the Royal Society 1764) Parish put on production after production and soon had them eating live locusts. "What was the point of that," asked one actor picking a wing out of his teeth. "To show that you are cattle."

One of his leading ladies left the university and only corresponded with her family via postcards posted by third parties from distant parts of the world, Chile, the Solomon Islands, Zululand. She refused to tell them where she was since she maintained that if anyone one else knew, there was always the possibility that Parish might find out. She moved on every three days "My life is devoted to keeping the maximum distance between myself and it."

But he knew how to make money. He staged Hamlet with a cast of two actors, one male, one female (a sort of proto-semi-Gerardism), both nude; an unparalleled saving on costumes and peerless box office. A lot of the audience left at halftime (I know I did) having indulged that most human of pastimes, genital-scrutinising, (but they don't collect the money at the curtain call).

Parish's room

Parish's room was a double-set, but of course his roommate had long ago moved out and no one had dreamt of moving in. "Eddie, do come in," he said affably, "I've been expecting you." He went and sat under a huge canvas of black not in the way an erring student should greet his booter-outer. I gaped at the canvas some fifty square feet of black; it was a black which went back into the wall like a mine shaft.

"I'm sure you love it. I did it myself since there is no end to my talents. I call it 'Black isn't what it seems.'"

Unsure how to start, I hadn't planned any exordium. To be frank, I had been hoping that Parish would say something like: "Dr Coffin, I've been thinking about leaving Cambridge and disposing of the Wing-Commander in a style in keeping with fin-de-millennium mores in England, all without the slightest fuss. Do you think that's the right thing to do?"

"How's the Wing-Commander?"

"In a safe place. It's amazing what you can get for a bottle of whisky."

I outlined the college's objections. Parish acted surprised but pointed out that nothing in college regulations stipulated against owning dead tramps.

"And anyway you have a stuffed zorilla." The dangers of not keeping your home in good order.

Weight mustered by myself

1. Parish had no experience of embalming
2. It isn't done, is it?
3. The crates of Chevalier-Montrachet (unprofessional to mention).

Weight mustered by Parish

1. To my first broadside: university should be an educational experience.
2. The Fitzwilliam Museum has mummies – who, unlike the Wing-Commander, hadn't agreed to be exhibited.
3. Why should only appalling foreigners be so well preserved?
4. Offer of donating the mummified Wing-Commander to the college so we can flog him in a couple of thousand years to the Fitzwilliam.

"I wonder," I said, "I wonder if you really are happy here? Is this the best place for you?"

"Happy? Unhappy? Doesn't matter when you have a job to do." He offered me a bowl of some stew he had been heating up, which I ate to be polite. "Old recipe. Old family recipe."

Another tack: "You know, some people think you rather odd."

"Like the Dean? You can't be an Antichrist and expect everyone to like you." This was said ambiguously, so that in a court, defence and prosecution could both use it. "And how was London last night?" he asked

"Fine," I replied, not wishing to give him the satisfaction of asking how he knew I'd been taking zakuski at the Soviet Embassy.

"Come on, Eddie, you're one of us." I didn't know what he meant by this, but I had the feeling he was right. "I think I can offer you a job later on. How do you fancy governing a couple of countries?" Bizarre 'n' bizarre.

I left, sensing that my avuncular promptings weren't doing it. But no entity is as dangerous as a cornered philosopher.

Eliminating Parish

The wisdom was that Parish was going to scrape through. A pity because failing his exams would be a no-quibble way of jettisoning him. He could make a scene about being sent down on any moral grounds, but if you didn't deliver in the exam hall, it was time to pack up your old tramp and warm your feet with leaving. Parish was a mathematician, which was encouraging, because with a science there was a chance of failure. With English, Modern Languages or History, you aren't going to fail unless you suddenly forget how to read and write during the exam. Failure in tripos = crates of Chevalier-Montrachet.

I was nurturing some panic. I had spent most of my life trying to flee the influence of the fens but now the ticket was being drawn up, I was getting clingy. I had fluked one career as a philosopher: that was it. Apart from making tea in a warehouse somewhere I couldn't see what was open to me. Knowledge can be very useless for an incredibly long period of time, then can suddenly be invaluable and of the greatest benefit to mankind. Science is rife with theories, observations, insights that have hibernated for decades or centuries until their glory called (Boolean algebra, binary system, falling apples).

So it was with Bev. I hadn't even seen her for many years, despite Cambridge not being of sufficient dimensions to make this possible. One of the amusing things about living long enough is that people who roomed next to you in your undergraduate days end up in important positions; such as Bev who was setting the Maths paper that year.

Bev greeted me znuzily. Although not at the top of the tree mathematically, she was a fine example of what meticulous work could achieve. Her room looked, as usual, as if a crew of zealous cleaners had just left every piece of paper, every book and every pen in its appointed place. There were one of two photos of naked women (taken by women and thus completely different from the representational evils perpetrated by male hets). And if she wasn't a highly decorated commando in the wars of knowledge, she handed the spanners to the people who were taking apart the universe.

As I looked at her, I wondered whether the sweep and speed of science could continue at the furious pace of the last hundred years or whether human limitations would slow it down and what about a book on that, but then I remembered I had come to blackmail her, which wasn't easy since every aspect of her life reproached mine.

"So what brings you here, Eddie?"

I gazed down at my right shoe and noticed that its sole lolled like a dog's tongue; reclined extremely in Beverley's sofa I also perceived two patches in my crotch that could only be slothful urine.

I nevertheless requested that Beverley fix the exam so that Parish would fail, by inserting whole sections not on the syllabus, and warning the other students in a last minute fashion. The other mathematicians in Parish's year at college had left, so he could be isolated from the changes. One of the few benefits of being the hard man of philosophy is that no one wastes time being surprised at your behaviour.

"What exactly have you been drinking, Eddie? That's insane, immoral, irresponsible and above all, impossible. The paper was set months ago. I'm off on holiday tomorrow. Nice seeing you, Eddie. We must have lunch sometime."

I've always found it curious how many people, when they are clearly in an unrivalled physical and mental state to arrange a lunch or a drink, don't do so, but merely say that they should.

Beverley's refusal had been anticipated.

Grossly inappropriate couplings

Although our undergraduate friendship had lasted only as long as our proximity, it had encompassed a unique confidence. Why she had chosen me for trust is beyond me, since in terms of world ranking for confidences, I must have rated a ten-figure number.

She had had a fling with a rugby player. Bad enough. A demon composed of whisky had been at her steering wheel. "It was about halfway through that I remembered I wasn't interested in men – it would have been rude not to let him finish."

Vogues for Rogues

A hundred years ago, the child out of wedlock would have been the blackmailable, but now not the illegitimacy but rather (x) the father who had become an illustrious MP in a party which was anathema in academic circles (y) who was well-known for business interests which contorted people in academic circles and (z) even more amusingly her son, adopted and uninformed of his stock was involved in another party even more anathamatic in academic circles whose members were very keen on beating up small, frail and lone immigrants. None of this had black and whited in newsprint. Nothing one couldn't live with, but in view of Bev's prominence in certain campaigns, not a bad thing to keep under a thick carpet of ignorance.

"I must thank you," I said, "for this chance to see what blackmail feels like."

"How does it feel?"

"Extremely unpleasant." I could see her calculating, she picked up the phone. "I'm calling my travel agent, Eddie. Goodbye. If this is ever raised again, it'll be much easier to kill you."

I went off, feeling that I had, possibly, solved a problem; I intimated to Featherstone that Parish was sliding towards the exit.

But I found myself agitated. Parish unsettled. What happened if he lucked the exam? I couldn't sleep, despite thinking of wax-modellers such as Zeiller, Ziegler and Zumbo, and it occurred to me, that a bit of insurance might be on.

Twice in the head

Twice in the head was the slogan used by Six, according to Wilbur who had been stationed in Vienna where he had shot an American operative following him around, under the impression he was a Soviet heavy, and left him bobbing in a fountain. "The Americans were getting suspicious of Cambridge graduates for some reason. We blamed it on the Russians. Cold wars have their fringe benefits."

I decided on another shot for Parish. I started following him around in the hope of unearthing something dismissible. This was excruciatingly boring, and I had problems being inconspicuous since I was working in the half-dozen streets where I was a well-known philosopher.

I decided to stop messing around and tipped off the police

that there was stupendous illegality in his room. I had been suffering from vicious heautomorphism; I had never had a moment in my life where there hadn't been a jail sentence lying around my room, so I couldn't imagine that there was nothing iffy in Parish's quarters. The police left disgruntled.

I should have known better. Before you tip off the police, you guarantee there's something to tip them off about. I thus took up Grew's *Anatomy of Plants* (1682) which had been missing from the college library for several months since I had been using it as a doorstop, and thinking about flogging it, and made my way to Parish's room along with a packet of gum-number.

Two hours' vigil, before I saw him lope out. I rushed along with my bundles, and gained access with a master key. I looked around the study, and decided it would be more convincing to secrete them in the bedroom.

Parish was lounging on the bed. "Nice to see you, Eddie."

I lost my aptitude for breathing. I could have been displayed as the man totally shocked. I knew that I was often lax and slapdash in my affairs, but I had shadowed Parish ocularly. He had gone.

I looked at the open window. He must have tagged me and dashed back to pelt me with his omnipotence. His serenity matched my astonishment.

"I brought you this. I recall you were fascinated by seventeenth-century botanical works ... or am I confusing you with someone else?"

"You may well be. I'll return it to the library for you. It's rather overdue. And is that a packet of high-grade cocaine on top of it?"

" ... Yes. I've been a bit worried about you. You know I feel responsible for bringing you to the college ... . I know it might seem improper but you need to unwind a little."

I retreated. Parish had wrought total worry, evicting all the regulars such as hunger, weariness, craving for pleasure from my frame. My zygomatics were cracking with anxiety.

The day of the exam I was delighted to see Parish portering concern as he came out. I watched him in a café where he made some actors lie on the floor but there was no question that he was distempered. I trailed around after him in a car with smoked windows I had borrowed from Zak. Several cyclists almost perished under my wheels but I kept him in my sights as he walked out fuming to Grantchester.

It was getting dark. I couldn't see what Parish would get up to in the countryside, but I was banking on it being something really damaging. We all piss in the kitchen sink (even if it's more difficult for some than others). He disappeared into some undergrowth, and after a while, I followed him on foot.

I save the world

Convinced I had lost him, I found him by tripping over him, or rather by tripping over four bare legs, that on inspection all seemed to belong to Parish. Parish was naked and was in the middle of shafting ... Parish. Or, if you prefer, Parish was shafting Parish. He had duplicated himself. My alarm and surprise outbid, outdid each other.

There he was, starkers, in tandem, with to metaphor politically, dick sieg heiling. Two sets of those terrible eyes fixed on me. My cardiovascular system had a lot of work.

"I told you this would happen." "I told you this would happen."

They spoke simultaneously, identically.

"You told me?"   "You told me?"

"Outdoors was your idea.""Outdoors was your idea."

It became apparent to me that what I was witnessing was not fission, but incest. Parish had a twin, and obviously, Parishs preferred Parishs.

"Twins," I said releasing my discovery.

"Took you long enough, Eddie, and you did just stumble on it . My one weakness, I like to look at the stars. At what will be my domain. Surely that's not disgust I can see?"

It wasn't. My face had stalled; my amazement containers were emptied, at zero, and I had serious difficulty feeding this scene to my credulity.

"So few people get the chance to make love to themselves. I'm so good, they made me twice." One Parish fondled another. Even with all the pluses of youth, the Parishs were not a sightly sight, and I speak as the veteran of sex shows from Amsterdam, Beirut, Tokyo.

"Why?" I asked, aware of the put-upon nature of the question. The long-line of previous users.

"Because belief is a thief ... "   " ... it takes reason."

"If you are thought omnipotent ... " " ... you are."

"When they fear you ... "   " ... they free you."

"What for?" I still couldn't see the good of pretending to be one person unless it was to halve the lectures you had to attend.

"The Spherical Empire ... "" ... the world is ready for one master, us."

"Armies can go around the.." " ... world in a day."

"Other empires fell ... " " ... because of outside forces."

"Now there is no outside" "the world is ready."

"One man couldn't" " ... but two see both ways."

"To rule you have to rise early ... " " ... we never sleep."

"Ten years for England ... "" ... ten years for the world."

"Then to the stars ... " " ... then to the stars."

It was a situation where you only think of the clever things to say afterwards, but I was discountenanced by being in a lea with not one, but count them, two ithyphallic maniacs. I cast my mind back to ideateers such as Aristotle or Cineas, who had tried to dissuade monarchs from grabbing as much reality as they could, to cut down on the conquering. I waved an inquiry.

"So. World domination. What's in it for you?"

"A laugh."

Then they exchanged a look which I was shortly to find out meant: it's time to kill him now. Parish grabbed me and with the advantage of surprise and an extra arms began to throttle me.

I was getting big pictures of black and trying to remember how long you had when someone was gladhanding your neck, as well as reflecting on how trite it would be for another Cambridge don to be strangled by naked boys.

However, Parish must have chosen this field regularly, because with the final smidgin of my self I was aware of the police zooming through the hedge, hastened I assume by my gurgling. Apparently the farmer was tired of people raping his rape. This was the only time in my life I warmly welcomed the police's dragging me off to the station.

I had a cell next to one Parish while facts were established. He whispered forcefully through the wicket-gate, of their childhood in Zimbabwe. How they had no more family there and they had come to the UK as one. How he had further planned to die and resurrect himself by killing his brother (perhaps Jesus had a brother too …). Of course, such dissimulation is as old as the biz itself. I thought of Pythagoras's slave, Zalmoxis, who was purported to have fooled the wooden cubes of Thrace into thinking he was immortal, by hiding in a secret chamber for a number of years, and then coming back to life.

But Parish's schemes were futile since I had discovered his duplicity.

Long Pig

Parish also hissed to me that the repast he had given me in his room had in fact been curried tramp. I'd had a drumstick of the Wing-Commander. Stringy. Very peppery. Don't feel you're missing much.

Saturday

As far as I can tell, Saturday had the requisite number of seconds and hours. Looking out of the window it appeared that Toulon hadn't decided to stop existing, which would have solved my problem.

Sunday

Late in the evening, Hube returned from Paris. From his eyes I could see that more than just travel had happened, that there were events seeking buccal escape.

"Well?"

"I spent the night with her," he confirmed. He had more precisely spent the night under her bed to satisfy his desire to be close to her, to milk her proximity and 'to breathe her breath'. He had watched her out on duty, and then had broken into her flat to sleep under her. He remained immobile and silent during the nocturnal hours, taking in her shiftings, throatings, lungings. As his zeb dawn infiltrated, he thought how much he wanted to talk to her so he waited until she went to the bathroom, let himself out and then rang her doorbell.

"We met twelve years ago, and I'm sorry to disturb you, but I can't stop thinking about you."

They went and had breakfast.

"Did she remember you?"

"No."

"Did she know who you were?"

"I think she did."

"Are you going to see her again?"

"No. Once was enough. They can build-up a picture of a dinosaur from one bone, can't they? That breakfast was enough for me to know." He showed a photograph of them seated at the table. "Can you tell how long we've known each other?" It was true, the eyes were on the same line; they glanced as one. "We're all moments. That's a moment. I can make the memories. That she exists is enough."

›››››››››››››??››››››››››››

"Do you take milk with your tea or not?" said Cécile. That was the only thing she said that wasn't a complaint. Politeness didn't cramp her moaning. She had more whine than the Zuluf has oil, though her domestic state was grim. Her thirteen year-old son sat with the patience of someone who knows he only has to wait a few more years before he can join a death squad, and who was eagerly awaiting another opportunity to stub out cigarettes on his seven year-old sister.

Cécile's invalid mother was upstairs playing computer games. "On her sixty-fifth birthday she said to me: 'I've worked hard all my life, I worked hard bringing you up, I worked hard looking after your father, I worked hard looking after the grandchildren; I've done more than most, now I'm going to play computer games'."

Her estranged husband was estranged.

Jocelyne gave me a sorry-but-be-patient glance. I wasn't bothered, I studied the zebra-wood cabinet. Cécile was perfect.

›››››››››››??››››››››››››

I shouldn't have got in the car. But the trouble is, with no specific task to avoid, no chores to shirk, no inkling of ink from the killer opus, why not? I listened to Hube when he said: "Let's go to a football match."

My interest in football is and has always been zero. I went to a football match for the first and last time when I was twelve and too small to argue successfully against an uncle. I was forced to play at school, and I did score a goal once.

A goal that had turned out to be an own goal since I had forgotten we had switched ends at half-time. My mind was elsewhere when suddenly I found myself with the ball, excited and unthinking, I dribbled a few yards in the mud and put it in the net. I was surprised by (a) my scoring a goal and (b) Guthrie being in goal, since he usually goalied for my team, but we did change line-ups quite often. When we got back to the changing room, I was spat on by the ten others in my team (despite our losing six nil) and punched in the mouth by the striker from the other team who had been denied a hat trick by my footwork.

"Some friends of mine are playing," Hube said. Football: you know what's going to happen. Approximately twenty-two people are going to kick a ball for ninety minutes or so. But by agreeing I could blame Hube for another day without any dazzling brainwork.

We zoomed out of town, Hube at the wheel, unusually quiet. We went at insane speed utilising Hube's theory that there is nothing more suspicious than driving in a law-abiding manner.

One week to go

"So what are you going to do afterwards," I inquired, "assuming there is some afterwards?"

Hube shrugged his shoulders. "I haven't thought about it. You know, the things you don't like to think about ... you don't like to think about. And there are things you don't talk about because to talk about them, because first you have to think about them. Like Emile."

We sped on in silence. Hube overtook a coach, bowing the accelerator. We whizzed past the profiles of the passengers.

Great coach-whizzing moments 1.1

As I had walked towards the coach station in Cambridge,

the coach roared past me, and I caught a profile, like a fast moving coin, Zoe, looking down, looking pensive, perhaps hand-bag delving. Pondering a final brushing. I ran the remaining half a mile to the bus station, so I could claim a few extra minutes with her.

Reflection on Great coach-whizzing moments

Why, when there were so many hours of enclosure to choose from, has that fleeting head stuck?

The Football Match 1.2

Not far from Nice, we pulled up outside a small stadium, the sort of thing that a large village with aspirations would cough up for.

Our progress into the patch of bare ground next to it that served as a car park was impeded by two thugs paid to be aggressive, who didn't seemed bothered that we had a large metal object powered by three hundred horse power, and they hadn't.

"Yes?" asked one.

"We're here for the charity," replied Hube. I wasn't fussed, because when you're involved in the sort of odd that has philosophers robbing banks, you don't worry much about shavings of strangeness. I was latching onto the notion that this wasn't going to be the kickaround I had been envisaging.

We parked and Hube started shaking hands with people, unfriendly and hard (some had to work at it, some didn't) but who were well-dressed in an expensive, tasteless way. I also noticed a couple of individuals with dark glasses and high-powered rifles on the stadium roof.

A van lumbered into the car park. It was one of those vans the police transport prisoners in. It was unmarked and tatty. Upon stopping, it disgorged a dozen muscular, short-haired, vicious-looking men, who didn't have sunglasses, probably because the sun wouldn't look them in the face. They all wore the same cheap tracksuit and reminded me very much of the zigs who used to punch me in the mouth at school.

"Who're this lot?" I asked.

"The police," Hubert said in a way which suggested he was clearly hoping what he had said wouldn't sound too much like what he had said.

"The police," I repeated carefully. He nodded, but very slightly, as if hoping I wouldn't notice it and not wishing to reutter the word and thus add to the accumulating body of evidence that it was the police.

I was taken aback, but not hugely concerned. I mean, getting arrested at a football match is no worse than getting arrested anywhere else.

"The police – as in the people who are employed to look for us?" I reiterated just to see in what minimal way Hube could affirm this. Hube didn't interpret this as a question and so didn't answer.

"You think they won't bother arresting us?"

Here Hube reverted to conversation. "I know so. Not on the day of the match."

The Match. According to Hube it had started years ago when a police chief had been horrified to discover a top dealer moving into the flat next door. "I arrested the bastard half a dozen times and now he's living in the flat next door, with a larger balcony! What does that say?" On exactly how this blossomed into an annual police vs. thieves fixture, Hube was vague, but its root was a park dispute between the two fathers, two sons and two footballs. A match was convened which the police, having nominated the officials, won. The discontented losers demanded a rematch with a Milieu ref, which they won. And so on.

As we gathered by the touchline, we learned that a disaster in a rich catastrophe sauce had been served up for the Milieu. Their first eleven (for whom they had high hopes, since the team included three pros who had been up on criminal damage) coaching to the match, (along with the subs) had been caught in a pile-up, and were being cut out of the wreckage and ferried to hospital; they didn't have enough unbroken bones between them to field a single player.

Hurried consultations. Volunteers from the audience stripped down to footballing levels of clothing. They got eleven out onto the pitch, but they didn't perform well. There were a few zippy players who could toe the ball and put on the pace, but their virtuosity were always cut short by the police racing off with the ball. The Milieu didn't play as a team, while you got the impression that the police had been sleeping in the same bed for the last five years.

Yet, in spite of the game being played around the Milieu's goalmouth, the police couldn't make the net jump. The ball bounced off the goalposts, brushed them, it rat-tat-tatted along the crossbar, teetered along the line, was punched, butted or seized by the goalie; but the police couldn't score. It was quite funny. The Milieu was greatly aided by their goalie whose bulk did a lot of the job for him. Six six, and about the same around. His preventive approach identified both those in a position to score as well as those who might reach that stage, and this was followed by hitting them very hard about the head, principally in the face. The police were awarded penalties, but they missed, and the goalkeeping style kept them out of kilter.

The more they missed, the less chance they had of scoring, but still, the ball only tasted the police's end half a dozen times before returning to its rightful habitat by the Milieu goalmouth.

The spectators were much more interesting than the match. Naturally, it's profitless to go to a football match, especially a match like this if you don't shake out your worst parts, sending out your imprecations as far as they'll go. Telling who supported whom was difficult, since the reviling gushed effortlessly with no discernible relation to the action of the boots. Names were called names with volleys of obscene gestures to such an extent that the footballers might have felt they were on the sidelines of an insult match.

Hube had disappeared in that worrying way he had, and reappeared, tendering a tracksuit to me.

"What am I supposed to do with that?"

"It's a real fake," Hube said. "Zip it up and sit on the bench for a while."

I didn't understand what all this was in aid of. I had a no leaning out of my mouth, but refusal didn't fit into Hube's ear. I fingered the tracksuit. It had the Hermes emblem, a knowing or an unknowing reference to the god of secret dealings, of theft, of business.

Time for an insight

It occurs to me that a skilled thief, like a skilled thinker, has to know what has value, and what can be carried off. End of insight.

The Football Match 1.3

I revealed to Hubert that I hadn't even attempted to kick a ball for nearly forty years. He insisted that it was just for show, to show that the Thought was on site (although in front of me he did confirm to someone that I had made my living as a professional footballer). As a zemi.

"We have to be here," he said.

"But we are here."

"We have to be on the bench," Hube pleaded. "I'd do it but it's obvious to everyone here that I can't play."

"It's equally obvious that I can't." Despite having twice the limbs that Hube did, I barely possessed a tenth of his vitality and energy; I'd have backed him against any pro footballer in a head-butt contest. I haven't reached a self-powered velocity of more than two miles an hour for ten years; the last time I had walked briskly for a bus I was ill.

Pulling corks is my most vigorous form of exercise, since even my tubular entertainment is conducted in the style of a beached whale.

Upshot

Why Hube, who knew me well enough to know that I had taken some of the shortest taxi rides in world history, thought this sensible was something my comprehension refused to touch.

I changed and sat down on the bench. Only a few minutes of the match remained with zero goals, a sterling result for the Milieu.

I sat and reflected how close I was to doing one of the last things on earth I wanted to do. Amidst the burdens and tribulations of adulthood, there were, I believed, a number of rewards, one of them was not being forced out onto an expanse of mud with bruisers with a predilection for studding you.

As I sat there, one of the team limped towards the bench, indicating that his right leg wasn't legging as well as it should. The whinging young fraud.

"Okay, you, the fat Englishman," said the manager, with a twist of his thumb. "Do your stuff." I indicated the other two ruffians on the bench, and the lack of proper footballing footwear on my part. The manager gestured again taking my objections not as a genuine desire to refuse but as a desire to be implored a little more. I glimpsed Hubert looking at me, desperately. If he had asked, I would have refused, but because he didn't ask, I couldn't refuse.

With a shrug I strolled out, trying to act as if I knew what I was doing, and that I was sauntering, not because I was decrepit and unfit (a sort of anti-striker), but because I was so up on the game that I didn't need to run.

I fortified myself with the thought that in playing football for a few minutes I was unlikely to do any more evil than in thirty years of tampering with further education in Britain.

I paid close attention to the ball (flitting around the Milieu goalmouth) because I wanted to ensure it would get nowhere near me. I hung around the police net to guarantee there was no way I could score an own goal. Hube gazed at me with great relief. Essentially, whoever, whatever you are, there's just a small coterie that can give you the nod. I pondered whether I should comment to Hube how rum the crowd was, but I immediately conceded that if you were to amass a group of philosophers, they would hardly be impressive in bulk.

At the last conference I had attended, an Oxford professor under my vision, who shall remain nameless but easily identifiable, had rolled up sheets of snot teased out from his nose into pellets and fired them off indiscriminately into the auditorium like a Serbian shelling Sarajevo. This was not a momentary mutiny by his fingers, just unremitting oafishness. His wife had committed suicide the week before.

Reviewing the participants of that conference, all in all, they were less likely to break your jaw and take your wallet than Hube's chums, but that was mostly because they lacked (a) a good right hook and (b) the guts to do it.

Close-up

A tour of philosophers, poring over their pores. The philosopher is the one, as Wilbur once observed, who has his tongue dangling out and his leg cocked since whenever an arse enters his zone he has to make a split-second decision whether to lick it or to kick it.

Integrity, diligence, rectitude, all these qualities, perhaps, are things that can only be seen at a distance.

Eye on the ball

It was fortunate that only a few hundred seconds were left to play, otherwise I'd have been polished off on the pitch. Despite being two-thirds of a pitch from the ball hard elbows sank into my midriff, into my ears, into my flanks. The ref didn't pay any notice to the spectators' catcalls.

My presence on the pitch was a gesture: a very rude one. If the truce of the game prevented the zarps from arresting me, it didn't prevent them from giving me a good hiding now that I had come out of hiding. A cruel kidney punch brought me to all fours, and as I hit the turf and watched other policemen approach to trip accidentally and violently over me, I wondered how it would look, my perishing in the service of a football team composed of pimps, dealers, ledger artists, hotters and armed robbers: bang on.

I forced myself up and fled. The action had been at the other end of the pitch but maybe I distracted the police as, to shouts of euphoria, a milieu striker suddenly pulled away with the ball. I saw the ref check his babylon.

To my horror, I realised the ball was coming into my vicinity. The striker, wearing ridiculous blue glossy shorts, went through the police challenges as if they were hired to make him look good. Irritatingly, he shot up the middle of the pitch. I couldn't guess which wing would be safe. As I looked around for the bit of the pitch least likely to see the ball, I turned back to be bashed in the face.

The ground leapt over me.

And as I lay on it, I was aware of frenzied applause, which seemed a trifle cruel, and which made me angry since I didn't think my getting hit again was so very amusing. But the applause was for the winning goal. A winning goal, I was soon to discover that I had scored as the result of the ball smashing into my laughing gear.

Hube described it for me with emotion: Glossy had taken a desperate blast at goal, a shot which, according to Hube, was going to fly past the left hand corner of the goal, but the intervention of my face had given the ball an eerie spin that had foxed the goalie.

There was another thirty seconds of desultory play but that was it. One nil. I didn't care much. Blood dived dropily from my nose, and even the violent backslapping from my teammates and the emotion liquating in Hube's eyes failed to dispel the powerful sensations of unwellness in me.

The police were sulking. Not many people like to lose, even to a good team, but to a team whose dangerman is a geriatric philosopher and the bank robber you'd most like to arrest: it's tough to swallow.

But Mr Glossy was the trouble. You could tell from his legs he footied a lot and he fancied himself. He asserted that his shot had been on target and he reproached me for my ontological whereabouts and maliciously manoeuvring my boat race to pilfer his glory.

Being someone whose trade lies chiefly in the precise use of language and who prides himself on swift and sustained transmission of information, I'm always perplexed by people who don't understand what they're saying, who seem to get stuck in an odd part of a proposition.

"You stole my goal." Glossy repeated again and again. This was odd because (x) it wasn't true and (y) if it were, what could I do about it? (z) snap my fingers and take us all back five minutes? The univalence of his thought was outlandish.

You would have thought having supplied the victorious pass would have been good enough but one of the things that emerges from the most superficial study of world history is that good sense gets few votes. Hube tried to be affable for the first five you stole my goals, but Glossy kept prodding him with his pecs. What I couldn't understand is why, instead of wittering on about my having purloined his goal, he just didn't ask Hubert to hit him very hard, because after a while Hube guessed that was what he wanted.

"I'm sure we can settle this peacefully … ," said Hube, stepping back a pace and kicking Glossy with tremendous zest. (One moment Hube's leg was under him, the next it was aiding Glossy's groin inches above its regular altitude.) But why bother?"

Glossy went down with no plans of getting up, overwhelmed by Hube's elenchus. Apart from the few small mammals and a number of invertebrates, I thought I'd seen it all. However, at Hube's instigation, everyone piled in. Although Hube's portfolio of pain had been directed at a fellow team member, it was like a formal dinner where everyone was waiting for the host to raise the first item of cutlery. The ceasefire ceased. Hostility was exchanged for hostilities.

Hube strode through the scrums with the perfect invulnerability of the truly reckless, not at all embarrassed about leaving so abruptly. A bar brawl you have a fair chance of plotting, but when a hundred fists are in search of a hundred jaws, it's beyond my computation. On the way to the car I collected some new violaceous patches for my lesioned features. As Hube pulled away, I indulged in some sarcasm, having earned the right: "Is that enough for one day? Or are we going to burn down a high-rise to round off?"

Hube was wise enough to limit his response to driving.

"There are going to be some arrests," I reflected.

"They can't arrest anyone. It's a truce. And we have hostages, you'll see." Hube's nonchalant changing of gears was too much for me.

Wig-out. Not keeping my hair on 1.1

"This is it," I proclaimed, "I'm a fucking philosopher, do you understand? Not a very successful one, but a philosopher." It was too much for me – the strain of top-class football had got to me. "This non-philosophical stuff has got to stop. No more football. No more bank-robberies."

The thing about losing your temper is that it rarely has any effect apart from making you look ridiculous. I go (I am told) a funny colour, my nostrils flare and my voice becomes that of a cartoon character. Hube was unconcerned which prompted me to further somersaults of rage.

But Hube played it right, just driving, knowing far better than me that when you're going nowhere, you've got nowhere else to go. If I had received a phone call at that moment offering me accommodation or an awaital somewhere, I'd have been off.

The Needle

We didn't go home and I had expended my anger. I was smouldering taciturnly in my seat, when Hube stopped the car and addressed his first words to me since my explosion.

"This'll be worth it. Have I ever been wrong?"

I seemed to be regressing further into my childhood. Hube hid around the corner and got me to ring the bell of a small flat.

"What am I supposed to do then, run off?"

"No, just speak some English and get whoever answers out."

"Good afternoon," I said to the cicatrised individual who opened the door, "do you speak English?" Scarface looked at me znuzily, as well anyone might at the spectacle of a cheaply-track-suited bruise appearing on their doorstep.

"No? In that case my postillon has been struck by death rays from Saturn and my meats cannot have a Merry Christmas. And if you come a little further out, I have an acquaintance who will do something to your disadvantage." Grudgingly, Scarface followed me out to the car while protesting that he didn't understand what was going on until Hube appeared behind him and stuck a gun in an uncomfortable place.

Inside we found another thuggy zig and the Corsican,

who had apparently been deposited there as a safeguard for the good behaviour of the police. "Stay calm," said Hube, "I think everyone here knows that there's nothing I like more than to pull a trigger. We just wanted to drop in and see if you're ready for next week."

If I had been in a foul mood, the Corsican left me standing. His words had trouble getting out through the solid hatred. "Please come. We're so looking forward to shooting you."

"Okay," said Hube, "I was afraid you might have forgotten. We'll be off then." As we handcuffed them to the radiators, Scarface commented: "You know, Hubert, Régis is very interested in seeing you. About Thierry." Hube didn't say anything which was a complete giveaway.

In the car, I delved. "So, who's Régis?"

"Someone." Sensing my supplementary question about to launch, he continued: "A big wheel. A man with a lot of success in the businesses they don't cover in the financial pages."

"And who's Thierry?"

"His nephew."

"And why would he want to talk to you about him?"

"He was in Les Baumettes with me. He was found dead the day I was released." I wondered whether I'd have to ask him, but he knew the zet was on. After a moment he continued: "I was just getting my things to be released. I was walking past one of the storerooms next to the kitchen, where Thierry worked. He must have felt safe because I was getting out, or because he's Regis's nephew.

'You've been in a long time, eh?' he said.

'Yes,' I said.

'And all because your getaway car was stolen, eh? I had no idea when I stole it it'd be so funny.' We knew each other from youth custody. That day in Montpellier he saw me going into the bank and helped himself to the car."

"And how did he die?"

"We were standing there, there was no one else around

and I saw on his face the resting place for the grandfather of head-butts. I couldn't resist the opportunity. It was the fall that finished him, though. They should arrest gravity."

»»»»»»»»»»»»?»»»»»»»»»»»

The Blaggiest Blag

It was odd, because not only was I ready on time, I was ready early. Very early. I, the man, whose mug-shot could be appended to the definition of late in an illustrated dictionary, the man who liked nothing more than to lie in bed contemplating fifteenth-century printers such as Zainer, Zanis and Zarotis. But there was no sign of Hube.

I had time to admire myself repeatedly in the mirror, to study the police uniform that Hubert had obtained for me. The uniform fitted me like ... like a uniform that fits really well. I looked rather good, a trustworthy village gendarme (one recently beaten up) too jolly to be promoted. The uniforms had been Hube's idea. They weren't essential to the execution of the robbery, but they were droll, and might make movement easier in an environment where every third person would be a zarp.

I was nervous. Moving along the coast of nervous down towards the islands of pure panic, because we had already consumed an allocation of luck for millions. I pedalled the cycle of fear faster and faster as Hubert failed to hubert.

My role in the day's proceedings was to be collected by Hubert and then the two of us would go and collect the lolly. Hubert's engine had been running hard that morning: "we are artists, artists of excitement, our work can only be felt in the blood, it goes straight to the heart."

Then, as agreed, Hube had gone off to kidnap and terrorise the old woman. However, he hadn't returned as agreed. He had allowed himself an hour to be wicked and to take into account traffic conditions. Ten was when we should have left for the bank. By five past ten I was exceedingly fidgety: by quarter past, I was bounding around the room like a ricocheting bullet.

I began to ponder whether I was doing anything wrong. I relived our conversations several times. Everything was clear, there was nothing to misunderstand. I was to wait, Hube to return.

By half past, I had had two showers, but I was still sweaty. Something was wrong. Had Hube been bagged? Would he be expecting me to soldier in and spring him? I'd do him more good by giving myself up and stating that I'd planned the whole thing and forced Hube to tag along.

I didn't know what to do. I was unaware of standard procedure when your partner fails to show for the greatest bank robbery of all time.

Had they nicked him? Was he on his way back to Les Baumettes? I switched on the radio to listen to the news. Not a sausage. I zebra'd around the corner to a phone booth and dialled the bank. Adopting a ludicrous accent I asked for Madame Juillet. "Her line's busy," was the reply.

Were they lying? Or was she in as she should be? I was crushed by questions and doubts. As a top toper, not an actionman, I was stumped. I went back to our base in the hope that Hube would have reified: he hadn't. He was over an hour late.

Leaving a note, I started for the old lady repository.

My participation in the preparations had consisted of passing on Jocelyne's idea.

The Coffin Method:

Get someone else to do the work.

However, I was lucky in that Hube, who had carried out all the logistics, had taken me to the flat we were using as the granny-container, so at least I knew her theoretical whereabouts. I didn't know what else to do. I could hardly ring the police to report Hubert missing.

I entered the flat with the keys that I had been entrusted with but unaccountably hadn't lost. I unlocked the bedroom door to find the old girl zapping away with the games console we had provided her with.

"Are you another kidnapper or are you a real policeman?" she enquired not taking her attention off the game.

"A kidnapper."

"Why bother dressing up as a policeman?"

"People seem to like it. I don't want to bother you, I can see you're busy, but you wouldn't have any idea where my colleague is?"

"We're talking about that skinny ziff who brought me here? He's quite thoughtful, this is first-rate equipment. I don't know where he is – he didn't say anything to me apart from he'd be back later on."

I was crestfallen. Crushed and crushed. I sat down to remove the effort of standing from my hard-pressed consciousness.

The game went beep, boop, phwatt, zaag.

"But you can ask about the last time I saw him. That's quite interesting."

"When did you last see him?"

"Outside. He locked me in very courteously. This is a nice neighbourhood, and I was just looking around a little out of the window, when I saw him leave the building. Three types who had been outside jumped on him and bundled him into a van. It looked very much as if he was being kidnapped, which seems unfortunate for a kidnapper. Tell me, my daughter isn't behind this, is she?"

"No," I said, with as much conviction as I could; Cécile wasn't behind it, but she wasn't in front of it either. I decided I might as well ask her if she had taken down the registration number, though I didn't know what I would do if she had. I might look like the police, but I wasn't.

"I didn't get the number. But it was a van for an olive company. It had that in big letters on the side. From Nice. I don't trust people from Nice at all. I don't think much of your colleague's prospects." Fortunately she was of a generation that had had to direct its animosity to people a hundred kilometres down the road, before they had imported enough foreigners to take over that function.

I now had a hunch. At the football match, in the parking

lot, I had seen a van which had 'Athena's Olives' painted on the side. I noted it, because although olives, like wine, are available everywhere, again like wine, pinnacle olives are hard to find, and because the address given on the van was the street where the young lady on the flagpole had ended up. (Forlornly I followed her there, not having enough maturity to know when a union wasn't on; she spent the weekend playing hard finds soft with three filmmakers on the roof, while I made coffee and other refreshments for them.)

Olives

There were many people I knew about in the Milieu who would like to spend a quiet hour kicking Hubert's head in, so why not a few more I didn't know about?

"You're not thinking of courting my daughter, are you?" she inquired.

"No."

"Good. You look like a decent sort." As I rose to leave, she added: "And if you don't want my memory to work too well when I give descriptions to the police about you, I would like soup at five o' clock. Asparagus is my favourite."

"Sorry. I'm going to have to lock you in again."

"As you wish," she remarked, as the international sounds of success zooged from the game. I resolved to phone Jocelyne to make sure the old girl would be all right if things went amiss. I had no choice but to seek out Hubert.

Second Floor

On the second floor I was accosted by an elderly man. "Excellent," he said grabbing me, "just the man I need." I certainly didn't want enter his abode, but he was a man who knew how to grab an arm. I was dragged into his bathroom. I had been anticipating finding something gruesome, something for zopilotes, but what greeted me was a well-maintained bathroom, one which looked as if it was expecting guests.

"Now," said my conductor, "I want you to look at this basin carefully. Don't rush, have a good look."

I scrutinised the basin. It was nondescript, a mild green, an exemplar that graced half a million or so homes. No antique value, no extravagant modernity; it was a basin about which you'd be pushed to make conversation.

"I've brought in an independent assessor," my host shouted towards the adjacent room, "an officer of the law. Is that good enough for you?" He turned his discourse on me. "My wife – she thinks she's punishing me by not speaking to me. So what do you say about the basin?"

"It's ... green."

"We are in agreement on that. Is there anything else you'd like to remark on?"

"Nothing comes to mind."

"Fine. Now, which of the two following adjectives would you feel most at ease using in relation to this basin: clean or dirty?"

I tested the basin ocularly once more; no expired insects, no zigzags of toothpaste, no humps of soap, no lingering lather, no hair, no scrapes that would propel it into the domain of filth. Indubitably, compared to any basins that had been under my jurisdiction, it gleamed.

"Clean," I said but in an easy way so that if it wasn't the right answer I could withdraw it.

"Clean! Ah-ha! A professional verdict. Official. A disinterested judgment. It's clean." He darted into the next room for face to face relaying of this news. I moved towards the exit, sensing that my usefulness was at an end, while his wife, having ditched the mutisme, was giving him a broadside: "Men. I don't know why they bother giving you names, you're all so interchangeably stupid. I ask you to do one thing. One thing. To clean the basin properly."

As I reached the stairs I heard: "Then why did he say it was clean? Is it a worldwide masculine conspiracy? You're always like this."

"So you regret marrying me now?"

"No, I don't regret marrying you. What I regret is not divorcing you straight away."

Ground Floor

Beginning to get my worry really working again, I bumped into a man carrying a carving knife, which if it had been angled slightly differently would have Z-plastied me. The man swore furiously. Here it is, I thought, Featherstone and the others will laugh themselves to injury when they learn that I, fraudster, serial blagger, was stabbed to death because someone mistook me for a policeman.

I was beginning to feel enormous sympathy for the profession.

"That was quick," said the man. He was well-dressed for someone prowling with a carving knife. Dull suit and tie.

"Quick?"

"Yes, I just phoned a minute ago. He's in there." He motioned towards his flat. I considered bolting, but the man had an assiduous air about him, plus a carving knife.

I went in and amidst some disarray was a skinhead cocooned by an extension lead on a chair, as contented as one would expect someone to be in those circumstances.

"I came back from work and found him helping himself," disclosed the knife carrier. "He smashed a window to get in."

"Well, if you've phoned the police," I said in a way which I realised implied that I wasn't part of that fine body, "there'll be a unit on its way. I'm off duty," I said, trying not to run to the door.

"Oh, so you want to leave him here, do you?"

"If a unit's on its way ... ."

"That's wonderful. I'm already doing your job for you, and you can't be bothered to take him. No, no. I'm already late for a meeting, and I'm not having this slime in my home a second more. You lot are all so concerned about that Swedish chiropodist who's hopping around robbing banks-"

"-it's an English philosopher," I interjected.

"Don't talk rubbish, it's a Swedish chiropodist. I heard it on the radio this morning. I have to go. You take the zozo and wait for your friends. I'll give you a statement later." He handed me his card. I suppose if you go around pretending to be a policeman you can't really complain if people take you for one. I decided that acquiescence was easiest.

I bundled the skinhead into the car and drove around the corner.

"Look," I said, stopping the car. "You obviously did something very silly this morning. But I can see that basically you're all right. I shouldn't do this, but if you promise me you won't do this again, you can just get out here."

"You'd like that, wouldn't you?" retorted the skinhead, "You'd like me to get out eh? Do you think I'm stupid? I get out, out comes your gun. Paf! Paf! resisting arrest. You can take me to the police station. You're all the same, you cops."

I tried to persuade him, but he wasn't having it. I even emptied my gun and tossed the bullets aside, but he didn't budge. I argued a bit, but I had other things to worry about.

So I drove to Nice with my prisoner saying sporadically, "I don't know what you're up to, but you're dealing with someone switched on."

Before storming an olive warehouse

I parked twenty yards down the road from Athena's Olives. There was an office, but no signs of activity.

Metrodorus the Epicurean put his finger on it. Does it really matter if a man doesn't know who Hector was? No, it doesn't. He is no richer, his dick no burlier, his supper no tastier. Even in the classics they argue against the classics (although I think it a pity to life without Homer – acceptable not to care greatly about him, but one should drag one's mind through once).

All dedicated. A knowledge of aorist infinitives, Diels-Kranz numbers and Descartes' Latin writings is invaluable if you want to teach the history of philosophy, but is of limited application when your friend has been abducted and is being held by stunningly violent miscreants. Regardless of almost drowning myself with small lakes, I wasn't willing to be shot by anyone who didn't know at least two of Zeno's paradoxes.

I inspected the unhoneyed gun to verify for the third time that the ammunition was there. After all, you don't implore a nut and a bolt, you get a spanner.

"You can sit here all day," said the skinhead, "I'm switched on, me."

The Olive

Heroes' laurels. Athene got a city named after her because of her generous provision of olives in Attica. Thales, our convoker, card holder number one made vast sums of money out of the olive, by having the monopoly on olive presses.

Would my death merely be a momentary distraction, like an unwelcome phone call or a wrongly-addressed letter?

I was afraid. The fear was not entirely for myself, it was fear that I would let Hube down; I was in that most dreadful of states: responsibility. Suddenly, lying in my bed in Cambridge composing zuihitsu on fifteenth-century printers such as Zel, Ziletus and Zwolle, supervising the spotty, housework, everything looked good. I would have done anything, (even storming an olive warehouse) to avoid storming the olive warehouse.

I stared at the building, waiting for something to happen, for guidance. For someone to come out and say: "Eddie, we have twenty questions on the Ionians; get them right and we'll give you Hubert."

Verity's severities

Truth: not always what we'd like. False hope, it must never be forgotten, is still hope. Hope is the rope that pulls us up.

I tried to think of something clever to do, without success. I had been in the car for half an hour, saving those phenomena as Plato 'n' the boys had recommended but the only phenomenon I had saved was the dull frontage, the sequestered street. Sitting in the car was beginning to feel and look stupid. Sitting in the car, if it could do Hubert any good, I would have done for the rest of my life.

What worried me as much as getting shot, was being laughed at, or wrong. What if I walked in to demand Hube, and they simply said "Who?' either with ignorance or dissimulation.

Since I couldn't think of anything clever, I settled for something stupid.

There comes that moment in your life when you have to get out of a car containing an unlosable criminal, and wearing a bombillatingly ridiculous uniform, force your way into an olive emporium in an attempt to rescue a one-armed armed robber and get shot dead.

Longevity

The funny thing is that, by genealogy, I should be entitled to a long life. My parents, and grandparents were all keen livers with good livers (up to a point). Perhaps it's my inherited resilience that has jeered at the doctor's prognostications. Certainly both my grandfathers had unusual endurance (like Zemaituka).

They had a lot in common. Both soldiers, both stout, both had faith in the selfless military tactic of surrendering to the enemy as quickly as possible, and thus sabotaging their martial progress by being a burden.

My maternal grandfather capitulated in 1941 in Singapore. He ended up building a railway in the jungle and losing a body's worth of weight. But he came back so thin my grandmother had doubts it was him (only accepting him because no one would bother impersonating him).

Due to war-heroness, he became Mayor, but after a few months, during a council meeting concerned with licensing, he got up: "I think I can hear someone calling me outside. Don't go away, I'll just check." He must have had superb hearing because he ended up in Florence (taking the seal of office with him), playing ziginette, eating zabaglione, making money by guiding tourists, though he never so much as bought a book on the city. "Why be encumbered by facts?" He retrieved his corpulence and used the name Churchill, insinuating to American tourists that he was a not so distant relative. "They're happy to have a good story to tell and I'm happy to get a weighty gratuity." He made enough to grappa himself to death.

Grandmother went to try and bring him back. She returned alone. "Would he be better off in an institution? Look how many women lost their husbands because of the war. I can't feel hard done by. He's lost, but at least I know where to find him."

My mother went. "You know you're better off without me. I'm dead. Dead and busy. Look after yourself."

My maternal grandfather I never met, but my paternal grandfather lived with us. He had been a career soldier, due to retire in September 1939 and was captured within hours of the first engagement of British and German forces in France.

He was virtually bilingual. He had spent a lot of time in Austria and in Zug as part of the Army's bobsleigh team (the ideal sport for beachballs) and had fluent German before his five-year stint as a prisoner of war.

He wobbled now and then, but instead of leaving for Florence, he would take a chair up to his room saying, "I'm going to have a funny five minutes." This would be every eighteen months or so. He would close his door and then smithereen the chair, tidy up meticulously, dustbin the fragments, and then go out and purchase a second-hand chair that would sit on destruction row waiting for its obliteration.

You could always (as my cousins did) get him to blast off by leaving food on their plate: a bread crust, a rind, a sole Brussel sprout or a single ziti would be enough. Abandoned food would contort him like a wrung towel. His mania for shining plates was not the only imprint of his incarceration: he had gone native and absorbed a mutant Prussian assiduity.

A zealous collector of editions of Schiller and Hölderlin (antiquarian and new), he would incinerate them in his fireplace during the winter. His pension was modest, but he would snap up the Schillers and Hölderlins wherever he could (though he did hint to me once that he did half-inch copies from libraries and the more pricey bookshops). Schiller and Hölderlin had been the only works available in the Stalag library.

Around the age of ten, when I was evolving the rudiments of reason, I asked: "But it wasn't Schiller or Hölderlin's fault, was it?"

"Yes, it was," he opined tossing another Schiller into the flames. "I'm not a rich man, but I must do my bit." He was undaunted by being an old soldier with a feeble pension in Macclesfield and that these two celebrated poets had a head start of hundreds of years. "Eddie, never be afraid of a job because it's big. I know the odds are against me, but you should always do what you feel is right."

His reasoning was that the world was trending for a crop

of croppers and that thinning out the Schillers and Hölderlins would reduce their chances of survival. Equally in anticipation of a scorched globe, he buried the works of Shakespeare in lead-lined casks in odd places. Whatever happened, his canon was that we were heading for a head-to-head with the Germans again.

"Show me the letter where I asked them to invade their neighbours? It wasn't me who recommended a motorcade through Sarajevo to Archduke Ferdinand."

He gave German conversation classes for a little pocket money and was for a while the honorary consul for the Federal Republic of Germany in the North West.

History : World War One

"One minute, you're in a lather about ablative absolutes, then someone walks into the classroom and says you've got to put your books down and go to a foreign country to be killed."

Get ready, get ready

My grandfather was most anxious to impress upon me the arbitrary nature of life on this orb. These lessons were nowhere as enjoyable as his German instruction. The most zany example: my going to bed to find a live alligator under the sheets (albeit a very young one), which was no problem as far as I was concerned since I wanted to keep it.

The most jarring incident: he hoisted me out of my bed in the middle of the night, pushed me out onto the doorstep, doused me with a bucket of water, and with the injunction "survive" slammed me out. It was December. However, before I had an opportunity to act, my father appeared. My grandfather's pedagogic influence diminished greatly after that, though there was a subsequent trial when we were taking a train up to Scotland and he slipped me half a crown at the railway station in Carlisle, telling me to alight and get him a coffee. "Plenty of time before the train leaves." Thus I was stranded at Carlisle railway station with my nine years of gathered phenomena. That was my first visit to a police station. They were very nice.

Grandfather's ideas

Religion made him laugh. Whenever he saw a priest, he would guffaw. The trenches had removed any possibility of respect for the divine. Religion was fancy-dress. "Oblivion first class, hmm?" he would say in uncivil tones to any cleric hapless enough to stray within range. "Got to keep working for that first-class oblivion, eh? Can't spend eternity in second or third, what?" His other favourite clergy-baiter: "I find I have an overpowering sentiment that I am the son of God. Would you be kind enough to clarify whether I am partaking of the godhead or merely deranged?"

He had an immense respect for ideas: "Ideas are what make thousands of healthy young men climb out from trenches like a vast centipede."

My parents were remarkably unremarkable. Perhaps the surfeit of eccentricity in the previous generation had made them as impermeable as the Zechstein to aberrancy. My father was a one-anecdote man. His war anecdote. He was working at an airfield as groundcrew when they got an air raid warning.

Uses of fat

My father received the nomenclature and sympathy someone of an obese disposition could expect in the armed services. When the siren went, everyone hotfooted it to the air raid shelter, leaving my father with their dust and barbs such as "save some shrapnel for us, porky". His comrades were all safely in the shelter, waiting for my father to waddle up, when a two hundred pound bomb bullseyed it. The relatives got sandbags.

Attribution of blame

My grandfather taught me German to an advance level. Since my parents didn't have a sentence of German between them, he boosted my acquaintance with the language by procuring not only a Zitatenschatz, but tomes of an erotic turn, rightly judging that erudition could hitch a ride on my dick. I got all the wordmen of Germany apart from Schiller and Hölderlin. He forbade me to touch them. "What are you going to do if you end up in a German POW camp? You don't want to take that risk."

Granddad crushes Germany

Every year, for two weeks, he would holiday in Germany. Apart from the largest cities, he never went back to the same place twice, because he invariably left powerful memories. He would take the ferry to Hanover, where he would patronise a pet shop that had special supplies for him.

He had imported his own paraphernalia (dead cockroaches and dead rats, suitably packaged) until one day a customs official had probed his suitcase and been dismayed about undocumented vermin entering.

My grandfather would plant the expired creatures around hotels, restaurants, doctor's waiting rooms, hospitals and town halls, creating mayhem, distress and quite often a reduced bill.

His Arsenal

1. Cruelty to waiters: ordering steak, then pretending he had chosen the zander.
2. His wartime in-camp profession as forger was deployed

to join innumerable libraries to clean out their stock of Schiller and Hölderlin. He also concocted letters purporting to be from local dignitaries or politicians to English newspapers containing proclamations of rearmament and keen anticipation of the next one.

3. "I'm taking you into my confidence because you have a honest face ... " His bamboozling was outstanding (he did have a whole year to dream up schemes). He had entire villages digging up the countryside for non-existent hoards of gold he claimed had been hidden there during the war. What he considered his best work: two former Zeppelin navigators apprehended in the basement of a new hospital in Bremen, at it with pneumatic drills, in pursuit of gold sovereigns stashed there, so they believed, by British intelligence.

4. No prank too small. He skipped paying in hotels; he left items that would rot with great effect such as prawns or cod fillets under the floorboards or in the curtain rails of his room. He phoned the fire brigade. He rewired the control mechanism for traffic lights. He would arrange deliveries of cement-mixers full of cement to people who had no interest in cement (such as the department of theology at Göttingen university – the driver waved a signed order from the professor).

5. He loved both showing off his imperfect subjunctives and pretending that he didn't speak a word of German. His summation: "The one big drawback to speaking German is that, by in large, you can only speak it with Germans."

His vendetta was self-financing. One of his superior routines was raising funds from former SSists (the first pan-European organisation) to spring Hess from Spandau jail, or to raise petrol-money for Hitler who was circling the earth in a flying saucer. "If it's what people want to hear, they'll hear it no matter how bad your accent or story is."

My father would leave package holiday brochures in my grandfather's path. One year, my grandfather did book a holiday in Spain and for the three months before he left my father floated around the house because (a) he didn't have to worry about my grandfather landing in choky and (b) he had managed to change his mind. This euphoria was erased when my grandfather returned, bronzed, with a suitcase full of dosh that he had swindled out of an SS zechtour in Madrid.

He bought a car (a Zephyr, the talk of the street) with the proceeds and permitted me to learn how to drive it, but not to sit the test. "An Englishman has no need of a piece of paper to certify his sense of courtesy and consideration for others: we are natural motorists."

I found myself chauffeuring him around the country, frisking the nation for obscure bookshops that might be harbouring some S and H, so they could be ssshhed by my grandfather. He wanted his gravestone to read "S? H? Who?".

Around this time my mother started to noticeably hope that he would be imprisoned or that some assassin envoyed by defrauded Bavarians would track him down. It galled her enormously that her curtains were thirty years old, but there was a car worth half the house parked outside.

My grandfather on being brought to book: "One finds it hard to imagine anyone tracing me to Macclesfield. It's a place that doesn't exist for the outside world. Just as for many people here the outside world has no existence."

Walking over to an olive warehouse 1.1

I closed the car door and traversed the street, which seemed to have swelled to almost unfordable dimensions.

Worrying amounts of my life are parking, double parking, triple parking on my consciousness.

What I won't write 1.7

?????????????????????????

Obituaries rained down as I approached the olive entrance. *He was on the verge of doing something quite unique with the Ionians when ...* I shoved them aside. If you haven't zetted hat-raisingly by the time you're fifty, you're working on forgetfulness's farm. As Featherstone once causticked, the only way I would ever do anything unique with the Ionians would be to stencil their fragments onto a hippopotamus' rump. I resolved, if I survived this, to hire a hippopotamus and after it had been suitably adorned, to deliver it to Featherstone.

I was one step away. I could see that there was no one around inside. The apparatus of office life was on display, but no employees. I tried the door. Closed. No bell. I hammered for a while. No one tried to shoot me. I didn't know what to do.

The door was manifestly capable of excluding an ex-philosopher with more calories than he knew what to do with and I was pondering whether it would be appropriate to ram the car through the frontage, when checking around the corner, I discovered a passageway which led to the back of the olivery, an iron stairway and an open door.

I gave my gun some fresh air; if I was in the wrong place, no one was going to laugh at me.

I ventured in a step or two at a time, poised for event. I advanced along a dark corridor for years, until I heard voices. Ahead of me was a large storage area, with a chain dangling from a pulley. Moving with stealth that would seem incompatible with a pudgy philosopher, I fermi'd forward and peered down over the railing.

Hubert was below me. I'm not going to be bending under the weight of plaudits for good looks, but he was looking rough. Suspended naked from the chain by his good arm, grume over his face and hair, he was a bizarre turkey in a strange butcher's window.

It must have been extremely painful, but Hubert didn't look bothered. Gagged, he had a watchful look that augured bad things for his captors if he managed to unsuspend himself and arm and leg himself. Hube's observation was fixed on the two zigs in front of him, with their backs to me, so we didn't tangle ocularly. Frankly, he was a lot cooler than I was, and I was exitable.

Congratulations

I had found Hube – an achievement which dwarfed the rest of my life – a triumph for someone who has difficulty keeping his bathroom in toothpaste. I shied away from visibility to think what next.

The sound of more people arriving. This was disheartening, but I was buttressed by the knowledge I had already reached the honourable death bracket.

"Take off the gag," a voice commanded. "Salut, Hubert."

"Salut, Erik," Hube responded.

"We're conducting an investigation, Hube."

"You a policeman now, Erik?" Hubert spoke so softly I could barely hear: was he weakened by pain or was he hushing his tones to lure them in so he could take a bite?

"A very public-spirited citizen. There are so many things

you can help us with. Thierry. Money. But first of all, how unbearable is your pain?"

"Pain, that's what I'm good at," Hube said (or that's what it sounded like). "You and the imbeciles here wouldn't have lasted five minutes in my life."

"Listen," said Erik, in the monotonous drone of a statistician doing a Z-transformation. "We know you're an honorary perpetual, we know you're hard. But you topped Thierry, you know where your money is, you may even know where Thierry stashed his money. You're going to hang there until you tell us. Why not get it over with?"

I raised my head to get a shot of the visuals. Erik, it had to be said, was the sort of person who got photographed a lot next to mass graves: paint-strippingly unpleasant. Not a man to be in proximity with in an olive warehouse.

Next

I studied the chain and wondered what to do. There were three of them, and I couldn't envisage any ballistic exchange doing me any favours. What I needed was the assistance of a PhD in violence such as Hube; it would help if he were liberated. I wondered if I shot at the chain, whether I had much chance of hitting it, and if I did hit it, whether it might snap. It was guaranteed that if I was trying to hit the chain, I would miss it. On the other hand, if I tried to be clever, and didn't try to hit the chain, I'd doubtless miss what I was aiming at, but I wouldn't necessarily hit the chain.

Hard vs. Hard

"I don't want to disappoint you," Hube said, "but I've got one arm, one leg, one eye, I'm haemophiliac and I'm dying of a very fashionable disease. To be quite honest, if you want something from me, you're better off buying me a drink."

This wasn't true, the robbery we should have been committing was as dear to Hubert was anything. Denying him that was the greatest torture, but Hube wasn't going to unharden. I had to (x) admire Hube's tranquillity and (y) do something and (z) do it quick.

How to get out of really hairy situations

The secret of extricating yourself from dangerous or dire predicaments is simple: don't get into them in the first place.

I would have agreed to several centuries of nine o' clock lectures to be unolived warehoused.

"I have to do something," I said with enough volume to feed this idea into my ears. I kept volleying this along the walls of my skull, aspiring by battology to battle.

More eavesdropping

"Says here in the paper, Hubert, you should be robbing a bank. But it looks to me as if you're hanging from a chain about to have your olives cut off with a pair of bolt cutters."

"It's no use being nice to me, Erik."

"They do remove inhibition, bolt-cutters. One guy, when I trimmed his zeb, it flew across the room like a champagne cork. But you can relax, Hubert, you're amongst friends, you don't have to put on a show for us. Régis is angry with you for descending Thierry. I'm not. I owed him a pile of money, so you saved me a wedge. But I tell you what, I'm off for a few hours to part the parts of a bored housewife, but then I'll come back and we can talk. You've just arrived, you have a nice breeze to keep your pecker up."

"Why don't I hit him a bit?" asked another voice.

"Because," Erik replied grabbing a claw of hair on Hube's forehead (he had never got the haircut right), "in here is the information we want. You tap him, and you might tap him into the next world. I won't insult Hube by asking him any questions yet, he's only been stretched for a few hours."

"I think we should move," Hube said, still softly.

"Why?"

"We were seen when your friends snatched me. The Professor'll probably be on his way here."

"No one saw us," intervened one of the shadows, crushing the loathsome silverfish of Hubert's assertion underfoot.

"He's honest," Hube commented, "but he's too zozo to have noticed."

"If the Professor wants to come, I can talk to him too."

"I wouldn't if I were you. He'll be furious."

"Angry philosophers don't worry me."

"He's not a philosopher. That's just a joke. He used to be in the Legion, but he kept on killing people without being asked to. You know the three Viets killed in Arles last month?"

"The drug business?"

"That's what everyone thinks. We were in town, we go back to the car. The Prof looks at the side of the car. I can't see anything but he screams there's some paint missing. Old man on a bench tells us some Viet brushed it parking his car, and Viet had gone into a bar. So we go in, these three Viets are at a table. Did he ask whose car it was? Not him. He just gave them two in the head each. 'I wanted to be sure,' he said."

Erik leaned in close to Hube, as welcoming as a Zettelmeyer wheeled dozer.

"Arles?"

"Yeah."

"Last month?"

"Yeah."

"Three Viets?"

"Yeah."

"That's strange because I thought I shot them. Or maybe it was another trio. A really bad day for Franco-Vietnamese relations."

Hube didn't have anything to say. Erik pushed his stare

for a moment and then laughed. "You see, Hubert, I can lie too."

Cretan Liar

I had cerebral space for: this is an interesting update on the Cretan Liar.

And: why was Hubert giving me such a build-up? However little credence they gave to Hube's fabrications, they would be zapping me on sight.

Where my life went wrong ?.?

My life: wasted. What I should have done was join a gun club at the age of eighteen and practise on the range for three or four hours every day. Then I could have sauntered down, distributed fatalities magisterially, and rolled off for lunch.

Here we go

Erik left. One of his minions took advantage of this to whack Hube's ribs with a baseball bat. It's interesting that the French adopt such hauteur towards the Americans when they are totally enslaved culturally.

My brilliant patience had paid off. The odds were evening out. Me and surprise against the two robber-chandelier guards. Mild annoyance towards Erik for exiting since I now had no excuse for waiting. I couldn't gull myself into thinking that it would be better to wait, that they might wander off and leave me to unchain Hubert.

I crouched some more. Every second felt fat, felt good. I noticed I had delayed ten minutes. All I had to do was get up on my legs and start blasting. The distance was fifteen to twenty feet. Hard to miss one would say, but then I miss the toilet bowl at closer range.

A phone faintly ripened with call. It rang until one of

them went to answer. Confirmation that it was a four-way. I was still revelling in the passage of time, when the one who had a black-eye (reverse head-butt?) picked up a comic and announced helpfully, "I'm off for a good crap."

The signal for my entrance. I gave him a few seconds to detrouser.

I crept down, sailing the stairs without creaks or reports. A long corridor, at the end of which would be the comic-reader. I forwarded. Turned the corner, a door was marked in slanting letters: Gents, Women, Visitors from Outer Space (offices encourage the proliferation of feeble but self-satisfied humour). As Solon observed some time ago, there are many things a man will see that he'd rather not. This door was one of them.

I was about to do something rather unsporting. Kill someone through a toilet-door. Remorse mantled me, but my mother hadn't raised me to be shot by a semi-literate in an olive warehouse (what she had raised me for I never ascertained). Academic life 'n' its zebra labels had grown endless joy.

I felt bad about my forthcoming unilateral declaration of fatal intent, but what worried me more than killing the enthroned reader, was not killing him. What held me back was that once the shooting started, I couldn't ask for a coffee break.

I trained the gun, centering it on the area of the door likely to be fronting for the comic-reader. "Oh well," I said, fully expecting my reception of that thing we dub reality to be abruptly terminated.

Nothing happened. The safety catch was the wrong way. I flipped it and fired. Deafening after deafening. Louder and longer shooting than I had expected, pock-marking the door. I let off three, but then, in the way you do when you're cooking, there's the temptation to add a little more of an ingredient. I emptied the gun, pulled out the police service revolver and hit the ground (no harm in a quick veneration to Zam), because it's the fashion in shoot-outs, and having reduced my target-area I waited for number two to appear.

I waited. Then I heard Hubert, hoarse and faint. "I got him."

Still counting on being shot, I peeked around the corner to see Hube continuing with his hanging, but number two lying on the ground, as if sun-bathing with clothes on. "I've been waiting to do that all day," Hube said. Evidently the gunfire had distracted number two from his most important duty, which was keeping a close eye on Hube, who, with the only limb that could be described as fulfilling its contractual obligations, had given him an almighty kick in the face, nulling all of number two's sensory revenue.

Unchaining Hube was tricky, because technical stuff has never been my forte. While Hube pulled himself together, I walked over to number two who sounded as if he was mumbling about Zemes mate, and gave him a series of vicious kicks. Then I went over to a corner and parked the contents of my stomach on the floor. Fear's tough to digest.

"You don't seem surprised to see me," I remarked to Hube.

"I'm not. Though you left it a bit late. We do have a bank to rob."

We chained up number two, making a woozy return to participation in the end of the twentieth century. "How did you find me?" Hubert asked, not making any attempt to conceal the barrel of his gun. "We were all out looking for you. We got lucky and spotted your car."

"Okay," said Hubert jamming his gun into number two's ear, "ready for the big one?" There was a click of an empty chamber, though I think it took number two, busy with terror, a while to appreciate this.

Hubert put a bullet in his pocket. "Keep this to remember you're dead, but that I've brought you back from the underworld. Lead a good life from now on." Hube checked the toilet and found the comic-reader had decamped, un-wounded, since there was no blood.

The skinhead was still sitting in the car. "We've got an hour to get back to Toulon," Hube observed. "Is there anyone, philosopher or non-philosopher, who can solve this problem better than you?"

I got us up to 200k, somewhat distracted by Hubert insisting that I read and construe from Epictetus, a fellow raspberry ripple, and Zenonian, the volume perched on the wheel-well. Hubert commented on the absence of the rat and the presence of the skinhead.

?????????????????????????

From the roof we looked down on the van which housed the Corsican and was acting as the mind of the vast police body spread out around the centre of Toulon, where the earmarked bank was waiting to be robbed.

We knew the Corsican was inside because he had started orbiting Jocelyne again and had outlined in considerable detail how the security would be managed. The sun seemed to be shining exclusively for me, its shine reaching into me to push the happiness button that only light can reach.

Our rooftop wasn't close to the main square, because all the buildings that bordered the square were cop-topped (large numbers of policemen are very sincere praise) but we still had a good, if distant view. The square wasn't terribly pedestrianed, but there were passers-by who seemed to linger longer than the attractions of the square merited, and as we recced, two kids who unfurled a banner reading, "Go, Thought, Go" incurred a massive police overkill.

"Our public and the history books await us," said Hube, unzipping. "Sorry about the blatantness," he added as he trained his urethra undercover policewards. He sent down, four storeys, a ticker tape of urine. Hube's rain made shrunken thunder on the van's roof. A woman in the building opposite watered zinnia in a window box.

We expedited ourselves to the ground floor and thence to the other side of town, to a small bank where Hubert had opened an account the previous month.

Some four minutes to closing time, we reached the counter. With a big smile, Hube watched the teller count out the money. A sum large enough to hurt, to prove that we could have done some real damage, but not too large. "We don't want people to think we're in it for the money," as Hube put it.

Outside, there was a tinge of melancholy, because although the concentric circles of policemen around the main square a mile away didn't know it, the robbery had taken place, the money squeezed into wires under their noses. The Thought Gang was in retirement.

???????????????????????????

We had the farewell supper.

"There's nothing more we can do," Hube said. "That was the end of bank robbery. All that's left is not to blemish our record by getting arrested in a supermarket with a frozen chicken between our legs. Know when to start, know when to stop."

I had been thinking the same thing about the zinziberaceous seasoning on our fish – another flake or two would have collapsed the gastronomic structure into monotaste; the border between getting it right and getting it wrong is poorly signposted.

We had left Toulon and driven up to Draguignan, where there was (a) a famous restaurant that had been recommended to us and (b) although no one said anything to that effect, our move to Draguignan did fit in with the time-honoured technique of making yourself scarce, a nod to the tradition of doing a bunk. Draguignan, like Macclesfield, is your seven figure guess for the hideout of big time criminals.

Who you know, not what you know

Without Jocelyne, we wouldn't have met Cécile.

Seeing Cécile had been Jocelyne's idea; the kidnapping Cécile's. Jocelyne knew that Cécile, who had skived off from her bank by pleading an iffy ticker, was running out of grace on medical grounds, and was prospecting for a new excuse to absent herself from work but still get the cheque to support herself, her kids and her mother.

Cécile would certainly come under heavy suspicion, transferring the money from the central police account (used to pay the Old Bill's bills) out to our account, and not alerting the authorities until she returned home to receive a message giving the whereabouts of her kidnapped mother.

But there was no way they could prove it. We weren't going to tell them it was a set-up, and neither was Cécile. Cécile didn't even want a cut, all she was seeking was a sound pretext for a nervous breakdown and a paid stay at home, which surely having your mother abducted by fearsome bank robbers was (though we did have an understanding that at some distant future Jocelyne would lend her a modest sum that couldn't really arouse suspicions, but that would be handy).

"Is it that easy?" I had asked Cécile in regard to the transfer.

"Well, in principal it takes two people to okay it, but in principal marriages are meant to last forever."

Draguignan supper 1.2

We were tired as we investigated the state of zymurgy.

I was, much to my horror, faced with choices again and to my surprise I sensed a taste for frugality, for solitude, for thinking some thoughts, which weren't catered for Chez Odile; a long buried Eddie was pushing his hand through the soil.

Hube was detongued; he drank more than usual, his cog-turning look gone. Since we had met, this was was his first evening off. He slurped his zeb wine unappreciatively.

I was put in mind of the ancient Egyptian thief, Amenkau, who having lifted precious metals from a tomb, gave half a deben of silver to the scribe, Oshefitemwese, for a jar of wine and half a deben to Penementenakht for a tub of honey. They were having a party to celebrate the smoothness of their getaway. "We took the wine to the house of the overseer, put two measures of honey in it and we drank it." Fine sentiments from their trial, over three thousand years ago, brought about by that deathless mistake, blowing your wad in public. As we were; the police would have done better to have staked out the high-class steak houses.

Where my life went wrong 1000.1

"No one has ever kissed me like that," Zoe had said.

I've always felt particularly grateful to Cheops for building his great pyramid, since, despite the discomfort of making love on stone, it was a memorable moment, even without the aid of the most monumental bed in the world. Although these things are slippery to bring to judgment, I'd wager that was the zeb moment of my life. Once I climbed down from that pyramid, it was all downhill.

The night was cool, the stars leered enviously, but the whole universe was our blanket. Zoe was, as the Egyptologist, benefiting most from the arrangement. I had reservations about the venue, but unlike a flagpole, it's hard to fall off a pyramid. After we nuked, I had confirmation, (not needed), that all the answers were packed into a 5'6, 34, 32, 34 Egyptologist, a book to be read in braille. We sent a column of passion fire up into the night as far as a column can go, a greater, more eternal construction than our stone mattress. Pinnacling at the pyramid's pinnacle taught me that there's an awful lot of darkness and cold in the extent of the extant, and real warmth comes not in suns but in skin packs.

Writing what I won't write

It's embarrassing that the answer is so simple, so right in front of us. The sages have said so, but like most of the truths, we're bored with it. Change it round, say it backwards, make it foreign: evol, evol, evol. Unstealable money.

Not that it's easy to get. Or to keep.

There can only be one. The one and the many. On top of the pyramid, I grasped perfection. I was young enough to have a powerful generator in my breast, but old enough not to be taken in easily. We went down to the Nile and watched the ziczacs zigzag.

I loved the way Zoe hitched, (with the elegantest thumb). I loved the way Zoe queued for the cinema; I loved the way Zoe looked with make-up; I loved the way Zoe looked without make-up. I could go on. The only thing she ever did I didn't wildly overapprove of was her telling me she didn't want to see me anymore, a fortnight later back in Cambridge.

"Philosophers make good lovers," she said, "but lousy husbands." She was joking. "You're too young. You're the kind kind, but you're not yet the marrying kind." She wasn't joking. She was two months older than me.

My profession is the science of knowledge, the polishing of thought, but if you were to ask me why is it that I'm sitting in a restaurant in Draguignan with a dicey set of boozed-up organs, and she's in Cornwall with two children, and barely remembers me when I phone every third year, I'd say: not a clue. It wasn't as if there was one argument, one failure, one dispute.

Zoe was the seventh daughter of a seventh daughter. Poor family from Salford. She was the complete opposite to me, the impractical only child. Tough. Organised. My pleas, in person, epistular and telephonic, were filed away in really ancient history.

The East End was my final assault. I had wangled her new address, but as I approached the street, there was a power cut, a complete blackout for miles ahead of me. I couldn't see the street names, couldn't see the numbers of the houses. I waited in the gloom for half an hour, then went to a pub in the electrified part of town. The next morning the police sledgehammered through my stupor.

That's it. So long, life. Did I love more than most, or am I just an oversensitive slob and zero?

When they crack open my heart, they'll find a perfect miniature of Zoe.

Draguignan 1.3

"So where's Jocelyne?" Hube asked again. She was nearly two hours late, which was particularly perturbing since she usually was encased in the minute she had promised. I was worried something nasty had happened to her, and worried (though to a much lesser extent) that she had owned up to her life being littered enough without an Eddie-sized mess to add. Normally I have the feeling with women that they've mistaken me for someone more interesting, more stylish, more amusing and that at any moment I'm going to reveal my true identity.

Having been unusually docile throughout the meal, Hubert came to life when he heard a group of citizens at the next table commenting that after the day's events the police should give their salaries to charity. Hube offered them all a drink.

We derestauranted into the night, arguably the two best-fed, most erudite, most successful bank robbers in this sector of the Milky Way.

Unfortunate exoduses from restaurants 1.1

One thing I would like to share is that it does your digestion no good, when, as you make your way to your car, you have a senior police officer jump out of the non-visible, especially when it is the senior police officer you have placed at the top of the list of most laughed-at police officers of all time, when it is the police officer whose career you have recently trodden on and heard go pop like a loathsome arthropod, when it is the police officer whose flat you have trashed and so on ... and when he's pointing a gun and you're not.

It was effectively the last thing I wanted to see, after (a) Featherstone garlanded with teenage prostitutes of every nationality and of good health and (b) an elephant's rear heading towards me with firm intentions of making contact with the ground underneath me. Nevertheless, there was a part of me that was cheered to see that the forces of law and order weren't completely hopeless.

The notion that we might deny our Thought Gangness passed through my mind without stopping. He knew. We knew he knew. We knew he knew[3]. He didn't seem to have a prepared speech, not even the utilitarian "you're under arrest". He glared at us, his face writhing with anger. Language simply didn't seem to be able to provide him with the services he required.

Taking into account the frequency of killing on this orb, it's odd that look hasn't been immortalised on Z-twists, but I can't recall seeing it in the galleries. Unmistakeable: man about to kill someone he's really looking forward to killing.

"Shouldn't you be taking statements instead of hanging around outside three-star restaurants," enquired Hube with what sounded like genuine curiosity. The stockpiling of rage on Versini's face made me realise we had reached that stage where (should we be in line for it) our biographers would be breathing out relief because they could go down the pub. That biography-concluding moment.

"I mean," said Hube, "it won't look good in court, will it".

I was uneasy, because although I couldn't summon up a single justification for the Corsican not shooting us, truth to tell, I was hoping he wouldn't. Much as I admired the purity of Hubert's nonchalance, it wasn't abetting our longevity. I knew that he wasn't bluffing when he had said that under no circumstances would he go back to jail. I suppose he was aiming to deride while he could.

Versini spoke: "I should have stayed. There's plenty to do. Every policeman of my rank or above has been phoning up to tell me what a cretin I am. I could have stayed and waited for my letter of dismissal." He spoke slowly and unevenly, like someone who had only learned to speak French that day. "But I walked out. I thought I might as well go somewhere quiet and have a good meal. Look what I find: my saviours."

I applauded the stomach-led evening, homage to Zao Jun. However, two ideas were vying for the title of most amusing in the front room of his mind: our getting a hundred years in the clink or our getting blown away.

"May I say two things?" asked Hubert, taking an avalanche of hatred that slid off the Corsican's face – who assented by not shooting.

"First, in case you didn't work it out, your van was pissed on this afternoon, and it was me that was doing the pissing."

"And the second?" The Corsican was beginning to find it funny; he was evolving that smile people wear when they are shooting people they could spend all day shooting. Time had time off, and I perceived a car that looked like Jocelyne's pulling into the far end of the car park.

Yet again, I wasn't in the mood to be ventilated, and it did enter my thought tureen how nice it would be if it were Jocelyne. If it were Jocelyne, silently getting out of car. If it were Jocelyne, silently getting out of her car, and slinking up behind the Corsican. If it were Jocelyne silently getting out of the car and slinking up behind the Corsican, carrying one of the home-made coshes Hubert had shown her how to make ("You can't beat cash in a cosh," he had said, demonstrating the explosive effect several francs in a sock could have). If it were Jocelyne, silently getting out of her car and slinking up behind the Corsican, carrying one of the home-made coshes Hubert had shown her how to make and hitting the Corsican so hard it would tighten his Zaufahl's folds.

I was really straining the will-muscle, striving to midwife that concept into the world; I was also thinking that it was vital to keep the Corsican talking, but as always on these occasions when you have to talk, you can only engineer the most inappropriate vowels and consonants. The only words I found in my mouth were: "So how does it feel to be the number one dickhead in France?"

"So," said Hubert, "how does it feel to be the number one dickhead in France?'

I could now see Jocelyne moving towards us, but there was too much car park between her and and the Corsican for the cosh to get indexed in my biography.

Opportunities

Don't say we don't get them. We do, we just don't use them.

There was no need for Jocelyne. Although it had looked as if the Corsican's rage had turned its back on the situation, leaving him with a merry executional mood, it bolted back into play. If he had stuck to pulling the trigger, he would have been all right; but he wanted to enjoy a dismissory word, and his fury was so gigantic, it was like trying to coax an outrageously fat zebra down a plughole. He didn't manage to fire some full stops into our life sentences because …

He gurgled a little and then slumped inelegantly, joining the ground in its insensibility.

"You see," said Hubert, not looking at all surprised, and

prodding the supine Versini with a toe, "we're untouchable. Destiny even does our laundry."

It did seem a bit soft, a senior policeman swooning like that. Cardiac? Epilepsy? On closer inspection Versini was breathing in a meek fashion, which seemed to disappoint Hubert who had been savouring the prospect of giving him the kiss of life.

A couple emerging from the restaurant offered assistance. "No, our friend will be fine," Hube assured them. Jocelyne, grousing about her two flat tyres, went into the restaurant to avoid straying into Versini's consciousness, while we loaded him into our car and started driving.

Hube no longer had the glint in his eye. Versini was manacled with his own handcuffs, and Hube did remark what a pity it was we had hung up our blag since it would have been bonus zest to have used Versini's gun in a robbery. "It would be super to strip him naked, paint a Greek tag on him, something pithy, and then dump him outside a police station." Hube trotted the idea verbally but you could sense he was talking about something that wouldn't happen.

He put his arm around the shocked Versini. "I'm sorry you're so angry. Because without you, we'd be nothing. You're as much part of the team as we are. I'd really like to buy you a present."

At Hube's suggestion we drove down to the coast. Versini looked worn, but not really twitchy, reasoning I suppose that if we had wanted to kill him we would have dusted him back at the restauro, and that whatever diversion we had in mind, it wouldn't be effecting his subsequent career as quailbreeder, newspaper vendor, whatever. I didn't question Hubert, I was merely the driver, not the driving force.

We stopped and promenaded out into the darkness. We were on some cliffs and it seemed to me our good fortune had been doing too much overtime for us to play footsie with a dark abyss.

"We're going to get you," Versini said mechanically,

probably not able to think of anything more original to say. And it's true – in the long run, you get nabbed, unless you're prepared to sit in a jungle somewhere or criminal big and run the country.

"So how would you explain our liberty?" Hube queried.

"You've been lucky."

Hube undid Versini's handcuffs. I couldn't understand what he was up to; I didn't share his fascination for the equations of law and order: all I wanted was a raid-free bed.

"I get the feeling," Hube said, appraising Versini, "that you'd like to hit me." Versini shrugged in affirmation.

"All right, since it means so much to you, I'll grant you a swipe. One on one, the Prof won't interfere." Hube tossed aside his weaponry ostentatiously and made the international gesture of come on, so beloved in bars all over the world. I debated whether Hube really meant it about me not intervening: he wasn't at his best.

But then neither was Versini, he took a swing at where he reckoned Hubert and his Zeis's glands should have been, but H had made himself unavailable for punching. Too fast for me to see, but not too fast for my ears to hear, Hube implanted his knee in Versini's love department, and threw in an elbow to the Zuckerkandl's fascia free.

"You're not much good at this, are you?" observed Hube as Versini was bunched up at his feet. "However, we have to discuss this idea of yours, that you have the right to arrest me. My question to you is: why should I let you arrest me? Let me promise, that if you can persuade me, I'm happy to put myself in your custody."

Versini was still quadrupeding. He wasn't used to (x) having his life destroyed (y) being kicked in the balls (z) people wanting to mix it dialectically. Whatever he said, I was wishing he was loading a succinctness. But his day had produced alalia (or senior police management courses didn't include courses on disputation with bragging blaggers).

"Is it that you think you're better than me? Let's test the

mettle," said Hube, "I've got one hand, it navigates the world for me." Hube produced a flick knife, fired it and then crouching down, fitted the grip behind his right knee, so as he crouched right down, the blade was firmly held in place by the backs of his leg. Then he slowly skewered his hand, pushing his palm onto the blade.

This made me rather ill – it's not what you want to see after a large meal. Versini sprawled untongued, perhaps hoping that we'd shoot ourselves in the temple for an encore: self-eradicating criminals.

Hubert, pallorous and saggy by the car's headlights, reached awkwardly into a pocket to draw out another knife and chucked it in front of Versini, in case Versini had inhibitions about using the one that had traversed his veins. "Your turn," said Hube. Versini peered at the butterfly knife in a fashion that broadcast his refusal to even pretend he was considering it, although Hube waited a moment to see if bravado would suddenly ride out.

"The conquest of the self ... ," here Hube, realising there was no need to elaborate, confined the rest of his discourse to his brainpan. The virtue of self-discipline is a great one, and one of my chief deficiencies, but I think I'll plump for pacification of the ego by easy stages of propaganda, inviting it to a zillion lunches.

Versini's hebetude was too early; I doubt if Hubert could have pulled a trigger, and it had occurred to me that the gun I had wasn't loaded. But it had been a long day.

"We're stopping," Hube announced. "We're stopping, not because we're afraid of getting caught; we're stopping because we've finished. Here's what I propose: acting on information received, you go to the restaurant, where, heroically, you attempt to arrest us solo, but a sympathiser mallets you and you're seized by the evil Thought Gang.

"You're brought here to the coast to be rubbed out, but you fight loose, you struggle to retrieve your weapon, you have a shoot-out with the gang, leaving ballistic evidence everywhere. Wounded and out of ammunition, the Gang jumps thirty feet into the water in a desperate attempt to flee justice, leaving their empty guns, covered in their blood and finger prints. You call for assistance but by the time it arrives, there's no sign of the bodies, they aren't found, which is surprising, but there are strong currents here, and you move from being a laughing stock and leading dolt to a hero.

"And, as you're no doubt thinking, should we turn up later, well, that's not so good, but it doesn't dent your bravery and your version. But as you can imagine, we're looking for a peace and quiet period."

Versini didn't move as he inspected the ramifications of this fabrication. For him it was if not a good exit, at least a respectable one; here he was a big enough arse for the whole of France to sit on, and now he was getting a chance to be mistaken for a policeman.

He didn't say yes, but he didn't say no. He didn't say anything as he lay on the ground zeros in his Z-charts.

Under Hubert's directions, I assumed a variety of positions to empty the guns, immobilising our car, firing Versini's right in front of him so he would be impregnated with gunpowder, so the forensic boys would find what they were looking for. Hube wanted some of my blood too, expecting me to slice myself like a loaf of bread; I picked at one of my cuts, like a small schoolboy, to haemoglobin my weapon and the undergrowth.

We left Versini, with warnings not to follow us or to move for twenty minutes, but he was giving the impression he wouldn't be rushing anywhere for a long time. We hiked back to the main road where Jocelyne was waiting.

"You two need your own hospital."

???????????????????????????

Each according to his abilities: Hube was getting rid of most of the money.

"I want to give it away," he said.

"That's a lot of money," I said.

"There are a lot of charities," he said.

Manumitting rats

I was detailed to free Thales, so I took him to Cannes, the biggest sewer I know of. Perhaps I'm being rattist, perhaps he would have preferred to be released into a museum or a concert hall, rather than an environment of corruption and waste, but that's what he got.

I opened the cage and Thales sniffed the air of freedom, then padded off like a zmudzin, not realising if goat cheese and gut-stuffing was really his bag, he was making a big error.

???????????????????????????

I spend a lot of time waiting for the sound of sledgehammered door or incoming gunfire, but things are ludicrously quiet.

Shock horror

I haven't been beaten-up, assaulted, or shot at for days. Inexplicably, I wake up early feeling like getting up; my mood is good, my health like a zaruk of limbo-dancers. Such haleness is a nuisance since it gives me no excuse for not doing something.

At the kitchen table, with piles of guns, and bits of guns, Hubert is sitting vacantly, like someone who has ordered too much and can't eat it all. He selects an item now and then and puts it away into a large orange hold-all.

"I was afraid," he says. "You're the only one I can tell that to."

We circumnavigated the silence, until, having worked out what he was referring to, I rejoined: "It didn't show."

"Perhaps that's it, the brave are those who do their whimpering in secret. Those who can afford a cowardice room."

"What would have happened if I'd had some money when you tried to rob me?"

"I'd have had some money, and I'd be nothing."

"What I don't understand is I remember explaining at the hotel reception that I was penniless. How come you didn't hear?"

"Maybe I didn't want to."

We viewed some memories on the skull screen.

Goodbye

"What are you going to do?" I asked, never having seen Hube sit in a chair for so long.

"After such a long career in bank robbery? Where can a hardened criminal such as me go? There's only one place: jail."

He wasn't joking. His intention was however to go to jail without the traditional assistance of those prison-feeders, the police. His plan: to break into Les Baumettes, a maximum security jail and to challenge Emile, the king of the perpetuals to a duel, a holmgang. I pointed out the unwelcoming nature of maximum security jails.

"That's true," Hube conceded, "but whatever they say about security, the place is designed to keep people in, not people out. And I do know the place well, don't forget."

Switching on the radio to full blast, he picked up one of the Mac-10s, and tugging the trigger obliterated a large zone of the wall separating the kitchen from one of the bedrooms. "Let's see what Emile has to say about that."

"Why not just go off and enjoy yourself somewhere?"

"There isn't much time, and there are more people I would like to say goodbye to inside than out. I don't want to wait for it by a swimming-pool. No, I want to see Emile's face. And I want it to be a fair fight, that'll tear him up. No, seeing his face and then blowing it off, that'll be something. If after all that, I'm still alive, I'll take it as a hint I should relax."

I tried dissuading Hube a bit. Frankly, at the end, whether you settle for grouting the tiles in the bathroom or breaking into a prison to dispatch the top dog, it's your choice.

Hube zipped up the bag.

"And when they catch me, I can always say I was putting myself inside because the police can't be relied on to do it. It'd be worth it for that one line. Beat that for an outro."

Reaching into a pocket, Hube pulled out a coin and thumbed it over to me, making it whirl through the air; oddly enough, I caught it.

A slightly irregular shape, I recognised it as an electrum stater, a recumbent lion looking backwards, a typical design of the early coinage of Miletus. Its complexion was impressive for a coin more than two and a half thousand years old, a timed traveller.

"Perhaps the boys themselves handled it," said Hubert. " wanted to leave you with a souvenir, something that's smugglable into prison; something that in emergency could buy you a few drinks."

This was perhaps the profit that Thales had made with his olive-presses; this was the fee that Gorgias and Protagoras palmed, the remuneration that Socrates shunned. A coin possibly knocked off by Ionian blaggers: a fertile region inventing coins and thought, enslaving metal, imprinting it with ideas. Strangely, holding the stater, I felt so close to the coin-coiners, as if I were shaking their hands.

Hube pulled back the sleeve of his sweatshirt to reveal a thick black Z on his forearm, a tattoo so solid, it was more as if Hube was attached to the Z, rather than the Z being attached to Hube.

"Z is for zetetic," he said smiling.

Z. The last letter of our alphabet, the seventh of the first alphabets, Hebrew and Phoenician, the sixth of the Greek. The Hebrew *zayin* from the Hieratic letter 𐤆 and linked to the Syriac *zaino:* weapons. Possibly descended from the Sumerian battle-axe sign, *zag*. When the Romans conquered Greece they were forced to borrow the letter Z. It stands like a brand on the forehead of Roman culture, skivy, porter to the Greeks. Z, the letter chosen as the most important symbol, the symbol for atomic number, the symbol for protons, the element of the elements, the things that give character to the universe. The one and the many. Z, in the international code of signals flags, means "I am commencing to tow" or "Ready to be towed". Z, the medieval Roman numeral for 2000. I could go on. "We might see each other again; stranger things have happened," Hube said as he left.

Leavings

As quietly as he had walked into my life, Hube walked out. Departures in themselves can be exceedingly dull. You hear the sound of receding steps and often there is no pull. Walking outs rarely reveal their significance straight away; usually you feel no different a minute after than a minute before. They're delayed action, they gestate. Even the weakest of us can sustain a loss for a few hours, a few days, a few weeks; it's the months that teach us what's missing.

Hube leaves me intellectually much as he found me: albeit with a selection of diverting memories, and something that if it's not optimism, would be hard to tell apart.

Bit of profundity for this page?

Perhaps it was Hube rescuing me in the olive warehouse, rather than me rescuing him.

Things to do

1. Move up to Normandy. No one is seriously going to look for me there. A whole region's worth of Macclesfield, where a strange Englishman might get some teaching work. Never too late to change?

Make Greeks. Get zet.

2. Phone Jocelyne.

3. Sort out Western Philosophy. Mere interior decorating? Is the mind mined? This feels like page one in disguise, but then as you get older, it's harder to kid yourself.

I think of
watch-makers, clock-makers,
such as Zach, Zachariah,
Zacharie, Zachau,
Zademach, Zagnani,
Zahm, Zahne,
Zahringer, Zanchi,
Zanker, Zanlich,
Zantner, Zantzig,
Zappeck, Zaringer,
Zaug, Zech (incorrectly
credited with the invention
of the fuzee),
Zehng, Zeissler,
Zeitelmeier, Zeitz and Zucker. But, as we all know, the solution to a really difficult problem ... is to leave it.

zabuton	flat cushion
zakat	(Islam) tax
Zajc, Ivan	1832-1914. Croatian composer.
Zama	battle where Hannibal was finally crushed by the Romans. 202 BC.
Zamzam	sacred well at Mecca
zam-zum-mims	"giants dwelt there in old time; and the Ammonites called them Zam-zum-mims." Deuteronomy 2.20
Zantedeschia	tropical African plants
zaotar	Ancient Iranian priest
Zapodidae	jumping mice
zapote	fruit
zaptieh	Turkish policeman
zaqqûm	(Koran) food of the sinner
zarp	policeman, the Transvaal
zaruk	Arab dhow
Zaufahl's fold	plica salpingo-pharyngea
Zeami, Motokiyo	1363-1443. Japanese Noh Dramatist
zeb	(backslang) the best
Zechstein	impermeable rock system
zechtour	(German) pub-crawl
Zemaituka	tough breed of pony
Zemes mate	Lettish earth-mother goddess

zemi	tutelary spirit
Zener cards	used in esp research
zensho	Sumo tournament with undefeated wrestler
zet/zetetic	(Greek ζητεῖν, to seek) investigating
zig	(French) type, man
Zin	biblical state
Ziphiids	family of whales
Ziusudra	Sumerian hero of the Flood
zmudzin	Polish pony
znuz	frost, frozen
zocle	socle, plinth
Zoilus	Fourth century BC, savage critic
zonitid	snail of the family Zonitidae
zonkey	offspring of a zebra and a donkey
zonule of Zinn	membrane adjacent to lens
zonure	lizard
zope	a bream
zori	Japanese sandal
zozo	(French) idiot, clod
Zuckerkandl's fascia	retro-renal fascia
zuclopoenthixol	generic anti-psychotic drug
zuihitsu	Japanese literary genre of random notes

zumbador	South American humming-bird
Zurvan	Iranian god of time
Zwaardemaker, Hendrik	1857-1930. Dutch physiologist, originator of system for classifying smells.
zygite	a rower in a bireme or trireme
zythum	Ancient Egyptian beer
zyzzogeton	South American leaf hopper

the
Collector
Collector

To a small flat in South London comes what looks very much like a Sumerian bowl: but the bowl is the Collector Collector, clay with something to say, foreverware, a ceramic quick-change artist who was 'old' before old was invented. The bowl is about to become best friend to Rosa, who has been asked to authenticate the bowl. As the Collector Collector offers her vast swathes of unrecorded history, Rosa stuggles to centre her life, and to settle the disturbances caused by an uninvited guest, Nikki. *1001 Nights* comes to the inner city, *The Collector Collector* is unquestionably the finest novel narrated by a bowl ever written.

The Collector Collector is published by Vintage in March 1998.

I've had a planetful.

Impending owner: old, obese, ooooorotund. Only one hundred and one hairs for his barber to worry about. Jowly. Flesh dripping off his face, melted by age. Balloon. A fat-filled balloon. His belt is nearly longer than he is. Lugal. Lugal number ten thousand, four hundred and sixty twooooooo.

'Smedley will be in touch with you,' he says.

Present holder: auctioneeress. She sells the world the world. Red cotton from India under ruffled blue tweed. Ten-denier stockings. Tomato-red lipstick. An expert with one child. She has rigid thighs where big men have whimpered like small dogs, but she is still lonely.

'I thought you only used him to sue members of your own family,' she replies.

Lugals aren't strong on humour. Power rarely has a use for humour. They don't have much interest in being entertaining or popular. This one tries to act as if he has; a project perhaps to help him imagine that people are drawn to him for his charm and wit and not his integrity-crushing riches. There are lugals like that.

'No. No. Not just that.' He exposes twenty-three per cent of his teeth as a smile. 'That's if all the checks verify it's genuine.'

Genuine? The genuine ones don't look as good as me. I'm better than genuine. I'm the original, so genuine, the genuine ones look like copies, which, of course, is what they are.

'I have a good feeling about this,' she says.

'And you'll use Rosa?'

'I'm going straight to Rosa's.'

'Good. I have a lot of faith in Rosa. A lot of faith.'

Street: paved. Called King. W.1. London. England. It's been two thousand and sixteen years since I've been near the Thames. Can't say I've missed it, though I could lead you to some fascinating burial sites. Surroundings don't matter much to me. Everything's been under or near a river. Rivers, if you watch patiently enough, flicker and jag like slow, dull lightning. Water, like a lumbering drunk, has pissed and slouched all over this planet.

'It's going to rain,' he says, quite concerned. There is one tiny, feeble cloud in view. With the information available to me, I would reckon the odds on rain in the next hour as 5000–1 against.

'If I get caught in the rain, I bleed,' he says in a tone that is aiming to hook sympathy.

The auctioneeress nods, slightly oddly. He probably interprets this as sympathy, because that's what he wants, so he can take a little odd-looking sympathy. I, on the other hand, interpret it as the auctioneeress biting the inside of her mouth to stop herself laughing, because he is, in addition to being a lugal, a clown, a multi-storey car park filled with jalopies of laughability, soooooo preposterous, a baboon of prodigious risibility; I adjust his position from the early ten thousands to bring him up to just outside the supreme thousand, though I am well aware that if I am in his company for much longer he will penetrate the supreme hundred laughing stocks. Of my collectors, he is already the most mockable.

The auctioneeress looks up to the sky as if pondering its cruelty, but more likely to give her teeth the chance to hang on to her cheeks. He is, to the core, a lugal, loaded. He has lots of money; she hasn't. And while he might feel obliged to take some ribbing, outright contempt might sour relations. She needs the money

2

otherwise she wouldn't be conducting an unauctioned sale for a backhander. Child-thinking-of. Her lips have the unmistakable pursing of someone with much knowledge and little chance of making money. So much and yet so little, that is what she is thinking.

With all my medical experience, greater than any three teaching hospitals you could care to name, I have never detected a condition where drops of rain can be traded for drops of blood. And besides which, it is a mark of the lugal that whatever their quirks, they bounce like balls. You can drop them from a great height, dump them into a volcano, clobber them with a whale. They never tire in loofahing their me's and feeding them grapes. No lugal ever perished in drizzle.

He signals to a car waiting down the street. It is a vehicle fit for a lugal, a limousine with smoked windows so that he need not be sullied by passers-by's gazes.

'I don't like taking the car. Cars are nothing but metal missiles hunting each other down on the roads. Huge metal monsters hurtling at each other. Designed to kill as much as a gun. Crazy invention.' He is getting panicky, he has to walk to the car and thus expose himself for eight feet to the risk of rain, and his ear wiggling betrays the thought that once he reaches the car he will be signing up for the risk of a pile-up. The great pity about the absurdly rich is that they become absurd because none of them have the foresight to buy a wanker-alarm, someone who would accompany them and just toll at apposite moments: 'You are being soooooo wanky.' That is the danger of wild wealth, it frees you from gravity. They could hire the poor for the job, who'd have to be changed every so often like batteries because their good sense would be dissipated in the plush restaurants and chi-chi boutiques.

'You're very lucky not to have money. So lucky,' he says, the foreignness in his diction rising from eighteen per cent to a peak of twenty-nine. 'When you have money, people are simply after you, all the time. All the time. You know, I have seven teams of accountants working for me. The second checks the first, the third checks on the second, the fourth checks on the third. And so on. The first also checks on the seventh. And even if they're not stealing, they might as well be for the fees they charge. And as for my family . . . there's no end to it. This bowl is just what I want.'

'So why are you looking so miserable?'

'I'm afraid it's a trick to get my money. Someone must have heard I want one for my collection.'

'You can give me some of your money, Marius.'

'I wouldn't wish it on you. And what can you do with it? Banks go bankrupt. Companies go bust. Even top-notch banks in top-notch economies go kablooey. Civil-isations drop dead like flies. There's no safety, you have to watch all the time. You have no idea how bad it is. Say hello to Rosa for me.'

You could take his words and grind them down to quarks and you wouldn't find the slightest trace of irony. I have now slotted him in at number one hundred and fifteen. He waddles off, his gait topped up with ridicu-lousness by the gold ingots he is carrying under his shirt. Gold, the shining shunner, so beloved of the rich and the poor, playfellow of the learned, so ungiving of itself. I wonder why he doesn't employ someone to carry the fire extinguisher he has grasped in his left hand.

The auctioneeress and I get into a rickety car and drive south, across the river. 'Why?' she asks. 'Why?'

She says this sixteen times on our journey, the world roller-coasting from bitterness to amusement. A prime timeburster. In the index of the billions of vocalisations I have catalogued, this is the import that occurs most often. A sound that's been around, too. Unripe apples

4

here, soul's sigh there. If you wait long enough any word or sound gets to mean everything.

But I can't help her with her inquiry.

Rosa

Everything. Been it. Seen it. Mean it.

You think you've had a demonstrably hard time? Your job, let me guess, is made of solid odium?

Now, I've been *used*: abused, disabused, misused, mused on, underenthused, unamused, contused, bemused and even perused. Any compound of used, but chiefly used: shaving bowl, vinegar jar, cinerary urn, tomb good, pyxis, vase, rat-trap, krater, bitumen amphora, chamber pot, pitcher, executioner, doorstop, sunshade, spittoon, coal scuttle, parrot rest, museum exhibit, deity, ashtray. If you're quiet, don't fuss and take it, it's staggering what people will dump on you. If it's vile, I've had a pile – *and* I know more than five thousand languages (even if you want to get dainty about what's a language and what isn't).

Rosa puts me on a low table, folds her arms and looks down at me sternly.

'Talk,' she commands.

This is an idiotic, if not deranged thing to say to a bowl, even to a bowl like me, thin-walled, sporting the scorpion look of Samarra ware that was the rage of Mesopotamia six and a half thousand years before Rosa was born. Pottery, after all, isn't renown for its chatty nature, so why futilely address a vessel thus, even me, the bowl with soul? But Rosa is far from being unhinged.

Inevitably, I've been talked to, more than anyone would credit. Being inanimate doesn't earn you any dispensation from being buttonholed. People prefer people, will accept pets, but failing all else, they will unburden themselves to the crockery. And, naturally, supplied with sonic tools, I could chatter. I could chatter until this young lady, her flat and her city were nothing but unremarkable dust.

I'm not sure what's going on here. Lately I stick to collectors of note. Moneybags. Lugals. Those deformed by excessive wealth, those who will lay down reverence all around me. The trials of being a utensil didn't bother me for a long time, but I've become soooooo tired of indignity, of some dullard keeping terrapins or Busy Lizzies in me.

Reverence is my quarry, and giving a hint of my pedigree achieves this, age and a dash of the flash equalling venerability in the pottery game. Old? How old? Oooooold. Old before old was invented.

Does this make me a snob? Yes, I do like my collectors destructively rich and obeisant. Granted, the oofy are goofy, the disgustingly rich are often disgusting, but that's an epithet that doesn't turn up its nose at escorting those who have only moderate amounts of money and those who have none.

Rosa: cordial, respectful, relaxed.

She is, I educe, some expert, scrutinising me; this is because my last few carriers have been poorly presented individuals from a region not enjoying a reputation for probity or rectitude, or any of the qualities that make a buyer feel better about a transaction – especially when it comes to pottery worth a lottery.

The vogue for savants is white coats and frowns, slipping some solemnity under their metier to raise its importance. They like props: gauges, drills, beakers. Their investigations don't fluster me; if you have no idea of what you're looking for, you're not going to find it.

Her home appears to be Rosa's place of work. She doesn't blend in with the scrutineers I have encountered.

There are a few books, nowhere near enough to suggest outstanding scholarly competence, and as she grades me she wears only minimal black underwear, which would, in isolation, be deemed unprofessional in most professions, unworkable in most workplaces.

She scratches the small of her back with her left thumbnail, and then, straightening herself, places her hands on my sides. But this is entirely different from her grip on me before. I'm not expecting this.

She's live.

This is a touch I've never experienced before; it is much more than a touch. Imagine you've been living alone for a long time and suddenly you hear the door open when it shouldn't, you hear footsteps in your bedroom where you know there shouldn't be any. A light comes on by itself, your clothes fall off by themselves, a breeze trespasses. For the first time I know what it is to be naked.

She's through, she can hear me. Rosa's in.

Fooled. But this is only the four hundred and twelfth time. She isn't a catalogue-turner, a contour-crawler, a holder of a magnifying glass. Rosa is a silence-taker. A diviner. A vase tickler. An intruder.

Diviners, like everyone, I've heard about, but to be frank I've never been much convinced about their trade. Before Rosa, the tally of my dealings with those ostensibly having abilities to receive the hidden: three. A former ropemaker in the Indus valley, a footman in Siam and a colour explorer.

As to my dealings with those purporting to have abilities to receive the hidden, but who were flimming the flam, they number one hundred and twenty thousand, four hundred and forty-two. The youngest being an eight-year-old shaman who had his head kicked in after his tribe had everything they owned washed away in a flash flood scouring their encampment, an encampment decreed by the shaman. The oldest was a ninety-two-year-old fortune teller in Byzantium who had been predicting winners in the chariot races for seventy-five years and had never got it right once. However, the perfection of his errors established, after twenty years he became greatly patronised by the gamblers, since his choice, while not a short cut to winnings, could be used to eliminate one element from their calculations.

As for the true soothsayers: the ex-ropemaker had been much in demand at the more vulgar celebrations at that juncture when modesty and decorum have been wholly dissolved, when, using his chosen agent of insight, his tongue, he would muzzle himself with the nautch girls and then delve into mysteries such as their places of birth, their fathers' occupations, their earliest memories, their favourite colours, their dearest aspirations, the names of their closest friends, their most-loved jewellery; the answers to which, garnered solely from his bridle of legs, earned him unbridled applause. Notwithstanding his redoubtable gift, I have to remark that the same information could well have been obtained by anyone using tools such as civil conversation and the odd bauble.

The footman: could always guess, unerringly, when it would rain. This gained him a popularity with many street-traders and hunters, but he was never invited (in the bounds of my knowledge) to any rousing debauchery. A pity he couldn't boost himself from the status of rain-teller to the more lucrative level of rainmaker (twenty-two bona fide on board, nineteen dubious, four hundred and ninety-eight frauds).

BY TIBOR FISCHER
ALSO AVAILABLE IN VINTAGE

☐	The Collector Collector	0099268191	£6.99
☐	Don't Read This Book If You're Stupid	0099283123	£6.99
☐	Under the Frog	0099438054	£6.99

FREE POST AND PACKING
Overseas customers allow £2.00 per paperback

BY PHONE: 01624 677237

BY POST: Random House Books
c/o Bookpost, PO Box 29, Douglas
Isle of Man, IM99 1BQ

BY FAX: 01624 670923

BY EMAIL: bookshop@enterprise.net

Cheques (payable to Bookpost) and credit cards accepted

Prices and availability subject to change without notice.
Allow 28 days for delivery.
When placing your order, please mention if you do not wish to receive
any additional information.

www.randomhouse.co.uk/vintage